A Winter's Dream

D0262597

About the author

Sophie Claire writes emotional stories set in England and in sunny Provence, where she spent her summers as a child. She has a French mother and a Scottish father, but was born in Africa and grew up in Manchester, England, where she still lives with her husband and two sons.

Previously, she worked in marketing and proofreading academic papers, but writing is what she always considered her 'real job' and now she's delighted to spend her days dreaming up heartwarming contemporary romance stories set in beautiful places.

You can find out more at www.sophieclaire.co.uk and on Twitter @sclairewriter.

Also by Sophie Claire

The Christmas Holiday
A Forget-Me-Not Summer

Sophie Claire

A Winter's Dream

HODDER

First published in Great Britain in 2020 by Hodder & Stoughton
An Hachette UK company

I

Copyright © Sophie Claire 2020

A CIP catalogue record for this title is available from the British Library

Paperback ISBN 978 1 529 39283 8
eBook ISBN 978 1 529 39284 5

Typeset in Plantin Light by Palimpsest Book Production Limited,
Falkirk, Stirlingshire

Printed and bound in Great Britain by Clays Ltd, Elcograf S.p.A.

Hodder & Stoughton policy is to use papers that are natural,
renewable and recyclable products and made from wood grown in
sustainable forests. The logging and manufacturing processes are expected
to conform to the environmental regulations of the country of origin.

Hodder & Stoughton Ltd
Carmelite House
50 Victoria Embankment
London EC4Y 0DZ

www.hodder.co.uk

To Jane Dodds, who inspired this story.

Chapter One

L iberty was ready for this.

Every year she wondered who delivered them, who sent them, and why. Well, this time she would find out.

The cottage was quiet. Outside, the night was a dark blanket tucked around the woods, and she pictured the wildlife curled up asleep. Although she usually left the porch light on, today she hadn't. Deliberately.

Liberty shivered and pulled her quilt tighter around her, wishing she could read a book to keep busy, but she didn't want the light to betray her. So she sat in the dark, waiting. Her eyelids were heavy. If it weren't for the mystery person who visited once a year on this day and always before dawn, she would still be in bed. She picked a loose thread off the leg of her blue pyjamas. Perhaps they weren't coming this year, she thought, as the minutes stretched on. Perhaps she'd wasted her time getting up ridiculously early. The clock in the hall ticked a lullaby rhythm and she leaned her head against the window frame . . .

She'd almost nodded off when the throaty purr of an

engine made her eyes snap open. She sat up and spotted headlights coming towards her. Whoever it was cut their engine, the crafty devil. No wonder Charlie, her ever alert Labrador, hadn't heard them in past years. He barked if he sensed a squirrel a hundred yards away, but right now he remained asleep in the kitchen.

Wide awake, Liberty watched as the small van dipped its lights and rolled silently towards the cottage. She strained to see the driver, but they were only a dark silhouette. She couldn't even tell if it was a man or a woman. They got out, bouquet in hand, and approached the cottage. Her heart jumped in anticipation of the beautiful gift – and of finally clearing up the mystery.

Liberty opened the window. 'Thank you for the flowers!' she called cheerily. 'I just wondered who –'

The figure jumped, dropped the bouquet and ran.

' – sent them,' Liberty finished under her breath. Okay, that wasn't the reaction she'd expected.

She hesitated. She couldn't very well chase after them – could she? She looked down at her pyjamas and dressing-gown. She wasn't exactly dressed for it, and she didn't know who that person was.

But the sound of their van starting helped her come to a swift decision. If she did nothing, they'd get away and she'd never know who was behind this. She couldn't let that happen. She was so close to getting an answer, she refused to give up now.

She raced to the front door, adrenalin pumping. The noise woke Charlie, who barked and came galloping into the hall. By the time she got outside, the van was already skidding away. Cursing, she grabbed her keys. Charlie followed, and it was easier to let him jump into the car too. She thanked her lucky stars that her beaten-up old Citroën 2CV started first time, and excitement mingled with nerves. She'd never done anything like this before.

'Who is it, Charlie?' she asked, as she yanked the gear stick into first and drove after the van. 'And why on earth did they run away?'

She wasn't sure why it made her so angry. Perhaps because she'd been close to seeing their face. 'I just want to know who's sending me the damn flowers! Is that too much to ask?'

Charlie blinked nervously as she careered round the bend. She knew the country lanes like the back of her hand, but she didn't normally drive so fast. In fact, since her friend Carys's accident six months ago she was more careful than ever. The van swung out onto the main road and shot away, but Liberty was catching up. She put her foot down, trying to keep up. The road was deserted, thankfully.

'It's a florist's van,' she mused, squinting to read the name, 'but it's definitely not Natasha, is it?'

Charlie whined.

'It's okay, Charlie. Don't worry.' She gave him a quick pat, then returned her attention to the road ahead. She gripped the steering wheel, determined not to let the van out of her sight. The mystery person was driving at lunatic speed. Liberty's heart was going nineteen to the dozen and she tried not to think about the risks of skidding or her brakes failing and the car spinning out of control. In all those American television programmes she'd watched as a girl, car chases had seemed exciting, but in fact speed made her queasy with fear.

Finally, they reached town and the van pulled up behind a flower shop. The driver – a woman – shot Liberty a glance before scooting inside the building. Liberty screeched to a halt, then jumped out and ran after her, shouting, 'Stop! Wait!'

Charlie bounded with her, barking his support. When the woman tried to shut the door, Liberty stuck her foot out to block it. Pain shot through her as the woman tried again to push it closed.

'Okay, I'm scared now,' said the woman. 'Why did you follow me all this way?'

Liberty fought to get her breath back. Seriously, if she didn't have a black toenail after this she'd be very surprised. Still, she kept her foot firmly wedged in place. She was determined to get answers to the questions she'd been storing up for years. 'Why did you drive like a maniac? I hope you don't break the speed limit like that every day.'

Guilt shaded the woman's blue eyes. 'Of course not. I was trying to get away because you're not supposed to know who sent your flowers.'

Charlie was still barking at her side. Liberty shushed him, then turned back to the woman. 'Why not?'

She remained tight-lipped.

Liberty went on, 'I just want to know who they're from. It's my birthday today and they've been coming every year since I was eighteen, but there's never a card or a name, and you wouldn't believe how many hours I've spent trying to work out who they're from, but I still have no clue and – and anything you can tell me, no matter how small, well, I'd like to know. I'd really like to know.' She paused to catch her breath, then added, 'Please?'

The woman bit her lip, and pushed a hand through her fringe. 'Fine,' she said, with a sigh. 'Come in. But not the dog.'

Liberty hesitated. She didn't have Charlie's lead with her to tie him up, but she was afraid that if she went back to the car the florist might change her mind and close the door. 'Sit,' she told him. He obeyed. Improvising, she yanked the belt out of her dressing-gown and used it to attach him to the drainpipe. It wasn't ideal, but he was a well-behaved dog – most of the time. 'Now stay there, okay? Good boy.'

Inside, she looked around. They were in a back room, sparse, with a bench littered with leaves and the ends of stalks. Another doorway led to the main shop and Liberty could see shelves stacked with silver buckets of flowers. It was bigger and more spacious than her friend Natasha's flower shop in Willowbrook. The air was cold, but the clouds of colourful flower heads were a warming sight. They were gorgeous. But, then, she should have guessed they would be. The flowers she received each year were always stunning: neon-coloured gerberas, her favourite flowers, interspersed with spikes of greenery and exotic blooms she couldn't name but which looked as if they'd been plucked from a tropical jungle. Artful and elegant, they always made her heart lift.

She pulled off her slipper and rubbed her foot. 'They don't show how much that hurts in the movies.'

'Perhaps because they're not wearing slippers in them,' said the woman, as her gaze swept over Liberty's dressing-gown and fleece pyjamas. She had long hair, white-grey at the roots fading into ice blue at the tips. It looked stunning. 'Sorry, but you scared me. And with your dog . . .'

'That's okay,' said Liberty, and put her slipper back on. 'This shop is gorgeous. Do you deliver my flowers every year?'

The woman nodded.

'Well, first, thank you. They're always beautiful.'

'You're welcome.' The florist's gaze didn't quite meet hers.

'Please tell me who they're from.'

The woman's mouth pinched. 'I don't know.'

'There's never a card. Is that deliberate?'

She nodded. 'They're to remain strictly anonymous. Those were the instructions I was given.'

Instructions? It all sounded so carefully planned. Calculated, even. 'Why?'

The woman shrugged. Liberty decided to try a different tack. 'Can you remember *when* you were given those instructions? Did someone come in personally?'

She threw Liberty a sidelong look, which suggested she shouldn't reveal this information. 'I inherited the order with the shop when I moved here ten years ago.'

So the person behind this had set it all up twelve years ago when she'd turned eighteen. 'So, wait – they've paid in advance? Or do you send them a bill each year?'

'That's confidential. Listen, I've already told you more than I should. You're not supposed to know who the sender is, okay?'

Sighing, Liberty couldn't hide her disappointment. 'I just really wanted to know.'

The woman's expression softened. 'I must admit, it is strange, and I've never known another order like it except one-offs for Valentine's Day. But perhaps the mystery is supposed to be part of the gift. It is quite exciting, don't you think?'

'I suppose,' Liberty conceded.

'They're expensive flowers, I'll say that much. Whoever ordered them doesn't skimp.'

'And gerberas are my favourite,' Liberty agreed. 'They must have known that because you always include them.'

'I'm sorry I can't help you any more.' The florist glanced at her watch. 'Listen, I've got a list of deliveries to make, so if you don't mind . . .'

'There's just one more thing,' Liberty said quickly. 'How long did they ask for this order to keep coming? I mean, it's been twelve years already, and I'm thirty today. Is that – is that the end of it?'

The woman pressed her lips together. 'No, it's not. But that's all I'm going to say.'

Liberty felt a rush of relief she hadn't been expecting. 'Right. Well, er, thanks. And I'm sorry if I scared you.'

Liberty pushed open the door to leave, relieved that Charlie was still patiently waiting where she'd left him.

'Enjoy your birthday,' the florist called after her.

★

7

Liberty drove home slowly and sensibly, mulling over the crumbs of information she'd gleaned from the florist. But she had more questions than she'd received answers to. What if she moved house? Would the flowers still reach her? And what if something happened to the sender? Was it just one person?

She turned off the main road and wound her way through the woods until she pulled up outside the cottage. The bouquet was on the porch where the florist had abandoned it. Liberty took the flowers inside and arranged them in a vase, then noticed the time. She was running late and her morning routine was completely out of the window, which was unsettling because Liberty loved her routine: she hadn't walked the dog or had breakfast or even showered, and there wasn't time to do all three. She compromised with a short walk (Charlie seemed so disappointed and confused when they turned back) and a super-quick shower (thank goodness for dry shampoo), then hurriedly made tea and toast with peanut butter and jam. No way was she missing out on that: she'd be growling at customers if she didn't have breakfast.

While she ate, she tried not to think about the day's significance. Thirty was a milestone. It made her feel . . . She couldn't put her finger on it. Unsettled? Adrift?

This time last year her best friend and housemate, Carys, had been waiting for her in the kitchen with a sparkling silver envelope. 'Happy birthday, Lib!' She'd looked so excited that Liberty had guessed the envelope contained a special gift.

Even so, her jaw had dropped when she saw two train

tickets for Paris. 'I thought we'd have a long weekend. We can go sightseeing and do some Christmas shopping, if you like.'

'That is such a lovely gift,' she gasped. 'Thank you, Car.' Tears of joy had made Carys's smiling face blur, and Liberty had hugged her. Then she remembered. 'But I don't have a passport!'

Carys handed her an application form and winked. 'So get one.' She'd thought of everything.

But Carys wasn't there now. She'd been in a coma since the car accident six months ago when an idiot who'd been driving way over the speed limit had hit her car head-on.

Liberty had known her birthday would be difficult without Carys, she'd prepared for it, but the house was quiet, and there was no gift waiting for her on the kitchen table.

She shook off the thought and began to make a list of who could have sent the flowers, just as she'd done dozens of times before. 'It can't be a secret admirer because I've been single over a year now,' she said out loud, 'which has been plenty of time to make a move. Unless they're too shy . . .'

Charlie glanced up, then carried on eating his own breakfast.

'And it can't be Carys.' Her best friend had always sworn it wasn't her and now it simply wasn't possible. 'Which leaves . . . just about anyone else I've ever met, and an infinite number of reasons why.' She put her pen down, frustrated. For Heaven's sake, who could it be?

She carried her cup and plate to the sink. And why were they doing this? Did the sender think she needed cheering up? Did they pity her? She scrubbed her plate harder than was necessary. Oh, God, she hated the thought that someone felt sorry for her. No, it couldn't be that. 'Oh, dammit! Why won't they just say who they are, and put me out of my misery?'

She slotted the plate into the drainer and looked out of the window at the back garden. She'd really hoped this would be the day when the sender finally revealed themselves. It was a big birthday, after all. She'd hoped they'd come forward, maybe deliver the bouquet personally this time.

And she'd hoped it would be a man.

A secret admirer, someone who'd known her a long time but kept their distance for some mysterious reason, yet now couldn't hold back any longer and simply had to admit the feelings he'd been harbouring for her. Someone handsome, kind.

Oh, Liberty. She'd been foolish to imagine an admirer waiting in the wings. It had been bound to end in disappointment.

Charlie trotted over to her. She reached down to fuss him and steal a quick cuddle. The Labrador nuzzled close, as if sensing her disappointment. A glance at her watch told her she had to leave for work so she got up. As she passed the bouquet, she touched the petals of a golden gerbera. They were as soft as the green velvet dress she was wearing.

'But they are beautiful,' she said softly, 'so thank you, whoever you are.'

Perhaps you could simply enjoy them, her mum had once suggested, years ago when Liberty was fretting over who the sender could be. She closed her eyes and tried to do that now, savouring the feeling of having been singled out, trying to appreciate the thought behind the gift and the attention that had been paid to selecting her favourite flowers. Someone cares about me, she thought, and warmth filled her. This is what I need to hold on to. This feeling of being . . . cherished. Someone's focus. It doesn't matter who sent them in the end. I'm lucky to receive them.

Despite the disruption to her morning routine, Liberty arrived at work on time and her spirits lifted, as they did every morning, when she pushed open the door of the Button Hole. It was almost a year now since she'd left her old job in a department store and she adored working here. Outside, the late November sky might be grey and the light weak, but Evie's patchwork and quilting shop was a bright star in the high street, an Aladdin's cave of colourful fabrics and sewing materials. Here, among the giant cotton reels and buttons that hung from the ceiling, and the display quilts that decorated the walls, Liberty felt perfectly at home. When she gazed around she saw infinite possibilities for exciting new designs. And in the back room those designs became real: bespoke quilts made for their online customers all over the world. This shop was her happy place.

Her boss, Evie, was leaning on the counter chatting to

Natasha, who owned the florist's across the road. Both greeted Liberty with bright smiles and hugs – although it wasn't easy to hug Natasha now she was eight months' pregnant.

'How are you feeling?' Liberty asked.

Natasha was petite, and her bump was neat but big beneath her flowery tea-dress. 'Like I'm being kicked about. I'm sure this baby's going to be a gymnast. I swear it keeps doing forward rolls and stretches.' She tucked her blonde hair behind one ear.

'How long until your due date?'

'Four weeks. Luc's getting overprotective and keeps telling me to stop work and put my feet up, but there's so much to do in the shop that I need to carry on for another couple of weeks. I've packed my hospital bag, though, just in case. And Evie's on standby to look after Lottie when I go into labour.'

Evie nodded.

'Sounds like you've got everything organised,' said Liberty.

Natasha's cheeks glowed pink, but she was moving slowly now, and Liberty wondered if her pregnancy was wearing her out more than she was letting on. Or perhaps it was just tiring to work full time as well as look after an active toddler.

'Happy birthday, Lib!' Evie thrust a gift into her hands. It was wrapped in a square of cotton material and tied with an orange ribbon.

'Thanks, Evie. Gorgeous fabric,' Liberty murmured, as she untied the bow.

'I know you don't normally read thrillers, but trust me, this one's brilliant.'

Liberty turned the hardback over and skimmed the blurb.

'What do you normally read?' Natasha asked.

'Small-town romance,' said Liberty. 'I love them. And cowboy heroes. The kind who look mean and hard but have a hidden soft centre.'

'The ones who seem like they can't be tamed?' Natasha's blue eyes gleamed.

'Exactly,' said Liberty.

'I like those too.'

Natasha gave her a pair of pyjamas in beautiful brushed cotton, downy soft and patterned with cotton reels. 'They're beautiful, Nat. Thanks.'

'I know you like a quiet night in quilting and watching a good film. These should be perfect.'

'Yes, I'll wear them lots.' She smiled.

But as she spoke, an uncomfortable feeling crept over her. She told herself it was about missing Carys, but it wouldn't be dismissed. It niggled insistently. Her friends' gifts were thoughtful and showed how well they knew her – but was this how she'd expected her life to be at thirty? Pyjamas, cosy nights in, and heroes who existed only in her imagination?

'Right. I'd better get back,' said Natasha. 'I'm changing the window display today. Going for something nice and Christmassy. See you both soon!'

'We need to think about a new window display too,' said Evie, when she'd gone. She pulled her long plait forwards and twisted the end around her fingers as she eyed the window thoughtfully. 'It's the first of December on Monday.'

Liberty tucked her gifts behind the counter. 'Last year's display was eye-catching.' When she'd started work there last December the window had been filled with giant baubles and fabric-covered gifts.

'It was, but this year I'd like to give people ideas for small projects they can make to give as presents. Customers are always telling me how much satisfaction they get from making gifts.'

Liberty gave this some thought. 'How about starter kits for cushions? We could include instructions, squares of fabric and matching thread. And I could make up a few finished cushions for the window display so they can see how they'll look in different colourways.'

Evie's eyes lit up. 'That's a great idea. They can either buy the kit and make it, or give it away to someone who enjoys crafting.'

They set to work, choosing which fabrics to use, and cutting out squares.

'Did you get another mystery bouquet, then?' asked Evie, as she sliced through the fabric.

Liberty picked up the four-inch squares and stacked them neatly. 'I did, and I got up early so I was there when it arrived.' She told Evie about the chase.

Her boss's eyes widened. 'You followed her all the way to town? Well I never . . .'

'Why is that so hard to believe?'

She reached for another bolt of fabric and measured

a four-inch strip. 'I don't know. I suppose I had you down as someone careful and sensible.'

In other words, dull, thought Liberty, for the second time that morning. 'Well, it was all for nothing because she wouldn't tell me who they were from.'

Evie's mouth twisted in sympathy, then she brightened. 'Perhaps that's a good thing,' she said, and her hazel eyes shone. 'You know – the mystery of it. If you knew who they were from it wouldn't be anywhere near as exciting.'

Liberty smiled. Evie always looked on the bright side, no matter what the situation. 'It's romantic, too – don't you think?'

'Definitely,' said Evie. 'I'd love to be sent flowers from a mysterious anonymous person.'

The shop bell jingled as their first customer arrived, and the morning passed quickly. At lunchtime, Liberty nipped out to the bakery next door to buy lunch.

'We've got some delicious new Christmas fillings if you want to try something different,' said Marjorie. 'Turkey and stuffing, smoked salmon and prawn, Brie and cran-berry sauce?'

'I'll just stick with the usual, thanks.' Liberty paid for the coronation chicken sandwich and vanilla slice.

Marjorie laughed. 'I dread to think what will happen if you come in one day and we haven't got it.'

Liberty was alarmed at the thought. 'That won't happen because you always keep one aside for me.'

'True. You're a creature of habit, Liberty, and a very easy customer!'

She took her paper bag with a smile, but as she left the

bakery Marjorie's words played on her mind. They reminded her of something her ex had said when he'd broken up with her last year: *You're too set in your ways.* She and Carys had laughed it off because he'd dumped her for a party girl, who had ditched him two weeks later, but now she asked herself if he had been right. Was she stuck in a rut?

Her routine was the same every day: she got up, walked Charlie in the forest, and drove to work. She helped customers in the shop, and ran sewing workshops. Then she went home, and spent her evenings working on her own quilts. All this used to be more fun with Carys for company, of course – they'd shared Damselfly Cottage for five years before the accident – but even now she couldn't imagine an evening without sewing. Her online name was Liberty Homebird, and for good reason. People loved the pictures she posted of her sewing projects with the log fire burning in the background. They said her cosy cottage looked dreamy, a world away from their city lives. But had she allowed her life to get *too* cosy?

Things had changed so much since Carys's accident. Problems that used to seem small had doubled in size now she had to face them alone. She'd never been a risk-taker, but now she was cautious in the extreme, and the thought of socialising with strangers made her break out in a sweat. And although she visited her just once a week, Carys was constantly at the back of her mind. What if she died in the night? What if she never woke up? What if she woke up but wasn't Carys any more? The gnawing questions were exhausting, and Liberty found comfort from the uncertainty in her quiet, familiar routine.

But thinking of her friend in a coma made her wonder: what if today was her last?

Back at the shop they had a sudden rush of customers, but Evie and Liberty had a system that worked well when this happened: one cut the fabric, while the other rang it through the till and took payment. That way they got through a queue of people in no time. When the last customer left, they began to put away all the rolls of fabric.

'So what are you doing tonight?' asked Evie, as she pushed a bolt of fabric back into place. She had to stand on tiptoe to reach the high shelf.

Liberty rolled up the remaining bolts left on the counter and stacked them one on top of the other. 'Oh just the usual. A quiet night in sewing. I've almost finished a Maple Leaf quilt.'

'Maple Leaf? Isn't that a bit traditional for you?'

Liberty smiled. Evie was right. Her quilts were always modern with bold blocks of colour against a plain background. 'I designed my own take on it with stylised leaves rather than lifelike ones. And I used those new woodland fabrics.' She pointed to the far corner of the shop.

'Ooh – nice! Which colours?'

'Orange, red, purple and brown.'

'Autumnal,' Evie said approvingly. 'I'd love to see it.'

'I'll bring it in when it's finished.' She hoped to finish and photograph it while the leaves of the oak trees were still clinging on. She always shot her quilts against the backdrop of the forest behind her cottage then posted the pictures on social media. This one would look gorgeous against the caramel tones of late autumn.

Evie's brow pulled a little as she returned to the till. 'But aren't you going out tonight to celebrate your birthday?'

Liberty picked up four bolts of fabric. 'I'm seeing Carys's mum and dad at the weekend. They've invited me round for tea,' she mumbled, and hurried away. She began to slot the fabrics back into place, tidying the shelves as she went, tucking in loose ends.

Evie frowned. 'But it's your thirtieth! You've got to celebrate it.'

'You know me. I'm not a party person. And without Carys . . .' It felt wrong to celebrate when her best friend was in a coma. They had had big plans for their thirtieth birthdays. After the success of their weekend in Paris last year, Carys had come up with the idea of a backpacking holiday around Europe – by train because Liberty couldn't fly – and they'd been saving up, excited at the prospect of visiting so many countries.

But Liberty's savings were gone now: she'd had to use them to keep up with all the bills for the cottage. Living alone meant her finances were stretched. She pushed the last bolt of fabric into place and realised her boss was watching her.

Evie's hazel eyes were warm with understanding. 'It doesn't have to be a party. How about something low key – a meal at the pub, maybe?'

'It's fine. I don't want to make a fuss.'

'Since when is celebrating with your friends a fuss? It'll be fun. Come on, Lib!'

She bit her lip. It was tempting . . .

'I'll take that as a yes.' Evie reached into her pocket for her phone. 'Right. I'll organise it. I'll invite Jake and Natasha. Luc will probably have to stay with Lottie. I can't believe you were going to let this go by without celebrating. You always look after everyone around you, but what about you?'

Liberty didn't reply straight away. They both knew that normally Carys would have organised it. 'I don't want a fuss,' she repeated.

'Oh, Liberty,' said Evie. She put her phone down and came over to hug her. 'I know you miss Carys, but it's important to keep living your life.'

Evie had lost her sister a few years ago. Liberty knew she understood. She nodded mutely, her throat suddenly tight.

The shop bell tinkled and a lady came in, clutching a piece of fabric. Evie greeted her brightly, then turned to Liberty and said quietly, 'I've an idea. Why don't you leave early and visit Carys this afternoon?'

Liberty's spirits lifted. 'Are you sure? Will you manage here?' She glanced at the customer.

'Of course I will. Go! It's your birthday.'

'Hi, Carys!' Liberty called, as she entered the hospital room. She hung her coat over the back of the chair and took her friend's hand. 'I know it's not Sunday, but today's special.'

Carys slept on, eyelashes resting on her cheeks. She looked so peaceful, which always made Liberty feel better.

She launched into her usual patter, updating her friend on everything that had happened since her last visit. She told her about the meal with friends that Evie had spontaneously organised for that evening, and how she'd chased the florist. 'I thought this was the year the sender was going to show themselves, Car. I'm so disappointed.'

Those damn flowers had really got her down this morning, and it wasn't the sender's fault: it was hers. She'd pinned her hopes on having a secret admirer, that he'd come forward and her life would move in a new direction. Before today's disappointment she hadn't realised how *dissatisfied* she felt with everything.

The hospital room remained silent, but she knew her friend so well she could imagine what her response would be: *Never mind Mr Anonymous Flowers. Get yourself out there and find your Dream Guy.*

But how? Liberty picked a thread off her sleeve and wound it around her finger distractedly. She wasn't brave like Carys. She was even less brave without Carys by her side.

It was hard to keep up a one-way conversation, so after a while Liberty began to sing. She began as she always did with Carys's favourite, 'Your Song', then worked her way through to Leonard Cohen's 'Hallelujah'. She was halfway through it when one of the nurses came to check Carys's stats and see to her drip.

'Don't mind me,' she said, when Liberty paused. 'You have a beautiful voice.'

'Oh, I can't, Jacqui. Not when people are listening.'

'Why not? As I said, you have a great voice. Not like

my husband. He thinks he's Tom Jones, but he sounds more like a tom cat howling.'

Liberty smiled but stayed quiet. Carys was one of the few people who'd heard her sing, and that was how she intended to keep it. 'Jacqui, can I ask you something?'

The nurse stopped. 'Of course.'

'Is Carys less likely to wake up now six months have gone by?'

Jacqui thought about this. 'I'm not sure what the statistics are, but in my experience there's no pattern. I've seen patients wake up years after.'

Liberty watched Carys's chest lift and fall with each breath. The ticks and beeps of machines beat a steady rhythm. 'But,' she said slowly, 'she could equally never wake up?'

The nurse nodded gravely and touched her arm. Liberty watched her slip out of the room. Until now she hadn't allowed herself to think like this. Giving up hope would be like letting her best friend down. She'd promised herself she'd keep hoping and praying and visiting Carys for as long as it took. But today Evie's words echoed in her mind: *It's important to keep living your life.*

Liberty and Carys had been best friends since primary school. Like sisters, even. They hadn't needed anyone else. And since Carys's accident – well, Liberty hadn't felt much like socialising. So she'd put her own life on pause. But six months had gone by, and now she had to face it: what if Carys never woke up from the coma?

And that was when she realised what had been niggling her all day.

She was lonely.

And because she'd turned thirty, which felt like a huge milestone, Liberty was afraid it would always be like this: just her and her dog and her quilts.

At the moment, anyone observing her could set a watch by her daily routine. But today's birthday had made her conscious of time ticking, and she saw now that she was stuck in a rut. If she carried on like this, she'd be hitting forty and still be alone. She never left Willowbrook except to visit Carys in hospital or occasionally to shop in town. She never met anyone new, apart from customers in the shop and they were mostly female. Liberty loved her cottage and she loved village life – but she hated being alone.

She blinked hard and tried to ignore the plunging sensation. She missed Carys, she missed her mum. But she was a firm believer that the best way to make things better was to take control of the situation. So what was she going to do? Something had to change. The only question was what?

Back at her cottage, she scrolled through her Instagram feed. One of those inspirational quotes caught her eye: *Open your mind to possibilities and suddenly they become realities.*

She paused a moment then flicked past it. Another post came up showing an Advent calendar. *The countdown to Christmas begins in five days!*

She shifted uncomfortably. If her birthday felt hard without Carys, how much harder would Christmas be?

Everything felt more acute then: the lonely felt lonelier, the days were darker. And it was creeping up fast. In the woods outside the leaves had almost all fallen, the early-morning air was frosty when she walked Charlie, and decorations were gradually appearing in the village: a bare tree had been placed in the green, the pub landlord had strung lights above the door of the Dog and Partridge, and the shops were filled with Christmas cards.

Liberty scrolled on, pausing to admire a beautiful quilt photographed against a snowy mountain background, then deliberately whizzed past pictures of cake and food because her tummy was already rumbling but dinner wasn't booked until eight. An ad popped up for a dating app. She flicked straight past it.

Then stopped and frowned. She wasn't going to meet new people in the Dog and Partridge tonight, was she? She'd lived all her life in Willowbrook, she knew everyone here, and there were no single men that she liked in *that* way. But a dating app? That was for extroverts, for fun-lovers, for pretty girls with long hair and perfect manicures – not dull home birds like her.

She blew out a breath, then whistled for Charlie. He poked his head up, instantly alert at the signal for exercise. 'Come on, boy. Let's go for a walk.' An idea was taking shape and she had some thinking to do.

The Dog and Partridge wasn't busy – it was Wednesday evening, after all – so they had no trouble getting a table for the four of them.

When the food arrived, they raised their glasses in a toast for Liberty's birthday.

'How do you feel about turning thirty?' asked Evie. Liberty knew her boss would be celebrating her own thirtieth soon.

'Erm . . .' Truth be told, she wasn't feeling good about this birthday and the sharp awareness it had brought of time passing and doors closing. It wasn't logical. There were still a million opportunities if she chose to take them. But until now she hadn't. '. . . I'd thought my life would be different by now.'

'Different how?' asked Evie.

'Well, Carys and I had talked about travelling around Europe, but that's not happening. And also . . .' she bit her lip '. . . I suppose I thought by now I would have met someone and settled down. But did you know it's been thirteen months since my last date?'

Jake, Evie's boyfriend, put down his pint and said thoughtfully, 'It's not easy to meet new people here in Willowbrook.'

His quiet observation reminded her that he'd moved to the village only a year ago and still saw the place through objective eyes. But he wasn't the surly loner he'd been back then. Meeting Evie had transformed him and he was definitely part of their close-knit community now.

'It isn't,' she agreed. She saw the same people on her way to work every day, she'd dated the only three men she found even mildly attractive, and her most recent relationship with Rob the plumber had ended badly, which made things awkward when she bumped into him.

(And when she needed a plumber.) 'But I've also been guilty of taking things for granted, living life as if I had all the time in the world, putting things off and being . . . safe.' Staying in and sewing was the easy option, she saw that now.

'Safe? What do you mean?' asked Natasha.

'Too predictable. I'm stuck in a rut.'

'You think so?' asked Evie, with concern.

'I love my job and I love living here, but – I can't help feeling there must be more.' She squeezed the stem of her prosecco glass. The question was, did she have the courage to put into action the idea she'd come up with earlier?

'Maybe you could go travelling by yourself,' suggested Natasha.

'I'm not that brave.' The thought of backpacking alone was terrifying. And flying? No way. Not after the last time. But wasn't that exactly the problem? She never did anything scary. Her life was all about the familiar and routine. 'The most exciting thing I've done all year was to chase after the florist's van this morning.'

'I heard about that.' Jake chuckled. 'A high-speed chase in pyjamas and slippers. Did you find out who the flowers were from?'

She shook her head. 'I was so disappointed. But it helped me come to a decision.'

'Ooh, exciting!' said Evie. 'What is it?'

Liberty hesitated. Once she'd said it out loud, she'd have to see it through. 'Well,' she began tentatively, 'what happened to Carys made me realise that we don't know what's round the corner, right? And if something were to happen to me tomorrow I don't want to have any regrets. So . . .' she took a deep breath '. . . I'm going to spend the month of December being brave.'

'You're going to join the SAS?' joked Evie. 'Become a stuntwoman?'

Liberty shook her head. 'Not *that* brave – just a little bit braver than normal. From the first of December until the end of the year I'm going to say yes to everything. Every opportunity, every invitation, I'll accept. Every difficult dilemma, I won't let myself go for the easy option. I'll do the opposite instead. And every day I'll do at least one thing that takes me out of my comfort zone.'

'Why?' Natasha looked thoroughly perplexed.

'Because that way I'll have to try new things and hopefully meet new people.' If she carried on like this following the same routine each day and living this quiet life, nothing would change and in another thirty years she'd still be sitting by the fire each evening, sewing. 'I want to know if my life could be different. If I could be different.'

Truth be told, she was terrified at the prospect of this challenge, but she kept that thought to herself.

'Go, you!' said Evie. 'That's a great idea.'

They chinked glasses in celebration.

'You know December has thirty-one days?' said Jake. 'It's a long month.'

'Yeah, with Christmas in there, too,' said Natasha. 'That might complicate things.'

'You should have picked February,' said Evie. 'Much shorter.'

'I can do it,' said Liberty. She was determined. 'And they don't all have to be big things. I might, for example, not have turkey for Christmas dinner, but eat something else instead.'

'Aren't you going to Carys's family for Christmas?' asked Natasha. 'So you'll have to eat whatever her mother makes, won't you?'

'It was just an example.' She laughed. 'But each day I'll say yes to one new thing. And the reason I've told you all tonight is so you can hold me to account. I have to see it through now.'

Evie twisted a strand of her hair around her fingers. 'Do you have any challenges planned or are you going to take it one day at a time?'

'I already had one idea,' Liberty said cautiously. She wondered what her friends would think of it. 'I might take in a lodger.'

'You'll rent out Carys's room?' asked Evie.

She nodded, ignoring the lump in her throat. 'I'm finding it hard to pay all the bills without her rent. I feel bad, though.' She dipped her head. 'It's like I'm giving up on her. What if she wakes up and wants to come home?'

A short silence followed and Evie sent her a look of sympathy. Natasha seemed thoughtful.

'You could rent the room on a monthly basis,' said Jake. 'That way if she does wake up, she can have it back quickly.'

'Yes,' Liberty said. 'I'm planning to advertise, but I'm not sure how to go about it. I can't let any old stranger move in with me. What if they're a secret axe murderer?' She winked, but she was only half joking.

'I might have an idea,' said Natasha, reaching for her coat and bag. 'I need to go now, I'm expecting an early delivery tomorrow morning, but I'll check with Luc, then talk to you about it.'

'Okay,' said Liberty, feeling brighter.

'This challenge is so exciting,' said Natasha. 'I think it's a great idea.'

Liberty smiled. She was determined to do this. She didn't want to look back in ten years' time and wonder what her life might have been like if she'd been braver. 'There's no going back now.'

Chapter Two

Say yes to everything. Be brave. It was a bold plan, but Liberty knew that for it to work she couldn't just sit and wait for opportunities to come to her: she had to make them happen. Set herself challenges. With a tiny orange notebook open on her lap, she started a list. Apart from trying new sandwich fillings, what would take her out of her comfort zone? What did she want to achieve? Getting out more, meeting new people . . . She chewed her pencil. What would Carys tell her to start with?

Dating. Without a doubt.

They used to go out together – to the cinema, restaurants or the pub. They used to double-date as well, or sometimes even go out as a threesome if one of them was temporarily single – but since the accident Liberty could count on one hand how many times she'd been out. She'd felt too guilty to have fun while her best friend was lying in hospital. But Liberty also knew Carys would be horrified at how quiet her life had become, how limited. She could hear her now: *Lib, you need to get out and live. Thirty is so old!*

Liberty smiled and reached for her phone. Maybe old was an exaggeration but today's birthday had definitely focused her mind. She wanted a partner, a loving relationship, and – one day – a family.

She knew what she had to do, although it was the most daunting of all the challenges she'd come up with so far. She was going to join a dating app.

Or maybe she'd just download the app and take a look. No, she'd join. How scary could it be?

The problem was, Liberty hated putting herself out there and she wasn't any good in social situations with strangers. Working at the Button Hole was fine because conversations revolved around sewing, and that was her passion, but anything outside her job was a different matter. Other people could recount funny stories and chatter away for hours, but not her. She just stammered and her mind went blank.

The app popped open and she searched through her photos for a profile picture, but the only pictures she had were of her and Carys together. Finally, she managed to crop one so it showed just her. It wasn't the best photo: her hair looked even redder than normal and her cheeks were flushed from the sun, but it would do, and she uploaded it.

So what kind of man was she looking for? She picked a couple of loose threads off her top and wound them around her finger as she thought about this. She supposed her ideal man would enjoy the quiet life. He'd prefer to stay in watching films than go to nightclubs or wild parties. And he had to be an animal-lover, she thought, glancing at Charlie who was asleep in front of the fire. It would be nice if he was good-looking, but not so much that he was out of her league, and he had to be tall. At least as tall as her, and she was five foot ten. She didn't have a preference for hair colour or physical stuff: it was the person inside who mattered. She'd never had much patience for fickle, unreliable sorts, but now she'd turned thirty she was even keener to find someone she could rely on. Someone steady and grounded, who was in it for the long haul. She filled in all the details, then decided that was enough for today and picked up her quilt.

Shame she couldn't find a quilting guy, she thought, as she stitched. He'd be her perfect man. Or even better – a quilting cowboy.

Thursday, 27 November

Next morning Natasha popped into the Button Hole. The shop bell jingled as she came in and her white-blonde hair gleamed under the shop's lighting.

'Hi, Nat,' said Liberty. 'Shall I put the kettle on?' She stepped forward to pluck a tiny sprig of pine out of her friend's hair.

Natasha laughed. 'I've been making Christmas wreaths all morning and that stuff gets everywhere. I can't stay for coffee. I just popped in to talk to you about taking in a lodger. Are you still considering it?'

'Yes – especially if it's someone who's recommended.'

Natasha smiled. 'Luc has a French friend who's coming to visit and needs a place to stay. We offered him our sofa, but he's going to be here for a few weeks so he's been looking into hotel rooms in town. But your place would suit him better. Living in the village will mean he's closer, and we can see more of him – if he's around, that is. I'm not sure what his plans are exactly.'

'That sounds good,' said Liberty, her brain automatically searching for problems. Don't be so negative, she told herself sharply. Remember, from now on, life is about saying yes.

'The thing is, though – he's arriving on Monday. It doesn't leave you much time to get ready.'

'Monday? How long for?'

'I don't know. I'm guessing he'll go home for Christmas, but he hasn't said. I can give you his email address if you like. Then you can contact him directly.'

'Okay,' Liberty said gingerly. 'What else do you know about him?'

Natasha smiled. 'He's a motorcycle racer. Very successful.'

Liberty frowned. Why did she say that as if it was a good thing?

'He and Luc go back donkey's years. When they were very young they went to school together in Provence. Then Alex's family moved to Paris. They didn't see each other for a while – a bit like you and me, only Alex was a teenager when he left.' Natasha had left Willowbrook when her parents died and she was sent to live with an elderly relative, but she'd moved back a few years ago and opened her flower shop. 'But they've kept in touch over the years.' Natasha smiled. 'So you don't need to worry. He's not going to murder you in your sleep.'

Liberty nodded, even though this wasn't as reassuring

as Natasha might have thought. 'I'll email him and see what he says. If he agrees, this will count as my first challenge.' She reached into her pocket and pulled out the orange notebook she'd bought especially to record her challenges. 'It's not every day you let a stranger come and live with you.' Others might not regard it as a hugely daring thing, but for her it was an important step.

'Think of the rent he'll pay. And I met him at our wedding.' Natasha winked. 'He's very easy on the eye.'

Saturday, 29 November

Liberty started clearing Carys's room as soon as she got home from work on Saturday evening. She had brought home some cardboard boxes from the supermarket to pack up her friend's possessions.

'They'll still be here waiting for you,' she murmured, as she stood in the middle of the room and wondered where to start. It still smelt of Carys, even though it had been six months since the accident. She sniffed the perfume bottle beside the bed and memories sprang up of their best times together: the films they'd watched, laughing until they cried; eating Carys's homemade cookies; getting dressed up for a special meal; confiding in each other over broken hearts or new romances. Liberty blinked hard. The most difficult thing about Carys's accident was that it had come out of the blue. They'd both believed those shared moments would go on for years to come.

She carefully wrapped up the photos of Carys's parents and her little brothers, and a handful of cards her pupils at school had drawn for her. There were more beside her bed in hospital, dozens in fact, but the ones at home had been sent before the accident and weren't get-well-soon cards, just heartfelt tokens of affection. *Your the best teecher in the world!* was printed beneath a stick lady with a brown face. Liberty's eyes filled and she put the card away quickly. Carys had been a brilliant teacher. She cared about the children she taught, understood each pupil and nurtured their individual talents.

Once the bedside table was empty, she folded the quilt on Carys's bed. It had been a gift from Liberty on her sixteenth birthday. A Friendship Star design, she'd made it using the cheerful colours that Carys liked against a white background. It wasn't as bright as the bold primary shades she used nowadays but it had her trademark modern touch. She hugged it, and laid it carefully in a box. Carys's clothes were the hardest thing to fold away: shoes they'd bought together, dresses they used to share. It hadn't felt right to borrow them so Liberty had left them untouched since the accident.

When she'd finished clearing the room, she stacked the boxes on top of the wardrobe and under the bed. It seemed more spacious now, ready to receive a guest. But was it too sparse? She wanted her lodger to feel welcome so she did a quick trail around the house collecting candles, lavender-stuffed hearts, and pine cones strung from white ribbon, which she hung from drawer handles and hooks around the room. When she'd finished she stood back and assessed it. Yes, much more inviting. All it needed now was clean bedding and a quilt to make it more homely: Liberty had a pile of those to choose from. She thought of the emails she'd exchanged with her lodger, Alex. He'd said he was planning to stay until Christmas. His messages were brief and to the point, and she wondered what he'd be like. At least she wouldn't have to wait long to find out.

Monday, 1 December

'I can't believe how little you've changed.' Luc smiled. 'You still eat twice as much as everyone else.'

Alex tucked into a second helping of the cassoulet, hungry after a long day on the road. He'd arrived an hour ago, and was glad he'd arranged to stop at Luc and Natasha's for a meal before going on to the place where he'd be lodging. 'I burn it all off. And this is delicious. Even better than my mother's. Did you make it, Natasha?'

She shook her head. 'Luc did. He does most of the cooking – when he's home, anyway.'

Alex stared at his friend, remembering the bachelor lifestyle he'd lived before he'd married Natasha. He was fairly certain Luc wouldn't have been able to boil an egg four years ago. 'Who would have thought you'd settle down like this, Duval? Nat, you're a positive influence on my good friend here.'

'Oh, he just decided to learn to cook one day. I can't claim credit for that.'

Luc and Natasha shared a look. 'You can,' he said quietly. 'I knew I had to prove to you that I could do commitment. That's why I learned to cook.'

'You changed in other ways, too. Learning to cook isn't enough to convince a woman you're dependable.'

'True.' Luc's dark eyes softened as he gazed at his wife. 'We were always meant to be together, and once we figured that out, everything else fell into place.'

Alex was amused that Luc still seemed slightly amazed at the way things had turned out, even though he'd been married for more than four years now. Memories rose in his mind of Luc and Natasha's second wedding in Provence. It had been a shock to hear they'd been divorced, then fallen in love all over again. He'd felt privileged to be invited to the small, relaxed celebration at Château Duval when they'd remarried.

'So what's brought you here?' asked Luc. 'You said something about looking for a relative?'

'That's right. After Dad died, Mum asked me to sort through his affairs, and I found some letters.' He sipped his water. Luc and Natasha waited for him to go on, but this wasn't something he found easy to talk about. If he was honest, he was ashamed. 'They were addressed to Dad and he'd kept them hidden. They were written thirty years ago, by a woman who wanted him to know she was having his baby. A girl.'

'Wow,' whispered Natasha.

'Your father was a dark horse.'

'That's one way of putting it,' he said. 'These letters had no address, no name, and they were simply signed M.

The only clue where they were from was the envelopes, which were postmarked from here.'

'Willowbrook?' Natasha asked.

Alex waved his hand. 'Not quite. The nearest town.'

'Still, it's a happy coincidence that your search has brought you here, near us,' said Luc. He leaned back in his chair. 'So you're hoping to find the woman who sent the letters?'

'Perhaps. Or the child. My half-sister.'

'How will you do that? Without a name it won't be easy.'

'It's not. I've started looking online. Now I'm going to investigate all the local birth records and see what I can find. Then, if I can get a lead, I'm hoping someone might remember something. That's why I wanted to stay somewhere local . . . My half-sister would be about thirty years old with an absent father. Do you know anyone who fits that description?'

Luc and Natasha exchanged a look. 'Well, Liberty's mum was single, but her dad was around and died when she was small,' said Natasha. 'She's the friend you'll be lodging with. And she's nothing like you – she's got striking red hair. Her dad's genes, she always says.'

Alex shook his head. 'I don't think it could be her. My father was dark-haired, like me.'

Natasha lifted a hand to her chin. 'Hmm. I'll let you know if I think of anyone else.'

'Have you thought about hiring a private detective?' asked Luc.

'It's a possibility.' Alex felt uncomfortable hiding the

real reason he'd come in person. He would tell Luc – later. He just wasn't ready yet. 'But it's a delicate issue. I thought it would be better if I handled it myself.'

Natasha's blonde hair glinted as she got up. 'Do you two mind if I turn in for the night? I'm really tired.' She touched her bump. 'This one's so big I feel ready to pop.'

'Of course I don't mind,' said Alex.

'We'll clear up here, *chérie*,' said Luc, and gave his wife a lingering kiss.

She closed the door quietly behind her and the two men began to collect up the dishes. Alex reached for the cast-iron casserole dish and winced as he picked it up. The flash of pain in his shoulder was biting.

Luc glanced up. 'Still suffering from the accident?' he asked, reverting to French now they were alone.

Alex stiffened, irritated with himself that he'd inadvertently drawn attention to it. 'Now and then.'

They carried everything through to the kitchen. 'I saw a clip on the internet. It looked like a bad crash,' said Luc.

Alex put the dish down. 'I was lucky to walk away. Or so they told me.'

'It definitely seemed that way. What were your injuries?'

'Shoulder and wrist.' He peered at his wrist. That was the damn problem, although it was his shoulder that was still painful.

Luc filled the dishwasher. 'So soon after last year's crash, too. You must have been gutted.'

Alex had spent a long year in rehabilitation, then crashed during his second race back. Gutted didn't even begin to describe how he'd felt as he'd hit the tarmac.

He thought of his last meeting with the boss just over a week ago. His manager, Eric, had shuffled papers on his desk. 'I've got the reports here from both doctors.'

Alex had insisted on getting a second opinion. 'What do they say?'

Eric had met his gaze and Alex's heart had sunk. 'They've done all they can.'

The doctor and personal trainer had been pessimistic from the start, but Alex had been determined to prove them wrong. It hadn't happened, despite all the hours of physio and physical training he'd done.

His goals, his dreams, his life were collapsing around him. His throat felt tight. He didn't speak. What was there to say anyway?

'But you're young, you're well thought of. You won't be short of other opportunities, I'm sure.'

Alex stared. Did his boss really think he was interested in that stuff? He'd seen the tacky commercials and sponsorship deals other racers had gone on to do in their retirement and he couldn't think of a more soul-destroying way to spend his days. He needed to race. Nothing else came close to the buzz of being on the track.

'I'll let everyone know, the team, the press—'

'No!' Alex had cut in. 'Not yet!'

Eric had raised an eyebrow.

'Please. I'm not ready.'

His manager had considered this. 'What shall I tell them, then? They're not stupid. When you disappear they'll put two and two together.'

Alex searched around for a credible reason. 'There's

something I've been meaning to do for a while – relating to my father's affairs. It will mean going to England.'

A short silence had followed. 'Fine. I'll tell the guys you're taking a break.' Eric threw him a warning look. 'But there's only so long I can stall, you know.'

'Give me a month. Until Christmas. Then we'll go public.'

Now, ten days later, he still didn't feel any readier to talk about it. Not even to Luc. It was still too raw. It cut too deep. He could imagine his friend's pity, the messages of sympathy from his colleagues – and rivals. He wondered if he'd ever feel ready to stomach all that.

'Are you in a lot of pain?' asked Luc, as he shut the dishwasher.

'Nothing I can't handle.'

'Cheese? Wine?' offered Luc.

Alex shook his head. 'Just a coffee, then I'll be off. It's been a long day.'

'No problem. I'm having decaff. Do you want that, too, or do you still sleep through anything?'

'Decaff, thanks.' Sleep didn't come easily any more. In fact, he dreaded the long nights.

Luc slid a cup under the coffee machine and pressed a couple of buttons. 'Remember that camping trip when you slept through the storm and –'

'– the tree fell down,' Alex finished in unison with him. He smiled. 'How could I forget, the number of times you reminded me?'

Luc handed him a coffee, poured one for himself, and they carried them into the lounge, where the fire was still smouldering from earlier.

'This is a great place you have here,' said Alex, looking around at the low timber-beamed ceiling and diamond-pane windows. The cottage was almost a caricature of how he'd pictured an English cottage to be. Slate roof and cream walls, a flower-filled garden, white picket fence. 'You and Natasha seem very happy.'

'We are. Extremely so. I'm a lucky man. And being a father – well, I recommend it.' Luc took a sip of coffee. 'So is there a woman in your life?'

'No.'

'Not since . . .?'

'No,' he said definitively.

The corner of Luc's mouth lifted. 'It's still a touchy subject, then?'

'No. I'm just . . . No. That's all.'

Luc nodded.

A sudden whimper made them turn to the baby monitor. Little Lottie murmured something unintelligible, then fell silent again.

'I take back what I said earlier,' said Luc. 'You have changed.'

Alex raised an eyebrow.

'You're quieter than you used to be. Not that you were a chatterbox before, but still.'

Alex tilted his head in acknowledgement. 'Life changes us, doesn't it?'

He wasn't used to opening up. His career had made him close down, raise barriers. The sport was seen as sexy and glamorous, so of course men and women flocked to him in the hope of muscling in on his life. He hated that side of his job. In fact, he hated the fame and the money as much as his father had adored them. For him it was all about the bike and the track. He just wanted to race.

'Everything okay?' asked Luc.

Alex nodded, but couldn't meet his friend's eye. He stared hard at the glowing embers in the hearth and absentmindedly rubbed his wrist.

'It's been a difficult year for you,' Luc said quietly, 'losing your father, then the crash. How's your mum coping?'

'Surprisingly well.' Alex brightened at the thought. 'She's really changed.'

'In what way?'

He gave a dry laugh. 'It's like the chains have come off. Without Dad, she's happy, she's socialising more, and she's met someone.' He pictured his mother's expression as she'd introduced Alex and his brothers to Bernard. He was a softly spoken guy with a gentle manner. Nothing like their late father. And as she'd introduced him, there'd been a light in his mother's eyes, a radiance, which Alex had never seen before. 'In fact, she sold her flat in Paris and they've bought a house together. Back in Provence.'

Luc raised a brow. 'You're all right with that?'

'Of course. My father never made her happy.' On the contrary, he'd caused her so much pain Alex wasn't sure he'd ever be able to forgive him. 'And Bernard treats her with the respect she deserves. He's devoted. It's nice to see.' He finished his coffee and glanced at his watch. 'Right. I'd better be off. It's late.'

Luc got up with him. 'It's great that you'll be staying

so close, in the village. You'll be well looked after at Liberty's. She's a good friend. She often helps us out when we need a babysitter. Lottie adores her.'

'Right.' Liberty McKenzie had emailed and sent photos of her cottage, but he had no clue what she looked like beyond the red hair that Natasha had mentioned. He rolled his shoulder. The ache was setting in. 'As long as she understands I just need a room and won't be around much.'

If he was honest, he'd been in two minds about the lodging arrangement, but Luc had twisted his arm, saying Liberty could do with the income and the nearest quality hotel was thirty minutes away. He wasn't used to sharing his personal space with anyone else. When he was travelling with work he even avoided hotels and preferred to rent apartments so he could be guaranteed privacy.

'I'm sure that you two will get on well,' said Luc, and held open the front door for him. 'Oh, one more thing.'

'Mm?' He was tired now. The long day was catching up with him and he just wanted to put his head down, get some sleep.

'The friend she used to share the house with was badly hurt in a road accident.'

'Recently?'

'About six months ago. She's been in a coma ever since. It's very sad.'

'Right.'

'Just thought I should warn you. They were very close.'

A gust of cold air slapped him in the face as he stepped outside. Moonlight glinted off his motorbike, and he looked up. The night sky was a sheet of smooth tarmac studded with broken glass.

'It's good to see you again, Alex. We'll meet up in a few days, yes?'

'*À bientôt.*'

Charlie tugged on his lead, eager to turn off the main road and onto the long path that snaked through the woods to Liberty's cottage. There were very few cars about at this time in the evening, but even so the wildlife kept itself well hidden. Liberty occasionally glimpsed the odd badger or fox, sometimes heard an owl call, but tonight it was silent and still. Just her and Charlie. She didn't mind. Night or day, she loved walking in the woods around her home, loved the damp, peaty smell, the quiet rustlings and the freshness of cold air washing over her face. Which was why she'd refused to stay in all evening and forgo her usual walk.

She reached the turning and the ground became springy beneath her feet as she left the tarmacked pavement behind, and darkness enfolded her with a hushed sigh. The beam of her wide torch cut through the darkness, bobbing as she hurried back to Damselfly Cottage. Her phone remained stubbornly silent in her pocket. The lodger was late, over an hour late, but he hadn't bothered to call or leave a message. Perhaps he'd changed his mind and wasn't coming. Perhaps he'd had problems on his journey from France, although she suspected Natasha would have let her know if that was the case because he'd been due to have dinner with her and Luc early in the evening, and it was almost eleven now. Her boots crunched over fallen beech nuts and crisp leaves.

Then, out of the darkness, came the violent roar of an engine. Charlie whirled round and barked. The explosion of noise crashed down on them from behind, like a giant wave, and she instinctively stepped back. She shielded her eyes against a blinding light and gripped Charlie's lead as a motorbike thundered past. Birds screeched and wings flapped, startled out of the treetops. She didn't blame them – she would have flown away herself if she could. The noise had been so loud it had shaken the ground and vibrated through her. It had felt like an attack, a violation. And it was heading for her home.

Angrily, she picked up her pace as she rounded the corner and the cottage came into view. She was just in time to see him dim the lights of the motorbike parked in front of her door. Charlie barked even more furiously.

'Hey,' she murmured, and gave the dog a reassuring pat. 'It's okay. This is our new housemate. He's not a monster – although, by the looks of it, he drives one.'

As she approached, the guy dismounted. He wore form-fitting leathers and in the porch light his eyes gleamed, like black treacle. A helmet dangled from his hand.

Liberty passed the bike. It was enormous. Almost as wide as a car. Why did he need such a huge noisy thing?

'This is Dragonfly Cottage?' he asked. His voice was rich and deep, and he had a strong French accent.

'*Damselfly* Cottage,' she corrected. 'Yes, it is.'

He peered at the cottage in the darkness, but she couldn't

imagine he could see very much: the lights were on inside, but the curtains were drawn. 'It wasn't easy to find.'

'Yes, well you're here now. You must be Alex,' she said. Her words sounded clipped. 'I'm Liberty.' She couldn't bring herself to sound friendlier. Her heart was still racing from the scare he'd given her.

They shook hands, and she waited for a greeting or an apology for his lateness but neither came. Instead, he frowned at Charlie, who was sniffing him curiously. 'You didn't say you have a dog.'

Her fingers tightened around the lead. 'Didn't I? I thought I did. Is it a problem?'

'Yes. I'm allergic.'

He pronounced it *allairjeek*.

'Oh.' Had she really not mentioned it? She made a mental note to spell it out loud and clear for any future lodgers. Charlie was non-negotiable. If they didn't like dogs, her cottage wasn't for them.

'I hope he won't be allowed in my room.'

She bristled. 'No, of course not. He's not allowed upstairs, but maybe keep your door shut, just in case.'

He was dressed from head to toe in fitted black leathers that made his shoulders look broad and his legs long and slim. She had to admit he was handsome, and she tried to ignore the feeling of self-consciousness that sparked in her. Something in his eyes made her wary. Impatience? Irritation? She couldn't pin it down.

Well, since he wasn't bothering with the niceties, she might as well tell him what was on *her* mind, too. She made a show of consulting her watch. 'You know you're nearly two hours late? You said in your email that you'd be here at nine.'

'Oh? Does it matter?'

His casual indifference pressed all her buttons. 'Yes, actually. It matters because I waited in all evening just for you. I put off walking my dog because I thought you might arrive any time.' The poor animal had been practically crossing his legs.

He cast Charlie a withering glance. 'Clearly you went out anyway.'

'Because we couldn't wait any longer! You could have messaged to say you were running late. It would have been polite.'

Usually she loved her evening walk with Charlie. It was calming and cleared her head before bed. Tonight she was far from calm. Instead, she was fuming and flustered, her usual routine totally disrupted, thanks to him.

He opened the panniers on the back of the bike as if she hadn't spoken and lifted out a couple of small bags. She glared at him. He had typically French dark hair and olive skin, like Luc, but none of Luc's warmth or charm. Fine, she thought. If that was how it was going to be. Rather than opening the front door to let him in, she got on with what she always did after a walk, and picked up the hosepipe. 'Charlie, come here,' she coaxed. The Labrador trotted over to the side of the house. 'Good boy.'

Beneath the dim outdoor light, she gently washed his paws, making sure she'd removed any dirt and burrs or sharp twigs and pine needles that might dig in and hurt him.

'What are you doing?' The Frenchman appeared beside her, scowling and clearly impatient to get inside.

Good. See how he liked to be kept waiting.

'Cleaning his paws,' she spelled out.

'Now? In the night?'

She straightened up. At times like this she was glad to be tall. She was only a fraction shorter than him so their eyes were almost level as she said pointedly, 'Yes. Just like you would wash yours if you'd walked barefoot through the woods.'

That seemed to leave him floundering because he didn't reply, but looked incredulously from her to the dog and back again. She turned the tap off and marched past him to the front door. Inside, she crouched and patted Charlie's paws dry with an old towel. Alex put down his bags and helmet, and she could feel him watching her disapprovingly. Charlie didn't pick up on his hostility, however, and seemed to have overcome his reservations about the stranger. As soon as she'd finished, he rushed over, tail wagging, excited to have a visitor in his home. The Frenchman stepped back, clearly horrified.

'Would you like a drink?' she asked politely. Now she'd recovered from his dramatic arrival, she recognised that they hadn't had the best of starts. It might be wise to get to know each other a little. 'I have some red wine open, or there's tea, coffee . . .' She'd baked gingerbread cookies too, and the smell of sweet spice permeated the air.

'No, thanks. I left early this morning to drive here and I've got a headache. I need to sleep.'

She stiffened at his curt tone. 'Right. I'll just show you round the house, then let you turn in.'

'Now? Can't it wait until morning?'

They might as well get it over and done with, then tomorrow she could keep out of his way. She was seriously regretting her decision to have a lodger. 'It won't take long. It's not a big place. This is the lounge.'

He followed her in, ducking his head under the doorframe. The fire was still smouldering, and the quilt she was working on was neatly folded over the armchair. Charlie was running in excited circles around them, much to the Frenchman's annoyance. He sneezed twice, then a third time.

'Bless you,' she said over her shoulder, and ducked through the doorway. 'Through here is the kitchen, and in—'

She heard a loud thump. Then, '*Aie!*'

She swung round. He was clutching his forehead. 'What happened?'

'Banged my head,' he said, through gritted teeth, and pointed to the doorframe.

'Oh! Ah – yes, I forgot to say. I'll get you some ice.' She rooted around in the freezer, but found only frozen peas. They would do. 'Here,' she said.

'It's fine.' He waved them away irritably and sneezed again.

'I'm afraid all the doorways are low. I think people used to be smaller in the days when this cottage was built.'

He sneezed again and glowered at her. She continued into the hall. 'And through here is my sewing room.'

49

Another sneeze.

She picked up a box of tissues and offered it to him. He took one and blew his nose. 'Have you got a cold?'

'No. I told you – I'm allergic to the dog.'

'Oh.' Her smile slipped. 'Charlie, come here,' she murmured, feeling a nip of guilt. Had she really forgotten to mention the dog in her emails? Charlie nuzzled her hand and she rubbed his ears. 'Well, I've got the day off work tomorrow so I expect I'll see you in the morning for breakfast. I can show you where the tea and coffee are then.'

'It's all right. I'll manage.'

'I'll show you your room, then.' She told Charlie to sit and he waited obediently in the hall.

Upstairs there were two bedrooms and the bathroom. Her cottage could only be described as snug, but she wouldn't want to live anywhere else. As she led him up the stairs he sneezed three times in a row, then cursed under his breath. She pushed open the door to his room and gestured for him to go in first. He cast an assessing gaze over it, but didn't say anything. Judging by his expression, it wasn't what he'd been expecting. She bit back a sigh of exasperation. There was really no pleasing this guy.

'Is everything okay?' She looked at the room, trying to see it through the eyes of a stranger. The candles she'd lit earlier gave it a warm glow, and a gorgeous grey quilt, with orange and red appliquéd triangles, lay on the bed, a pile of fluffy towels at the foot. In the morning, he'd open the curtains to a beautiful view of the woods at the back of the house. Carys had adored this room. It wasn't big, but it was homely.

His shoulders lifted in a typically Gallic shrug. 'It's fine,' he said, without enthusiasm, and put down his bags heavily.

She gritted her teeth. What had he expected? She'd sent him photos and dimensions.

He sneezed again. 'I'm going to bed.'

'Goodnight, then.'

Alone in the kitchen she made sure Charlie was settled for the night, and rearranged the flowers in the vase, moving an orange gerbera that had been hidden at the back to the front. She could hear footsteps above as Alex moved around his room. Disappointment made her shoulders slump. Well, that was a fantastic start, wasn't it? Maybe taking on a lodger hadn't been her best idea. Maybe the whole challenge had been naïve. The hopes and optimism she'd had for her brave new start suddenly dissipated. This was reality: a rude, surly stranger with a horrifically loud motorbike. She shuddered. She didn't like the way he'd walked around her home with narrowed eyes. And Charlie. *I hope he isn't allowed in my room.* The cheek of him. This was her – and Charlie's – home. He was just a guest. Sharing with him would be very different from sharing with Carys.

You don't have to like him, Liberty. Just tolerate him. Say yes to everything.

Even unfriendly lodgers. And it's only for a month. Not long at all.

Chapter Three

Alex closed his bedroom door and clutched his shoulder. The pain was always worse late in the evening, but tonight, after a day on the road, it bit into him. He knew it would have been more sensible to travel by plane and car, but coming without his bike had been out of the question. Of course, it wasn't the one he'd raced but his tourer; far better suited to the long journey he'd made. He rubbed a hand over his face, exhausted. Still, he'd arrived now. And what a welcome he'd had, he thought, picturing Liberty's angry red hair and brown eyes, which had glinted in the porch light. A barbed comment about the time and a smack on the wrist because he hadn't messaged her. She was only his landlady, not a friend. He didn't owe her an explanation. He just wanted a bed to sleep in.

She was *Luc*'s friend, he conceded, with a shadow of guilt. But he was too tired and sore to think about that now. As he rolled his shoulder to ease the pain, he looked around the room. The bed was supposedly a double, but it was small, and the décor – well, it wasn't his taste at all. On the bedside table candles were flickering. Scented candles, judging by the sickly smell. He blew them out.

There'd been candles burning all around the lounge, too.
Fire hazards, although she clearly wasn't worried because
she'd left them while she was out with the dog. Next to
the pile of towels was a hot-water bottle with a red-and-
white-striped knitted cover. He picked it up. Why had she
thought that could possibly be of use to him? Sighing,
he shoved it into the bedside-table drawer and rubbed
his head. It was still throbbing and he could feel a bump.
He needed to sleep. He opened a case and unpacked only
his toothbrush. The rest could wait until tomorrow. Eyeing
the big chest of drawers and the embroidered red felt
heart that hung from one of the handles, his nose wrinkled. Why on earth had Luc recommended he stay here?
He hadn't expected the cottage to be in the middle of
nowhere with death traps for doorframes – and he
certainly hadn't expected a dog. How could she have
forgotten to mention something so important? He sighed
and went to brush his teeth.

A little later he pulled back the quilt and got into bed.
In the darkness, he listened to the unfamiliar sounds:
creaks of wood, the faint hammering of pipes. It had been
good to see Luc, to visit his home and see how happy
and settled he was with his little family. He and Natasha
were excited about their new baby, too.

Alex stared at the shadows around him. In contrast,
his own future stretched ahead of him, bleak and overwhelming.

What would he do now? Without racing, he had
nothing. His life was empty. Meaningless.

He felt sleep begin to drag him down, and he didn't

put up a fight. His body was too tired and ached too much, and his head welcomed a reprieve from the dark thoughts he'd hoped to leave behind but had followed him.

Tuesday, 2 December

The long drive must have tired him out because Alex slept later than he'd planned the next morning. He blinked and looked around him, then remembered where he was – and why. He sank back against the pillow, emotions roiling in him like poison.

He should be on the other side of the world, not in this backwater. He should be training, preparing for the next race. Speed was what he lived for. He missed it, craved it. Despair sucked him down. He wasn't just cut up about his career, he was angry, too. Angry with the doctors, with his body – and with himself for not having been able to prevent this.

He sat up and held his head in his hands, trying to push the dark thoughts out of his mind. He had to remember why he'd come and stay focused on the search for his sister. Reading his father's letters had set alight in him such a burning sense of rage, of injustice at what the man had done and how he'd behaved. Alex had thought it wasn't possible to cause more hurt than his father had already caused, but those letters had proved him wrong. To ignore his responsibilities, to turn his back on someone who'd reached out for help, who'd clearly been desperate:

it made Alex's stomach twist. His father's selfishness had truly known no bounds.

Well, he intended to put right his father's wrongs. He might not be able to change the last thirty years, but he could step in and help now – financially, emotionally. Think how incredible it would be to find his sister and get to know her. They'd have a lifetime of catching up to do. Would she look like him and his brothers? Would she have children of her own? The hope of finding her raised his spirits, like a lamp glowing in grey mist.

He got up, showered and dressed. He desperately needed coffee, and then he'd get on with his search. As he made his way towards the kitchen he looked around. It was a curious place, this little cottage in the woods, and it certainly didn't look like the home of a young woman who lived alone. With its tiny rooms and low doorways he felt like Gulliver in Lilliput, and it was how he'd imagined a typically English cottage to be: stuffed with knick-knacks, candles and – he bent down to peer at a doorstop in the shape of a hare – quirky objects. In the lounge he spotted an antler ceiling lamp, and there were quilts everywhere: strewn over sofas, armchairs, folded in a basket; they'd even been used as wall-hangings. Pine cones were strung with ribbon from every hook and door handle. His bedroom window, when he'd opened the curtains, had given onto nothing but trees, and he wondered why anyone would want to live in such an isolated place.

He heard a low rattling coming from the front room, and it was only when he saw Liberty sitting behind a sewing machine that he realised what it was. He'd intended to slip past unseen, but she spotted him.

'Good morning.' She followed him into the kitchen. 'Did you sleep well?' She smiled, but her expression was wary.

He was wary, too. He didn't want to argue again. He hated hotels. He hated the attention he got when he was recognised, as he invariably was, and he didn't want questions to be asked about why he was in England. 'Yes, thanks.' He opened a couple of cupboard doors. 'Where's the coffee?'

'It's here. Would you like toast? I've also got cereal in this cupboard, and fruit here. Help yourself, and if there's anything else you need, I keep a shopping list by the fridge – just write it on there.'

She seemed friendlier today, and more helpful. He wondered what had changed. Last night she'd been on the attack from the moment he'd arrived. 'Just coffee is fine.'

She had a machine, thank goodness. At least there'd be decent coffee. He flicked it on and placed a cup underneath.

'I'll join you,' she said, opening the fridge and reaching for a bottle of milk.

Oh, great. Just what he needed. After last night he'd planned to stay out of her way and hoped she'd do the same. He wasn't interested in getting to know her. He always kept himself to himself, and friends like Luc were rare in his life. The only people he trusted were his mum and brothers.

The kitchen fell quiet. Outside in the woods, birds

chattered. When the coffee came through he seized the cup and blew on it. The dog trotted into the kitchen and came straight to him. Before Alex could pull away, it was licking his hand as if he were a long-lost friend, not a perfect stranger. He snatched his hand away. Too late: a red rash sprang up and he sneezed.

'Charlie, come here,' said Liberty. She held on to his collar to keep him away. 'Sorry. He really likes you.'

'Dogs always do,' he said wearily. 'If there's a group of people in a room you can bet they'll always come to me, even though others want to stroke them and I show no interest. I think they see me as a challenge.'

'I'll send him out into the garden,' she said, and ushered the dog through the back door.

Through the kitchen window he saw the dog scamper around, then stop and bark at a tall tree. Alex felt a nip of guilt. The forest looked damp, the bare branches of the trees glistening in the wintry December light. 'Will he be all right outside? It's not too cold?'

'It's fine. He loves it out there and the garden's fenced off. As long as you don't mind him barking at every squirrel in the vicinity.'

'It might irritate your neighbours.'

She laughed. 'My nearest neighbours are Jake and Evie and they live a mile away on the other side of the woods and up the hill.'

Her long hair was a vibrant red and swung around her shoulders as she moved. She was dressed casually in a velvet tunic and leggings, nothing special, yet there was something graceful about her.

'So why are you here?' she asked. 'Natasha said you're trying to find someone. A relative?'

'That's right,' he said, deliberately keeping it vague. His reason for coming here was deeply personal. The last thing he needed was for news of it to get out into the public domain. 'There's some personal stuff I have to see to concerning my father. He passed away last year.'

'That must be difficult for you,' she said, her tone unexpectedly gentle. 'It took me a long while after Mum died before I stopped being hit by the grief at unexpected moments.' Her eyes were the deep rich brown of chestnuts and they filled with sympathy.

'We weren't close.' He drank down his coffee.

There was a surprised silence. 'No?'

He shook his head.

'Right. So – er – do you need any help with your search? I've lived here all my life. I know the place well.'

She really was trying suspiciously hard to be friendly, and instantly his barriers went up. This happened all the time on and off the track: people of all ages taking a keen interest in him, always with a self-centred motive. 'I can manage. I have a list of places I need to visit.'

Hurt flickered in her eyes, and he remembered he'd seen it last night, too. She was a curious combination of haughty and vulnerable, but the vulnerability reminded him that, whatever her intention, she was Luc and Natasha's friend. He tried to backtrack on his curt answer. 'Actually, do you know where is the nearest local records office?'

She brightened. 'Yes, it's in town. Would you like me to take you there?'

'I'm sure I can find it.'

'The traffic's bad round there,' she warned. 'It can be difficult to park.'

'My bike gets through where cars can't.'

'Oh, yes. Of course.' Her tone was cool. 'Well, suit yourself.'

Liberty knew Alex was going out, but still the noise of the engine starting was so loud and fierce it made her jump. She looked up from behind the sewing machine and peered through the window as he fastened his helmet and gunned the engine yet again. Birds scattered from the treetops, terrified. Was it really necessary to rev it repeatedly – and so loudly? Finally, he rocketed off at speed, and calm was restored.

She shook her head. Why would anyone choose to use such a dangerous mode of transport? Worse still, why would anyone choose to risk their life racing profession-ally? It was one thing to enjoy the rush of wind on your face as you pedalled a pushbike downhill, but quite another to race around on a machine at such high-octane speeds that one small error could cause carnage.

Like the idiot who'd been speeding and hit Carys head-on.

She pushed away the thought and reminded herself that this morning she'd vowed to make a fresh start with her lodger. She'd woken up regretting the way things had unravelled last night. Yes, he'd been late and had got off to a bad start with his noisy bike and bad attitude, but what if he left and booked himself into a hotel?

The idea had made a shiver of panic touch her spine. She was counting on his rent to help cover her winter bills. This old cottage was expensive to heat and she couldn't imagine there'd be many people looking for a room around here before Christmas. So she'd resolved that from now on she'd try harder to be hospitable and friendly.

Well, maybe just hospitable – because he wasn't making an effort, was he? This morning his body language had screamed, 'Keep away', and their conversation had been clipped, awkward. And why had he looked so suspicious when she'd offered to take him into town?

Shaking her head, she went into the kitchen, flicked on the kettle and topped up the vase of flowers with water. They reminded her: it was day two of her challenge. What was she going to say yes to today? Perhaps she could cook something out of the ordinary – a curry, maybe. She wasn't keen on spicy food, but Alex might like it. And perhaps he'd appreciate the gesture as the olive branch she wanted it to be. Her spirits lifted. Also, she had the whole day free to sew, and once she'd finished stitching the binding onto this Maple Leaf quilt, an idea for a new design was buzzing in her head, begging to be started. She'd received a delivery this morning of gorgeous new orange, black and white geometric fabrics, which would look great in a chevron design.

But an hour later her plans were interrupted. She had just begun cutting triangles of orange material when she got an alert from the dating app: it was an invitation for lunch today from a chef who had a rare day off.

Liberty pushed it away. She wouldn't have time to get ready at such short notice. And it was her first blind date. She didn't want—

Every opportunity, every invitation, I'll accept.

She had to say yes. Simple as that.

Taking a deep breath, she looked again at the invitation and answered, 'Yes,' before she could change her mind. On the bright side, short notice meant she wouldn't have time to get nervous.

This was exactly what her challenge was about, she told herself, as she left her sewing room and ran upstairs to get ready.

As she drove into town Liberty gripped the steering wheel to stop her hands shaking. What if he was gorgeous and she got completely tongue-tied? What if he took one look at her and walked away? What if they had nothing in common and nothing to talk about? She'd tried to prepare some questions, but each time she thought of one, she ruled it out because it sounded dull or judgemental or just plain silly.

Oh, this was such a bad idea. She wasn't interesting or confident, and she wasn't any good at cracking jokes. Carys had been the bubbly, outgoing one. She could bond with strangers within five minutes and have a roomful of people laughing their socks off. Liberty didn't have that gift. It took her a long time to get to know anyone, which was why she missed Carys so much. With her best friend, she didn't have to try. She could just be herself.

She did her best to ignore the fluttering in her stomach. It was just lunch, she told herself. Even if it was a disaster, it wouldn't last more than two hours. Once she'd parked the car and found the restaurant, she paused outside the door, taking a deep breath and smoothing her dress. It was black velvet with red flowers, which she'd been told brought out the colour of her hair, and she'd picked her favourite high-heeled suede boots, which always made her feel a million dollars. She was satisfied with her appearance, but the urge to turn and run was still strong.

Think of the challenge, Lib. Think of how wonderful it would be to meet The One. And even if you don't meet him, just doing this will shake up your routine and earn you a tick in your orange book.

'Fake it till you make it,' she whispered to herself. It had been Carys's catchphrase and it made her smile.

Holding on to that thought, Liberty drew back her shoulders and went in.

Merde, merde, merde. Alex strode out of the town hall into the icy wind and stamped down the steps, cursing under his breath. What a damned waste of time that had been. Unfriendly, unhelpful staff, who'd been about as much use as a bandage on a wooden leg. He'd hoped they would at least be able to get his search started, if not provide him with information on the births recorded for the autumn and winter of thirty years ago. But no. They'd apologised, but without the child's name they couldn't help him. And there'd been no record of anyone with his surname: he'd made sure of that by checking page after page himself and wasting most of the day.

He took a deep breath, glaring at the passing traffic while he regrouped and planned what to do next. He rolled his shoulder and winced. The pain was a crushing weight and he found it ironic that the wrist injury, which had ended his career, barely hurt at all. He tried to knead the ache out of his shoulder, but it was difficult to reach and impossible to apply enough pressure. Sighing, he pulled out his phone. The journey here and having to grit his teeth against the pain were taking their toll and he'd had enough.

The team doctor answered on the third ring. 'Alex?'

'I've run out of painkillers,' he said. 'Can you email me a prescription?'

A long silence followed. Alex frowned.

'Alex,' the doc said. His tone was careful. 'I'm not your doctor any more. You're not part of the team. I can't treat you.'

Alex could have kicked himself. He hadn't even given it any thought, just hit speed-dial. 'Who should I see, then?' The doc had been treating him since he was a kid when he'd first signed with the team as a teenager.

'You need to register with a family doctor. Where are you – Paris?'

'No. England.'

'England? Oh. I can't help you there. Let me know when you're back in Paris and—'

'It doesn't matter,' he said quickly. Heat rushed to his face. 'Forget it.'

'Alex, I—'

He hung up before his humiliation could be prolonged any further. Then he thumped the seat of his bike and cursed. How could he have been so stupid?

It was nine p.m. when he got back to the cottage but that call was still at the front of his mind. Would the doctor tell the rest of the team? Alex could picture their incredulity, their amusement, their pity. And none of this was helped by the fact that this afternoon's efforts to find his sister had yielded nothing. He'd visited another office, checked through the records himself again, because as soon as he told people he didn't have a name, they were reluctant to help. They had a point: it was like searching for a needle in a haystack.

He shut the front door quietly. He was in a dangerous mood. It was best for everyone if he kept to himself.

Liberty was in the lounge. The fire was burning and a quick glance told him she was watching a comedy film and hand-stitching a quilt. Her dog stopped barking when he recognised Alex and greeted him with a lick. Alex jerked his hand away and muttered a curse beneath his breath.

'How did you get on?' she said, and came into the hallway. 'Did you find the town hall?'

'Yes.' He pulled off his boots. They were wet and sticky with mud.

'Were they able to help?'

'No. No luck there.'

'Oh dear.' She threw him a look of sympathy. 'So what will you do?'

He unzipped his jacket, hung it next to her coat, and shrugged. He could really do without the barrage of questions.

'You could try the church records. I could call the vicar if you like, make an appointment for you.'

'It's fine. Thank you.' He was trying to be polite, but he wished she'd stop interfering.

'Right.' She glanced behind her at the kitchen. 'I made chicken curry. Would you like some?'

'No, thanks. I had something while I was out.' Not that he'd been impressed by the Greek restaurant in town. He'd never eaten such tasteless tomatoes, and what they called pitta bread hadn't even faintly resembled the genuine Greek version.

'Oh.' She tried to hide it, but she was evidently disappointed.

He followed her into the kitchen where she took a dish out of the oven and spooned curry into a bowl. He frowned. Had she been waiting for him to eat her own dinner? He felt a twist of guilt. On the other hand, he didn't want to get drawn into sharing meals or anything else. He poured himself a glass of water and flinched as a sudden shaft of pain fired through his shoulder.

'What's wrong?' asked Liberty.

'Nothing,' he said through gritted teeth. It felt as if a metal spike was stabbing him. He didn't have the energy or the patience to answer her questions.

'What do you have planned for tonight?' she continued, as she poked a fork into her food.

'I have things to do.' He started to leave.

'Would you like to watch a film?'

He stopped in the doorway. He'd rather stick pins in his eyes than watch the rom-com she'd had on earlier.

Perhaps he should make this clear, once and for all. He didn't need an interfering landlady questioning him all the time and trying to intrude in his life. He was fiercely protective of his personal space. He needed – wanted – to be alone. Especially now, while he came to terms with the monumental change of direction his life had taken.

Taking a deep breath, he turned around. 'Listen, I don't know what Luc told you, but I don't want to watch movies, and I don't need meals or help with what I'm doing or anything else. I just want a room and a bed.'

As soon as he'd tracked down his half-sister and resolved things with her, he'd be out of here.

Liberty stared at him. Then her eyes narrowed and glinted angrily. 'I see.'

'I'm quite happy to look after myself.'

Her expression was stony. She reminded him of a purebred horse, tall and dignified. 'Yes. You've made that perfectly clear,' she said, and stalked away into the lounge.

Chapter Four

Oh, my goodness, how cringeworthy had that been? Liberty sat alone on the sofa, mortified and angry. She ate her meal in quick, snatched mouthfuls, furious that she'd waited all evening to eat with him, only to have her offer thrown back in her face. For goodness' sake, she'd only been trying to be welcoming. There was no need to be so rude and arrogant and – and—

She gave up trying to find the words, and pictured instead his dark scowl. What had she expected? Men who raced motorbikes were hardly known for being friendly, were they?

Actually, she had no idea. She knew nothing about racing of any kind.

She heard Alex moving about upstairs, then it went quiet. She carried on watching the film she'd started (she'd been offering to pause it and start a new one with him, for Heaven's sake!) but she wasn't really paying attention any more. He'd been so sniffy about watching television, yet she'd like to bet he was watching a film right now up there by himself.

Picking up the remote, she gave up on her film. She was too ruffled even to sew. She glanced at her watch. It

67

was a little earlier than usual, but taking Charlie for a walk seemed like the best way to get rid of her frustrations, so she called the Labrador, put her boots on and stamped outside into the night. She'd had a rubbish day, not just because of this tiff with her grumpy, rude lodger. Her blind date had been disappointing, too. He'd been a nice guy, but there'd been no chemistry.

James, the chef, had spotted her as soon as she'd walked in. (The advantage of having red hair: it was distinctive.)

'Sorry. Sweaty palms,' he'd said, wiping his hand on his trousers as he stood up, then shaking hers. 'I'm so nervous.'

She'd laughed. 'I'm nervous too.'

They both sat down and he tugged at his collar. 'This tie is strangling me. I don't normally wear clothes like this.'

'You wear a chef's whites?'

He nodded. He was overweight, and Liberty noticed the beads of sweat accumulating on his brow.

'Do you mind if I take it off?' he asked.

'Course not.'

His hands shook as he pulled at the tie and unfastened his collar and she realised he was terrified. Curiously, her own nerves shrank and she did her best to put him at ease. 'Where do you work? Is it near here?'

He named a smart hotel on the other side of town. 'I enjoy it there, but it's hard work. I rarely get evenings off and my social life's really suffered. That's why I'm doing this dating malarkey. Trying to get out more. I'm a bit out of practice, though. You'll have to excuse me if I don't know what to say or the right questions to ask.'

Liberty laughed. 'This is my first time on a blind date so you don't need to worry. I'm no expert either.'

But he continued to look worried, and as the conversation progressed it became clear that a lot of his anxiety was centred round his appearance. 'I didn't always look like this,' he told her. 'But working with food makes it difficult.'

At the end of their lunch they said goodbye, but Liberty knew she wouldn't see him again. She liked him, but there was no zing of attraction. In fact, what she felt most was sympathy for him, and that was hardly the basis for a relationship. It was disappointing, but it was only her first date, and hopefully there'd be plenty more.

She trudged through the woods, breathing in the refreshingly cold night air and enjoying the calm that spread through her with every step. That date might not have been successful, but it had been a confidence-booster. It had made her glad that she had no hang-ups about her appearance. Apart from her hair colour, she was ordinary-looking, but now she appreciated how blessed she was to be tall and slim and have no trouble finding or making clothes that suited her. And spurred on with new confidence, she'd already arranged another date for Friday night.

When she got back, the house was still quiet. She topped up Charlie's water bowl and settled him for the night. 'Sleep tight, gorgeous boy,' she said, as she patted his head. 'See you in the morning.'

Warily, she climbed the stairs and brushed her teeth quicker than usual, not wanting to linger in the bathroom in case she crossed the arrogant Frenchman on the landing. Then she got ready for bed. Normally she would have lounged in her pyjamas and slippers all evening, and she really missed that. She'd made so many concessions for her lodger, and for what? She patted her quilt straight and absently traced the quilted cable pattern with her fingertip. Despite her efforts today to be friendly, Alex Ricard was not good company, and she was so disappointed.

Why disappointed, Lib? What did you expect – another friendship like the one you had with Carys?

It was then that she realised she'd secretly hoped there would be at least the spark of friendship with her new lodger, if not more. Someone to watch movies with and chat with over supper. Something like the closeness she'd felt with Carys.

Oh, you stupid girl. What were you thinking – that you could replace your best friend? How ridiculous.

Liberty sighed. She'd never had a stranger lodge with her before so she had no idea how it worked to share a house but lead completely separate lives. How would they each cook their own meals in her small kitchen, for example? She and Carys had agreed that if one cooked, the other washed up, and it had worked well: they'd enjoyed eating together and it had been harmonious. Things with Alex, however, were awkward and prickly and made her feel uncomfortable. And it was all complicated even more by him being Luc's friend. She would have had lower expectations if he'd been a complete stranger.

She sank back into her pillow and pulled the quilt up

higher to ward off the chilly night air. She hated living alone, she thought, as she turned off the light, but she wasn't sure that sharing with Alex was any better.

A while later Liberty was woken by the squeaky floorboard on the landing. She listened groggily, half expecting to hear the bathroom door. Instead, there were light footsteps on the stairs, the front door closed, and then the harsh growl of his motorbike made her start.

Wide awake, she jumped out of bed and pulled the curtain back, only to catch a glimpse of his tail light disappearing round the corner. Liberty frowned. What the hell was he doing at this time of night?

Alex sped along the main road. It shouldn't have surprised him that it was deserted at this time: this was the back of beyond, not the city where life happened around the clock.

After he'd gone up to his room, he'd scrolled through emails and done a little more research on his laptop in the hope of finding a new lead to his sister, then given up and switched off for the night.

But the ache in his shoulder had kept him awake. He'd tried everything: pacing his room, rolling his shoulder to loosen the muscles, listening to soothing music through headphones – nothing had worked. So he'd scooped up his keys and gone out.

Now the night air washed over him like iced water, but he didn't mind. He needed this: the adrenalin, the pounding in his ears. Previously, his days had been filled with training and riding, testing himself and his bike to the limit. Then, suddenly, nothing.

How would he fill the void in his life where racing had been?

He couldn't. It seemed impossible, and despair sucked him under.

But as kilometre after kilometre of tarmac whipped by, his thoughts quietened. The speed calmed him, concentration on the road distracting him from the pain. He focused on learning the bends and the straights as he used to learn tracks. There were no chicanes or hairpin corners, but he automatically memorised the roundabouts, junctions and possible flashpoints. He soaked up the solitude and the darkness. They asked no questions, they didn't judge. It was a relief to be in the moment.

When he got back to the cottage, the pain had dulled, the ugly thoughts dispersed, and his body was weak with exhaustion. He was ready to sink into bed and embrace the respite of sleep. He closed the front door silently, but the dog heard and came scampering into the hall to greet him. Alex led him back to his bed, made sure he was settled, then crept up the stairs as quietly as possible. It was one thirty and he was conscious that Liberty was probably asleep.

But as he reached the top step, her bedroom door opened. She was wearing pyjamas and her fiery hair was messy. There was a sleepy softness about her that made him feel a tinge of longing. It was obvious he'd woken her and for the briefest second he felt guilty – but her confrontational stance instantly dispelled that.

'Do you have to ride that thing so late at night?' she snapped. 'You've probably woken the whole valley with that noise.'

He climbed the last step and drew level with her. 'I didn't realise there was a curfew here.'

'Of course there isn't, but you could show a bit of respect for those of us who have work in the morning.'

The guilt crept back. He went on the defensive. 'I had to go out.'

She folded her arms. 'Oh, really? At this time?'

'Yes.'

'Why? What on earth was so urgent it couldn't wait until morning?' A thought seemed to occur and her brows knotted. 'You weren't looking for drugs, were you?'

He was shocked, and her suggestion raised his hackles even more. 'If I'm going to be interrogated on my movements, then I'll move out first thing in the morning.'

'You know what? Maybe you should! I'm not sure I want to share my house with someone who has such little thought for other people.' She stamped back into her room and slammed the door.

Wednesday, 3 December

Alex heard the front door shut as he got up the next morning and guessed that Liberty had gone to work. Through the bathroom window he watched her start her old 2CV. In front of the cottage there was a wide clearing, yet she manoeuvred the car as slowly and carefully as if

73

she were navigating through heavy traffic. He felt relief that he'd missed her – and guilt too.

She'd caught him off guard last night, springing out of the darkness, and then that barb about drugs – was that really the kind of man she thought he was?

But that was no excuse. He regretted what he'd said, how he'd lost his temper.

He'd been on a short fuse ever since he'd arrived here and somehow she seemed to light it each time they met, he wasn't sure why. He pictured her mane of richly coloured hair and deep brown eyes, but it was her parting shot that preyed on his mind: *I'm not sure I want to share my house with someone who has such little thought for other people.*

Was that really what he was like?

His father had been the epitome of selfish. He'd swanned through life causing nothing but hurt as he'd pursued his own pleasure and thought of no one but himself. Alex bristled at the thought that perhaps he'd done the same.

Was she right? Had it been selfish of him to go out on his bike late at night?

Perhaps she had a point. He wasn't used to living with others. He eyed his tiny room and the quilted bedcover critically. And his lifestyle couldn't be more different from hers.

He sighed, knowing he'd have to speak to her.

Once showered and dressed, he went downstairs to the kitchen, careful to duck under the low doorway. The dog seemed excited to see him and followed him around hopefully. Alex sneezed once, twice, three times. Still, the dog trailed him like a shadow while he made breakfast. His stomach growled and he found a loaf of bread and dropped a slice into the toaster.

After his altercation with Liberty last night it had taken him a while to calm down. He'd lain in bed seething and replaying the confrontation in his mind. He wasn't used to conflict, apart from the obvious rivalries on the race-track. He spent a lot of time alone, and that was how he liked it, how he'd lived for the last ten years. After his relationship with Solange had ended, he'd decided it was better this way. His lifestyle, being constantly on the move, made relationships difficult. And a solitary existence meant that no one got hurt.

So last night had thrown him, but as the clock had ticked into the early hours, sleep had eventually begun to tug him down, and this morning he was astonished by how well rested he felt.

The toaster popped and the dog looked at him with big hopeful eyes.

'What do you want?' Alex asked. 'A walk? Food? I'm sure Liberty wouldn't like it if I overfed you.'

The dog perked up, and rushed away into the entrance hall. He reappeared moments later with a lead in his mouth.

Alex muttered a curse. 'You understood? You're cleverer than I thought.' He bent and gave the dog a friendly pat on the head. Then remembered he shouldn't have done that, and pulled his hand back. 'Sorry, my friend. I don't want to get it wrong and get in even more trouble with your mistress. Another time, okay?'

He buttered his toast and left it a moment to make himself a cup of coffee. When he turned back, he stopped.

His plate was empty, bar a few crumbs.

'What—'

The dog, who was now in his basket, kept his head down and his gaze averted.

Alex frowned. The Labrador looked . . . guilty. 'Did you just steal my toast?'

The dog thumped his tail.

'I don't believe it.' Shaking his head, Alex got another piece of bread. This time he made sure to keep a close eye on it.

When he'd finished breakfast, he washed his plate and cup. He noticed Liberty kept everything spotlessly clean and tidy – apart from the dog hairs, which were everywhere, especially in the lounge, clinging to all the quilts and the thick carpet. When he'd dried the crockery and put it away he looked around the lounge. What was the word Liberty had used to describe her cottage? 'Cosy'. It was tiny and would feel more spacious if it wasn't crammed with furniture and knick-knacks.

He examined the photo frames that covered the sideboard. In one Liberty was waving at the camera and beside her was a black girl of the same age, with a wide smile and glossy hair. He peered at the rest. There was Liberty as a child with the same friend, Liberty in school uniform, Liberty with an older woman – her mother? Liberty and her friend in front of the Eiffel Tower. This must be the friend in a coma. The girls' closeness was almost palpable: he could practically hear their laughter and see the intimacy of a lasting friendship in their eyes.

He looked out of the window. Even the little garden at the back, fenced off from the forest, was cluttered with gnomes and coloured jam-jars suspended from the branches of trees. He presumed they held tealights in summer, but against the sparse winter landscape they looked mournful. This place felt unbearably claustrophobic with that army of trees assembled outside, closing in on him, the low ceilings and tiny doorways.

Alex closed his eyes. Maybe he shouldn't have come here. Maybe he should have taken a few weeks off to lie on a beach and get his head around the fact that his career was over. But a beach holiday would never have worked for him. He was too restless. He had too much energy. At least here he had his bike with him, and if he could find the woman who'd written those letters to his father it would make the trip worthwhile.

'So how's it going with your lodger?' asked Evie, as they tidied the counter after a busy morning in the Button Hole. 'What's he like?'

Liberty pictured Alex's exotic dark looks and deep frown. 'He's not what I expected,' she said tactfully.

'What do you mean?'

'I thought he'd be like Luc – charming, friendly – but he's not. We've had a couple of disagreements already. And he's allergic to dogs.' His angry words from last night rang in her ears and she remembered how he'd threatened to leave. For all she knew, perhaps he'd gone already.

'Oh dear,' said Evie. 'What were the disagreements about?'

But Liberty didn't get a chance to answer because a customer came over needing help with fabric choices. While Evie was serving her, the bell tinkled and Natasha came in.

'Is this a good time for a coffee?' she asked.

'It's fine.' Liberty smiled and gestured to the back room. 'I'll put the kettle on. You sit down and put your feet up.'

Her friend didn't argue and lowered herself carefully into a chair. A few moments later, the customer left with her bag of fabric, and Evie joined them in the back room. Liberty handed out drinks and reached into the cupboard for the box she'd bought from the bakery. 'Here. Have a mince pie.'

Evie beamed and helped herself.

'Eves, what did you do to your finger?' Natasha asked, spotting the big plaster.

'Accident with a rotary cutter. Fortunately Jake was home.' Evie grimaced. 'There was a lot of blood.'

Natasha winced.

'It's not as painful as it sounds,' Evie said cheerfully. 'I've had worse accidents.'

Liberty laughed. Evie was one of the clumsiest people she'd ever met.

Natasha suddenly clutched her stomach and gasped.

'Nat? What's wrong?' asked Liberty.

She let out a long slow breath and relaxed back into her seat. 'It's nothing. Just another Braxton Hicks. Practice contractions. I keep getting them.'

Liberty and Evie exchanged a worried glance.

'You look a bit tired,' Liberty said carefully. 'Is everything okay?'

Liberty's gaze dropped to Natasha's bump and she felt a shiver of wonder that a little being was safely nestled in there, growing and developing.

'I'm fine. Just a little weighed down by this one.' She patted her stomach. 'Mm, these mince pies are delish.'

Evie studied her with concern. 'Perhaps the early mornings are taking it out of you.'

'You sound just like Luc. But I really want to get all the books in order before I go on maternity leave. Plus, I don't think I'd get much of a lie-in with Lottie anyway. She's an early riser.'

Liberty smiled. Natasha's three-year-old daughter was adorable but demanding. She talked constantly and asked endless questions. Liberty loved to babysit her, but she always went home exhausted. 'Well, any time you need a hand looking after her, just ask. You know I love to help.'

'Thank you.' She licked a crumb of pastry from her finger.

Evie turned to Liberty. 'What were you going to say before – about your lodger?'

Liberty glanced at Natasha and hesitated. Her friend would worry if she knew how bad things were between them, and Liberty didn't want to add to her problems when she was already exhausted with her pregnancy. 'Oh, nothing. He just . . . wasn't very happy about living with a dog, that's all.'

'Is it true that he's really good-looking?' asked Evie.

Liberty pictured his mesmerising eyes. 'Unfortunately, he knows it.'

Natasha peered at her. 'You don't seem too enamoured of him.'

'He keeps himself to himself.' She didn't say that he was sullen and snappy. She didn't say she'd be glad if he left, and last night she'd paced up and down in the darkness, too angry even to think about sleeping. Ever since he'd arrived he'd turned the air sour, pushing her away every time she tried to be friendly, sulking moodily, and thundering around on that beast of a motorbike.

Although perhaps stomping onto the landing and yelling at him in the heat of the moment had been rash.

She didn't say anything, but Natasha must have sensed there was more because she waited expectantly for her to go on.

Liberty sighed and made light of it. 'I suppose I'm disappointed he doesn't want to chat like Carys, or watch romantic comedies while drinking hot chocolate and wearing knitted slipper socks.'

Natasha laughed and touched her hand in sympathy. 'Oh, Lib.'

The pity in Natasha's eyes made her cringe. She didn't want anyone's pity. 'On the bright side, he doesn't hog the bathroom.'

Natasha absently stroked her bump. 'Luc said he's not fully recovered from the accident he had earlier in the year. It can't be an easy time for him.'

Liberty's head jerked up. 'He had an accident?'

'A bad one. Haven't you looked him up?'

'What do you mean?'

'On the internet. He's a bit of a celebrity, you know, in the racing world.'

'Is he?' She wasn't impressed. She equated celebrity status with arrogance and wealth and big egos.

Actually, thinking about it, that explained a lot.

'And his dad died last year,' Natasha continued.

'Yes, he mentioned that.' She remembered his icy tone. *We weren't close.*

'All in all, he's got a lot going on. Luc said he didn't seem his usual self when he arrived. Still, at least he's with you and not in some impersonal hotel. That would be really lonely for him, wouldn't it?'

'Yeah,' Liberty said guiltily. She sipped her coffee, careful to avoid her friend's eye: what if he'd already moved out?

Now she wished she hadn't shouted at him. She could have waited until morning when she'd calmed down, and had a quiet word with him instead of being confrontational. But that bike of his infuriated her – it was so big and noisy. *He* infuriated her.

But Natasha's friendship was more important.

She frowned. If he was still there when she got home tonight perhaps she should try a little harder to make things work with him – if for no other reason than that she didn't want to upset Luc and Natasha.

Later that day Liberty was checking through their list of online orders and the last dates for posting before Christmas, when the shop bell jingled and a blond guy

81

came in. He closed the door, then headed directly towards her. She felt a quick kick of excitement – and recognition because he'd been in a couple of times before, shopping for his mother. He was tall, and his eyes were a startling slate blue. Usually he was casually dressed in jeans, but today he wore a long coat and a smart suit, and looked even more dashing. She thought of the dating app. If his profile came up she'd definitely say yes.

'I wondered if you could help me,' he said. His voice was deep and low. 'I'm on my lunch break so I haven't got much time.'

'Of course.'

Reaching into his inside pocket, he produced a few scraps of fabric and a piece of paper, then placed them on the counter. 'Mum's sent me on an emergency trip to get more of these,' he explained, with a rueful smile, 'and half a metre of another coordinating mid-blue.'

Liberty smiled. 'I'll show you where the blues are.'

He followed her across the shop, seeming mildly alarmed. 'Oh, I don't want the responsibility of choosing. Mum will be much happier if you recommend one.'

'No problem.' Liberty held up the swatches in front of the shelf. They were mostly ditzy prints with tiny flowers, but one or two were plainer with geometric designs. From what she recalled about his mother's taste, she seemed to err towards traditional floral prints. Definitely nothing too modern. 'This one would work,' she said, pulling out a tone-on-tone scroll-patterned print, 'or this one.' She showed him another with butterflies outlined in navy. It was plainer, but the perfect colour.

His blue eyes creased as he smiled. 'Which do you prefer?'

Liberty examined the swatches again. 'If she only needs half a metre, then I'd go with the first,' she said, careful not to answer his question, because her personal preference would likely be the opposite of his mother's. 'It's more in keeping with what you have already and she's finishing a quilt she's already started, right?'

'How do you remember that? I'm impressed.'

She pulled the bolt of fabric off the shelf. 'We don't get many male customers in here. You stand out, I'm afraid.'

He chuckled and followed her back to the counter. Hurriedly, she pushed aside the laptop. 'How's your mum?' she asked, as she measured the blue material then sliced through it. If she remembered correctly, his mum was ill.

'Not bad.' His eyes clouded and she recognised the pained look of someone worried about a loved one. 'No change, really.'

Liberty wondered what illness prevented his mother from coming into the shop herself. She was clearly a keen quilter, judging by the amount of fabric and quilting thread he'd bought over his last couple of visits. 'Does she have mobility issues? Because we have a wheelchair ramp at the back, you know.'

'It's not a physical illness.' He rubbed a hand over his beard. 'She's agoraphobic.'

He must have logged her confusion because he explained, 'She can't leave the house. She gets panic attacks.'

Liberty felt a tug of sympathy. That must be difficult for both of them.

'It's hard for her,' he went on. 'But at least she has her sewing to keep her busy.'

'Has she been ill for a while?'

'It started two years ago, when Dad died. I suppose she was an anxious person before then but Dad was good at calming her down, and without him she can't face the world.'

Liberty put the rotary cutter down and folded his material. 'That's so sad.'

He lifted a bag onto the counter. 'Want to see the quilt so far? I brought the middle section with me. She's working on the outer border now. It's nearly finished.'

'Oh, yes, please.' Lots of customers came in with examples of their work and Liberty was used to giving polite praise, but when he unfolded this one, she blinked. This wasn't run-of-the-mill squares or triangles. It was a collection of complex blocks clustered around a Mariner's Compass in the centre. The points of each long triangle were as sharp as pins, the colours and patterns had been carefully chosen to blend or contrast, and the whole quilt spoke of great skill and meticulously neat workmanship. 'Wow,' she said quietly. 'That's amazing.'

'It's some kind of online challenge. Apparently people are taking part all around the world, following the same design but choosing their own colours and fabrics.'

'I know the one you mean. From what I've heard it's very difficult. Your mother has serious talent.'

'You think so?' He sounded proud.

Liberty felt a tingle in response. 'Definitely. Believe me, this is way above the standard we usually see here in the shop. Do you mind if I show my boss?'

He looked surprised and even prouder. Liberty opened the door to the back room. 'Evie, come and take a look at this.'

Evie came in, her dimples showing as she smiled at the customer. She flicked her long plait over her shoulder before leaning in to study the quilt. Immediately, her expression changed to one of serious awe. 'Did you make this?' she asked him.

'Not me. My mum.'

Liberty explained, 'This gentleman comes in to buy fabric for her because she can't come in herself.'

'My name's Ethan,' he said, and his gaze locked with Liberty's, making her heart give a little bounce.

'I'm Liberty,' she said, 'and this is my boss, Evie.' She wasn't sure why her cheeks heated.

'Ethan,' said Evie, 'does your mum enter her work for shows?'

'No,' he said. 'I didn't know there were shows for this kind of thing.'

'There are, and this deserves to be on display so other people can enjoy it too. I'm fairly certain it would get high praise from the judges. It's really very good.'

'I don't know anything about that stuff. But it might give her a boost just to know it was on display for others to see.'

Evie nodded. 'There's a big festival in Birmingham in the summer, but if you don't want to wait that long there's one starting at the end of this month. It's in the South of France, but I'll be entering a few of my own quilts and I could send hers, too, if she can finish it in time.'

'Oh, that won't be a problem. Time is the one thing she has in abundance.'

Evie grabbed a piece of paper and scribbled something. 'This is the website. Why don't you ask her and let me know? If she's interested she'll need to enter it online and the deadline is soon because they print programmes listing all the entries. They won't need the finished quilt until just before Christmas, though.'

'I'll speak to her. Thanks.'

They exchanged business cards, and Evie disappeared into the back room to finish machine-piecing a quilt.

Liberty pointed to the scraps of fabric he'd brought in. 'I'll get these for you.' As she cut them, she asked, 'Do you think your mum might be persuaded to go to the show if her work was going to be on display there?'

He shook his head sadly. 'Not a chance, I'm afraid. Even going out into the garden is too much for her at the moment.'

Her heart went out to the woman. The thought of being trapped indoors was terrible. It must be a worry for him, too. She glanced at him. He was clearly deeply caring. A nice guy.

'Do you look after your mum alone or do you have help?' she asked casually.

'It's just me and Mum. My sister lives in New Zealand.'

'Right.' No mention of a wife, but he might have a girlfriend. She folded up the fabrics. 'Is there anything else you need?'

He reached into his pocket and produced a cotton reel. 'Yes. Some of this blue thread, please. She asked me to buy the biggest reel you have.'

Liberty picked one from the rack and keyed everything into the till.

'Mum enjoys the emails you send out with pictures of all the new fabrics that have just arrived. She used to love shopping for fabric. Now she does it online, but she says it's not the same as touching the fabrics and seeing them for real.'

'Where does she live? Is she local?'

He told her the name of the village. It was only ten minutes away. Liberty thought of her stuck at home, so talented yet unable to share her passion with anyone. Perhaps she could help.

No. Don't get involved, Lib—

She stopped herself. This month's challenge was supposed to be about doing new things and shaking up her routine. 'Do you think your mum would like to have company for an hour or so? I could bring her samples of our new stock if she'd like, and perhaps stay an hour to sew with her, too.'

His eyes lit up, turning a brighter shade of blue, and Liberty felt a burst of pleasure. 'She'd love that. I try to be in most evenings, but sometimes I have to work late, and I worry about her being on her own.'

She jotted down her phone number and handed it to him. 'I'm free tomorrow night. Why don't I pop round after supper? Is eight o'clock convenient?'

'I'm sure it will be, but I'll check and confirm with you.'

Liberty smiled and enjoyed the rapid tapping of her heart. Would it count as a tick in her book? Yes. Visiting a stranger wasn't something she did ordinarily, even if quilting was. And, yes, she was happy to admit she had an ulterior motive, because this stranger had a very handsome son.

Chapter Five

Alex zipped up his leather jacket and sneezed. He reached for his boots, keen to get out of the cottage and away from the dog, which was intent on following him everywhere and didn't take the hint that he was allergic. He slipped his foot into one boot, but while he fastened it, the dog snatched up the other and scooted away with it.

'Hey!' He went after him, racing through the kitchen and into the lounge. The dog stood by the fire. The boot was nowhere to be seen.

'Where have you put it?'

Alex began to search. It couldn't be far. He looked behind the sofa and the door, in all the corners, he moved chairs and bent down so he was at dog height.

Eventually he crouched in front of the dog. 'I give up. Show me where it is.'

The dog gazed back at him long enough that he was certain he was wasting his time. Then Charlie turned and trotted into the kitchen. He looked back, as if to check Alex was still following. He was. The dog led him to his bed and there it was, next to a ragged monkey and a hair-covered blanket. Alex picked up his boot with two fingers. 'Is this your idea of fun? Or are you trying to show me who's boss? Either way, you don't need to worry. I'm not planning on staying any longer than I have to.'

Outside, he put on his helmet and mentally scrolled through his options, working out where to go next with the search for his half-sister.

The census information wasn't available for the last hundred years, so that was no use. Church records, maybe, as Liberty had suggested. But that depended on the baby having been christened.

He unlocked his bike and swung his leg over. He might as well try. He'd visit all the churches in the area and ask to examine their parish records. Without the mother's surname his task was difficult, but he had an approximate date of birth, which was a start. He could look for the name Ricard around that time, and search for mothers whose first names began with M. There couldn't be that many births recorded in each individual parish, could there? He gunned the engine of his bike, determined to give it a go. It was a long shot, but it wasn't as if he had many other options, was it?

Stepping out of the church into the wintry air, Alex tucked his helmet under one arm and pushed a hand through his hair, disappointed that the parish records hadn't yielded anything. It was the fourth place he'd visited today without success. The light was fading fast and the village green was deserted, apart from a pair of men in high-visibility jackets who were winding lights around a large tree. Alex rolled his shoulder, trying to dispel the ache. It seemed worse in damp weather, and England was renowned for that, wasn't it? Unfortunately, the pillowy clouds showed no sign of lifting. He sighed. Perhaps he should call it a day, he decided. Head back and face Liberty.

But when he got there, the cottage was empty. The cup and plate on the draining board suggested Liberty had been in and gone out again.

He had a quiet evening by himself. He made himself a snack, then retreated to his room (upstairs, thankfully, was free of dog hairs so he had a respite from sneezing), and tapped away on his laptop. He heard Liberty come home, heard her go out with the dog, and when she got back she went to bed too. By eleven the house was quiet, lights out for the night. The soft hoot of an owl rang through the air.

Alex was determined not to disturb the peace, but tonight the pain in his shoulder was worse than ever. He tried lying on his left, then his right, then his back, but the ache grew deeper, eating into him, until he could bear it no longer. He got up and paced the room, rolling his shoulder forwards, back, trying to relax the muscles. He lay down again.

But it was no good. So he got dressed, grabbed his keys, and tiptoed down to his bike.

He pushed it until he reached the main road, then climbed on and started the engine. He accelerated hard, head down, savouring the force, the power, the freedom of being alone, just him and his bike.

But following a straight road was nothing like steering round a racetrack. It didn't demand his total focus, there was no challenge, and the speed was nothing like he was used to. He turned off onto a side road, hoping to mix things up a bit.

What the hell would he do without racing? How would he fill his days? The years stretched ahead of him, as endless and intimidating as an ocean. He'd always known his career wouldn't last for ever, but he hadn't given much thought to what he'd do when he hung up his helmet. He supposed he'd hoped to have a long career, like his father. He approached a junction and slowed to a stop. He realised it was the end of the road and turning left or right were the only options.

Just like his career, he thought bitterly, as he swung the bike round and headed back towards the cottage in the woods. He was being forced to do a U-turn, and he didn't like it one bit.

He dismounted at the last turning and pushed his bike back the last two hundred metres. It was dark on the tiny lane. The trees arched over it, covering it so even the moonlight couldn't penetrate the tunnel of darkness. A sharp rustle made him swing his headlight to the right, certain something must be there, but the bushes revealed nothing. And as he swung it back all he could see were networks of roots protruding from the ground, like skeletal limbs ready to trip him up.

He let himself into the cottage so quietly even the dog didn't stir. He padded warily up the stairs, eyeing her door. When it remained shut, he breathed a sigh of relief.

Thursday, 4 December

Alex came downstairs, to be greeted by the overenthusiastic Labrador that was frantically wagging its tail and trying to lick his hand. 'Don't lick me!' Alex warned, and pulled it away.

'*Aie!*' He cursed. He'd only walked into the doorway again.

Rubbing his head, he ducked under it – then frowned as he spotted Liberty outside in the garden. Her fiery hair was a burst of colour against the dull brown of the trees. He peered closer. What was she doing? She'd draped a quilt over a tree branch and appeared to be photographing it. She adjusted it so it hung at an angle and shot it again. Then she moved in and snapped some close-ups of the orange and red leaves in the pattern. He guessed that she'd made the quilt, but why was she photographing it in the woods?

He stepped away from the window. He didn't need to know. Whatever she was doing was her business.

He was having breakfast when she came inside, carrying the quilt over one arm. Her eyes narrowed warily when she spotted him and she murmured, 'Good morning.' He returned the greeting, watching as she locked the back door and folded the quilt. He noticed she was careful to avoid eye contact.

'You want some help with that?' he asked, as she stretched the two corners apart.

'It's fine.'

'Liberty, about the other night . . .' He ran a hand

through his hair. She finished folding the quilt and pressed it against her chest. 'I'm sorry I disturbed you with my bike. I shouldn't have gone out so late.'

She looked surprised by his apology but it was a relief to get it off his chest.

'You were right,' he went on. 'It was inconsiderate of me. I didn't think of the noise. I'm not used to living in the middle of nowhere like this. It's such a small and . . .' he looked at the doorway where he'd banged his head again '. . . quiet place.'

A whole array of emotions flashed through her brown eyes before her expression finally settled on apologetic. 'I'm sorry, too. You woke me up, and I was tired and snappy. I just saw red. Your bike's so noisy.'

He laughed softly. 'Yes. And Willowbrook is very quiet.'

Her chin lifted. 'You don't need to keep saying that.'

'Sorry.' He was only digging himself deeper. 'You like it here?'

'Yes. Of course I do. It's my home.' She paused. 'Where is home for you?'

His toast sprang up, but he ignored it. 'I move around. Wherever the next race is.'

'Such as?'

'You know – all the big tracks.'

'I'm afraid I don't know anything about motorcycle racing. It's not something that interests me in the slightest.'

He was a little thrown by her withering tone. Yet it was refreshing, too. Most people were *too* interested in his career. 'Australia, Malaysia, Dubai . . . There are tracks

94

all around the world. I stay in city apartments mostly, places where no one cares if you go out on a motorbike late at night. Or if they do, you never find out.'

She kept her gaze level with his. Her eyes were remarkably expressive. Everything she felt was there to see: her wariness of him, a whisper of disapproval, curiosity too. They were enchanting, and he had to force himself to refocus when he realised she'd asked him a question.

'What about where you grew up in Provence? Isn't that quiet? Luc's family live on a vineyard.'

'We moved to Paris when I was twelve. I haven't been back since.'

'You don't have a place of your own in France?'

'In Paris, yes, but it's just another flat.' No different from the ones he rented.

Her eyebrows lifted. 'I don't think I could live like that, without a place to call home.'

'I love it. The travelling, moving from continent to continent, preparing for each new race . . .' He'd only been away from it a week but he already missed the build-up, the preparation, working with the engineers to fine-tune the bike and his race plan. 'I love the constant change,' he said longingly, and gazed out of the window at the grey trees and the carpet of dead leaves beneath them. 'Each race takes me to a new location and it's a chance to start again, to win.'

At least, that was what he *had* loved. He gripped his coffee cup. Was this how his life would be from now on? Stuck in a backwater, yearning for all that he'd lost? He touched his wrist and the doctor's words rang in his head:

It would be easier if you'd accept this, rather than fighting it. For your sake.

That was easier said than done. No matter how hard he tried, he couldn't shake off the feeling that he was balanced over an abyss, looking down.

Chapter Six

Liberty glanced at the toaster. 'Your toast will have gone cold. Want another slice?'

It might sound like polite concern, but really it was a diversion tactic while she absorbed what he'd just said. *I'm not used to living in the middle of nowhere . . . It's such a small, quiet place.* She was still bristling at the disdain with which he'd spoken. Granted, the woods weren't at their best in early December when half the trees had lost their leaves and the ground was muddy. But, even so, she'd choose quiet and peaceful over a noisy concrete city any day. Damselfly Cottage was her home. How dare he look down his nose at it, implying he'd rather be anywhere in the world but here?

'No, it's fine.' He grabbed a plate and began to butter his toast.

At least they'd cleared the air, though. Was he really so self-centred that he'd never thought about how his bike's noise might disturb others?

'There's jam in here,' she said, pointing to a cupboard. She was careful not to try too hard since most of her efforts to help him feel welcome had been rebuffed. Yesterday, he hadn't even wanted breakfast.

He opened the cupboard and hesitated over the jars of peanut butter, marmalade and blackberry jam. He had beautiful eyes, she noticed grudgingly. Dark, with really long lashes.

'I've never had marmalade before,' he said, picking it up.

'Good choice. I recommend it.'

He carried it with his plate and coffee to the kitchen table. She hesitated. It was tempting to leave him to have breakfast alone, and she needed to go to work soon. But his apology had been an olive branch of sorts. So she made herself an espresso and sat down opposite him, smiling to herself when he took a bite of toast because the surprise on his face was priceless.

'This tastes good,' he said. 'Tart yet sweet. Delicious.' He took another bite.

'It's homemade. Dorothy in the village gave it to me.' So you can stop being so uppity about Willowbrook, Mr I-Like-My-Jetsetting-City-Life, because I bet you don't get homemade marmalade in Singapore or Monaco or wherever you'd rather be.

Liberty McKenzie, those thoughts are not welcoming.

She cleared her throat and asked politely, 'So do you get a chance to see much of these countries you go to?'

'Only the racetracks. Sometimes I go to the odd restaurant or hotel for a party.'

'Right.' So not only was he missing his globetrotting life, but also the glamorous parties. No wonder he and she didn't get on: they were chalk and cheese. Parties were not her thing, and she couldn't think of anything more daunting than constantly travelling around the world, waking up in different places where she couldn't speak the language or read road signs. She'd miss Charlie and her cottage, the Button Hole and, most of all, the comfort of knowing exactly how each day would unfold.

She watched as he ate hungrily. 'You know, Willowbrook might be a quiet village, but everyone knows everyone and it's really friendly.'

His eyes creased as he smiled. 'You think that's a good thing?'

'I do.' She held his gaze. 'You don't?'

'I prefer the city – where it's more impersonal.' He sipped his coffee. 'Aren't you afraid, living here?'

'What do you mean?'

'In the woods, with no other houses around. It's so . . .' he searched for the word '. . . isolated.'

She wanted to laugh. 'I'm not afraid at all. It's a beautiful place to live.' She looked out of the window at the familiar woodland tapestry. The trees stirred in the winter breeze, and light trickled through the filigree branches. 'There's birdsong and wildlife all around.' Well, there had been before he'd arrived with that enormous noisy machine.

'What kind of wildlife?'

'Owls, foxes, pheasants. Sometimes we get the odd deer.'

He quirked an eyebrow. 'All you're missing is the Seven Dwarfs.'

Deadpan irony. She liked it. And she felt a tingle of awareness, but quashed it. A man like him must have hundreds of admirers and she was definitely not going to join their ranks. 'Oh, they're in the back garden.' She smiled sweetly.

'Funny.'

'I'm serious. Look.' She got up and beckoned for him to come to the window too. She pointed to a cluster of garden gnomes on a small rockery. 'My mum collected them.' She noticed they were a little faded now and made a mental note to repaint them.

Alex frowned. 'Aren't gnomes a different species?' He remained serious, but the glint in his eye told her he was joking.

She smiled and put her hands on her hips. 'If you're going to be racist you can leave right now. Those guys are my friends. Happy, Sneezy, Dopey, Doc . . .' Grumpy was in the kitchen beside her, but she kept that thought to herself.

'Right.' The corners of his mouth twitched.

She felt a burst of warmth. Or was it relief that they'd reached a kind of ceasefire? She glanced at the clock. She really needed to go, but something was niggling and she knew if she didn't ask now, the opportunity would be gone. 'Where did you go in the night?'

'What?'

'On your bike. You said you *had* to go out. Where did you go?'

He dipped his head, as if about to make a shameful confession. Liberty tensed. Oh, no. It *was* drugs, wasn't it?

'When I can't sleep, going out on my bike helps me relax.' His gaze met hers, and what she saw in his eyes made her still. Despair: black and weary. 'It's the only thing that helps.'

She blinked. 'Riding a motorbike is your cure for insomnia?' She couldn't think of anything that would make her blood pressure spike more. Well, she could: aeroplanes. But a motorbike would be a close second.

'Yeah.' His smile was sheepish.

'Have you tried the more conventional solutions like hot milk?'

He laughed. 'Yes.'

'Well, listen, if you have to go out on your bike late at night again could you maybe keep the noise down until you get away from the woods? So you don't scare the wildlife. Or me.'

'I did this last night. I was as quiet as possible,' he said defensively. 'I wheeled the bike away from the cottage before I started the engine.'

She couldn't hide her surprise because she hadn't heard him go out at all. 'I appreciate that. Thanks. Have you always suffered from insomnia?'

Now she glimpsed bleakness in his eyes. 'My shoulder is painful. I injured it when I crashed earlier this year. For some reason it's most painful at night when I'm trying to get to sleep.'

'Have you seen a doctor?' she asked.

He laughed unhappily. 'Yes. Several.'

'Can't they help? Give you painkillers?'

'They did but I've run out.'

'You should see Dr Hartwood. Jake. He's my boss's boyfriend and a great doctor. He'll help you.' He didn't answer, so she went on, 'This weather can't be helping, either. My mum used to get arthritis in her hips when it was cold and damp like this. She found a hot-water bottle helped.'

He remained tight-lipped, but she could tell from the scepticism in his eyes that he didn't buy into hot-water bottles.

'How does going out on your bike help?' she asked, genuinely curious.

'It takes my mind off the pain and helps me relax.'

Her eyes narrowed. 'I suppose you like to go fast on the main road. You do know what the speed limit is, don't you?'

'Speed limit? What speed limit?' His eyes sparkled, and she got the feeling he was teasing her again.

'Very funny. There are speed cameras all along the main road, you know.'

'Are there?' His casual tone made her hands ball into tight fists. She'd heard him revving the engine of that enormous machine: she was in no doubt that it could easily reach top speeds. 'Yes, there are. And if you're caught speeding, you'll get a fine. You might even get a prison sentence. That happened to one guy last year. The judge said he wanted to make an example of him.' She wished he'd lock away more people who drove danger-ously and put innocent people's lives at risk.

Alex's teasing smile vanished. 'Why do I get the feeling you disapprove of my bike, Liberty? Or is it just me you don't like?'

Thrown by his questions, she battled the anger that

flashed through her and the jagged memories of Carys's accident. Yes, she did disapprove of his bike and people like him who raced around, scaring everyone and everything around them. Her spine stiffened. 'Do you ever think about others when you're speeding? Do you ever think about all the people who would be hurt if you crashed? You put everyone else on the road at risk of being hurt or worse, just so you can get a few cheap thrills from going fast.'

A long pause followed before he said quietly, 'It's usually the person on the bike who comes off worst.'

Their gazes met and locked, but she wouldn't back down.

He studied her closely. 'Why are you so angry, Liberty? What have I done to you?'

'You haven't done anything,' she snapped. She wasn't angry, she just felt strongly about this. Memories hooked at her heart like barbed wire.

He said nothing. She folded her arms and glanced at him. He kept his expression neutral and waited.

Seconds passed. Her heart beat rapidly.

Then she swallowed and admitted quietly, 'My friend Carys was hit by an idiot speeding – he was in a car, not on a bike, but even so. He hit her head-on. She didn't stand a chance.'

Hot colour rose in her cheeks. Suddenly her words sounded foolish. Emotional. He wasn't responsible for Carys's accident. It was irrational of her to tar everyone who drove fast with the same brush. Yet she knew if she looked out of the window at his bike she'd feel the same rage. It wasn't fair that Carys had been hurt like that. It wasn't fair that, while her life had stopped and she lay in a coma, the guy who'd hit her was serving a ridiculously short prison sentence and in a couple of years he'd go free.

'That's terrible,' Alex said.

She was completely wrong-footed by his gentle, sympathetic tone.

'What happened to your friend is very sad.' He appeared to choose his words carefully before he continued, 'My friend Thomas died in a crash, too. But he was a racer, doing what he loved, and knew the risks. It was a tragedy, but it must be a hundred times harder for you because your friend was just going about her life.'

'She was driving to school where she teaches. Taught.'

He nodded. 'Thomas was young, too. He was talented, he had so many plans. It's difficult to accept when someone dies so young.'

'She's not dead,' she said quickly. 'She's in a coma.'

'I know, and I sympathise with what you must have been through.'

His sympathy was genuine – she could see it in his eyes. She couldn't speak because her throat was a tight knot.

'I was teasing you before. I never speed on the road. Never have.'

'No? Most bikes do. Especially round here on the quiet country roads.'

'I love to go fast, but I save it for the track where we're all in the same . . . galley.'

'The same boat, you mean?'

'*Oui, voilà.*' There was a long pause. Then, 'I'm sorry

for your friend. You care deeply for her, I see this, but being angry won't change anything. It will only make you bitter. You are punishing yourself this way.'

She knew he was right. And suddenly she saw how angry she'd been with him – irrationally so – for having a bike that went fast. He said he didn't speed, and he'd lost a friend too. It felt like a fragile bridge had narrowed the distance between them.

Yet she still couldn't fathom why he enjoyed something as dangerous as motorcycle racing. 'When you're on the track, aren't you afraid? Of the speed? Of crashing?'

He laughed. 'Life would be dull if you only focused on what could go wrong. I'm aware of the danger, but I concentrate on what I need to do. I memorise the layout of the track and anticipate each bend and straight so I'm always thinking about my next move, my position, and so on. I don't have time to think about anything else.'

'Do you enjoy it?' She peered at him, curious to understand because she genuinely couldn't see the appeal.

'Of course. I wouldn't do it if I didn't.' A stricken look flashed through his eyes and his gaze slid away from hers. He must hate it here – he must be so bored.

'*What* do you enjoy about it?'

He considered this. 'The adrenalin rush, the speed and the power, the thrill of winning and coming first. It's about pushing the bike and myself to the limit.'

He looked so animated talking about it, and she contrasted this with what she enjoyed most: sewing quilts. She wasn't bothered one jot about going fast or coming first in anything. All the things he'd just described – speed and adrenalin – made her shudder with dread.

'I could take you out on the bike, if you like,' he said. She glanced up, surprised. 'Then you could see for yourself what it feels like.'

'Me?' She choked a laugh. She wanted nothing to do with anything that went fast or could take a life. 'No, thanks. I can't think of anything wor—'

The word died on her tongue as she remembered her challenge.

Oh, damn. She was meant to say yes to everything. *Everything*. No excuses.

But a motorbike? Her hands became clammy just thinking about it. She fiddled with the skirt of her dress. Alex was apparently amused by her indecision. It was a simple yes-no question, and the easy answer, her instinctive answer, had been no.

Therefore . . . she had to say yes, didn't she?
Drat.

She swallowed. 'Yes, please.' Her words were a tiny squeak.

He peered at her, lips curving. 'You don't sound too sure.'

'I'm not. I'm really scared, but I – I feel I ought to do it.' Her heart was beating nineteen to the dozen just thinking about it.

'Ought to?'

'I'm doing a challenge for the month of December. Saying yes to everything.'

His eyes lit up. It was the first time she'd seen them so animated. Until now he'd had such a desolate air about him. She could tell he liked this idea. It was probably the kind of thing he'd find fun and not challenging at all. 'You have to say yes?'

She nodded.

'This is all?'

Ouch, that hurt. She wished she hadn't told him now. Her chin went up. 'One challenge each day, yes. But they have to be things I wouldn't normally do. Things I'm nervous about or scared of doing.' Like riding a motorbike. That would be a big, scary 'yes'. Positively terrifying.

'Who set you this challenge?'

'I did.'

'Why?'

She hesitated. 'Because I'm hoping it will make me braver. Shake things up a bit.' She deliberately kept it vague, not wanting to confess that she was a coward stuck in a routine of dog walks and cosy nights in. She was still feeling stung by 'This is all?' and had a feeling that he, with his powerful motorbike and leathers, would definitely not understand.

'What have you done so far?'

She pulled out her notebook and showed him what she'd written on page one. 'Took in a lodger.' She didn't mention the sandwich fillings. He'd find that ridiculous.

'Me? I am part of your challenge?'

She nodded. 'I'd never had a lodger before.'

He took a moment to absorb this. Her gaze lingered on his beautiful long lashes. They lifted and he met her gaze. 'You were scared?'

'Not scared, exactly. More apprehensive.'

'Why?'

She shrugged. 'This is my home. I've only ever shared it with my mum and my best friend.'

'What's tomorrow's challenge?'

'I don't know. I'm making it up as I go along.'

'So you want to go for a ride on my bike as part of your challenge?' he asked.

'"Want" is a little strong.' She gave him a weak smile.

'Should we go now?'

Cold white fear filled her. 'No! I – I mean I can't.' She checked her watch and hurried into the hall where she grabbed her coat. 'There's no time. I have to go to work and I'm late already.'

'How about tonight, then?'

She wound her scarf around her neck. 'I'm going out.' Funny how going to sew with a stranger had seemed out of her comfort zone – until the prospect of riding a motorbike had put that completely into perspective.

His lips twitched. 'Tomorrow?'

'I'll be at work.' She scooped up her car keys, then stopped. Even to her ears it sounded like she was making excuses.

'Where is your shop? In the village?'

'Yes.'

'I could take you there, if you like? Tomorrow.'

She bit her lip. 'I suppose. And I could walk home at the end of the day.'

'Or I could pick you up.'

She smiled. 'I think one journey would be enough, thanks.'

'Okay. Tell me what time you need to leave and I'll be ready.'

So now he knew why Liberty McKenzie had disliked him – and his bike – from the start, thought Alex, as he spread generous amounts of marmalade on his toast. He'd never tasted anything like this deliciously sticky stuff. He had to admit, he understood her point of view. And although her anger had been irrationally directed at him, it showed how deeply she'd been affected by her friend's accident.

He thought of his own crash. The tilt, just a fraction of an angle too far, then the spinning away from his bike, whirling across the tarmac, his hands outstretched, grasping at thin air. And the endless seconds before the final impact. The crunching stop.

It had taken months for him to recover, months of gruelling physio, rehabilitation and pain. From the start, the doctors had been pessimistic. They'd all told him the same thing – that he might never fully regain the strength in his wrist.

But he'd refused to believe them. He'd vowed that he would recover through sheer determination. If he'd known then how futile it would be . . .

The dog trotted into the kitchen and watched him with soulful eyes. 'Hello, Charlie. And, no, don't even think about it.' He hurriedly ate his toast.

But when he'd finished the dog was still staring up at him.

'What do you want?'

Charlie went to the back door and began to claw at it.

'You want to go out?' Would Liberty approve? She'd let the dog out the other day and told him the garden was safe. 'Okay then.' He gave in.

The dog scampered out and Alex closed the door against the chilly winter air. He sipped his coffee while checking emails.

Then he heard a clawing at the back door. He frowned, and opened it. 'You want to come in already?'

Charlie bounded inside. Alex shrugged. Maybe he'd needed the toilet. He returned to his emails. But as soon as he sat down, the dog was back at the door, clawing and whining unhappily.

'Again?' The dog made big eyes at him. Alex sighed and got up a second time.

He sat down. Immediately the clawing started again. 'I'm not playing this game any more,' he called. 'You wanted to go out, now you live with it.'

But guilt crept in. What if he was cold out there? Or hurt?

Eventually, he got up and let him in. 'That's it now. You're staying in and that's final.'

He tried to sound authoritative, but as he left the room he felt the dog's gaze follow him and had the distinct feeling he'd just lost another round of a game he hadn't asked to play.

'Do you have a helmet I can buy?' Alex asked.

The garage was just beside the turning for Willowbrook

village, and although it wasn't the most modern, Alex had noticed it had a workshop for repairs and hoped someone there might be able to help him. As he went in, he inhaled the familiar smells of oil and grease.

The mechanic wiped his oil-stained hands on a rag. 'A helmet for a motorbike?'

They both looked at his bike. The orange paintwork gleamed in the rain, like a shimmering sunset. 'Yes, for a motorbike.' Alex tried to hide his impatience. He was hardly going to be seen riding a pushbike, was he? 'It's for a woman,' he added.

The man's brows lifted and deep grooves creased in his forehead. 'Liberty?'

'How did you know?'

He grinned. 'There aren't many French motorbike riders in Willowbrook. Friend of Luc's, aren't you?'

Alex hesitated, but the man clearly knew who he was already. 'Yes, I'm Alex.'

'Guy. Pleased to meet you.' He held out his hand for Alex to shake. 'I take it Liberty's only going to be needing this helmet for a few weeks while you're here.'

'Maybe not even that long. One day.'

'In that case I can lend you one, mate.' The man beckoned him into the back of the workshop.

Alex sidestepped tyres and spanners scattered across the floor. An old bike in the corner – a Triumph – caught his eye. But Guy had moved on already.

'I've got this one here, or if you prefer I've got a pair with inbuilt radios. Might be useful for reassuring a nervous passenger.' Guy winked.

Alex smiled. 'You know Liberty well, then?'

'Put it this way, I'm surprised you've managed to persuade her to go out on your bike at all.'

He'd been surprised too. But he'd be happy if it helped break down her prejudice. 'The pair would be good. Thank you. How much will it cost?'

'Oh, there's no cost, not for Liberty.' He pulled out a stepladder and reached for the helmets, passing them down to Alex one at a time.

'Are you sure? I don't mind—'

The mechanic shook his head. 'She's a good girl, is Lib. I've known her since she was a baby.' Alex was surprised. The only people who'd known him all his life were his family. 'Make sure you take good care of her.'

'Of course.'

'She won't like it if you go too fast. You know what happened to her friend, don't you?'

He nodded. 'I won't go fast,' he promised. Did everyone around here assume that because he owned a motorbike he had no respect for speed limits or other road users? He'd meant what he'd told her: he kept the adrenalin rush for the racetrack and never broke the speed limit on the road. It simply wasn't worth the risk of losing his licence. He couldn't imagine anything worse than not being able to ride at all.

'Thanks for these helmets. When do you need them back?'

'There's no rush. They're only gathering dust in here.'

As they walked back through the workshop Alex

stopped beside the old Triumph. 'She's a special piece of history. Mind if I take a look?'

'Be my guest.'

Alex inspected the bodywork, which was sound, but she was missing a few key parts. 'Needs a bit of work, doesn't she?'

'She does. Dr Hartwood bought her – have you met him?' Alex shook his head. 'You've probably seen him driving an old Bentley. He collects classic cars, but this bike caught his eye and he asked me to restore it. It's taking longer than I'd like, mind, because I'm having trouble sourcing the parts.'

'Which ones?'

As Guy explained, the two men crouched to examine the bike more closely.

'Are you looking for new or used parts?' asked Alex.

'Either. Ideally New Old Stock, but it's rare.'

Alex nodded. He'd heard of New Old Stock. Boxes of unused original parts, which occasionally came to light when an old garage or warehouse was cleared. Collectors of classic vehicles pounced on them, making them extremely valuable. Clearly Jake Hartwood was restoring the bike properly, using only authentic parts. He straightened up, and tucked one helmet under his arm so he could shake the other man's hand for a second time. 'Thanks again for the helmets.'

'No trouble at all. Oh, and tell Liberty to go slow on that bike, won't you?' His eyes danced with humour.

Alex smiled. Clearly he wasn't the only one who'd

noticed how carefully she drove. 'I don't think that will be a problem.'

Liberty knocked at the door. If she'd been at all nervous about visiting a complete stranger, she was more than a little reassured by the neat house at the end of a cul-de-sac. It was already decorated for Christmas with lights strung below the eaves and glowing reindeer in the front garden. She must get her own decorations out soon, although she always waited until the middle of the month to buy a tree because she hated to see it lose its needles.

The front door opened. In the golden light Ethan's hair looked blonder than she remembered.

'Come in,' he said. 'It's cold tonight, isn't it?' he said.

Liberty stepped inside, clutching her sewing bag. 'Freezing. I had to scrape the ice off my car this morning. It definitely feels wintry now.'

Mini quilts hung all around, and Ethan drew a quilted curtain across the front door to keep the draught out. It was made from ochre and crimson silks, some decorated with sequins, and it reminded Liberty of Indian saris. The rich colours evoked exotic lands and added to the warmth of the house. Everything was immaculately tidy, and the smell of furniture polish and cinnamon baking filled the air.

A woman with short, spiky salt-and-pepper hair bustled through from the kitchen, wiping her hands on a tea-towel. Her nails were painted a deep shade of blue. 'You must be Liberty.' She smiled. 'Hello, love. I'm Brenda.'

Liberty wasn't sure how she'd imagined Brenda would look, but she certainly hadn't pictured her so trim and with such an air of energy and purpose.

'Come into the lounge, and I'll make us a hot drink. What would you like, love?'

'Tea would be great. Thanks,' said Liberty.

'I'll get it, Mum,' said Ethan. 'You two go ahead and get comfortable.'

'Thanks, Ethan.'

Liberty followed Brenda into the lounge. As she sat down on the sofa, she noticed everything was immaculately tidy, not a cushion or a coaster out of place, and not a single thread on the furniture. A lap quilt was draped over the back of the sofa, like a throw, and in the corner of the room a slim artificial tree was covered with knitted decorations: snowmen, Christmas puddings, choirboys holding tiny paper hymn sheets, reindeer. They weren't like anything Liberty had seen before, and she suspected they were homemade.

Brenda took the armchair beside her. 'I know it's early,' she said, following her gaze, 'but I love Christmas. I like to have the decorations out as soon as possible, and get a whole month's enjoyment out of them.'

'It's not so early. Some of the shops in town put their trees up straight after Halloween.'

Brenda smiled. 'Yes, that's pushing it a bit far.'

Liberty spotted the large folded quilt next to her. 'Ethan showed me your quilt. Is that it there?'

'It is.' Brenda unfolded it and held it up for her to see. Liberty got up to take a closer look at the detail. She couldn't believe how much progress Brenda had made in less than a week. 'Don't look too closely,' Brenda joked. 'There are lots of places where I had to fudge it.'

'Really? You can't tell. These pieces here are thumb-size, they're so small.' Yet the triangle corners were as sharp as pins, and the stitches tiny, precise and even. 'Ethan said it's an online challenge.'

'Yes. You make a block a day over a year.'

Liberty had heard that a lot of people had dropped out partway through because it was so technically challenging. Each day's block was different, and some were so intricate and complicated that they took more than a day to complete, especially for people who worked and only had evenings free to sew. Clearly, Brenda had had no trouble in keeping up. 'Has the challenge finished? Aren't there more blocks coming in December?'

'That's right. It's supposed to continue until the end of the year, then you have a finished top to quilt in the new year, but Ethan mentioned the show in France, so I thought I'd better get ahead. I contacted the challenge organiser and she's let me have the remaining block patterns in advance. I've done them all, added the wadding and the backing, and now I'm quilting it.'

'You're not having it longarm quilted?' Many people paid a professional with a specialist machine to do the quilting.

Brenda shook her head. 'They're all fully booked until the new year, which would be too late, and anyway, I love hand-quilting. Plus, if I'm entering it for a show I want it to be all my work. I'm very excited about it. I've never entered one before. Are you sure this will be good enough?'

'There's no doubt in my mind whatsoever,' said Liberty, glancing at another quilt draped over the sofa. Made of hexagons in a Grandmother's Flower Garden pattern, it had been quilted by hand with tiny neat stitches, and the attention to detail showed it was clearly the work of a perfectionist.

'Do you enter your quilts?' asked Brenda.

'Yes, and so does my boss, Evie. Sometimes we win the odd prize, although that's not really why we enter. It's nice to get your work seen and it challenges us too. The quilts we send to shows are usually very different from our usual commissions, more artistic, less conventional.'

Liberty's quilts were simple and striking, whereas Evie used slightly more traditional designs and fabrics.

'Here are your drinks,' said Ethan. He came in with a tray and put it down on the coffee-table. On it was a plate of what looked like home-baked carrot cake, and two mugs of tea.

'Thanks, Ethan,' said Brenda. 'Now you go out and enjoy yourself.'

He smiled. 'Don't sound so keen to get rid of me.'

'I can't wait to see the back of you.' Brenda winked at Liberty. 'I'm worried he's never going to find someone to settle down with because he's always staying in with me. He doesn't believe me when I tell him I'm happy on my own.'

So he *was* single, then. Liberty felt a buzz of excitement. 'Going anywhere nice?' she asked him.

'Just to the pub,' he said. 'The Dog and Partridge in Willowbrook. Do you know it?'

'It's my local,' she said. 'It's nice in there.'

'It is.'

Their eyes met briefly, but she looked away. She wondered who he was meeting there. A woman?

'I'm just seeing the lads,' he told his mum. 'I won't be late.'

Liberty felt a spark of relief. Not a woman, then.

'Stay as late as you like, love,' said Brenda.

When he'd gone, Brenda had a look at Liberty's orange and black chevron quilt. Then they started to sew.

'Who taught you to quilt so well, Brenda?'

'I learned in America.' Liberty looked up, surprised. Brenda went on, 'Oh I wasn't always housebound, you know. Once upon a time we used to travel a lot. Ethan was born in New Zealand.'

'Really? He mentioned that his sister lives there.'

'Yes, but that's another story. Anyway, when we moved to America, I didn't know anyone, not a soul, and I was lonely. One of the first people I met was a keen quilter and she invited me to join her quilting bee.'

'A quilting bee? Is that a group who sew together?'

'Yes. Just like we're doing now, only there were a dozen of us. She assured me it didn't matter that I couldn't sew, so I went along. They saw I was keen to learn, so they showed me the basics and off I went. What started as an excuse to meet people quickly became a passion. And cotton fabric was really cheap over there, as I'm sure you know.'

'Yes. I'd love to go to America.'

'I recommend it. Just make sure you take two suitcases – that way you can fill one with fabric to bring home.'

Liberty chuckled. 'That's a great idea.'

But her smile faded as she remembered the trip she and Carys had planned to travel by train around Europe. They'd been going to visit Rome, Seville, Vienna, Prague, sunny beaches in the south, mountains in the north, the unspoilt areas in the east. They'd had their plans and all the time in the world – or so they'd thought.

Liberty kept her eyes down as she pulled her needle through the quilt.

'Have you heard of the Paducah Quilt Show in Kentucky?' asked Brenda. 'I went once. It was fantastic! You've never seen so many quilts. You should go, a keen quilter like you.'

'Oh, I can't.'

'Why not? It's expensive but worth saving up for.'

'It's not just that.' She stopped stitching. 'I'm afraid of flying.'

Brenda's blue eyes widened, but they were warm with understanding. 'Oh dear. That's too bad. Have you ever tried?'

She nodded. 'Once.' It had been mortifying. She and Carys had gone to Spain when they were twenty-one, and Liberty had had a meltdown. She'd hyperventilated and honestly believed she was going to die. She couldn't explain why it had happened, and no one could help. Worse still, she'd spent the rest of the holiday dreading the flight home, which had been just as bad.

She'd vowed never to put herself through such an ordeal again.

Brenda clicked her tongue. 'Look at me telling you to go to America when I can't even step outside to hang up the washing without having a panic attack.'

'Ethan said it started when your husband died.'

'It did. He had a heart attack. It felled me. One day he was here, the next he was gone. And then I started having these panic attacks. And now I feel terrible because Ethan had to move back in with me. It's the last thing he needs at his age. He should be getting on with his life, not caring for his mother.'

Liberty tied a knot in her thread and buried it in the fabric before snipping the end off. 'Does he work in Willowbrook?' She reached for her cotton reel to cut a new piece of thread.

'No. He's a solicitor in town. Here, have another piece of cake.' She was smiling again, but Liberty could see the shadows in her eyes, and guessed she must spend a lot of time worrying and feeling guilty about how her illness impacted on her son's life. Liberty admired how she tried to keep a brave face, and her heart went out to her. It must be so difficult, never being able to feel the wind in her hair or the sun on her face. Even when it was raining, Liberty loved walking in the woods. The smells and sounds of the forest, the fresh air, and the feel of the soft springy earth beneath her boots always left her happy and invigorated.

'How long have you been working at the Button Hole?'

'A year.' She smiled, remembering how excited she'd

been to start last Christmas. It really was her dream job: she was doing what she enjoyed most every day. 'I love it there.'

'I didn't think the young ones sewed nowadays, but Ethan tells me your boss is young too.'

'Evie's my age, yes. I used to shop in the Button Hole and when she advertised for an assistant I jumped at the chance. I was working in a department store, but that involved selling sewing machines rather than fabric. This job is much more fun. I get to help customers choose colours and patterns, I help to make quilts for our online customers, and I run workshops, too.'

'Did you learn to sew at school?'

'No. My mum taught me. My earliest memories are of watching her sew, and I desperately wanted to help so when I was little she let me cut fabric and paper pieces at first. Then she taught me how to tack them, and I was sewing properly before I was eight.'

'That's very young. Your mum likes to sew by hand, then?'

'She did, yes.' Liberty paused. 'She died twelve years ago.'

'I'm sorry.'

Her mum's illness had come on very suddenly, and within a couple of months she'd become too weak, too shaky to do the fine work any more. So, in a reversal of roles, her mum had tacked hexagon pieces for Liberty. She'd used them to make cushions for the lounge. 'Mum was a very patient teacher, she taught me so much. When I was little what really captured my imagination were the names of all the different designs: Flying Geese, Bear Paw, Log Cabin . . . I used to make up stories around them.'

She remembered all the hours she and her mum had spent working on quilts together. Her mum had always encouraged her, listening to her ideas and giving her free rein to try new designs and not feel constrained by the pattern books. Liberty felt sure this was why she'd developed the confidence to design her own quilts so young. She hoped to do the same with her own children one day.

The rest of the evening passed quickly, and when Liberty had to leave Brenda saw her to the door. 'It's so good of you to visit,' she said. 'I'm sure a young lady like you has better things to do with her time.'

Liberty smiled. 'I would have been sewing tonight anyway, so whether I was here or at home makes no difference to me.' She'd come hoping to help, but was surprised by how much she'd enjoyed it. It had brought back fond memories of stitching with her mum, and she and Brenda had so much in common. Liberty knew she'd come back soon. She got into her car, feeling a swell of satisfaction because her challenge had already brought a new friend (and her good-looking son) into her life.

However, as she started the engine, her thoughts turned to tomorrow's challenge and the motorbike, and her smile vanished.

Chapter Seven

L iberty got up as quietly as she could. She crept out of the cottage with Charlie, trying hard not to disturb Alex and secretly hoping he might sleep in. She shut the back door softly, and set off along the usual trail through the woods.

She'd had a restless night with vivid dreams about a monstrous motorbike speeding out of control: there'd been a deafening growl, a splintering crash, smoke and glass everywhere, the scream of tyres skidding, and a thunderous impact before she was hurled into the air. She'd woken shaking and drenched with sweat.

Now, as she breathed in the fresh morning air, she tried to reason with herself. What was the worst that could happen? It was only a couple of miles to the Button Hole, no distance at all.

But the image of Carys lying inert in hospital punctured her thoughts. That was what could happen.

Her hands were clammy inside her gloves. She tried to take deep breaths but she felt sick and the humming in her head wouldn't stop. This was not a good idea. Her challenge had been meant to nudge her a little out of her comfort zone – not propel her way beyond it and make her blood pressure rocket into outer space. Pine needles crunched underfoot as she walked, and she whistled for Charlie to come back when he scooted out of sight. He returned, wagging his tail, and she fed him a treat. 'Good boy.' She patted his head, made a fuss of him, then they looped around the pond and headed home.

When she got back to the cottage she'd explain to Alex why she couldn't go through with it. He'd probably be relieved. She'd read on the internet yesterday how dangerous riding pillion could be if the passenger was inexperienced: simply leaning the wrong way, especially on a bend, could throw the bike's balance and end in disaster. Besides, with any luck he might still be asleep, and if she hurried she could leave for work before he stirred.

She was disappointed to find Alex already up and dressed. He was wearing a navy sweater and jeans, but his hair was messy: glossy dark strands fell over his eyes and stuck up wildly where he'd pushed a hand through it. 'Ah, there you are,' he said, as she closed the front door. 'What time do you need to leave?'

Charlie pushed past her and raced over to Alex. She was surprised to see that the Frenchman didn't snatch away his hand today, but gave the dog a quick pat on the head instead.

'Actually,' she said, 'I've had a rethink and I can't do it after all.'

'You can't? But what about your challenge?'

'The thing is, you haven't got a spare helmet, have you? And it's not safe to ride without one. In fact, I'm pretty sure it's illegal, so we'll have to leave it.'

He raised an eyebrow.

She ignored his amusement and went on, filling the silence with nervous chatter: 'I'm sorry if you got up early especially I should have left you a note last night. It was a silly idea anyway. I mean I have no interest in or desire to—'

'Woah,' he said, raising a hand in the air.

She blinked. 'Sorry?'

'You don't need to worry. I have a helmet for you.'

'You do?'

'*Oui*.' His lips curved into a smile and his eyes creased. 'I went to the garage yesterday and I have everything you need.'

'Guy's garage?'

He nodded. 'I even have leathers for you, too. You'll be completely safe.'

'Oh.' A heavy weight plunged to the bottom of her stomach. How did she get out of this now? And had Alex really been to the garage? She would have said it was considerate of him if he hadn't looked so pleased with himself right now. She realised that Guy must know about the plan for her to go out on the bike, which meant the whole village would know. Which meant there was even more pressure on her to do it now, wasn't there? 'Well – that was very kind of you, but . . .' She faltered. Damn. She'd had it all worked out with the helmet thing. She'd never expected him to be so . . . helpful.

He stepped forward and studied her more closely. Then he said quietly, 'You're very afraid, aren't you?'

She opened her mouth to deny it, then changed her mind. 'Yes.'

'Don't be. I promise I won't go fast. I wouldn't put your life – or anyone else's – at risk. And I've been doing this a long time. I have total control of that bike.'

'Right.' She believed him. Something in his eyes reassured her. And, besides, you couldn't race bikes professionally without knowing what you were doing, could you?

Unless you were a nutcase, an adrenalin junkie, a speed demon—

She made herself take a deep breath.

'Think of your challenge, yes? You said you wanted this tick in your book. It will be a big one. And it will be over in ten minutes.'

She gave a strangled laugh, although she could just as easily have cried. 'Is that what you say to all the girls?'

'What?'

'Doesn't matter. You're right.' Think of the challenge. Be brave, Lib. Be brave. But her stomach was churning like a washing-machine, and her legs felt weak and shaky.

He looked at his watch. 'Do you want to have breakfast, or shall we go now?'

'Let's go now,' she said. She couldn't face eating, and she might as well get this ordeal over and done with. It was just ten minutes of her life, she repeated silently to herself.

He waited while she went upstairs and put the leathers

on, then packed a bag with a change of clothes for work. Outside, he helped her with her headset and helmet, then put on his own.

'Can you hear me?' he asked. His voice sounded surprisingly clear over the mic. There was something very intimate about it. She realised he could hear her just as well, too.

'Yeah.' The helmet felt huge and heavy, and her limbs liquid. What if she didn't hold on tight enough? What if she fell off? What if she leaned the wrong way and made him lose balance?

He climbed smoothly onto the bike and patted the seat behind him.

'Promise you won't lean the bike too much?' she said, breathless with nerves. 'Promise you'll keep it vertical. I've seen pictures of people racing with their knee almost touching the ground as they go through a bend.'

His laughter came through deep and throaty on the headset. 'We only do that on the racetrack. Don't worry. I'll keep you safe. Now remember what I said about following what I do, and try to relax.'

She nodded, her mouth too dry to speak. Could he hear the thumping of her heart?

'Put your foot here, hold on to me, and jump on.'

Feeling pale, she climbed on behind him. The bike was enormous. The slope of the seat meant she was higher than him, and her feet didn't even come close to touching the ground. She placed them on the footrests. Her legs were bent, her knees next to his hips, and she wondered if you could fall off a bike before it had even started moving.

'Hold on to me,' he told her. 'That's it.'

She gripped his chest and was surprised by how solid he felt. A ripple of heat flashed through her. She looked back at the cottage. Tonight when she was sitting in front of the fire, quilting, she'd be able to laugh about this and make jokes about what a bag of nerves she'd been.

He snapped his visor down and gunned the engine. 'Ready to go?' he asked.

No. She wanted to run back inside the cottage and hide under the stairs. 'Yes,' she said tightly.

'*Alors on y va.*'

Liberty squeezed her eyes shut, but they flew open again when the bike sprang forwards. It felt as if the air had been knocked out of her lungs. She gripped Alex's chest hard, and her legs clenched the seat as he steered them carefully along the forest lane to the main road. The familiar route felt very different today. Even through the helmet and protective clothing she could feel the wind sliding past and smell the peaty fresh forest air. The trees seemed to lean in and watch curiously as the bike went by.

When they reached the main road, it was busy with rush-hour traffic. To reach Willowbrook village they had to cross the main road, but once they'd done that it would be a quiet route into the village.

'I don't fancy trying to speed across this road,' Alex told her, 'so I'm going to turn left and drive to the next roundabout, then come back.'

'Good idea.' She didn't tell him that she always did the same in her car too.

She watched as he waited for a lengthy gap in the traffic before turning onto the road. The acceleration caught her by surprise again, but he kept his speed steady all the way, and manoeuvred carefully around the roundabout, glancing left and right the whole time, presumably keeping tabs on the traffic. She didn't loosen her grip on his chest.

'How are you feeling?' he asked, as they headed back towards the Willowbrook turning.

'Okay,' she said, and realised a wide grin had crept across her face. White-knuckle fear had been replaced with a soaring sensation, and her blood was fizzing through her veins. 'It's not as bad as I thought it would be. I quite like it, actually.' She sounded as shocked as she felt by this revelation. Who'd have thought?

She heard the smile in his voice as he asked, 'Want to go faster?'

'A tiny bit.' She clung to him.

His right hand twisted a little and the bike increased in speed. She yelped and laughed as they sped along the main road. 'Oh my God oh my God oh my God! That's so *faaaast*!'

'Too fast?' He eased off the throttle.

'No!' She heard the amazement in her voice. 'I like it. It – it's exciting!'

He chuckled, speeded up again, and her heart somersaulted. Then, in no time at all, they reached the sign for Willowbrook and he slowed down, indicated left, and turned off. The lane zigzagged as it followed the stream. They crested the stone bridge and the village centre came into view. Her heart was still banging and she couldn't stop grinning. He slowed right down as they travelled past the low cottages, and Liberty was glad because it would be dangerous and disruptive to roar through the quiet village on a big bike. When he saw a couple waiting to cross the road, Alex stopped to let them cross. Liberty hoped she wouldn't be recognised with her helmet on. Though when they waved and smiled, she suspected she'd been rumbled.

Finally, they came to a halt outside the Button Hole.

'How was that?' asked Alex.

'Great.' She was beaming as she clambered off the bike. 'Much better than I expected.' She didn't need to look at her reflection in the shop window to know her cheeks would be the colour of holly berries.

'I thought so. You almost deafened me.' He lifted his visor, and his dark eyes creased as he smiled.

'Did I? Sorry.' She giggled. She unclipped her helmet and lifted it off. 'Tell me truthfully, is that the speed you normally travel at?'

He shook his head, laughing. 'I went at a snail's pace for you.'

Her shoulders sank with disappointment because it had felt fast. But she appreciated that he'd listened to her.

'Maybe we can go for another spin some time.' He winked.

She giggled again and stepped back onto the pavement. 'We'll see. But thanks for the ride.'

He nodded. 'See you later. And if you change your mind about riding home, call me.'

Liberty watched as he rode off, threading his way gently

through the narrow streets towards the main road. What a start to her day. Adrenalin was rushing through her and she had a feeling it would take a while before it returned to normal. She pushed open the door to the bakery.

'Liberty!' said Marjorie, the owner. 'What are you doing here so early?'

'I missed breakfast. Can I have a bacon sandwich and a coffee, please?'

'Course you can. Love the leather. Is it a new look?'

She laughed. 'No. It's definitely a one-off.'

Or was it? She'd really enjoyed it. And that was exactly why she had to try new things. Why she had to be braver.

In the back room of the Button Hole, she changed out of the leathers and folded them neatly. She'd seen a whole new side to Alex today, a side she hadn't expected: the way he'd reassured her and driven slowly for her, he'd been considerate and understanding. Perhaps she'd been too quick to judge him when he'd first arrived. She realised she knew nothing about him, apart from the odd little snippet Natasha had told her. The shop was empty and Evie wasn't due in until lunchtime so she used the opportunity to do a quick internet search of his name.

The results appeared and she did a double-take. He was a world champion. He'd won countless prizes, and there were photos of him on podiums all over the world holding up big trophies. 'Well I never,' she muttered, under her breath.

There were similar black-and-white photos of his dad. In some he was racing, but there were many of him taken at red-carpet events with women clinging to his arm.

And there were pictures of Alex's most recent accident. Video clips, too. Liberty hesitated, then clicked on one. As the footage played, she saw his bike lean into a corner. Then he lost control and it spun across the track. She held her breath. He was an orange blur catapulting through the air, then bouncing roughly over the gravel until he came to a stop. Her heart was in her mouth as he lay still while race staff rushed to him. Then the clip ended. She clicked the tab shut.

No wonder his injury was keeping him awake at night. It looked really bad. How could he still want to race after surviving something so horrific?

'So how are you finding it here?' asked Luc.

Alex's gaze slid from his friend to the garden of Poppy Cottage. Little Lottie and her friend Annabel were outside playing some kind of game that involved ducking in and out of the playhouse. Luc had brought coffee and pastries into the orangery so they could keep an eye on the children while they enjoyed a late breakfast and a catch-up. 'Honestly?'

'How long have we known each other, Alex? Of course you can be honest with me.'

'It's too quiet.'

'Too quiet? I thought you'd enjoy having a break from it all.' He pushed the plate of pastries towards Alex, who took a cinnamon swirl.

'You don't find it quiet, too?'

'Not at all. I love coming home to Willowbrook. It's a

haven. It's . . .' he gazed fondly at his daughter in the garden '. . . home.'

'Because your family is here. You'd say that wherever Natasha and Lottie were.'

'True. But Willowbrook is special. There's something about this place . . .'

Alex frowned. He couldn't see it at all. What was special about a tiny village, in the middle of the English countryside, that hadn't changed for the last two hundred years? They still had cobbled roads, for Heaven's sake. He ripped off a chunk of pastry and savoured the buttery cinnamon sweetness.

'You'll understand,' Luc went on, 'when you settle down and have a family of your own.'

Alex tensed. He loved kids, but he'd never be a father. A good father should be stable, committed, reliable. He was none of those things. He thought of his own father. Some people should never bring children into the world. He'd rather grow old alone than repeat his father's mistakes.

'Anyway,' said Luc, 'how's your search going? Have you found anything yet?'

'Nothing whatsoever.' He counted off on his fingers all the places he'd tried. 'The town hall, the records office, and most of the parish registers in the area. I don't know where else to look. I'm losing hope, to be honest.'

'Have you spoken to people in the village?'

Alex drew his coffee cup towards him and felt the familiar dark thoughts enfold him. He'd never been the type to open up easily, and now he had even more reason to shy away from attention. If word got out that he was here and not on the circuit, questions would be asked. 'It's a delicate matter. I don't want to broadcast to the world what my father did. Plus I don't know anyone here. Who would I ask?'

'There's Old Dorothy. She's lived in Willowbrook a long time. And I presume you've spoken to Liberty already?'

'Not in detail.' Alex ducked his gaze away, but he saw his friend's eyebrows lift.

'Why not?'

Alex picked up his spoon and tapped it against his finger. 'We got off on the wrong foot,' he said carefully. He wasn't sure how to explain that the pain, insomnia and his recent news had been eating away at him, or that he seemed to have done everything possible to anger her. 'But things are better now.'

He thought of her breathless excitement when he'd driven her to work that morning. When she'd taken off her helmet she'd glowed with delight. And he'd been surprised by the twist of joy he'd felt, sharing her excitement, and by the rush of awareness, too.

'What happened?' Luc pressed.

'She had a problem with my bike.' He hesitated. 'And she didn't like it when I told her I don't want to be involved in her life. She wanted to cook for me and spend evenings together. She kept asking lots of questions. She was . . .' he tried to find a more tactful word for 'interfering' '. . . trying too hard.'

A short silence passed. Finally, his friend said, 'You're complaining about that?'

'I need my own space. And the injury's been giving me a lot of trouble. But I took her out on the bike this morning. She seemed to enjoy that, something about a challenge she's doing.'

Luc didn't look impressed. 'But you've told her about your search, right?'

Alex shook his head.

Silence. Luc studied him briefly, then said, 'You know, you don't have to be on guard here, Alex. You can relax, you're among friends. Liberty's never had a stranger lodge with her before. Natasha said she was nervous about it and she only came round to the idea because she needs the money. She might have tried too hard, but I'm sure her intentions were good.'

Alex felt the bite of guilt. He was so used to holding people at arm's length when they tried to get close to him: everyone he'd met for the last twenty years had seemed to have selfish motivations. There was only a handful of people in his life he could trust – like Luc. And his family. People he could be sure were not out to profit from him. Other than those exceptions, he'd long since decided he functioned better alone. 'You're probably right,' he muttered. 'I'm not normally this snappy. It's just . . .' He rubbed his shoulder absently.

'Maybe you should make an appointment with the doctor.'

Alex laughed. 'Liberty said the same thing.'

'Jake's a friend of mine. He'll be able to help with the pain. And anything else you want to speak to him about.'

'What do you mean?' he asked sharply.

Luc met his gaze steadily. 'I've known you a long time, Alex. Long enough to know something's eating at you. You might not be ready to speak to me about it, but maybe it would be good to get it off your chest, whatever it is.'

'I don't know what you're talking—'

'It's okay, Alex,' Luc cut in gently. 'I'm not prying. And nor will Jake. He's a professional. Anything you tell him will be strictly confidential.'

Alex opened his mouth to speak, then sighed. 'Luc, I'm sorry,' he said finally. He wasn't ready to talk. It was still too raw, too new.

His friend smiled. 'When you're ready, you'll share. But go and see the doctor about that shoulder, because the pain's making you short-tempered.'

Alex gave a dry laugh.

'And talk to Liberty about your search. Perhaps she can help you. If she can't, she'll know who you should speak to. She grew up here so she knows everyone.'

A short while later, Alex left Luc's and put his helmet on. He climbed onto the bike, then stopped. Ahead was the village, and behind him the main road. At this time it would be quiet, and the thought of the empty tarmac stretching away from him was simply too tempting. He turned left and gunned the engine.

Ten minutes later, he arrived back where he'd started, his face flushed, blood pumping pleasure through every vein. Yet it wasn't a substitute for the high speeds and adrenalin rush of racing. How was he supposed to live without that?

He forced aside the wintry thoughts and concentrated on the directions Luc had given him for Old Dorothy's cottage. It wasn't difficult. Five minutes later, he knocked on her door, helmet in hand. He waited.

He'd almost given up waiting when she finally opened it. Alex tried to hide his surprise. Luc had called her Old Dorothy, but he hadn't been prepared for quite how elderly and frail she was.

'Hello, dear. You must be the French racer. Luc called to say you might drop in. Step inside. I've just made a pot of tea.'

He wiped his boots carefully.

'I do like a man in leather,' she murmured.

At least, that was what he thought she said. 'What was that?'

'Nothing, dear.' She set off at a shuffle towards the tiny kitchen. 'Make yourself at home,' she called, over her shoulder, and waved in the vague direction of the lounge.

Instead he followed her and waited while she made the tea. 'Here, let me carry that tray.'

'Good manners, too.' She smiled as if she wanted to eat him. 'Put it on the coffee-table, there. Yes, that's right. Now, do you take milk and sugar?'

Alex hated tea and drank only coffee. But seeing how long it took her to shuffle across the room, he bit his lip. 'Black is fine, thanks.'

'So you're trying to track someone down?' said Dorothy, once they were both comfortable with a china cup in hand.

Alex reached into his inside pocket and drew out the

envelopes, yellowed with age. 'I found these letters when I was sorting through my father's things. He died earlier this year.'

She nodded for him to go on.

He opened the first and handed it to her. 'They're dated thirty years ago and addressed to him. But there's no return address, no name. Only the postmark tells me they were sent from round here.'

Dorothy took the letter and put her glasses on. They were attached to a beaded chain around her neck that chinked as she moved her head and read the handwritten note. Alex knew the letters word for word. The black ink of a fountain pen, the loopy neat handwriting, which suggested the writer had been young, possibly not much more than a schoolgirl.

Dear Gérard,

This will come as a shock – I'm still shocked myself – but I am pregnant.

Please write soon. I'm scared.

Mx

'Well I never,' murmured Dorothy. Her blue eyes sparkled.

'There are more.' Alex handed her the remaining two.

Dear Gérard,

I don't know if you received my last letter. I am pregnant with your baby. I should have explained that it can only be yours – I promise.

Please write or call or something. I can't do this by myself!

Mx

'The last one is postmarked a year later,' he said.

Dear Gérard,

You have a daughter. She's beautiful and smiles all the time, and – well, she's perfect.

It would be good if you would acknowledge her. For her sake. Doesn't she deserve the chance to know her father?

Mx

Dorothy finished reading and removed her glasses. 'So you want to know who sent them?'

He nodded.

'Why?' she asked, her shrewd gaze fixed on him.

'Isn't it obvious? Wouldn't anyone want to track down family they'd never known they had?' He had a sibling out there somewhere and that mattered to him. 'When I read those letters, I felt something. Here.' He held a fist to his heart. 'She sounds so desperate, so dignified. And if I'm right – that he never replied – then I have to go to her and explain. Apologise. I can't change the past, but perhaps I can make amends.'

He felt passionately about putting right the wrongs his father had done. He just wanted to make things right, prove that he wasn't like his dad.

He stilled. Prove it to whom?

To himself.

He shook his head, startled by this realisation. Was it really so important? Yes. Yes, it was. He was like his father in so many ways – the racing, the winning, the drive and ambition, the risk-taking. He needed to prove that he wasn't an unreliable, fickle bastard too.

And the best way to do that would be to find his sister and atone for their father's wrongdoings.

'Very noble,' muttered Dorothy, approvingly. 'How do you know he never replied to them?'

'I can't be certain, but when he died our family lawyer made us aware that there had been other women in his life.' He cleared his throat. 'None of them was British or had a child.'

'I see,' said Dorothy.

'You don't look shocked.'

She smiled and a gold tooth glinted. 'Oh, at my age, dear, I've seen it all. Although, I must admit, perhaps not quite on this scale. But your father was wealthy, wasn't he? Most of us are limited by our circumstances. It's not so easy to hide a secret lover if you've lived in the same village all your life and have no money to spare.' She picked up her knitting and the needles began to click rhythmically. 'It is interesting that your father kept these letters, though, don't you think?'

'I found them in a folder of other documents relating to that time. I'm not sure he intended to keep them, and he certainly didn't treasure them. It looked as if the folder hadn't been touched for a long time.'

'Ah.' She shook her head sorrowfully. 'I'm afraid I don't

know who your mystery woman could be. There have been a few surprise pregnancies over the years, but I can't think of anyone whose name began with M.'

'You don't recognise the handwriting?' It was a long shot, he knew.

She shook her head. 'But, then, why would I? I worked at the grocer's. I wasn't a schoolteacher or a—' She put down her knitting. 'You should go and see Peter. He worked in the post office for years.'

Luc had been right, Alex thought. He had to start talking to people. Perhaps someone would remember something. 'Yes. Perhaps my father visited. Perhaps someone from Willowbrook spent time in France or abroad, had an interest in motorcycle racing.'

'Perhaps. Try Peter. And if I think of anything else I'll call Liberty.' She reached for her tea and took a sip. Then a thought seemed to occur and her eyes glinted with mischief. 'You know your landlady is about the right age, don't you?'

'Liberty? It's not her. Natasha told me her father died when she was small, and he had red hair.' He pictured his landlady's beautiful long tresses.

Dorothy put the cup down. 'I don't mean that. Liberty is the right age to have been friends with your half-sister. Perhaps they were at school together.'

'How old is she?'

'She had her thirtieth birthday at the end of November. Did she tell you about the mystery flowers?'

He shook his head.

She tutted. 'Liberty receives a bouquet every year on

her birthday – sent anonymously – and this year she chased after the florist to ask who they were from.'

'Chased?' His lips twitched.

'Yes. In her car.'

He couldn't help smiling because he'd seen how slowly and carefully she drove. 'Did she find out?'

'Why don't you ask her yourself? You won't get very far with your detective work if you don't see what's right under your nose.'

'No . . .' He cleared his throat. He hadn't been scolded like this since his schooldays.

'So now, young man, what are you waiting for? You have a mystery to solve, and Liberty might be just the person to help you solve it.'

Liberty was having her lunch in the back room when Evie came in. She'd been to the wholesaler's and was laden with bags and boxes, which she put down with a clatter.

'Hey, I've heard the news!' she said to Liberty. Her dimples appeared as she smiled and her cheeks were flushed from the cold so they almost matched her cherry-red coat.

'What news?'

'That you came to work on a motorbike this morning.'

Liberty groaned. It must have spread round the village like wildfire. But that shouldn't surprise her. 'Who from?'

'Marjorie next door.' She held up the sandwich she'd bought from the bakery. 'I take it you did it for your challenge? Was it fun?'

'It was terrifying. And cold.' Liberty grinned. 'But, yes, lots of fun.'

Evie laughed. 'I'm so glad. This challenge is going to make you fearless.'

'I hope so. But I was so scared beforehand that I'm wondering if it might count for a week's worth of challenges. What do you think?'

Evie tried not to smile. 'It's your challenge, Lib. Your rules.'

She thought about it. 'Just one day then, but it means I don't have to experiment with lunch.' She looked guiltily at her coronation chicken sandwich and vanilla slice. 'So much for trying new things, eh?'

'Don't beat yourself up about it,' said Evie, as she took off her coat and hung it up. 'If you make the challenge too difficult it'll feel like a punishment – or, worse,' she wrinkled her nose, 'a diet – and you'll give up before the month is over. One challenge per day is plenty and I'm proud of you for going on a motorbike.'

'You're right.' Evie was like a cup of hot chocolate: she made you feel warm and everything in the world seem sweeter.

Liberty took another bite of her sandwich. Without the guilt it tasted so much better.

'Want to see what I bought?' asked Evie, as she unpacked the bags she'd brought in. 'I've got lots of cushion pads to sell with our starter kits, and look at these layer cakes.'

Liberty examined the packs of ten-inch squares cut from coordinating fabrics. They were modern with quirky designs like postage stamps and handwritten script. 'I love those. The colours are so fresh and zingy.'

'And I also got a couple of mini Christmas trees,' Evie said, as she sliced open a box. 'We can put one in the window and one by the till, and hang our felt decorations from them.'

'Great idea.' The heart- and star-shaped confections had been so popular last year that Evie had started making them in January ready for this Christmas.

Liberty helped to assemble the trees, but her mind was stuck on that morning's excitement and she kept wondering if she was brave enough to take Alex up on his offer.

When they'd set up the first tree by the till, she pulled out her phone and gave Evie a bashful smile. 'Alex said I could call him if I want a ride home tonight. I think I might.'

Evie clapped her hands. 'I said it – you're fearless now! So, he's not as bad as you first thought?'

Liberty called his number. 'The jury's still out.'

Alex answered almost immediately, but he sounded breathless. 'Liberty. I'm just on my way to see you.'

'You are? Why?' He must be walking, she realised.

'*Une minute.* I'm nearly there . . .' The shop door swung open and there he was, still in his leathers, helmet in hand, hair ruffled and messy as always. But there was something different about him, too. He didn't look as scowly. He seemed more . . . relaxed.

Evie's eyes widened. Her mouth worked, but no sound came out. She was clearly speechless – which was a first. She grinned at Liberty.

'Alex,' said Liberty. 'What brings you here?'

'You tell me first – why did you call?'

'Oh – ah – to ask if I could have a ride tonight. Please?' She smiled at the irony: she who'd been set against the motorbike was now asking for a second turn.

The glint in his eyes told her he'd had the same thought. 'On one condition,' he said.

Evie muttered something about giving them privacy and disappeared into the back room.

'What is it?' asked Liberty.

'You have dinner with me.'

Chapter Eight

It was Liberty's second blind date, and as she drove there she was pleased to find she wasn't at all nervous. In fact, her mind wasn't on the evening ahead, but playing back this afternoon's happenings in the Button Hole, wondering why on earth Alex wanted to have dinner with her.

When she'd told him she was busy tonight, he'd looked disappointed. 'Are you free tomorrow instead?' he'd asked.

She lifted a finger to her lips and pretended to think. 'The thing is, Alex,' she teased, 'I distinctly remember you telling me you *didn't* want to eat with me.'

He had the good grace to look ashamed. 'I shouldn't have said that. I'm sorry. I – I've had stuff on my mind.'

Stuff? She peered at him, curious. His gruff arrogance did seem to have been smoothed away, but why? 'What's changed?'

He rubbed a hand over his face. 'I saw Luc this morning and . . .' he weighed the helmet in his hand '. . . he told me I've been behaving like *un imbécile*.'

She tried not to laugh. Stripes of colour touched his

cheekbones and he looked genuinely contrite. 'In what way have you been an *imbécile*?'

'I've not been . . . friendly.'

'No, you haven't.' She was enjoying this more than she should.

'So – will you have dinner with me?' he asked. 'I'll cook for you.'

Her heart beat a little faster. She tilted her head to one side. He seemed almost . . . desperate to make amends. And he *had* taken her out on his bike, even before his dressing-down from Luc.

Still, she couldn't resist teasing him just a little. 'I usually have pizza and watch a film on Saturday night . . .' she began apologetically. His shoulders sagged in defeat. '. . . but I'm willing to make an exception this weekend.'

His smile lit his eyes and looked so heartfelt it was completely disarming.

Now, Liberty turned into the car park and found a space. Her date tonight had suggested they meet in a restaurant she didn't know, but she found it without any problem. She pushed open the door and was hit by a blast of noise and faces. The restaurant was heaving, which was only to be expected on a Friday night in one of the trendiest new places in town, but that made it difficult for her to spot her date.

Fortunately a waiter approached. 'Can I help you, madam?' he asked.

'I'm meeting a man called Sean.'

'Ah, yes. He's waiting for you. Follow me, please.'

Sean looked relieved when he saw her approaching. A nervous smile flickered across his features.

The waiter pulled out her chair for her, then left them with menus.

'You're Liberty, right?' said her date.

'That's right.' She smiled and was pleased with the first impressions: he was good-looking and seemed friendly. This was hopeful.

They ordered wine and food, then exchanged a shy glance. Liberty fiddled with the hem of her napkin and tried to think of something else to say or ask. She wished she could skip the awkward getting-to-know-you part of dating and whizz straight to the close-friends-and-more stage. It would make life so much simpler. Since she'd turned thirty she'd had a nagging consciousness of time passing and it was making her impatient. 'Do you live nearby?' she asked.

'Yeah.' He described where his flat was in town. 'I moved recently. I was sharing before. Now I'm renting on my own.' There was a dejected air about him as he fiddled with his cutlery.

'You don't like your new flat?'

'It's okay . . . I haven't been there long. I suppose it doesn't feel like home yet.'

She wondered why he kept glancing at the door. Was he planning his escape?

'What about you?' he asked. 'Where do you live?'

She gave him Brownie points for showing an interest in her. But when she described Willowbrook and Damselfly Cottage he barely seemed to listen.

The waiter brought their food.

When they were alone again, Liberty asked, 'Is this your first date, Sean?'

'What? Oh – yeah.' His smile was crooked. 'You can tell, then?'

'You just seem a little nervous,' she said warmly. But inside she sighed because she'd been here before with the chef. Was this going to be a repeat?

'I'm just . . .' He shook his head. 'I was in a relationship for a long time – until recently. So I guess I'm out of practice.'

Understanding dawned. 'Ah. When did—'

'Sean!' someone gasped.

Liberty dropped her fork. A woman with long tight curls had been walking past, but suddenly stopped and made a beeline for their table. She was beautiful, perfectly made up and wearing a sparkly dress that showcased her incredibly long legs, but she was glaring at Sean as if she wanted to murder him.

He clearly wasn't surprised, and Liberty remembered how he'd been darting nervous glances at the door all evening.

'Jessie—'

'What's this?' the woman spat, gesturing at their plates of food.

A couple of diners turned, and a prickling sensation crept over Liberty.

'What does it look like?' he said carefully.

Liberty frowned. He looked defiant yet guilty – she didn't understand why. What was going on?

The woman's anger seemed to mushroom. 'You said you wanted to try again. You begged me to give you another chance. You said it was over with her.'

Liberty stared at them both in turn. This was his ex? He'd been unfaithful?

The scary woman turned to her. 'Maybe you can tell me what the hell is going on.'

'Me?' Liberty swallowed. She glanced at Sean for guidance or an explanation, but he ducked his gaze away. 'Um – we're just having dinner.'

'You're having dinner with *my* man.' The woman pointed a finger at him.

The room had hushed completely. Heads turned, the waiters had all stopped, and Liberty's cheeks flooded with lava-like heat. Oh, great. Now she must look as guilty as Sean. 'There must have been a misunderstanding,' she said. Again, she turned to Sean to clear this up, but he was staring at Jessie. In fact, he seemed pleased with himself. Why?

She sat up tall and tried again. 'Listen, I've no idea who you are or what's going on, but this is our first date and—'

'So you admit it, then? You're dating him? And don't think for a second that I believe you about the *first* date thing. I know what you did.'

'What?' Sean, the dirt bag, continued to ignore her. 'That's not—'

'You're a man-stealing witch!' Jessie's expression was venomous, and the restaurant was completely silent now. 'You two did this on purpose, didn't you? You knew this was my favourite place, you knew I'd be here tonight and you came here deliberately to – to flaunt yourselves in my face!'

Beneath the table, Liberty's legs were shaking. This was mortifying.

'Jess—' he began.

She held up her hand to silence him, and turned back to Liberty. 'You cheated with him and now you think you can have him all for yourself, do you?'

Her eyes were black with rage.

'No. You've got it all wrong.' Liberty turned to Sean in desperation. 'Tell her. Tell her we'd never met before tonight.' She could feel the other diners' stares burning into her. Everyone in this room would think she *was* guilty.

'So you *do* feel something,' Sean said quietly, his gaze on Jessie.

The penny dropped. He'd set this up to make his ex jealous. Liberty felt sick. She'd been used, she'd—

A waiter approached and said to Jessie, 'Madam, I have to ask you to leave now.'

A wave of relief washed over Liberty.

Sean stood up and placed a hand on Jessie's arm. 'He's right. Come on, Jess.'

She shook it off. 'I've not finished!'

Sean and the waiter steered her, still yelling, towards the exit. 'That witch needs to know she can't go round stealing other people's men! She's a—'

The door swung shut behind her and the room became quiet again. Everyone was staring at Liberty.

She smoothed the napkin on her lap and waited for Sean to come back. But time ticked by and he didn't appear. Liberty looked around. This had to be the most embarrassing situation she'd ever found herself in. *How* had it happened? Her skin prickled, and she decided she didn't want to stay: she wasn't interested in hearing Sean's explanation even if he did come back.

The waiter appeared. 'Are you all right, madam?'

'Yes,' she whispered, and moved to get up. It was clear Sean wasn't returning. 'I – er – I think I'll go too.'

'I'll get the bill,' he said firmly.

'The bill?' She blinked hard.

The waiter's features hardened. He gestured at the wine and plates of barely touched food. 'I need payment for this.'

'But he— That's not fair. *He* should pay for what he ordered.'

The waiter remained hard-nosed. 'He's not here, madam.'

Her throat was so tight she couldn't have argued even if she'd known what to say to that. She sank down into her chair, defeated as the waiter clicked his fingers and someone hurried over with a slip of paper. She could feel dozens of accusing eyes boring into her. He put it in front of her, and tears blurred the number at the bottom of it.

This was mortifying. And to top it all, she was footing the bill.

Saturday, 6 December

'Morning, Liberty!' Evie greeted her with her usual cheeriness.

Liberty held her hand up to shield her eyes, 'Wow, that's bright,' she said. Evie was wearing a sequined red dress with a sparkly gold tree design. The light bounced off it, like little arrows. Liberty peered closer. 'Did you sew all those baubles on yourself?'

'Yep.' Evie grinned. 'You don't think it's too much, do you? Jake raised an eyebrow when he saw it.'

Liberty said diplomatically, 'It looks very . . . Christmassy.'

'How are you today?' Evic asked.

'Been better.' She put her handbag down and began to unbutton her coat.

'That doesn't sound good. What's wrong?'

She mustered a smile. 'Oh, I just had a really bad date last night.'

'Bad as in ugly with bad breath and body odour?'

'Much worse than that.'

Evie listened while she recounted what had happened. 'A bunny-boiler, eh?' she said, wide-eyed. 'Like in *Fatal Attraction*? At least she wasn't armed with a knife, like Glenn Close.'

Liberty laughed at her attempt to find the bright side. 'I suppose. But, Evie, it's made me seriously rethink the whole challenge. I don't know whether to carry on. Am I just opening myself up to humiliating situations?'

'Ah,' Evie said sheepishly, and glanced down. She picked up a carrier bag.

'What is it?'

'I just had an idea for a challenge, that's all. Something to get into the Christmas spirit and make our customers smile.' She opened the bag and Liberty saw the tip of a green felt hat and a very long pointed ear. 'But if you'd rather not . . .'

Liberty smiled. 'Show me. Nothing in that bag can be as upsetting as what happened to me last night.'

They had a really busy day at the Button Hole, and by the time Liberty got home that evening it was after seven. Charlie bounded up to greet her, and when they'd finished saying hello she hung up her coat and went into the kitchen to investigate the delicious smell of cooking.

Alex was nowhere to be seen. On the hob a couple of pans were on a gentle heat. She lifted the lid of one to peep inside and the fragrant scent of exotic spices rose to meet her. Her mouth watered. She was itching to know what this meal was all about. In the other pan noodles were cooking, and the table was set with her best napkins and goblet wine glasses. Her birthday bouquet had been moved and left by the back door, and she guessed this was because the flowers were half dead. The gerberas had lost their vibrant edge, and the roses were nodding piti-fully. They were almost two weeks old now – perhaps they'd simply reached the end of their life. But Liberty decided to give them the benefit of the doubt and began to sort them, removing the dead flowers and snipping the ends off those that remained.

These flowers had triggered the idea of her challenge, she thought, as she refilled the vase with fresh water, but last night had been so awful she still wasn't sure if she should carry on with it – or, at least, not the dating aspect. As she plucked off a shrivelled leaf, Jessie's furious face flashed up in her mind, and Sean's triumphant expression too.

But she also had to remember why she'd started the challenge. If she stopped now, she'd be the one who lost out.

She put the vase back on the kitchen table with fresh resolve. This challenge was about being brave, and a truly brave person wouldn't give up at the first hurdle. She had to carry on.

Footsteps in the hall approached and Alex snorted when he saw her. 'Why are you dressed like that?'

Her hand lifted to touch her hat. She'd completely forgotten she was wearing it. 'I'm a Christmas elf. It's my challenge for today. Which reminds me.' She pulled out her orange notebook and scribbled in it *spent the day dressed as an elf*. 'Do I have time to get changed before dinner?'

'If you're quick. It'll be ready at seven thirty.'

'I'll only be five minutes.' She went to go, then paused. She'd been thinking about this all day and still couldn't work out why he'd been so keen to have dinner with her. 'It smells delicious.'

'Thanks.'

She glanced at the table, which he'd laid with such care. 'So . . . are you going to tell me what this is all about?'

'I will,' he said. 'Over dinner.'

'Oh. Right.'

He looked at the clock, which was edging towards half past. 'Are you getting changed, then?' he asked, with a mischievous grin. His gaze swept over her slim-fitting green leggings, and was that a gleam in his eye? 'Because I don't mind if you want to stay dressed as an elf.'

Chapter Nine

'So you want help with your search?' Liberty asked, as she dug her fork into the Thai noodles with chicken and a rainbow of vegetables. The meal Alex had cooked was delicious, fragrant, and not too spicy. But she couldn't relax.

She felt jittery around him. On edge. She wasn't sure why. Maybe because they'd got off to a bad start and she was still wary of him. Or maybe because of his dark eyes and that heart-stopping smile. She darted a glance at his messy hair. Although he was far too unkempt ever to be her type.

Alex nodded. 'I'm not getting anywhere with official records. I've realised I need to talk to people who know the area, see if anyone remembers anything that could help. Everyone said you know Willowbrook well, and my half-sister must be about your age. Perhaps you know her.'

'Perhaps, but how would I work out who she is? You don't even have a name, and those letters were written thirty years ago. A lot can change in that time: the mother could have moved away, or the baby grown up and left.'

'I know.' He dipped his head in defeat.

He looked so sad she wanted to reach out and comfort him. 'Can I see the letters?'

She noted, as he gave them to her, that the envelopes were old and thin, yellowed with age. She opened them one by one, carefully smoothing out the satin-soft paper. Once she'd scanned them, she put them down. 'Do you know what the M stands for?'

He shook his head.

She ran through the possibilities; 'Maud, Maura, Melanie, Marianne . . . But I can't think of anyone I know whose name begins with M.'

'I'll never find her,' he said despondently.

She studied him more closely. He seemed so serious and intense, it was difficult to imagine his father had been the womanising type. She asked cautiously, 'Did your dad do this a lot – sleeping with other women?'

His features hardened. 'Yes. Sadly. He was the archetypal Casanova.' He pointed to the letters. 'This is typical of him. He behaved selfishly – all his life. When I think of what this poor woman must have been through, how scared she must have been when she wrote those letters . . .'

He sounded so angry, so passionate, and his desire to put right his father's wrongs roused a wave of admiration in her.

'We have an online group for residents of Willowbrook,' she said, picking up her phone. 'Would you like me to put a picture of the letters on there and ask if anyone knows anything?'

He shook his head. 'I don't want this to get out to the press. It's too personal.'

'You're worried people will judge you for what your father did?'

'I'm worried people will go to the papers with this piece of gossip about the Ricards. It would be terrible for my mother. She's already been through enough.'

'You don't need to worry. No one around here will talk to the press about you.'

He didn't look convinced. 'How can you be so sure?'

'Because that's not what people are like. We look after each other.'

'I'm an outsider, though.'

'As long as you're staying here, you're one of us.' Her phone was still in her hand, poised and waiting for his assent.

He hesitated, then nodded. She took a picture of one of the letters and posted it online with a brief explanation, then put her phone down. 'So what are you going to do next?'

'I'm not sure. Keep asking around, talking to people, I suppose. Hope someone remembers something. I've been to the post office, the school, the church. No one knows anything.' His long lashes lowered as he picked up his dessert spoon and absently twisted it this way and that. He looked dejected, and her heart tugged.

'When did your father die?' she asked softly.

'Last winter.'

He'd said he was never close to his father, and now she could see why, but she wondered if perhaps he hadn't worked through his grief yet. Maybe that was the reason he'd scowled so much when he'd first arrived.

He went on, 'He was never home. Always travelling. My mother raised us like a single parent. She did everything for us.'

She could tell from the warmth in his voice that he cared deeply about her. Liberty smiled. 'My mum was single, too.'

'You were close?'

'Very. I had the perfect childhood.' As a child, Liberty had always been envious of families larger than her own, but now she knew better. She and her mum had enjoyed an exceptionally harmonious relationship. Some of her schoolfriends had been constantly at war with their parents. She'd been lucky.

'Where did you grow up?'

'Here. In this house.'

'You lived here all your life?'

'Yes. So did Mum. This cottage has been in our family for three generations.' Her proud smile faded, however, as she remembered his dismissive words: *I'm not used to living in the middle of nowhere.*

'And your father?' he asked carefully.

'He died when I was very small. But he was never really in the picture. Mum and he split up when I was a baby. She always said we were fine just the two of us – and we were. We didn't need anyone else. I loved growing up here. I can't imagine ever living anywhere else.' She paused. 'I know that must sound dull to you when you travel all over the world.'

'It is a nice place,' he conceded. 'The unspoilt countryside, the traditional stone cottages. I'm the unusual one for having itchy feet.'

She was surprised by this admission. Perhaps he wasn't so snooty about the place, after all. It made her warm to him a little. 'Yes. We're very different, you and I.'

'But you enjoyed going out on the motorbike, didn't you?'

When he'd picked her up after work yesterday she'd been a little nervous again and had made him swear he wouldn't go too fast, but as soon as they'd set off, the exhilaration had kicked in and she'd arrived home buzzing. 'Yes, I did. And it was really kind of you to get the helmet and gear for me. Thanks.'

He waved this away. 'Perhaps you've overcome your fear.'

'Perhaps.' She smiled. 'I still wouldn't like to go fast, though.'

'Tell me more about your challenge. What else scares you?'

Where did she begin? Last night's humiliating scene was still fresh in her mind. 'Meeting new people, going to new places – anything dangerous, fast, or the unknown. I really like routine.'

Oh, well done, Liberty. Now he'd take her for a real stick-in-the-mud, just like her ex had said she was.

'This challenge is a good idea.'

'You think?'

'Definitely. It's not good to live a timid life. How can you realise your full potential if you're too scared to try new things? Life is more fulfilling when you push yourself to go faster or take a more difficult line. More rewarding.'

'It wasn't last night.' He was puzzled so she explained. 'I joined one of those dating apps and I had a really bad date.'

'A dating app?' he said, in horror. 'Why?'

Wasn't it obvious? 'Because I want to meet someone. A man.' Why did her cheeks suddenly feel toasty hot? She ducked her gaze away and picked a couple of threads off her sleeve.

'You don't need to do this.'

She was surprised at how earnest he sounded. 'I do.'

'Of course you don't. A woman like you – you're young and beautiful and – and you don't need a dating app.'

Was that a compliment he'd just paid her? 'I really do. Until this month I hadn't dated for over a year. That's another reason why I'm doing the challenge.'

She prepared herself for him to be appalled or pitying, yet he simply shrugged. 'The right man will come eventually. Why can't you just wait until Fate makes your paths cross?'

'I could be an old woman before that happens. I never meet men in my job.' She thought of Ethan and blushed. 'Well, not many men anyway. And I know everyone in Willowbrook. I've either dated them already or have no interest in them in *that* way. How else am I going to meet anyone?'

'Show me this app.'

She picked up her phone. While she waited for it to load, he asked, 'What kind of man are you looking for?'

'Someone who's ready to commit. Someone who's happy to live around here.'

He shot her a sharp look. 'Why?'

'Because I like it here. This is my home.'

'What if you meet someone who likes living in the city? What if he's perfect in every other way except his address?'

'He wouldn't be perfect for me if he didn't want to live here.'

'If you moved somewhere bigger you'd meet new people.'

'Oh, I can't imagine living anywhere else.' She laughed.

'Not even in the town ten miles away?'

She shook her head.

'Why not?'

'Because it's beautiful here. There's nowhere like it. It's . . . home.'

He whistled. 'You're just like Dorothy in *The Wizard of Oz*. But you know he can't possibly exist, don't you, this perfect man?'

'Perhaps I'm being too fussy. Perhaps that's why I've had no luck finding the right one.'

'Show me the contenders.'

She moved to sit next to him and together they scrolled through a series of faces and names. Smiling eyes and moody frowns flew past, one after another. Close up like this she caught a subtle hint of Alex's aftershave, and she could feel his warmth too – or was that her imagination?

He stopped and his finger hovered over the screen. 'What's wrong with him?'

'He looks . . . intimidating. Overconfident.'

'This one?'

She screwed up her nose. 'He's a fitness freak. We'd have nothing in common.'

'Him?'

'Too old.'

'Him?'

'Too young.'

'He's twenty-eight. That's not much younger than you.'

'But he wants to go travelling.'

'What's wrong with that?'

'It's unlikely that he's ready to settle down and have a family.'

He sat back. 'You want a family?'

'Yes. Why are you so shocked?'

He handed her phone back. 'You're young, you have a job you enjoy and you're successful. Don't you want to pursue that further before you settle down?'

'I'm happy with my job as it is. What is there to pursue? And I really want to be a mum. I'm thirty, I don't want to waste any more time.' She couldn't believe she was revealing so much to the man who, until yesterday, had been the Motorbike Menace. But he was easy to talk to, he seemed interested. *And he'd said she was beautiful.* She couldn't get that out of her mind.

'So you're hoping to find a man who wants to live here, who's ready to settle down and have children?'

'It's a tall order, I know, but I'm certain he exists somewhere out there.'

'Maybe. But I'm not sure internet dating is the best way to reach him.'

'After last night, I agree. It's really put me off dating.' She paused. 'Although . . .'

'Go on.'

'Well, there's this guy I met at work. He came into the shop because his mum can't get out, but she's a keen quilter and he's . . .' she hesitated '. . . really nice.'

She was suddenly reminded of how she and Carys used to confide in each other when they liked someone. The only difference was that Carys would have squealed, not looked serious as Alex did now. 'You like him?'

'I really like him. He's single, dependable and devoted to his mum. It's quite sweet.'

'You make him sound like a pet dog.'

She laughed. 'He's good-looking, too. Blond, tall and tidy.'

He lifted one eyebrow. 'Tidy?'

'You know, hair neatly combed, clothes never creased. He's always impeccably turned out.' She glanced at Alex's messy hair.

'A well-groomed pet dog, then. Does he feel the same way about you?'

'I don't know.' Heat rushed to her cheeks. She'd thought about inviting Ethan for a drink, but each time she'd gone to call or type a message, she couldn't find the right words. And what if he said no? What if he was so appalled by the idea that he never came to the Button Hole again?

Anyway, she might see him on Thursday when she'd arranged to visit Brenda again. Wasn't it better to let things develop in their own time?

'Have you asked him out?'

'No.'

'Why not?'

'Because he might say no. Anyway, I'm not sure I want to after last night.'

'This isn't a blind date like last night. You know him.'

'True. And his mum too.'

'So he's not a dumbass with a vengeful ex.'

She smiled. 'If he is, Brenda hasn't mentioned it.'

Alex studied her more closely. 'Are you really going to let one bad date stop you dating ever again?'

'No, but . . .'

'What if he meets someone else?'

The thought triggered a spike of panic. She wanted to be brave. She didn't want to live her life alone because she was too afraid to leave her cottage and go into the world. She had to keep pushing herself out of her comfort zone. Finally, she said, 'You're right. I suppose I could . . .' Maybe if she and Ethan found themselves alone for a moment at Brenda's, she could ask him then.

'Well?' said Alex, and nodded at her phone. 'What are you waiting for?'

'What – now? I can't!'

'Why not? *Carpe diem!* Seize the day. This way you don't have time to be nervous.'

Her heart was racing so fast it felt like a woodpecker drilling. 'But what will I say?'

'Would you like to have children with me?' He was deadpan, but his eyes danced with humour.

She thumped him playfully.

'How about "Would you like to go for dinner?"' he suggested more seriously.

'He'll say no, I know he will.'

'Why?'

'Because a man like him, he could date anyone he wanted.'

'But he isn't. He's single. And if he says no, so what? You move on, you find someone else.' His shoulders lifted in a dismissive shrug. 'Do it now, Liberty.'

Do it for the challenge. She took a deep breath and pulled out her phone. 'Fine. I'll call him.' Her hand was trembling. While the phone rang she said, 'He's probably out. It's Saturday night. He's—'

She was startled when he picked up on the second ring. 'Ethan?' The words stuck as her brain took a moment to catch up. 'It's – ah – this is Liberty. You know – from the quilting shop, the Button Hole?'

He chuckled. 'Of course. You're the only Liberty I know. Good to hear from you. How are things?'

They exchanged a little chit-chat, but Alex motioned impatiently for her to move on. She cleared her throat and mustered all her courage. Her hand was damp as she squeezed the phone. 'Ethan, I – ah – I just wondered if you fancy going out one evening? We could have a meal or a drink . . . if you like.'

Her heart beat wildly as she braced herself for his polite refusal. It felt like minutes passed, though it was probably only fractions of a second.

'That would be great.' She heard the pleasure in his voice. 'I'd really like that.'

Relief rushed through her and she smiled. 'Good.'

'When were you thinking?'

'When? Erm . . .' That threw her. Alex mouthed, 'Tomorrow', but would that make her look too keen? Oh, stuff it. Seize the day, as he'd said. 'How about tomorrow?'

'That works for me. Let's go for dinner. If you text me your address, I'll pick you up and we can take it from there.'

She put the phone down and beamed at Alex. 'He said yes! He actually said yes!'

'Of course he did. No man in his right mind wouldn't.'

The compliment triggered an explosion of fireworks that only added to her elation. This was such a result! Thanks to Alex she'd got a date with someone she liked. She could really learn from him and his bravery. A thought occurred and her smile slipped. 'Oh, no! I should have arranged to meet him at the restaurant, not here.'

'Why?'

Last night's experience had taught her she needed to be able to get away if necessary. 'In case it's a disaster. If he's driving, he's in control.'

Alex waved this away. 'If it's a disaster, call me and I'll come and get you.'

'Like a knight in shining armour,' she laughed, 'on a motorbike.'

Sunday, 7 December

Alex padded downstairs, amazed at how well he'd slept last night and how much better his shoulder felt as a result. Surely it couldn't be because of the hot-water bottle Liberty had insisted he take to bed with him and he'd felt he couldn't turn down.

She was already in the kitchen and the worktop was covered with open packets, bowls and spoons. She was humming to herself as she lifted a small bowl out of the microwave, and when she saw him she smiled. He noticed the wariness was gone and she was relaxed and comfortable as she pottered about the kitchen. Her hair swung loose and she pushed it back over her shoulder.

'I'm making waffles,' she said. 'Would you like some?' She poured melted butter into a large bowl filled with other ingredients and stirred.

'Er – yes, okay.'

She laughed. 'You don't sound very sure. They're delicious, I promise. I'm a bit of a pro. I've been making them every Sunday for the last . . .', she tilted her head to make a mental calculation, '. . . five years now. The machine was a birthday present from Carys.'

'Five years, huh? You must like waffles a lot.'

She smiled. 'I love them. And so does everyone who's tried them.'

'How many people is that?'

She thought about it. 'Carys, and a few of our ex-boyfriends.'

He tried not to laugh. 'That's not many.'

'See how privileged you are?' She grinned. 'They make me feel happy. They're a celebration to mark the weekend. Sundays wouldn't be the same without waffles.' She added, 'And visiting Carys. I always go to see her on a Sunday.'

She gave the mixture a final stir, then checked the waffle machine was hot enough by holding a hand over it. Apparently satisfied, she ladled some of the mixture into it, then set a timer.

'Do you have bacon and maple syrup?' He opened the fridge and peered inside.

'Yes. Bacon's on the bottom shelf and the syrup is here.' She reached into a cupboard and pulled out the bottle.

He placed a frying pan on the hob and lit the gas ring. The bacon sizzled as it hit the hot pan. 'What is it with you and your *programme*?' he asked, as he poked the rashers.

'What do you mean?'

'You have a time and a day for everything. Waffles on a Sunday, pizza and a film on Saturday, walk the dog at ten o'clock each evening . . .'

She shrugged. 'Don't you have a routine?'

'No. Every day is different for me.' He was constantly stepping on and off planes. And in racing, new challenges were always cropping up, which required adjustments either to the bike or to his race plan. His life was about being flexible.

Had been, he corrected himself, and tensed. He picked up a fish slice and pressed the bacon flat, not wanting to think about the monotony that the future held for him now. The hot fat sang and spat.

'I like routine,' she confessed. 'It makes me feel . . . safe. It's comforting.'

Alex studied her curiously. She kept her gaze down as she picked up a tea-towel, shook it out and folded it.

'I know other people find it dull, and I'm trying to

shake things up by doing my challenge, but I've found that excitement isn't always a good thing.'

The kitchen became quiet. 'Carys's accident?'

She nodded. 'And when Mum became ill.'

He turned the bacon over, remembering all she'd told him last night about her challenge and her hopes to find a partner. She was so alone in this cottage in the woods. Not that she felt sorry for herself. She was haughty, proud and beautiful, and he was filled with admiration for how she'd challenged herself to be brave.

She said brightly, 'But you can't go wrong with a cosy night in – a good film and a quilt to stitch.'

Alex laughed. 'Did you always like things to be predictable?'

'Yes. My mum was really scatty, you see, so as soon as I was old enough I took charge.'

'Scatty?'

'Disorganised.' Liberty smiled at the memory. 'But disorganised like you wouldn't believe.'

'Give me an example.'

'I could give you hundreds. Where to start?' She thought. 'Okay, example one.' She began to tick them off on her fingers. 'She worked at the high school in town and she would run out of petrol on the way to work because she'd forgotten to fill up.'

He gave the frying pan a little shake and the bacon sizzled. 'That can happen to anyone.'

'Yes, but then the same thing would happen the following week. And the one after that. And she could never understand why her boss got so annoyed.'

He put the fish slice down. 'Ah.'

'Example two: she was really messy and could never find anything when she needed it. I'd bring home a letter from school for her to sign and she'd lose the letter. I learned to forge her signature so I wouldn't miss out on school trips.' She ticked off a third finger. 'She often went to work with odd socks or even odd shoes. She used to forget to pay the bills and the gas or electricity would be cut off. She was a ball of dizziness,' her voice softened, 'but she was also the most loving mum in the world. She always had time for me, to do whatever I wanted – baking, sewing, playing and having imaginary adventures. She was loving but chaotic, so I learned to do things myself early on. I learned to cook so I could make dinner when she forgot. As soon as I could drive, I took over doing the weekly shopping so there was always food in the house. I did the washing and ironing too, and I tidied up.'

'It sounds like you were a domestic slave,' he said.

'Not at all. I did it because I wanted to. I needed things to be ordered and predictable, and the only way to get that was to do it myself.'

'And now you still like things to be ordered and predict-able,' he observed quietly.

'Yes.'

Their eyes met and held, and understanding rippled through him.

The timer rang, making them start. 'The waffles are ready,' she said, lifting the lid to take a look.

'So's the bacon.'

They sat down opposite each other.

'This bacon's good,' she said approvingly. 'Nice and crispy. And your meal last night was delicious too. When did you learn to cook?'

'I've been living on the road since I was nineteen. I had to be independent from a young age.'

'I thought someone like you would eat out or buy food in.'

'Someone like me? You have a low opinion of me, don't you?'

She grinned.

'I've always preferred to stay in a rented apartment, alone, and look after myself.'

'That's admirable. You could have been such a spoiled brat, getting successful so young.'

'Thanks.'

'You're welcome.'

His smile faded. 'My father was the living embodiment of how money and success can rot your soul. I suppose he's the reason I didn't go down that route.'

She glanced at him with sympathy, then seemed to remember something. 'Oh, yes – someone responded to my post about your letters.'

He sat up. 'What did they say?'

'Don't get your hopes up,' she said quickly. 'Just that they remembered your dad coming to visit. He was in the area for a few weeks apparently in the run-up to some race.'

'They didn't say anything else?'

She showed him the message on her phone. When he'd

finished reading, his shoulders slumped. 'Just a few weeks yet he managed to get someone pregnant.'

'So do you have any plans for today?' she asked.

'I'm seeing Luc and Natasha. You?'

'I'm going to visit Carys, and tonight I have my date with Ethan.'

'Is that a tick in your book?'

'Definitely.' She drizzled more maple syrup over her waffle. 'I'm really hoping it will go well. If it does, I might even delete the app. Thank you, by the way, for encouraging me to call him.'

He shrugged. 'You did it.'

'But you gave me the confidence to do it.'

'I'm happy to help in any way I can.'

She hesitated before asking, 'Why are you helping me so much with my challenge?'

He stopped. The question had him stumped.

She wasn't a friend, and until a few days ago he hadn't even known her, so why *was* he so keen to see her succeed? 'I – I just want to help . . .' Since he wasn't having any luck finding his half-sister he had time on his hands. Masses of time. Helping Liberty could be a distraction from his own problems.

But wasn't there something more? When he'd taken her out on his bike hadn't he derived some satisfaction from it too? She'd gone from disapproving of all fast-moving machines to laughing breathlessly in his ear and he'd felt a ripple of joy. The first glimmer of light in weeks.

'I can help you,' he went on. 'The things you find difficult, I find easy.'

'Right.' She was about to say something else, then seemed to change her mind.

'What?' he asked.

She eyed him warily. 'It's just . . . I didn't have you down as the helpful, caring kind, that's all.'

He was taken aback by this. All his life he'd tried to do the right thing. He'd seen what selfish was like, and he was determined not to be that man. He liked to think that those close to him could depend on him for support of any kind.

She continued, 'You've got to admit, you were quite scowly when you arrived. *I'm allairjeek to dogs, I 'ave a 'eadache,*' she said, imitating his deep voice.

'I *am* allergic, and I *did* bang my head,' he protested. Her laughter was like bells ringing. He smiled. 'But you're right. You've not seen me at my best.'

'Or you me. I think we got off to a bad start.'

'Maybe we should start again.'

Their eyes met and held, and he felt the same kick as he had when he'd done a winning overtake.

Liberty stood in front of her open wardrobe, trying to pick the right outfit for her date with Ethan tonight. The perfect outfit. She pulled out a green, floor-length dress: it was flattering, but too dressy. She didn't want to look like she was trying too hard, so she put it back, then took out another: too revealing? The next: a bit drab?

Sighing, she stepped back. She hadn't been this nervous before meeting her other dates, so why was she now? She frowned and looked out of the window at the bare branches of a horse chestnut tree.

There was more at stake tonight. That was why.

She liked Ethan. *Really* liked him. Although she'd tried to hold it back, hope had unfurled its fresh green shoots and she wanted tonight to go well. That was why her stomach was a cloud of tiny beating wings. She wasn't sure how she was going to swallow food at the restaurant. What if they got stuck for things to talk about? What if he found her boring?

She paced her room. Perhaps she should call and make her excuses, stick to her usual Sunday-evening routine instead. Think how relaxing it would be to stay in and spend the evening sewing. Familiar. Safe.

But it was lonely on her own, she thought, remembering her birthday. She drew her shoulders back. No, scary as it might seem, she was going to do this.

She picked a burnt-orange velvet dress with a boho skirt and dressed it down with knee-high boots, then tied a little scarf around her neck to complete the outfit. She'd blow-dried her hair for a change, and tried to curl it like Carys used to do for her. It didn't look as good as when Carys did it, but the big loopy curls fell nicely around her shoulders, softening her face.

When she came downstairs, the clock struck seven thirty. Alex was putting on his leather jacket to go to Luc and Natasha's for dinner. He frowned when he saw her.

'You look as if you're preparing to go to the guillotine. What's the matter?'

'Nerves,' she said. 'About my date.'

'Ah, yes.' His gaze swept over her. 'You look beautiful.'

Beautiful? Why did he use that word so carelessly? He didn't mean it, she told herself. He was being polite. Still, she lit up inside like a string of fairy lights. 'Thanks.' She jangled her keys and stared at the clock.

'Why are you nervous? You said he's a nice guy.'

'He is. But first dates can be awkward, can't they?'

'If it is, then he's not the one for you.'

She smiled at his dismissive shrug. It felt good to know his number was programmed into her phone and she could call him if there was a problem.

He glanced at Charlie. 'Would you like me to walk Charlie if you're not back at ten?'

'That would be great, thanks.'

The noise of a car pulling up made them both turn.

'Right. Wish me luck,' she said.

'You don't need luck. Have fun.' He smiled, and slipped on his helmet as he stepped out into the night.

Ethan got out of the car and walked up to the door to greet her. He looked dashing in a long smart coat and well-polished shoes. 'Who was that?' he asked, as Alex roared away.

'Just my lodger, Alex.' She locked the cottage and Ethan held open the car door for her. She was impressed by this chivalrous gesture.

But when he got in, he didn't start the engine. Instead,

he turned to her. 'Before we go any further, there's something we need to talk about.'

Liberty tensed. Oh, no. Was this when he warned her that he liked her but not in *that* way? That he'd got a promotion at work and was moving overseas? 'Erm – okay.'

He seemed to choose his words with care. 'The thing is, I don't want to risk spoiling your friendship with Mum.'

Her heart sank. He'd changed his mind. She knew it. Asking him out had been too easy. Now reality was catching up with her. 'You don't want to go out tonight?' she asked.

'No!' he said, clearly appalled when she reached for the car door. 'That's not what I meant at all.'

'Then what?'

'Just that if things don't work out between us I hope you won't feel you have to stop visiting Mum.'

Relief flowed through her. 'Oh. Right. Of course I won't. Unless she asks me not to, that is.'

'Right. Good.' He smiled, his relief obvious, and suddenly she saw how nervous he'd been. Perhaps even more nervous than her.

They settled on a Chinese restaurant he knew, and when they arrived it was quiet, with only two other couples and a family sitting in the corner. They ordered drinks and Liberty opened her menu. The choice was a little overwhelming. When she'd gone for Chinese with Carys they used to share a banquet.

'So – ah—' she began.

'You know, Mum—' he started simultaneously.

They stopped and smiled.

'Go ahead,' said Ethan.

'No, you,' she insisted.

'I was just going to say that Mum's really enjoying your visits. She loves talking sewing. She said you're very knowledgeable.'

'So's she,' said Liberty. 'She's really talented. I hope she'll win something at the quilt show in France.'

He nodded. 'So do I. Mum loves quilting, but it would really boost her confidence to win a prize.'

The waiter approached, notebook in hand. 'Are you ready to order?'

'How about we share the banquet?' suggested Ethan.

'Great idea.' Once the waiter had disappeared, she said, 'So tell me about your work. What do you do?'

'I represent clients who have been injured and can't work any more. Some of the cases I deal with are heartbreaking. I see a lot of people who are housebound or have mobility issues.'

'It must be very rewarding if you can help them.' She was impressed. His work was about helping others and she could tell from his tone that his concern for his clients was genuine.

'It is. If I can secure compensation for them at least they know their quality of life will improve. This alleviates one of their worries at least, even if it doesn't solve all their problems.'

The waiter brought their starters and she took the opportunity to watch Ethan surreptitiously. Her gaze lingered on his neat hair and gentle blue eyes. She liked that he was smartly dressed and took his responsibilities seriously. Most of all, though, she could relax with him and be herself. He knew she loved quilting, and having grown up with a quilter himself, she was certain he wouldn't judge her for the quiet life she led.

He glanced up and caught her looking at him. She smiled bashfully, then picked up a spring roll and concentrated on dipping it in its sauce.

'I'm glad you suggested we go out for dinner,' he said, smiling. 'It's tricky with Mum and everything – I don't often meet new people.'

'Me neither.' She smiled, enjoying the warm feeling that spread through her. 'What about through your work?'

'They're clients and they're usually in a vulnerable situation, so even if there was interest, it wouldn't be professional to act on it.' He took a sip of his drink. 'I must confess, I thought you'd have lots of admirers, possibly a man in your life already.'

'I don't, but thank you for the compliment.' She smiled graciously.

He returned her smile, and as their eyes locked she had the same feeling as when she was playing around with different-coloured squares of fabric, lining them up, then rearranging them – until suddenly the perfect combination appeared before her eyes.

The sensation of everything falling into place.

At the end of the evening Ethan turned off the main road and drove slowly through the woods. The cottage came into view, and although the porch light was still burning, the rest of the house was in darkness.

'Your cottage is on its own out here,' Ethan observed, as his headlights swung over the trees and bushes that surrounded it.

Liberty tensed, remembering the similar observation Alex had made when he'd first arrived. Was he going to criticise it too, and say it was too quiet? Or creepy? 'It is.'

'You're lucky. It must be incredible to look out on the woods, all that greenery and wildlife.'

'Yes, it's a beautiful place to live. Although I know some people don't like it out here. They think it's too isolated.'

He switched off the engine. 'I haven't seen it in daylight, but I'd love to live in a place like this, with woodland all around and nature on your doorstep.'

They got out of the car and beechnut husks crunched underfoot as they approached the front door. 'I really enjoyed tonight,' she said quietly.

Ethan's blue eyes gleamed in the golden light. 'Let's do it again,' he said. 'Soon.'

'I'd like that.' She held his gaze, enjoying the flutter of anticipation. Tonight had worked out exactly as – no, better than – she'd hoped. It felt as if their paths had crossed at the perfect time. He leaned in a little and she looked up, loving that he was taller than her, how at ease she felt around him. There were no jangling nerves, no sparks flying: it was harmonious and easy. His gaze dipped to her lips and he kissed her. She moved closer, wrapping her arms around his waist, and he did the same. It felt warm and sweet.

Chapter Ten

Monday, 8 December

Alex left the building and stepped out into the dreary wet weather. It matched his mood. He had to face the fact that he'd run out of leads in the search for his sister. He'd checked all the local parish records in person – every single damn one – and found nothing. And today's visit to a different department of the town hall, suggested by someone on Willowbrook's online forum, had been as fruitless as he'd expected. He'd been desperately clinging to the hope of finding his half-sister as a distraction from his own problems, but now despair sucked him under. Without a name, his search was fruitless; without racing his future was empty. Where the hell did he go from here?

Shivering, he peered up from beneath the stone porch and rubbed his hands together. Low clouds the colour of bruises emptied their contents onto the street with a persistent drumming and, judging by the puddles all around, they'd been doing so for a while already. Alex scanned the road for the spot where he'd parked his—

An icy chill slid through him. The severed chain was lying on the ground where his bike had been. Cursing, he strode over, looking left and right, but he knew it was futile. The thief would have driven away in seconds, and even if they'd loaded the bike onto a truck, it would have taken less than a minute. His fists clenched.

He was livid. It was an exceptional bike, a piece of beauty and engineering prowess. But that was precisely why theft was always going to be a risk no matter where in the world he took it. He'd known that. He raised his eyes to the heavens. Still, it felt like a double blow on top of everything else.

What would he do now? How would he get about?

He stamped back inside the building and pulled out his phone. There was nothing he could do except call the police.

The shop bell jingled as another customer left, carrying bags full of fabric. Liberty breathed a sigh of relief. They'd been rushed off their feet all morning and she was looking forward to a cup of tea once they'd tidied the cutting table and straightened all the shelves.

Evie scooped up several bolts of fabric and carried them away, whistling a tune from *West Side Story* as she slotted them back on to the shelves. Liberty smiled to herself. Her boss was always cheerful, but today even more so than usual. Liberty cleared the cutting mat, sweeping up all the scraps and threads. A loud thud made her start.

'Ow!' Evie's voice was muffled, coming from the other side of the shop.

Liberty ran over and found her on the floor with bolts of fabric scattered all around.

'What happened?'

'I tripped.' Evie rubbed her back as Liberty helped her up. She grinned. 'Good job I was only carrying fabric and not the tea tray.'

Liberty laughed. 'Why don't I finish tidying up and you put the kettle on?'

'Good idea. While it's boiling, I'll nip next door and get some mince pies, too. We deserve a treat – we haven't stopped all morning.' Evie brushed herself off and disappeared into the back room.

Five minutes later, they sat down with their tea. Liberty was eager to tell her about her date last night, but Evie got in first. 'Lib, I've got some news.'

'Good or bad?'

'Good. Definitely. Fabulous, in fact. Amazing, brilliant, incre—'

'Okay, okay!' Liberty interrupted. 'Tell me!'

'I asked Jake to marry me . . .'

Liberty gasped.

'. . . and he said yes.'

'Oh, Evie, that's wonderful!' She hugged her. 'I'm so pleased for you both.'

'Thanks. To be honest, I wasn't sure about the whole marriage business after what happened with my ex, and I wasn't sure Jake would want to remarry either, but we've been together almost a year now and, well, it feels right.'

'Of course it's right. You're perfect for each other.' Liberty's gaze automatically went to her left hand. 'Have you chosen a ring?'

'I don't need an engagement ring. I'm happy to wait for the wedding band instead.'

'Oh.' She was surprised, but Evie had been engaged before to a horrible man who'd cheated on her. Perhaps that was why she was approaching marriage in a slightly unconventional way. 'You don't want something more than a plain band?'

Evie shook her head. 'I used to work in a jeweller's, remember? I've seen all the rocks, and I know they aren't what matters. More important is the pledge of loyalty and love between two people, and you don't need a ring for that.'

A ring would be nice, though, Liberty thought. She'd love a dark ruby. Or a garnet. Something vibrant and bold. Not a boring diamond like most people went for. 'Have you decided when the wedding will be?'

'Spring next year.' Evie smiled. 'And we're going to combine the Christmas ball with our engagement party next week. Since everyone in the village is invited, it seems the perfect time to announce it.'

'Great idea. I won't breathe a word.'

'I've got the invitations with me.'

While Evie riffled through her bag, Liberty wondered what to get for an engagement gift. She decided she'd make them a quilt, and immediately began to plan the design. It would be black and white with a burst of colour in the middle – but what? A red heart? No, too twee. A double wedding ring design? Too obvious. A Celtic love knot? Yes, that was it. The symbol consisted of two interlocking hearts made from one continuous length of material, so it had no beginning and no end. And if she used a strip of gradated colour, all the shades of the rainbow would be in there, representing the joys and sorrows of life. Perfect.

'Lib, are you listening?'

She blinked. 'Sorry?'

'I was asking if you'd like to bring your lodger to the ball? Luc's friend.'

'Alex? Oh – well, I can ask him.'

Evie peered at her. 'I thought he was being friendlier now. Didn't he cook dinner for you?'

'He did. And he is being friendlier. But would you mind if I bring a date too?'

Evie raised a brow. 'Of course. The more the merrier. Who is it?'

'I thought I'd ask Ethan. You know, the guy who comes in here. We went out last night and it was . . .', she searched for the word, '. . . perfect.'

Evie's eyes widened and she clapped her hands. 'Tell me everything, Liberty McKenzie.'

Liberty drove home looking forward to a quiet night in. After a run of dates and dinners she welcomed the prospect of her Monday-night routine: a bottle of wine and some hand quilting. Approaching the cottage she noticed Alex's motorbike wasn't there and wondered where his search had taken him today.

She shivered as she got out of the car. She'd have to light the fire: it was distinctly colder today, and there was talk of snow later in the week. She opened the front door and Charlie bounded up to greet her.

'My favourite boy!' She grinned as he nuzzled her affectionately. 'How are you, gorgeous?'

'Liberty, hi.' The male voice made her jump.

She spun round. Alex was standing in the lounge doorway. 'Alex!' she gasped. 'But your bike isn't there. I thought you were out.'

His eyebrows were knotted in a scowl, and she wondered if his shoulder was causing him pain again.

He held up his hand apologetically. 'I didn't mean to frighten you. And my bike has gone. Someone stole it.'

'Where from? Not here, surely.'

'In town.' His eyes glinted like sharp metal. Silent fury rolled off him.

'That's terrible. Have you been to the police? Are you insured?'

'Of course. It's a very valuable bike. The police are not hopeful they'll get it back.' He threw his hands into the air. He often did that, she'd noticed, gesticulated and shrugged and used a million other gestures, so that words were just a tiny part of how he communicated.

'Can you hire another for the rest of your trip?'

'I'm sure it's possible, but I haven't looked into it yet.'

He sounded so despondent that her heart tugged. She knew how he adored that bike. And after going out on it herself she understood a fraction more than she would have done before. 'Oh dear. That really is bad luck.' And so early in his stay, too.

He hadn't seemed happy here anyway, and now he had even more reason to scowl.

She reached into her bag for the thick cream envelopes Evie had given her and handed one to him. 'Here, this might cheer you up.'

'What is it?' He took it but peered over to read hers, which was already open. 'To Liberty plus one.'

'Evie and Jake are holding a Christmas ball next week.'

'Oh,' he said, and put the invitation down without opening it.

'Are you going to come?'

'They're your friends, not mine.'

'Oh, it's not like that at all. Everyone in the village is invited.'

'Everyone? That's not possible.'

'It is. Willowbrook isn't that big. And the party's a tradition at the Old Hall. They've held a Christmas ball there every year for the last two hundred years.'

'You love your traditions round here, don't you?'

Liberty frowned. She knew he was upset about his bike, but there was no need to take that sarcastic tone. 'I'm sure even Parisians have their traditions too,' she said with a proud lift of her chin. 'Anyway, Luc and Natasha are going. And Ethan. He won't know anyone either.' When she'd called him earlier, he'd readily agreed.

'When is it?' he asked wearily.

'This Saturday.'

He shook his head. 'I might not be here.'

'Why?'

'I'm not getting anywhere with my search, and now this . . . Maybe I should just cut short my trip.'

She was surprised at the flutter of disappointment she felt. They'd just been starting to get along. 'That's a shame,' she murmured, and held up the invitation. 'You're always saying this place is too quiet. This would have been a chance to let your hair down and party.'

His lip curled. 'No, thanks.'

Alex tried to stay focused on what Liberty was saying but it was difficult. His mind was elsewhere, trying to assimilate the fact that his bike was gone and with it his ability to get about independently, to get adrenalin kicks – his only source of pleasure. It felt as if part of him had been taken.

At least he was sleeping better now and hadn't needed it to make nocturnal escapes for the last few nights. Small comfort.

So what was he going to do? He owned half a dozen bikes, but none were in England, and they weren't tourers anyway.

'Even his job is about helping other people. He's so caring, and I felt so relaxed with him. None of my other dates have been like that. The whole evening was just perfect. He even asked me about—' Liberty stopped abruptly. 'Alex, are you listening to me?'

'What? Oh. Sorry.'

'It's my fault. I'm boring you, aren't I?' Her smile was sheepish. 'I keep forgetting you're not Carys. She always wanted to know *all* the juicy details.'

'You're not boring me,' he lied. 'I'm glad it went well. Sounds like you found your perfect date.'

'Yes. I really think I have.' Her eyes were bright, like morning dew on autumn leaves. Enchanting.

He felt an unexpected stir of desire. Frowning, he pushed away the thought.

'I'm so grateful to you,' she went on. 'I wouldn't have had the nerve without your encouragement.'

He shrugged.

'I bet you can't imagine feeling fear. You love danger, speed, competition. Is there anything that scares you, Alex?' She picked up her glass and took a sip.

A bitter chill touched his bones. He was terrified of the empty future facing him. What reason did he have for getting out of bed each day now he couldn't race? He had no skills beyond the track. He was useless, hadn't even been able to achieve the one thing he'd come here to do.

'Not the kind of things you're talking about,' he said gruffly.

He was grateful for the distraction when the kitchen door nudged open and Charlie came in, one of Alex's boots dangling from his mouth. He dropped it at his feet. Alex gave a weak laugh and scratched the dog's ears. 'Not now, Charlie. I'm not in the mood for that game.'

He sneezed and the dog did his pitiful-big-eyes routine.

'Are you still thinking about your bike?' Liberty said quietly.

'Yeah.' How would he get his fix of speed, get rid of his frustrations? He pictured the bleak forest outside and the dull limp clouds that had hung over him all day.

He'd believed this trip couldn't get any worse, but it had now.

'Can't you rent another?' Liberty asked.

'It wouldn't be the same.'

'Buy one, then?'

'It was bespoke.' Even an expensive bike would never compare with his own, a design he'd tinkered with and refined. It would be like losing a Rolls-Royce and being given Liberty's 2CV as a replacement. Perhaps that was the solution – he should rent a car.

'And off the shelf wouldn't do? Not even as a temporary measure?'

'You don't understand.'

'Alex,' she said carefully, 'do you think maybe you're being a bit . . . picky?'

'You're probably right.' He sighed, black thoughts clouding his head. Who *was* he without a bike? Racing was all he'd ever known since the age of eighteen. He hated the thought that his identity was so bound up in something that could be stolen, in a machine. He hated how he felt right now. Marooned. Useless. Lost.

Maybe he should go cold turkey and see if he could live without a bike – simply for his own peace of mind. Until his anger had subsided, there was no point in deciding anything. He'd manage for a couple of days getting about on foot or in taxis, then decide.

'Look at the time!' Liberty pushed her chair back. 'I'd better take Charlie out for his walk. Why don't you come with us? It might make you feel better.'

'Colder, you mean.'

'Happier,' she corrected.

'I don't think so. It's dark and the temperature's close to zero.'

'So? Walking in the woods is uplifting. There's scientific research to prove it. The plants give off chemicals that alter our biochemistry. They do!' she insisted, when he lifted an eyebrow. 'Obviously it's better in daylight when there's sunshine and birdsong, but still.'

He got up. 'Thanks, but I'll pass. You go. I'll clear up here.'

Tuesday, 9 December

'Alex.' Guy greeted him warmly as he emerged from the back room. He leaned on the desk and asked, 'How did you get on with taking Lib out on the bike?'

It had been a few days ago but it felt like an age. 'I think she enjoyed it.'

'Well, that's a turn-up for the books. Normally she hates anything fast or dangerous.'

'We didn't go fast,' Alex said drily. 'And there won't be a repeat because my bike's been stolen.'

'I heard about that. Bad luck, mate.'

He'd heard? It seemed that in Willowbrook news spread faster than the speed of light. But he hadn't come to talk about his bike.

'How did you get here?' Guy asked.

'On foot.' It hadn't taken as long as he'd expected.

Guy grinned and nodded at the forecourt. 'You should

ask Jake if you can borrow his quadbike. I've just serviced it for him.'

Alex smiled politely and placed a cardboard box on the counter. 'I brought you this. Three other parts are on their way, and I'm still trying to track down the headlight.'

Guy's brows shot up with surprise – then delight. 'Holy moly, that's fantastic! Thanks.' A low whistling noise started up in the back room. It grew louder and more urgent. 'That's the kettle,' he explained. 'I was making a coffee. You want one?'

Alex hesitated.

'Go on,' said Guy. 'Dad's in the back. It'll make his day to meet you.'

'Thanks,' Alex conceded. Why not? He had nothing better to do. And he fancied taking another look at the Triumph. It was a treasure of a bike.

He followed Guy and shook hands with Bob, who had the same cheeky grin and twinkling blue eyes as his son.

'Good to meet you, lad. I remember your father coming to visit.'

'You do?'

'He came to watch the Grand Prix at Silverstone. Guest of honour. They made a real fuss. He stayed in town at the Grand Hotel.'

Alex's hopes lifted. 'Do you remember anything else?'

'Sorry, son. Guy told me you're looking for a woman he got cosy with, but I don't recall anything that would be of use.'

Guy had opened the box. 'Look what Alex brought, Dad. An oil pump for the Triumph.'

Bob winked at Alex. 'I suppose you'll be asking me to fit it next, won't you?'

'Well, you've got to earn your keep somehow.'

'Guy's rushed off his feet with all his regular customers,' Bob explained, and got up to pat the Triumph. 'Doesn't leave him much time to work on this old girl.'

'She's a beauty,' Alex said admiringly.

Bob plucked a set of overalls from a hook on the back of the door. 'Come on,' he said to Alex. 'Help me wheel her out into the workshop and you can pass me my tools. Once I kneel down, I'm there for the afternoon. My knees aren't what they used to be.'

Alex did as instructed, and while he helped, they chatted about how bikes had developed since his father's days. And when Bob's arthritic fingers meant he couldn't tighten a bolt, Alex gave him a hand.

As Alex left, Guy thanked him. 'Any time you want to come down and have a coffee or a tinker, feel free, mate.'

'Thanks,' Alex said politely. He didn't mention that he wasn't sure how much longer he'd be around.

Chapter Eleven

Wednesday, 10 December

When Alex woke, the first thing he noticed was the silence. He listened for the rattle of leaves in the wind or the chirp of birds, but heard nothing. Even the cottage's old timbers weren't creaking.

He got up, padded heavily to the window, opened the curtains – and stilled.

Snow covered everything. The dazzling brightness glistened as if diamond confetti had been sprinkled from the sky. Every branch, every twig was coated with a thick white quilt; even the sky was white. Only the woodland floor still harboured patches of copper and bronze where the dead leaves and bare earth had been sheltered by the canopy, although a layer of icy frost made them gleam, like pearls.

A blur of movement drew his gaze down to the garden where Liberty was crouching, phone in hand. She'd draped a brightly coloured quilt over the branch of a tree, and was photographing it from different angles. Curious.

His gaze was drawn up again as birds flitted in the trees, dislodging small showers of snow that fluttered to the ground silently. It was mesmerising. Magical. The cottage had been transported to a new enchanted place.

But the magic wore off when, ten minutes later over breakfast, Liberty explained what this meant.

He paused in buttering his toast. 'What do you mean, all the roads are closed?'

She finished folding the quilt and repeated patiently, 'The roads are completely blocked. No one's going anywhere.'

'Even the main road?' It was the only way in or out of this place, for goodness' sake.

She nodded and passed him the marmalade. When he reached for a teaspoon she handed him a tablespoon instead and winked. 'I know how much you like it.'

He smiled, but it faded quickly. 'I don't understand. Don't you get snow here normally?'

'Oh, yes. Last year it snowed for most of December.'

'Then why are the roads closed? Won't they send snow ploughs out to clear them?'

'They will, but the forecast is pretty bad for the next couple of days. This is the downside of living in the country, I'm afraid. We tend to get cut off. But don't worry, I have lots of food and wood. You won't be hungry or cold.'

'So I'm stuck here.'

'I'm afraid so.' Hurt flickered through her eyes and he felt bad.

But the feeling of being trapped was intense. Without his bike too. Not that it would have been any use in these conditions. He sighed.

She eyed him warily. 'Were you planning to leave?'

'I hadn't decided,' he said truthfully. But now the decision had been made for him and this cottage was his prison.

She got up to wash her plate and cup. 'Well, Evie rang to say the Button Hole is staying closed, so I'm looking forward to an extra day of sewing,' she said, with relish.

He finished his breakfast alone, then filled a few minutes by drying and tidying away all the dishes. Upstairs in his room, he tinkered around online, but the few replies he'd had to his enquiries were all negative. Sighing, he snapped shut his laptop and went down again. Liberty was busy at her sewing machine, and he noticed she hummed to herself as she worked. She looked peaceful and calm.

Unlike him. He was a ball of pent-up energy, restless, aimless. In the lounge he did sit-ups, press-ups and all the exercises it was possible to do in a confined space, while the dog watched him curiously. Still restless, he switched on the television for a while, much to Charlie's delight, and the dog curled up at his feet. But after twenty minutes he switched it off. The dog opened one eye and looked at him enquiringly. 'Daytime television is too depressing,' Alex told him. 'I'm not *that* desperate.'

He did feel he might go crazy if he didn't find something to do, though.

The dog picked up a squeaky toy and carried it over to him. 'Thanks.' Alex grimaced, as the saliva-coated ball was dropped in his lap. 'This is your cure for claustrophobia?'

He rolled it away and Charlie excitedly chased after it.

Tail wagging, he brought it back. Alex smiled and rolled it again; Charlie fetched. They kept up this game for ten minutes, then Alex heard Liberty's footsteps in the hall. He found her in the kitchen.

'I can't understand it,' he told her. 'I've been stuck in the house all morning and I haven't sneezed once.'

'Oh, that's because I hoovered this morning,' said Liberty. 'I gave the place a good dust, too, washed all the quilts and put clean ones out. There shouldn't be any dog hair left anywhere. I thought if we were going to be snowed in for a few days, it might help you with your allergies.'

He blinked. 'Wow. Thanks. If I'd known that was all it would take, I would have done it myself.' It would have given him something to do. He was going out of his mind, stuck inside this tiny cottage with nothing to keep him occupied.

He watched as she went into the hall and wound her scarf around her neck. Instantly, the dog appeared, bright-eyed and excited.

'Where are you going?' Alex asked.

'For a walk. Clever boy, Charlie!' She beamed as the dog presented its lead to her. 'Thank you.'

'Didn't you already take him out this morning?'

'Yes. But he loves his walks, and since I'm home I thought we'd do an extra one.' The dog wagged his tail and panted, eager to go.

Alex rubbed a hand over his face. 'I'm going to go mad stuck here with nothing to do. It's so quiet, so dull, so . . .' Her smile faded and he realised too late how that sounded.

'Yeah, well,' she said, straightening up, 'I didn't ask to be snowed in with you either. Perhaps you should borrow some boots and visit Luc.' Her chin lifted and she reached for her hat.

He'd thought of that already but Luc was away with work. 'I'm sorry. I didn't mean to insult you. It's just this place is not what I'm . . .'

They finished in unison: ' . . . used to.'

Liberty smiled. 'I know. You like cities, living the high life and fast bikes. Well, I'm sorry, but you've chanced upon the quietest cottage in the whole village. Even Old Dorothy's is noisier because she has the telly on full volume so she can hear it.' She grabbed her boots and stuffed her feet into them. Her movements were quick and angry.

He silently cursed himself. 'Liberty, I'm saying all the wrong things . . .'

'Yes, you are.' She yanked her coat off the hook, and went to leave.

But he planted himself between her and the door. Face to face, she couldn't ignore him. Startled, she stared at him with those big brown eyes. Heat rippled through him. He ignored it. His mind was playing tricks. He *was* going stir crazy. 'Can I come with you?' he asked. 'Please?'

'I told you, I'm going for a walk in the woods. It won't be exciting and there won't be any fast bikes or adrenalin rushes or beautiful women. Just me. I don't think you'll enjoy it.'

He laughed. 'You *are* a beautiful woman, but I understand and I'd still like to come. In fact, I'd *love* to come,' he corrected himself, 'if you'll let me. I'm going crazy stuck inside.'

She didn't answer immediately but met his gaze with a level stare. 'Fine,' she said eventually, and pointed to a pair of green wellies. 'Those boots there should fit you.'

They set off along the path in silence, and the quiet sounds of the woods welcomed them. The snow wasn't as deep beneath the bare branches of the tree canopy, but it was still a few centimetres thick and their boots crunched and squeaked, leaving prints in the pristine whiteness. The cold air sliced at him, and Alex pushed his hands deep into his pockets, wishing he had gloves and a scarf too. Liberty seemed oblivious to the icy temperature and her hair was a brilliant sunset against the white backdrop.

'Do you really think my life is about beautiful women in every city?' he asked, breaking the silence between them.

Her shoulders lifted in a shrug. 'It's the picture you've painted.' Was it? Or was it how she'd interpreted his words? 'And it's what you see on the internet. Flash bikes with scantily dressed women draped over them.'

'It is not like that.'

'No?'

He shook his head. 'I'm not interested in mannequins, only women who go to race. The others are there for photo opportunities. It's demeaning. I avoid all that.'

'Really?' She seemed to be seeing him with fresh eyes, and he wondered how he'd managed to give her such a false impression of his life.

'Really. I'm single and I like it that way.' He slanted her a crooked smile.

A bird took flight overhead with an urgent trill and the quick beating of wings.

'You don't get lonely?' she asked.

'No.' He breathed in the fresh air and his head began to clear, the tension dispersing like the small clouds his breath left in the air.

He and Liberty trudged on, following Charlie, who was way ahead now.

After a long pause, Liberty asked cautiously, 'Did you have a bad experience?'

He thought of Solange. 'You could say that.'

He could feel her watching him expectantly, but kept his gaze fixed straight ahead. A gust of wind shook flakes of snow from the branches of a tree and they fluttered to the ground. He realised he didn't often pause to look around him. He didn't spend much time in nature, either. The only reason he monitored the weather was to know how it would affect the tarmac and his tyres: would it be hot, wet, humid? The bite of loss sank its teeth into him again.

'You seem unhappy, Alex,' Liberty said quietly.

He looked up, caught off guard by this observation, and its accuracy. He didn't know how to answer.

She went on, 'Ever since you arrived you've looked . . . sad. Can I make a suggestion?'

'Is it going to involve a film and a hot-water bottle?' He tried to make light of it. 'Or seeing a doctor? Because if it is, Luc already said it. He told me I'm a grumpy bastard. Not those exact words, but it's what he was thinking.'

She laughed. 'No. None of those.'

'What, then?'

'Perhaps you should get back to your jetsetting life and search for your sister another time.' The only sound was their feet as they walked in step with each other. 'Or pay someone to find her for you.'

Alex frowned. Pay someone to do something so personal? He was appalled at the thought of a private investigator turning up on the doorstep of the poor woman who'd written those letters. It would be a heartless thing to do. Almost as heartless as when his father had ignored the letters thirty years ago.

'I can't go back,' he said, his jaw tight.

Charlie scurried towards them, panting.

'Because you're injured? It won't be long before you're feeling better, I'm sure,' she said, and bent to scratch her dog behind the ears. Charlie bounded ahead again.

Alex wished he could share the animal's energy and enthusiasm. Instead, every muscle in him was tense. 'I can't go back because my career is over.'

'Over?' Liberty stopped and stared at him. 'What do you mean?'

Reluctantly, he stopped too. The forest hushed and the trees seemed to lean in to listen as if they were as surprised as he was that he'd just confided his huge secret to someone he'd only met ten days ago. 'It's over. Finished. *Terminé.*'

'Your racing career?'

'Yes.' He lifted his wrist to the light and absently traced his fingers over the neat red scar line. The skin felt raised and smooth beneath his fingers. 'The doctors can't do any more to help me. They can't repair the damage. I'll never race again.'

She looked at his wrist and her fine brows pulled together. 'I thought it was your shoulder that caused you pain.'

'I damaged that too. But it's my wrist that means I can't race any more. It's too weak. It will never be strong enough.' The doctors had been telling him so for months, but it was only now as he spoke the words that he finally accepted it. Curiously, he had the sensation that something which had been tightly bound was suddenly released.

'Wow, that's tough for you,' she said. 'What will you do?'

He gave a bitter laugh. 'I have no idea. Racing was my life, what I lived for. Without it I don't know who I am.'

Chapter Twelve

Liberty heard the tremor in his voice, saw the fear in his eyes, and suddenly it all made sense: his brooding black moods, and the edge of angry tension. She'd believed he hated the solitude and stillness of country life, hated her cottage – but now she saw that he'd been wrestling with the news that the career he loved was over.

Her heart went out to him and she cast about desperately for something consoling to say. 'You'll always have the trophies, the titles. You're still the man who won, who was the best. No one can take that away.'

He set off again, his pace energetic, as if he wanted to leave it all behind him, but she had no trouble keeping up. 'They took away my career. They dropped me. The titles are in the past now. Where do I go from here? Racing was my passion, my reason for getting up each morning.'

She heard the vicious bite of his words, the rage, the feeling of injustice. Passion was exactly how she felt about her sewing and when she imagined being told she could never sew again her chest tightened. She remembered when her mum had become ill and could no longer hold a needle. She sympathised with the emptiness he must be facing. She understood his terror.

'Do you have a back-up plan?'

'No,' he said sheepishly. 'My father rode until he was well into his forties, and even after retiring he still did it for pleasure. I thought if I crashed it would be all or nothing, and I didn't want to think about a back-up plan because I always knew nothing else could fill that place in my life.'

They climbed over a fallen tree, their boots knocking the top layer of snow, then followed the path as it twisted sharply to the left, around the frozen pond, and looped back towards the cottage. The pristine snow squeaked with every step they took, and there was an awed hush, as if all the woodland creatures were watching, spellbound by the beauty of the snow – or the shock of what Alex had told her.

They were probably just curled up trying to keep warm, she thought drily, and made a mental note to put out some nuts and seeds when she got home.

'You'll find something else,' she said quietly. 'Give it time and something will come along.'

He hung his head. 'Without the training and the travelling my life is so different now – so static . . .' His words trailed off.

By static he meant dull. She tried to ignore the nip of hurt. A career-ending injury couldn't be easy to deal with. And on top of that, he was stuck in a forest in the middle of nowhere with no bike, and the search for his sister had so far proved fruitless.

'Perhaps I should steal cars,' he said. 'That would give me an adrenalin rush at least.'

'You're angry.'

His head whipped round. 'I am?'

'That's how it seems.'

A long pause unravelled, filled only by the sound of a blackbird's alarm call. She checked where Charlie was, but he was harmlessly sniffing around a tree stump. She called him, and he returned to the path.

'I suppose you're right,' Alex said finally.

'Who are you angry with? Your boss – for dropping you?'

'No. Yes. Well, not just him.' He speared his hand through his hair, which left it sticking up in spikes. There was something strangely endearing about how he always did that, even if it did make her want to comb it back into place. 'I spent months in rehab. I'm angry that all that was for nothing,' he glared at his wrist, 'and I'm angry with my body for letting me down, angry I had the accident – if I'd braked sooner, leaned in less . . .'

That was a lot of anger, she thought. A rustling made them turn to the bushes on their right. But whatever had made the noise became perfectly still and silent.

'Most of all, though,' he finished, 'I feel angry with myself.'

'Yourself? Why?'

'Because I failed.'

'How? You had an accident. It's no one's fault.'

He shrugged. 'This is how I feel.'

She considered this for a moment. 'Were you always good at racing?'

'I started winning races very young, yes.'

'And before that, how did you do at school? I bet you got top grades in most subjects, didn't you?'

'Yes.'

She noticed his cheeks darken with colour, and was surprised. Perhaps he wasn't so arrogant after all. Perhaps she'd misjudged him in more ways than one. 'That explains it, then,' she said.

'What? I don't follow.'

'You've never failed in anything before. You've always been top of the class, world champion – it's no wonder you're finding this adjustment difficult to make.'

'You think?'

She nodded. 'What would you say if a good friend was standing here telling you that their career had been cut short by an injury?'

He pressed his lips flat as he thought about this. 'I'd say he's had bad luck and advise him to find something else to keep him busy.'

'But you wouldn't tell him he was a failure, right?'

Alex gave her a pointed look. 'I'm not that cruel.'

'And you wouldn't think it either? You wouldn't judge him.'

'No, I wouldn't,' he conceded, with a sigh. 'I see what you're saying. I'm being harder on myself than I would with someone else.'

'Exactly. And maybe you should follow your own advice,' she said. 'Keep busy.'

'There is nothing. Believe me, I've gone through every possibility.'

'There must be something.'

'Racing was and always will be my life.' His mouth pressed flat and he sounded very certain and defiant, but now Liberty knew a little more about him she detected vulnerability too. Perhaps he was afraid of what the future held.

'At least you're still here,' she said quietly. 'I mean, you didn't lose your life, and you're not in a wheelchair.' She thought of Carys. 'It could have been worse. Much worse.'

They turned the last bend and the cottage came into view. It looked beautiful in the snow, as if it had been coated with sugar icing. The snow was thick and soft and deep, not the feathery kind that would melt and be gone by mid-afternoon. No, it was here to stay. Carys would have loved it. She'd have been pelting them with snowballs.

Liberty had been planning to make lunch, then get back to her sewing, but now she had a better idea. 'Do you want to build a snowman?'

Alex threw her a sceptical look. She scooped up a ball of snow then rolled it into a bigger one.

'Isn't that the wrong shape for a snowman?' he asked.

Charlie peered at it too. Alex was right: it was more sausage-shaped than round. She peered at it, then improvised. 'It could be a snowdog!'

Charlie barked his approval, and Alex laughed. He reached down to scoop up a handful of snow, and the two of them set to work.

Half an hour later, they stepped back to admire the finished snow sculpture. 'That looks good,' said Liberty. 'A snowdog eating a bone. No!' She pulled Charlie back. 'It's not real, silly, and it's not for you.'

'That dog is cleverer than he looks,' Alex murmured.

She couldn't tell if that was admiration in his voice or disapproval. 'He is. I'm going to make lunch now, if you want some.' Even though they'd been getting along much better since Saturday night, she was wary of being over-friendly.

'Good idea. I can warm my hands up.'

She gasped as he held them out. 'They're blue!'

'It's cold.'

'You should have said. I could have lent you gloves.'

He waved this away and headed inside. 'Doesn't matter now.'

Liberty cleaned Charlie's paws, and Alex went straight to the kitchen. 'I can make soup if you like,' he said, when she came in.

'Great.'

His meal on Saturday night had been delicious. She was happy to be cooked for. While he chopped carrots and leeks, she opened a packet of bread rolls and warmed them in the oven. She cast him surreptitious glances. It was curious, but he seemed more relaxed, and she wondered if it had done him good to talk about his problems. Or perhaps the woodland walk had cured his cabin fever.

'Does Luc know you're not racing any more?' she asked. 'Natasha never mentioned it.'

'No one knows. Not even my family. Please don't say anything to anyone. If the press find out . . . I'm not ready to face them yet.'

'I won't breathe a word. I promise.'

He searched around in the cutlery drawer. She handed

209

him a wooden spoon and he nodded his thanks. As he made the soup, she watched him thoughtfully.

'Why did you tell me?'

He put the spoon down and turned to her. 'I don't know.' He threw her a lopsided grin. 'Because you were there?'

'Oh, thanks. That's flattering.'

When he smiled like that it made her heart flip.

But he'd made it very clear he'd rather be anywhere but here, she reminded herself. And although he'd said he didn't date, she could imagine he had glamorous women throwing themselves at him everywhere he went.

'Could you work as a commentator or television presenter?' she suggested, still trying to think of an alternative career for him. After Carys's accident, she'd found that keeping busy helped. Having no direction and nothing to occupy him must be making his situation ten times harder.

He wrinkled his nose. 'It doesn't interest me much, and there aren't many openings.'

'Sports journalism?'

He barked a laugh. 'Words are not my forte.'

On reflection, she agreed. He was blunt and perhaps a little too open about his opinions. 'Maybe you could help Luc with his business.'

'It's very technical. Anyway, construction doesn't interest me.'

'I could teach you to sew.' She grinned.

'No, thanks.'

'Perhaps you could—'

'I don't need career advice,' he cut in.

'I was only trying to help.'

His expression softened to one of remorse. 'I know. Sorry. But I don't want to talk about it.'

She nodded her understanding. 'You need time to get used to it.'

'That's right.'

'Something will come to you, I'm sure.' She picked up the vase of flowers. 'I'd better bin these. They've definitely given their all now.'

'Is it true they were from a mystery admirer?' He poured stock into the pan, gave it another stir, then put the lid on.

'A mystery sender,' she corrected. 'I don't know if it's an admirer or just someone trying to show they care.'

He hesitated, then asked, 'You don't think it's a bit creepy – to send flowers without a note? It could be a stalker.'

She laughed. 'You're so cynical! I refuse to believe that. I'm sure they were sent only out of kindness.'

She popped out to drop the flowers on to the compost. When she came back she said, 'I need to think of a challenge for today.'

'Something scary?'

'Or new, different. I'm a bit limited while we're snowed in.'

He thought for a moment. 'I could teach you a few words of French over lunch?'

'That's a brilliant idea!'

★

Alex stood by the lounge window, hands in his pockets, glaring at the feathery whiteness outside. At least two inches had fallen over lunch and it was still snowing now. He willed it to stop, but the flakes collecting on the window-sill only grew thicker and heavier. He wondered where his bike was now. In his imagination he could feel the vibrations of the machine beneath him, the power of the engine as he opened the throttle, the forward surge, the explosion of speed and adrenalin. Frustrated, he jammed his hands deeper into his pockets.

'You've got that look on your face again.' Liberty came in, carrying a folded quilt. She laid it on the sofa.

'What look?'

'The I-don't-want-to-be-here look. You're really suffering from cabin fever, aren't you?'

'Cabin fever?'

'Being bored and frustrated because you're stuck indoors.'

'Yes. I'm missing my bike too,' he confessed. Although he'd felt better after walking Charlie this morning, he couldn't do circles of the woods all day every day.

She unfolded the quilt. He glanced at it, then did a double-take.

'What is this?' he asked, shocked.

'It's just a quilt I'm making.'

'These are – *were* – my racing colours.' Orange, black and white. He felt a sharp stab of pain.

'Were they? I didn't know.'

And the triangles of fabric had been laid out in a chevron pattern. It was as if the quilt had been designed especially for him. He turned away and glared at the snow outside again.

Liberty watched him pensively. 'I think I know what you might enjoy.'

'What?'

'Come and see.' She gestured for him to follow her.

At the back of the house, by the kitchen door, a tidy stack of logs was sheltered by a sloping roof and, next to it, was a small shed. Liberty opened the door and showed him a sturdy wooden sledge.

'*Une luge.*' He grinned.

'*Deux*, actually.' Smiling, she pulled them out. 'Want to test drive them?'

'Go on, then.' He winked.

'Here, you have the wooden one. It's heavier and it goes faster. I'll take the plastic one.'

A short while later, having fetched coats and boots, they set off, leaving Charlie at home. They walked a fair distance before they reached the top of a hill that overlooked the valley. From there he could see Willowbrook village, with its church spire and sand-coloured buildings nestled at the bottom. The slope was humming with people, adults and children alike, and their shrieks of laughter rang through the air.

'Best if you aim for that dip at the bottom.' Liberty pointed. She climbed onto her sledge and straightened her hat, grinning. 'See you down there!'

He followed, and soon they were speeding down the hill. He leaned back for maximum speed, pulled the rope and tilted left and right to get the fastest course possible down the hill. Sunlight ricocheted off the snow as he flew along, and the ice-cold air on his face made him feel alive, made him feel like a child again. He waited for Liberty at the bottom.

She laughed as she slowed to a stop. 'I'd forgotten how much fun that is!'

He held out a hand to help her to her feet.

'Did you enjoy it?' she asked, as they trudged back up to the top of the hill.

'Not bad,' he said, scanning the area, planning the route for his next run. Why restrict yourself to the busiest part of the slope when there were other possibilities?

'Just not bad? You looked like you were having fun.'

'It could be faster.'

She rolled her eyes.

'Why don't we go that way?' He pointed to a stretch halfway down the slope where it dipped away to the left at a steeper angle. It was quieter. No crowds.

'There's a stone wall at the bottom,' she explained. 'And it's too steep anyway.'

They reached the top of the hill again, and Liberty sat down, preparing herself for a second run. He dug his sledge end up into the snow and sat behind her. 'Hey!' She laughed. 'What are you doing? You can't come on my sledge!'

'Why not?' He pushed off with his feet, pedalling them towards the steeper slope.

'Because you're too heavy!' She shrieked as the sledge suddenly speeded up. 'Stop!'

'Why? It's more fun with two. We'll go faster.'

'I don't want to go faster. Get off – aaah!'

Chapter Thirteen

Liberty screamed and held on tight as they streaked past the other sledges and Alex steered a zigzag course around a pile of people who'd collided, then turned sharp left to take the steepest, most hair-raising course downhill.

The slope Liberty had always avoided because it was far too steep to be safe. The slope most people avoided, but not Alex. Not daredevil, speed-loving adrenalin-hungry Alex.

He tugged on the rope, his bare hands tinged blue with cold, and she yelped again as the sledge tilted and swerved, and the wind whistled past her ears, and snow sprayed up into her face like confetti. She could feel his face next to hers, she could feel his arms around her, and the warmth of his legs against hers. Tears streamed down her face from the cold, the wind, and from laughing.

But her laughter died when she saw they were heading straight for the stone wall.

Her throat squeezed so she couldn't speak. She knew what was going to happen: there'd be a loud smack and the crunch of bones. And she was at the front – she'd never come out of this unscathed. She screamed again and closed her eyes, which only made it feel faster. Fear snowballed inside her. She opened them again, the wall was coming at her at sickening speed and—

Alex leaned in and they swerved sharp left, throwing up a wave of snow and skidding to a stop.

Liberty gulped air. Heart racing, she reached out and touched the wall she'd been so convinced she'd be flattened against. Even through her woollen mitten, the stone felt cold and unyielding. Alex was laughing. He might even have been asking her if she'd enjoyed it, but she wasn't listening.

She was livid.

'I can't believe you did that,' she said, through clenched teeth.

'What? I was completely in control.'

'No one can be completely in control, especially going at that speed on a plastic sledge, which has no steering mechanism apart from a thin piece of rope that could have snapped at any time. You are so lucky no one got hurt.' She pulled herself to standing and glared at him.

He had been laughing, but his expression changed to surprise when he saw her angry face. He quickly recovered. 'Oh, stop with the outrage, Liberty!' He beamed that gorgeous smile. It would be almost impossible for anyone to stay mad at him when he looked at you like that.

Almost.

'It was fun, admit it.' He got up too and reached to dust the snow off her coat, but she batted his hand away. He frowned.

It *had* been fun – until it became terrifying.

There was no one nearby. No one else was foolish enough to take the course they'd taken, so she couldn't understand why he added quietly, 'I heard you laughing. I saw your beautiful smile.'

Beautiful. Her heart thumped hard. Why did he always used that word? He probably didn't mean anything by it. And yet his dark eyes were fixed on her face, intense and inescapable. It confused her. It made her glow inside, despite the sub-zero temperature.

She tried to stay focused on her anger towards him. She was still shaking, for Heaven's sake. 'I was scared,' she said. 'Really scared.'

His smile vanished. He looked genuinely perplexed. 'But—'

'We're not all like you, Alex. Not everyone is desperate for a fix of adrenalin or speed. We – we could have hit the wall!' She swiped away a tear from her cheek with her glove.

For a moment he seemed to grapple for what to say. Then he told her, 'We were never going to hit the wall. Trust me, I was totally in control. Loosen up a little.'

'Loosen up?' She stared at him, enraged. Those words pushed all her buttons. He thought she was dull and set in her ways, didn't he? Just like her ex. She remembered the disdain in Alex's face when he'd first arrived and described this place as too quiet. She spun on her heel and began to stamp away from him. Well, she tried to stamp, but her boots sank into the snow, slowing her down.

'Liberty?' he called. 'Where are you going?'

'Home.'

He caught up with her, the sledge tucked under his arm. 'What's wrong? What did I say?'

'It's what you did that's the problem! I don't like people who think they know better than I do what I want and what I need.'

'But isn't this what your challenge is about? Pushing yourself to have new experiences?'

He was right, dammit, but now she'd worked herself into such a fury she was not ready to admit it. So she marched on up the hill, past the clusters of sledges and people with brightly coloured knitted hats and rosy faces, towards the woods.

Alex watched her storm away. He winced as a shaft of pain forked through his shoulder. Damn. Just when he'd thought it was getting better. He went after her, but her fierce scowl warned him not to persist with the questions, so he collected the wooden sledge and they trudged back to the cottage in hostile silence.

Their breath left little clouds in the air, and the snow sparkled in the sunlight. He went over and over in his mind what had happened, but couldn't make sense of it. Something didn't add up. He'd genuinely believed she was enjoying herself as much as he was, but she'd been scared and upset, and he felt bad that he'd been the cause. Still, her fury seemed disproportionate to his crime.

Charlie must have heard them approaching because he barked excitedly. Alex hung his head. How was he going to repair this? He couldn't remember the last time he'd upset a woman so much—

Actually, he could. The memory of Solange flashed up in his mind and made him wince.

Damn it, Ricard. Not again.

As they reached the little gate at the back of the house, Liberty stopped unexpectedly.

She turned to face him, but didn't meet his eye as she said, 'My last boyfriend broke up with me because he said I was too dull and set in my ways.'

Alex puzzled over this. A long pause followed before he said warily, 'I don't understand. Why does this matter?'

'You said I should "loosen up" and you made me feel small, just like he did. Old before my time.' Her beautiful brown eyes flashed fire. Only now he saw the hurt in them too.

He groaned. 'That's not what I meant—'

'Yes, it is. We both know you hate it here, that it's too quiet and you think I'm way too attached to my boring routine.'

'That's not true.' He hadn't been the easiest person to be around, and maybe he'd made one or two comments about how quiet it was, but he'd been talking about the place, not her.

He should have known better. She'd told him about her challenge, and he knew she had hang-ups about leading a small life. And now she was upset because of him. Guilt twisted through him. Despite her air of being in control, a shadow of vulnerability followed her and made him want to wrap his arms around her.

She lifted her chin. 'Isn't it?'

'I'm not judging you,' he said finally.

'Yeah, right.' She pulled her hat off, and her hair was a burst of flames against the white woodland.

'It's true. You were out almost every night last week. And I don't hate it here. I've had stuff on my mind and I'm angry my bike got stolen, but . . .' He looked at the cottage behind her, the honey-coloured lights glowing in the windows, and he felt a rush of warmth as he remembered their walk this morning and how light he'd felt afterwards. His troubles had lifted for the first time in weeks. He said softly, 'I'm enjoying being snowed in with you.'

'You're only saying that because you're trying to win me round. What you said – about loosening up,' she blinked hard, 'it hurt, Alex.'

Her honesty felled him. 'I'm sorry.'

'I know I'm boring and a coward, but I don't need you to point it out to me. I'm trying my best to change.'

'You're not a coward and you don't need to change. You're perfect as you are.'

Her eyes widened and he could tell she was as surprised as he was by his words. But she *was* perfect, and he genuinely hadn't been criticising her. 'I like speed, but I forget that not everyone is like me. You are not like me.'

'You can say that again. We're complete opposites.'

'But this doesn't mean you have to change.'

'I do. But you' – she waggled a finger at him – 'need to change too. You're living in the real world now, with real people, not Celebrity Land where everyone kow-tows to you. You need to respect other people's wishes and not drag us all along with you on your high-speed . . .', she cast around for the word, '. . . joyrides!'

'Joyrides? What is this?'

'When thieves take a car and drive it dangerously for fun.'

'You're comparing me to a thief?'

Her pale cheeks bloomed with colour and her lips curved. 'Yes. I am.'

Charlie barked again, and they glanced at the cottage.

Alex shook his head, smiling. 'No one has spoken to me the way you do for many years – with such disapproval.'

'Yeah, well, maybe it'll do you good, Mr World Champion. Stop you getting too big for your boots.'

He chuckled. 'I'm sorry I took you for a joyride.'

'You already apologised.'

'But you don't believe I'm genuinely sorry. I thought you were enjoying it. You were laughing, smiling . . .' On an impulse he didn't stop to question, he stepped forward and brushed the hair out of her eyes. He was so close, he could smell her perfume.

'I enjoyed it at first,' she admitted quietly. 'Before you took us off-piste.'

He tried to take his eyes off hers, but they were spellbinding, sparkling with humour and vulnerability. 'So if we could rewind to the top of the hill, would you still tell me to get off your sledge?'

She weighed this up. 'Perhaps not,' she conceded, with a crooked smile.

He grinned. 'Could it count as your challenge for today?'

'I suppose.' She smiled, and he knew he'd scored a winning point. 'But,' she added quickly, 'I was scared, and you can't assume everyone is like you with the speed and adrenalin thing.'

He placed a hand on his heart. 'I will respect that. I promise.'

She went on, 'You can't pursue your own thrills regardless of other people's feelings.'

Her words made him still.

His father. The man who'd cast a dark shadow over his whole life sprang up between them, like a jack-in-the-box.

He tried to force the lid back down on it, but the image was so ugly and vivid, and it caught him off guard. He wasn't like his dad. He wasn't.

'You had no reason to be scared, Liberty,' he said, stepping away from her. 'I was in complete control. I would never let anything happen to you.'

She opened the back door and Charlie greeted them with excited barks and frenzied tail-wagging.

'Hello, Charlie,' said Alex, rubbing him behind the ears. The dog jumped up and he flinched.

'What's wrong?' asked Liberty.

He bit back the pain that lanced through his shoulder. 'Nothing.'

'Is it your shoulder? I thought it was better.'

'I must have strained it sledging.' He gripped it, trying to knead away the pain with his hand.

Concern flooded her eyes. 'Can I get you anything? A hot-water bottle? Painkillers?' She bit her lip. 'Sorry, I forgot – you don't like it when I fuss.' She turned to go.

'Yes, please.'

She stopped and turned, surprised.

'Both would be good, thanks.'

'What happened to Mr I-Just-Need-A-Room-And-Nothing-More?'

He shrugged – then winced again as another flash of pain hit. 'He was an idiot.'

Her smile was like sunshine reflected on ice. 'Yes. I agree with you there.'

'So what are you doing this evening?' Liberty asked, as they had dinner.

'I have no plans.'

'I'm going to watch a film. Want to join me?'

His eyes narrowed. 'What kind of film?'

She lifted a finger to her chin. 'Let's see.' Her eyes sparkled mischievously. 'A Disney princess movie?'

'No, thanks.'

'I'm kidding, Alex.'

As he'd walked past the lounge he'd caught glimpses and the films she liked all featured the same tall blonde Hollywood actress, who ended up either in slapstick situations or in the arms of her male counterpart. 'I don't think you and I have the same taste in films.'

'What do you like?' she asked. 'Wait – don't tell me. Sci-fi?'

He shook his head. What made her think that?

'War films?'

'No.'

'We could see what's on and pick something we both like.'

He hesitated. But what else was there to do?

In the lounge they went through the channels. 'Motor racing.' She grimaced. 'I suppose you want to watch that?'

He shook his head quickly. 'No.'

'Phew.' She continued to scroll through the guide. They settled on a box set neither of them had seen.

They sat side by side with mugs of hot chocolate and marshmallows. Charlie curled up on the floor, and Liberty picked up the orange and black quilt and stitched. The fire made the room snug, and the candles she'd lit gave a warm glow. He realised the cottage was growing on him. Now he knew to duck his head under the doorways, and he appreciated that what he'd seen as clutter held special meaning for Liberty. She'd talked about the quilted throw her mum had made, the cushion they'd stitched together when her mum became ill and couldn't sew unaided any more, and her photos of Carys. All of it was precious to Liberty and told the story of who she was. Someone loyal and loving, with deep roots in this place.

She couldn't be more different from him and his nomadic life.

'Canada looks like such a gorgeous country,' she said wistfully, as the camera panned over snow-covered mountains and the first episode ended. She turned to him. 'Have you been there?'

'In summer. The scale of it is incredible. Breath-taking.'

'I'm so jealous.'

'You should go.'

Her thimble-covered finger pushed the needle up and down through the quilt in quick, tiny stitches. 'I can't,' she said softly.

'Why not?'

She didn't answer for a long time. Finally, she darted him a shy glance. 'I can't fly.'

Spots of colour touched her cheeks and he understood. 'You're afraid?'

She nodded.

'Have you tried?'

'Once. A few years ago. Never again.'

'What happened?'

Reluctantly, she put down the needle. 'I had a panic attack on the plane. I thought . . .' Her eyes glazed with fear at the memory. 'It felt like I was going to die. I was petrified.' She drew breath. 'Now I stick to trains.'

Smiling, she picked up her stitching again, feigning cheerfulness.

But he wasn't fooled. He wanted to draw her to him, to help her. She was an intriguing combination of fiery strength and timidity. He felt a rush of protectiveness.

'Want a chocolate?' she asked, handing him a box.

He took it, but his gaze was fixed on her as she popped one into her mouth. Heat smoked through him unexpectedly.

Frowning, he looked away. He wasn't interested in getting close to her – or anyone. Anyway, she wanted a serious relationship, and he definitely couldn't give her that.

'Have you arranged to see the lawyer again?' he asked quickly.

'Ethan. His name's Ethan. And we were supposed to go out tonight, but we had to cancel because of the snow.'

'Shame. You could call him, though.'

She cast him a surreptitious glance. 'Yes. I could. I might do it later.'

'Good.'

Thursday, 11 December

'Are the roads open yet?' Alex asked over breakfast. Not that he had any means of transport. Still, once they did reopen he might be able to arrange to rent something.

Liberty looked up from her laptop and sighed. 'Every time you ask me that you make me feel like you're desperate to get away from me.'

'Not from you. It's being stuck indoors I don't like. Being static. I need . . .' He cast around for the word.

'Speed?' she suggested.

'I was going to say purpose.' He supposed what he was missing was having a goal, direction, and being snowed in only made the feeling of being adrift more acute.

Liberty tilted her head as if to think. 'There is something you could help me with, if you like.'

She had piqued his curiosity.

'But it doesn't involve speed or danger so you might not be interested.'

'What is it?'

'There's a tree farm on the other side of the village. We could pick a Christmas tree.'

'Normally I don't do this until the fifteenth of December,' said Liberty, as they put their boots on. She'd explained it was an hour's walk to the farm. 'But since we're snowed in we can bring it forward a little.'

'The fifteenth of December?' He fought a smile. 'Not the fourteenth or the sixteenth? Why this date?'

'Because it's the middle of the month and real pine trees shed their needles if you bring them indoors too soon. I like it to look fresh on Christmas Day.'

He zipped up his jacket and chuckled.

'What?' she asked.

'You and your routine,' he teased.

Her face fell. 'It's dull and predictable, isn't it?'

'No. It's charming. And it's you. It's how you are.'

She blushed.

He went to open the door.

'Wait!' she said, as if she'd just remembered something. She ran to her sewing room and reappeared seconds later with a pair of mittens. 'I made you these – for the snow. So your fingers don't go blue again.'

They appeared to have been made from an old pair of jeans with a cream fleece lining, so they were soft and warm. 'Thanks,' he said, touched by the thoughtfulness of the gesture. When he'd first arrived, he'd been suspicious of her offers of help, but now he knew that she simply wanted to look after everyone around her.

'So you just point to a tree and they cut it down for you?' he asked, when the pine-covered hillside came into view.

Liberty grinned. 'Yes. Amazing, isn't it? Still think Willowbrook is a bad place to live?'

'I didn't say it was a bad—'

'You thought it,' she cut in. His mouth snapped shut. Okay, he'd thought it. 'Here we are,' she said, as they arrived. She pushed open a wooden gate.

A surreal scene greeted him as he followed her in. Beneath a gazebo, a long table had been set for a celebratory meal, decorated with greenery and candles, and beyond that was a circle of trees glowing with fairy lights and baubles that caught the light as they spun in the breeze. A wide sofa was pushed up against them, with a stack of extravagantly wrapped gifts piled up either side. Beyond all this, a forest of snow-covered pines stretched up the hill. It looked like a winter wonderland with all the snow, pine trees and men in green elf costumes tugging trees around – although the effect was slightly spoilt by the hi-vis jackets thrown on over the top.

It was busy already. Everyone must have had the same idea and walked there too, with wheelbarrows or sledges to lug their trees home.

'Come on,' said Liberty, and she set off into the forest. 'Remember, it can't be too big because my ceiling's low.'

'I noticed,' he said drily.

'And not too wide because there isn't much space in the lounge.'

'How about this one?' He pointed to a small compact tree.

She wrinkled her nose. 'That's too small. It will look lost.'

'This one, then?'

'I'd like it to be fuller. Not so sparse.'

'This one?'

She shook her head. 'I don't like blue spruce. It has to be green.'

He hid a smile as he stepped around the wooden toadstools that marked the path. It seemed she was as choosy with Christmas trees as she was with men on her dating app.

They walked on, weaving through the Norway spruce to the area signed Lodgepole pines, then Nordmann firs.

'You really don't like any of these?' Alex asked.

She looked serious as she examined each tree and found them all wanting. 'They're not quite right.'

'None of them?'

She shook her head. 'I'll know when I find it.'

He pushed his hands deep into his coat pockets. His feet were so cold he could hardly feel his toes any more. 'Do you do this every year?'

His mum liked to buy a real tree too, but in Paris this had involved having it delivered to her apartment. She'd love to come to a place like this.

'Yes. One year we had to chop the top off because it was too tall.' She smiled. 'It looked so silly, but I was only nine.'

'Your mother let you pick the tree when you were nine? Didn't she see it was too big?'

'I doubt it. The next year I brought measurements with me. Aha!' She stopped suddenly. 'That's the one.'

He peered at the tree more closely, puzzled because, to him, it was just the same as all the others they'd passed.

Her eyes lit with excitement. 'What do you think?' she asked.

'It's fine,' he said.

'Just fine? It's perfect.'

She called an elf guy over to cut the tree down. Snow trickled from its branches as the elf lifted it onto his shoulder and carried it back to the entrance. Once she'd finished paying, Alex bent to pick it up, but she stopped him. 'We can leave it here for a little while. Let's go to the café for a mince pie before we head back.'

'Café?' He looked around but couldn't see anything.

She led him behind the decorated Christmas trees and pointed to a gleaming railway carriage with a sparkling sign that read 'Polar Express'. Through the windows he could see customers sitting at small tables, their hands wrapped around steaming mugs.

Liberty grinned. 'Their mince pies are homemade, and they do the meanest hot chocolate.'

When they got home they lit the fire in the lounge, put some Christmas music on, and began to decorate the tree. They'd got back just in time: the snow was now coming down in a thick, frenzied blizzard.

A Winter's Dream

As Liberty plucked old ornaments from a box, she smiled fondly at the memories they sparked. 'I loved Christmas when I was little. Mum made it really magical.'

'Was it just the two of you?' Alex was trying unsuccessfully to untangle a couple of baubles. His brow was furrowed and he sighed impatiently.

'Yes. Then when Mum died, Carys's family invited me. We joke that Carys adopted me, and it's kind of true – she's always been like a sister to me. Here, let me.' She took the baubles from him, untwisted their strings, and handed them back.

'What are you doing this Christmas?'

'I don't know.' She stared unseeingly at the red felt heart she'd just hung up. 'Carys's family have invited me, which is kind of them, of course, but . . .' It would feel strange going there without her best friend. If she was honest, she wasn't looking forward to it.

'It won't be the same without her?' he finished, and she was surprised at the warmth and understanding in his voice.

She nodded, her throat suddenly tight. Trying to shake off the thought, she stared out at the thick curtain of snow and the delicate patterns of ice that laced the windowpane. 'I hope Carys is okay,' she said quietly. 'I rang the hospital and they assured me they had enough staff despite the weather, but no one's been able to visit. I hope she doesn't think we've all forgotten about her.'

The radiator creaked as the ancient heating system worked hard to fend off the wintry temperatures.

'I'm sure she doesn't think that,' Alex said gently.

She reached into the box of decorations and briskly changed the subject. 'So what about you? Do you like Christmas – do you have fond memories of it from your childhood?'

He considered this. 'It was . . . tense.'

She looked at him, surprised.

He went on, 'We were never sure if my dad would be there. Usually he turned up at the eleventh hour, but things were more relaxed without him. And now – now we're a growing family with my brothers' wives and girl-friends and a baby. It's great. We'll all be together this year. My mother will be very happy.'

'You're going to Paris?'

'No. Provence. She's bought a house there with her new partner, Bernard. She's making a new departure.'

'A fresh start,' she corrected, and smiled. His English was near perfect, but every now and then he used strange expressions, which she guessed were literal translations from the French. 'Natasha loves visiting Luc's family in Provence. She says it's beautiful, even in winter.'

'It is. We lived there when I was a child before my father made us move to Paris. Maman always wanted to go back.'

'Going there might bring back memories for you, then.'

'I'm sure it will.'

'White Christmas' began to play and he hummed along as he reached up to hang a patchwork star on one of the high branches. In the last couple of days she really felt they'd turned a corner in their relationship and become – well, friends. Being snowed in together had been intense, but they knew each other better now. She felt more relaxed and guessed he did, too, because he began to sing along with Bing Crosby for the chorus. She smiled because he had more confidence than talent.

'You could have a second career playing in a band,' she teased.

His eyes glinted. 'I'm not that good.'

She laughed. 'No, you're not, but you're rich. You could form your own band and pay people to perform with you.'

In mock outrage he grabbed the nearest cushion and threw it at her. She threw it back but he ducked and it bounced off the wall. She grabbed another and stepped closer before throwing it. He dodged behind the sofa. She threw a third. He poked his head up and a missile flew at her. It took her a moment to realise it was one of Charlie's toys, a ragged monkey with one ear missing. Another toy flew at her, a squeaky one this time, then a third. 'Ew!' she cried. 'That one was wet with dog slobber!'

He laughed and rooted around for more.

'Right,' she said, snatching up a bigger, heavier cushion. She darted around the sofa and swiped at him with it. Feathers exploded as it burst. 'Oops!' She giggled.

'What the—?' he said, as they showered over him, clinging to his top and his hair. He moved to get away.

Damn, he was fast. She chased after him, and they both ran in circles round the room.

'Stop!' he cried. 'You can't do that. I'm allergic to feathers!'

'Oh.' Contrite, she stopped.

He grinned. 'I'm kidding.'

Her outrage made him laugh. 'That's playing dirty, Ricard.'

'You started it.'

She got him again, and he swiped the feathers away from his face. She threw a couple of lavender hearts at him too. 'Hey!' he said, as one hit him in the stomach. He sneezed and grabbed a quilt from the sofa to shield himself as she continued to pelt him.

Breathless, she caught up with him and threw the last lavender bag at him.

He peeped over the quilt. 'Have you finished?'

She laughed and showed her empty hands. 'Yes,' she panted. 'Nothing left.'

He put the quilt down. 'Phew.'

'Apart from this one!' She grabbed the half-empty cushion and showered him with more feathers.

'That's low, McKenzie. Really low.' He closed his eyes, resigned, and she laughed as the white feathers drifted down and clung to his clothes, his hair and even his stubble. 'I'm glad you find this funny.'

'You look –' laughter choked her '– like a white chicken!' She bent double with uncontrollable hysterics.

He stalked towards her, plucking feathers off his clothes until he had a fistful, then grabbed her sweater and pushed them down the back of her neck. She shrieked.

'Still find it funny?' He grinned.

'That tickles!' She squirmed, trying to retrieve the feathers. But he was stuffing more down. 'Stop!' she yelled. She tried to wriggle away from him, but he caught her by the waist. She yelped again and pressed her palms against his chest to push him away, but he'd stopped.

He was staring at her, his eyes dark.

The room suddenly emptied of noise, the air crackled, and she could hear someone's heart thudding. Her own? His? It was difficult to tell, he was so close.

She ran her tongue over her lips. His hand was still around her waist and her palms were still pressed against his chest, but she didn't push him away. She was mesmerised by the intensity in his eyes, and those soft lips so close to hers.

The moment seemed to stretch endlessly, and although no words were spoken a conversation was taking place silently. Breathlessly.

Her stomach tightened. He was so frighteningly, dangerously sexy. She lifted her fingers to touch his dark stubble. It felt deliciously rough, his skin so warm. He closed his eyes, and they moved closer, their hips touched.

Oh, God, it felt so good. Heat rushed through her. He didn't resist as she leaned in to kiss him. His lips were soft, her body pressed against his, and the kiss deepened. She gripped his shoulders, his back, his arms: all were firm muscle. His hair felt like satin as she laced her fingers through it.

The sharp trill of a phone made her jump.

She sprang away from him, but it took her brain a few seconds to realise where the noise was coming from – it was her mobile, and she patted her pockets until she found it.

Ethan's name lit up the screen. Red-faced, heart hammering, she hesitated.

'Aren't you going to answer?' asked Alex. His expression was unreadable.

'I— Yes.' She jabbed the phone and turned away to answer.

Ethan's smiling voice greeted her. 'How is everything?'

She pictured his blond hair, his kind eyes, and guilt made her feel a little queasy. He had no idea what he'd just interrupted. What she'd done. 'Oh, f-fine. You know . . .' She couldn't formulate a sentence or even a coherent thought.

'Not bored of being cooped up inside yet?'

'No, I've got plenty to keep me busy.' Belatedly she realised how that had sounded and, blushing, glanced at Alex. 'You know, sewing, sledging, walking the dog. How about you?'

'We're fine. Mum says hi by the way.' There was a pause before he said quietly, 'I wish it would thaw so I can see you.'

'Yes. So do I.' And she meant it. She really liked Ethan. So why had that kiss happened? Her fingers touched her lips. What on earth had possessed her?

Charlie trotted in from the kitchen. Curious, he sniffed the feathers. She reached down to rub his ears, but he ignored her and headed straight for Alex. Her dog kept doing that, she thought irritably, and watched as Alex greeted him affectionately.

She tried to focus on her conversation but she was too flustered. 'Ethan, can I call you back? I'm just in the middle of something.'

'Yeah? What are you up to?'

She cringed and her cheeks blazed. What would he think if he knew? 'Erm – the tree. Decorating it.'

He chuckled. 'There's no need to call back – I just wanted to say hello. Hopefully the snow will have melted before the ball on Saturday and I'll see you then. Can't wait.'

She hung up and took a deep breath while she tried to work out how a cushion fight had morphed into a moment of madness. Of desire. What had they been thinking? She felt guilty and mortified in equal measure.

Alex pushed a hand through his hair. He looked as shocked and embarrassed as she felt.

She couldn't meet his gaze as she blustered, 'Listen. I don't know what happened – *how* that happened. I mean, of course I know how, but not – not why . . .' Her cheeks prickled, her clothes felt sticky against her skin.

There was a long pause, which only made her feel worse. Oh, God, now things would be all kinds of awkward between them. Because of a stupid kiss.

She tried again: 'Look, just promise me you won't breathe a word about this to anyone, okay? If Ethan finds out he'll get the wrong idea. He'll think I like you.'

Alex raised an eyebrow and she could tell she'd offended him. Oh, great one, Liberty. Talk about digging herself in deeper.

'You kissed me like you liked me,' he said drily.

She didn't know what to say to that – so she ignored it. 'It was a mistake. I don't know why—' She began again, 'I shouldn't have done it. I don't know what came over me. You're not my type at all.'

She shook her head in disbelief. She was very clear who her perfect match would be and that definitely wasn't a thrill-seeking Frenchman.

His chin lifted. 'No?'

'You know you're not! We're opposites.' She remembered how it had felt on the sledge with him, the incredible rush of wind on her face, the terrifying speed, the fear as they'd stopped inches away from the stone wall. He was all about danger and excitement, whereas she was – she gazed at the cosy room stuffed with quilts, candles and cushions (admittedly, one less cushion than an hour ago) – a home bird. 'That was a mistake, Alex. The biggest mistake.'

Chapter Fourteen

Alex was as bewildered as she was by what had just happened, and by her reaction now. He knew she fancied the blond guy, he knew she wasn't interested in him in that way – look how often they'd argued since he'd arrived here.

But that kiss had been . . . incredible. The passion, the potency. It had blown him away, and if she hadn't kissed him, he was fairly certain he would have kissed her. Something that powerful couldn't be one-sided.

Which was why he was baffled by how she'd responded – with regret. Shame.

'So why did you do it, then?' he asked stonily. He wanted to understand and his brain raced through the possible reasons, trying to catch up. A thought suddenly occurred that made his eyes narrow. 'Don't tell me – it was another of your challenges. Kiss the lodger. No – kiss the *racer*. Does that count for more?' He couldn't keep the bitterness from his voice. He'd believed she was different, that she wasn't interested in that side of his life. But he also knew she was taking her challenge seriously.

'What?' She stared at him. Her cheeks bloomed with colour, then her eyes sparked fire. 'Yes. That's exactly it.

It'll be a nice fat tick in my book. You have a very high opinion of yourself, don't you?'

'I've helped you with your challenge before.'

'Let me set this straight, I did not kiss you for my challenge.'

'Then why? Why kiss a man and immediately tell him it was a mistake?' He was aware as he spoke the words that his pride was talking. His wounded pride.

'I told you before – I don't know. And I don't understand why you're so angry anyway. You told me you don't do relationships.'

'I don't. I never stick around, so don't read anything into it. Don't get attached.' The words tripped from his tongue automatically. Yet they sounded lame in the face of a woman who'd just told him that kissing him had been 'the biggest mistake'.

'There's no danger of that,' she said, her words clipped and curt. She went to leave. 'No danger at all.'

Alex paused from pacing in his room as he heard her locking the front door, running the tap in the bathroom, then finally closing her bedroom door and going to bed. The cottage became silent, but her mortified expression wouldn't leave him. Nor would the regret. She was right. Totally right. That kiss should never have happened.

Agreed, the cushion fight had come out of nowhere, but still. He could have stopped it – should have stopped it – yet instead he'd been mesmerised by those deep brown eyes and her pulse flickering furiously at the base of her throat. He'd wanted to run his fingertips over it. Touch it. Touch her. And then she'd kissed him and her lips had felt softer than he'd dreamed they would. She'd fitted perfectly against him, matching him in height. Her cheek had been velvet beneath his fingers.

We're opposites. She was right. One hundred per cent right. His head filled with memories of Solange, and warning bells sounded. Liberty, with her desire to settle down, was not for him.

He lay on his bed and stared at the ceiling, trying to remember the last time he'd lost control like that. He couldn't.

Restless, he got up and strode to the window, yanked it open, and dragged in lungfuls of frosty night air. Just when they'd been getting along. He cursed himself yet again. How was he going to fix this? He couldn't.

Or could he?

The white forest glowed in the moonlight, like a fairy-tale scene in a snow globe. An idea suddenly occurred, and he closed the window quietly.

He couldn't change what had happened, but perhaps there was a small thing he could do to put things right.

Friday, 12 December

Liberty was in the kitchen when Alex came down the next morning. She said hello, wrapped her hands around her mug of tea, then kept her eyes down and went back to reading the news on her laptop while he made coffee.

Had he really thought she'd kissed him for her challenge? And what had he been implying – that he was a challenge? That she was afraid of kissing him? Why on earth would she be afraid? She stared distractedly at the computer screen as she relived the dizzying sensation of his mouth on hers. It had been an explosion of fire and colour, and her body had lit up like a string of Christmas lights.

She squeezed the mug. Her body might have responded like that, but her head knew better. Alex was attractive – especially with his endearing accent and gorgeous smile – but she was looking for more than appearance in a man.

'Any news about the letters?' he asked.

She was surprised at the question after they'd parted on frosty terms last night. But his wary tone told her it was an olive branch. She realised he meant on the online forum. 'Sorry, no. Nothing.'

He was clearly disappointed. He leaned against the worktop, coffee in hand, keeping his distance. Although she didn't look at him she was aware of the covert glances he cast her way. She wasn't sure which was worse: his hostility when he'd first arrived, or this new awkwardness – magnified by being snowed in with no escape from each other.

'I have a surprise for you, Liberty,' he said unexpectedly.

His body language was wary, his tone conciliatory. She wasn't sure what to make of that. 'I don't generally like surprises.'

'You'll like this one.' There was a pause. 'I think.'

Her lips twitched. 'You're not filling me with confidence.'

'Well, we'll soon see if you like it or not.' He downed his coffee and went to leave.

'Where are you going?'

'To get your surprise.'

She jumped up and followed him into the hall. 'Now? What is it? *Where* are you going?'

He tapped his nose and smiled the gorgeous smile that made his eyes crinkle.

'When will you be back?'

'I'll be less than thirty minutes.' He fastened his jacket and slipped his hands into the mittens she'd given him.

What on earth could his surprise be? Her shoulders tensed. The things that excited him were terrifying to her. This could be disastrous.

'Should I prepare anything?' she fished, hoping for a clue.

'Just prepare to be brave.'

'Oh.' Her heart sank. 'That doesn't sound good.'

'It will be. You'll see.'

She watched him trudge away from the cottage, then closed the door against the biting cold air. This did not bode well.

Exactly thirty-six minutes later she was sewing the binding on to the chevron quilt when she heard the sound of a rough engine. She left the sewing machine and went to the window. A quadbike was pulling up, and when the driver removed his helmet it revealed a shock of messy dark hair. Alex ran his hand through it, but only made it messier.

'Is that Jake's quadbike?' she asked, as she opened the front door.

'Yes.'

'This is the surprise?'

'Sort of.'

'What do you mean?' She eyed the machine suspiciously. It wouldn't be as scary as riding his motorbike, but it wasn't something she'd do for fun. He really didn't know her well, did he?

'We can use this to go to the hospital and visit Carys,' he explained, as he stamped the snow off his boots and shut the door behind him. 'I'll drive you there.'

She stared at him.

He watched her reaction and added cautiously, 'If you like. We don't have to.'

Perhaps he *did* know her, after all. Visiting Carys would be—

She couldn't find the words. She was so touched that he'd thought of it. 'Alex,' her voice sounded rough, frayed around the edges, 'that's so . . . thoughtful. Thank you.'

His worried expression was instantly replaced with one of relief. 'Not too scary?'

'As long as you don't go too fast, no.'

'You said you were worried she'd have no visitors. Now she will.'

He'd not only listened but gone out of his way to arrange this for her. 'I didn't know you'd met Jake.'

'I hadn't before today. Luc helped. Will this count as today's challenge?'

Their gazes locked and she knew they were both remembering their angry words yesterday.

'Yes,' she said, in a conciliatory tone. 'It will.'

He winked. 'And if you want more of a challenge, you could take the driving seat.'

The smell of hospital hit Alex head-on. It caught in his throat and took him straight back to his accidents. Both of them. The first had been in Malaysia, the second in Spain, and eventually he'd recuperated in France. But hospitals smelt the same wherever you went in the world: of disinfectant, and the desperate wish to be anywhere else.

'You did well to get here in the snow,' said one nurse. 'A few of us have had to stay at the hospital because the roads are so bad. Did you walk?'

'No. We came on a quadbike.' Liberty grinned.

'Hi, Liberty!' another nurse called.

He watched as she greeted all the nurses by name, and they paused to chat by the desk. 'Hey, I love the latest quilt you made. The one with the orange, pink and red blocks. It looked amazing against the snow. So colourful.'

'Thanks. I'm missing Carys to hold them up for me.'

'Can't you get your lodger to help?' They all eyed Alex. 'Aren't you going to introduce us?'

She did so and all the nurses smiled. 'Lovely to meet you, Alex.'

He pretended not to notice that one or two exchanged secret glances. It didn't help that he was wearing his leathers, but they'd seemed the most suitable clothes for riding a quadbike in this weather.

As he and Liberty continued down the corridor, he asked her, 'What did that nurse mean about helping with your quilts?'

'Oh, when I finish a quilt I photograph it outside and post pictures on social media.'

'Why outside?'

'The light's better and it looks nice. The trees set off the colours.' She reached for her phone and showed him her photos. The colourful bold designs stood out against the trees and leaves of the woods. And her photos tracked the changing of the seasons: the zesty green of summer, the chestnut and gold of autumn through to the muted shades of winter. 'See what a gorgeous background the snow gives? With a colourful quilt it's especially effective.'

He ran his gaze over the brightly coloured bricks of fabric and the black border. Her quilts were striking and modern and, photographed in this way, they took on an artistic quality. He glanced at her, seeing her work in a different light. He'd regarded it as a quaint, old-fashioned hobby when, in fact, it spoke of years of training, not to mention innate talent and skill. She was an artist, working with fabric. He was seriously impressed.

'How many of these things have you made?' he asked, scrolling down the page.

She laughed and held open a door for him. They turned sharp right into another corridor. 'Dozens. Roughly one a week. More if you count the ones I make at work for Evie's shop.'

'Do you sell them?'

'Yes. That's why I post them on social media. It's my shop window. They always go quickly.'

'How did Carys help you?'

'She held them up so I could get the whole quilt into the shot. See? Like that.' She pointed to the older pictures at the bottom of the screen. 'But I've found that if I drape them over a branch, that looks good too.' She put her phone away and stopped outside an open door. 'This is Carys's room.'

He nodded, but as she moved to go in he stopped her. 'The – ah – the nurses were right. I could help you take pictures of your quilts. If you want me to, that is.'

She beamed. 'That would be great. Thanks.'

In Carys's room, Liberty bent to kiss her friend's cheek. 'Carys, it's me.'

Alex watched the sleeping woman and wondered if she could hear the smile in Liberty's voice. She was so still. The machines she was hooked up to ticked away calmly beside her.

'And this is Alex. You know, the lodger I told you about.' She beckoned him closer.

He touched Carys's hand, feeling a little self-conscious, but he understood what Liberty was trying to do. And who knew what her friend could hear? If Carys were his friend he wouldn't be able to give up hope, either. Besides, all he'd learned about Liberty the last few days told him Carys was more than just a friend. Like a sister, perhaps. Family.

'Hi, Carys,' he said. 'You should see the snow. It's incredible. Like a picture book.'

Liberty laughed and drew up a chair. 'He says that now, Car, but he wasn't happy when it first snowed. He was really grumpy to be trapped inside the cottage with me.'

'The place is growing on me,' he conceded. There wasn't another chair so he remained standing.

'You make that sound like someone made you eat sprouts.' Liberty smiled.

'What?'

'Doesn't matter.' She turned back to her friend. 'I've lots to tell you, Car. We've been sledging and built a snowdog in the garden . . .'

She chattered on and he watched her animated expression while her friend slept motionless.

'And you'll be pleased about this,' Liberty said to Carys. 'I've met a guy. His name's Ethan.'

Alex tensed.

'I told you about how he comes into the shop for his mum. I asked him out, can you believe?' She glanced shyly at Alex. He shuffled his feet, uncomfortable with the conversation. 'With a little encouragement from Alex, but anyway, Ethan said yes and we—'

Alex cleared his throat. 'Why don't I get us coffee from the machine? Give you some privacy.'

Her eyebrows lifted. 'It's okay. I'm not going to say anything X-rated.'

'Even so.' He didn't wait for her reply but left the room, relieved to escape. He didn't need to hear the ins and outs of her date. He knew her better after three snow days together, but there was a limit to how involved he wanted to be in her life.

He strode down the corridor, trying not to think about that kiss but it remained vivid in his mind: the velvet of her lips, her shocked delight and pleasure. He shook off the unwelcome memory and fed coins into the coffee machine. The thick black liquid that dribbled into a paper cup tasted as vile as he'd expected and he was almost glad of the distraction when a male nurse stopped to ask for his autograph. Clearly word had got round that he was in the hospital.

By the time he got back to Carys's room, a group of nurses had clustered outside and were listening to Liberty. He recognised the slow melody of 'Silent Night'.

It was incredible. Liberty's voice carried, silky and clear, reaching the highest notes with ease, and his skin prickled as the music stirred something inside him.

'Isn't it beautiful?' one of the nurses whispered.

'It is,' he replied. The haunting melody was mesmerising. 'Why don't you go in?'

She shook her head. 'Liberty stops singing if anyone goes in.'

'She's shy,' said another nurse. 'I could never sing in public, either.'

'The way you sing that's a relief,' her colleague teased. 'But where Liberty's concerned it's a waste of a beautiful voice that no one else hears it.'

Alex frowned. Liberty had all these talents, yet they remained as hidden as her cottage in the woods. The nurses were right: it was a waste.

★

'You don't mind hospitals?' Liberty asked, as they trudged through the hospital grounds to the car park. 'Some people hate them.'

Truth be told, she'd been worried he might be quiet and awkward around Carys – but he hadn't at all. In fact, she was impressed at how relaxed he'd been, chatting to her and to the nurses. She'd noticed, too, the looks the nurses had exchanged with each other when he'd arrived. It shouldn't have been a surprise. His leathers made his shoulders look so broad, his legs long and slim.

'I often get asked to visit kids who are sick. Fans, you know?'

'Poorly children? Oh, that must be really sad.'

'It's heart-breaking, but when I see how happy it makes them just to see me, I know I've done the right thing. And they're so brave, it's extremely humbling.'

And, just like that, Liberty was forced to adjust her view of him yet again. Who'd have thought a speed demon would do such good deeds? Perhaps she'd been a little quick to judge him. Perhaps her own prejudices – the speed thing and the jet-setting lifestyle – had clouded her judgement. She felt a needle of guilt. Well, at least the last few snow days had given them the opportunity to get to know each other better. And, thankfully, they had put yesterday's kiss behind them.

'It must be difficult,' he said softly, 'seeing your friend in a coma. Not knowing if she can hear you, or if she'll ever wake up.'

Difficult didn't begin to describe the complicated knot

of emotions. 'It is. Whenever I'm happy I feel guilty, but if I spend too long thinking about it I feel down. It's so . . . draining.' She threw him a weak smile and added quickly, 'But I can't complain. It must be far worse for her family.'

'Not necessarily. You lived with her. And it sounds like you were very close.'

She felt a rush of joy at his understanding.

He went on, 'I imagine it's harder than if she'd died. At least then you could grieve. But this – it's like . . .'

'Limbo,' she finished quietly. 'Yes, it is.'

They reached the quadbike. It was alone in the car park. 'So what's the plan tonight?' asked Alex.

'What do you mean?'

'What's the routine for Friday evenings? Does it involve wine?'

'No. I have work tomorrow. If the roads are clear, that is.'

'I think they might be. Look, it's melting in places.' He pointed to where the snow was turning to slush.

Her hopes lifted, like a hot-air balloon. Tomorrow was the Christmas ball and she'd see Ethan.

'It's a shame,' he said. 'The snow made this place look like something from a picture book. Although it has its charm without snow too.'

'I thought you hated it here.'

His lips curved. 'Maybe I'm getting used to it after all.'

She felt a kick of triumph at this turnaround.

'What are you doing?' he asked, when she climbed on the quadbike and gripped the handlebars.

'Taking the driving seat.'

A wide smile spread across his face and lit his eyes. He handed her the keys and climbed on behind her. His arms came around her waist and she tried to ignore the charge of electricity that flashed through her.

He showed her how the controls worked. It wasn't complicated. She gunned the engine. 'Ready?'

'Ready.' He chuckled.

'What's so funny?'

'You,' he said. His voice was deep and warm in her ear. 'On the way here you clung to me like a mussel—'

'A limpet,' she corrected.

'And now you're revving the engine like one of Hell's Angels.'

She grinned. 'Yeah, well, I feel braver now.'

When she was with him she always felt braver, it seemed. The realisation took her by surprise.

Saturday, 13 December

'This quilt looks great. Did the customer ask for Liberty fabrics?' Liberty smoothed the flowery material flat. It was their first day back at the Button Hole since the roads had been cleared of snow, but the shop was quiet so they were in the back room basting one of the three quilt tops Evie had made while she'd been snowed in. They'd laid out the backing fabric, smoothed it flat and clamped it to the big work table. Next, they added the wadding and flattened it.

'She did.' Evie clamped her corner of the quilt. 'I know they're not your thing, but they're very popular.'

'I prefer plainer fabrics, that's true, but Liberty fabric suits this style: romantic, classic. You've used your snow days well to get so much done.'

'Well, Jake walked into work – he didn't want to let his patients down – so I was at home on my own. I enjoyed it, actually. It's not often I get the whole day free to sew and now we've converted one of the spare bedrooms into a sewing room I have everything I need to keep me busy.'

Satisfied that the two layers were perfectly flat, they peeled back half of the wadding and Evie sprayed it with basting glue.

'It's good to be back at work,' said Liberty, as she carefully pressed the wadding back into place, working her way slowly from the middle to the outside. Evie did the same on the other side of the table, and they repeated the process for the second half. 'Being snowed in is fun for a few days, but it quickly loses its novelty. I missed this place.'

'I was worried about you, stuck inside all that time with moody Motorbike Guy.'

'Actually, he's not so bad once you get to know him. He's just got . . . things on his mind.' Her palms smoothed over the soft wadding and she remembered the heart-break in his voice when he'd told her his career was over, the heat in his eyes before they'd kissed.

Evie stopped. 'Are you blushing? Lib, is there something you're not telling me?'

'We've just got to know each other better after three

days of being snowed in, that's all.' But she avoided Evie's gaze as they laid the final layer – the quilt top – over the wadding and made sure it was perfectly flat and central before folding it back and gluing it in place.

'That's all?' Evie's eyes glinted with mischief.

'Honestly, Eves. It's nothing like that. Alex isn't going to be around long and, anyway, I'm really looking forward to seeing Ethan again tonight. I know it's early days, but I've got a good feeling about us.'

'I like him. He's so polite.' Evie clamped her side of the quilt in place. 'I'm glad you and Motorbike Guy are getting on better, though. It can't be easy to share with someone if there's an atmosphere.'

'You're right. Actually, I'm having second thoughts about taking in any more lodgers. I've been lucky this time, but it could go horribly wrong.' She unscrewed the small tub of quilter's safety pins. In the unlikely event that the glue didn't hold, these would keep the three layers secure until they'd been machine-quilted. Liberty poked a pin through the quilt, and said quietly, 'Plus I'm still hoping Carys will wake up and come home.'

Evie's eyes were warm with sympathy. 'She will. I'm sure she will.'

Liberty took a deep breath, fighting down the emotions. 'She'll be sorry she missed the ball tonight. She always loves it.'

Evie looked at the shop window. 'We're lucky the snow thawed in time.' Her dimples showed. 'I can't wait to tell everyone our news.'

Liberty smiled, glad for Evie that she'd found someone

who made her happy, the person she wanted to spend the rest of her life with. The ball tonight would be one to remember.

Liberty checked her reflection one last time before she went downstairs, trying not to catch her hem with the heels of her sparkly shoes. She wore a long chocolate satin dress and her hair was loose in big loopy curls. She'd darkened her eyes and painted her lips a deep matt red.

In the kitchen she opened the drawer where she kept her house keys and dropped them into her purse. Alex was preparing a salad. He glanced over his shoulder, then did a double-take. 'You look amazing,' he said.

Her heart jumped. She blushed and muttered her thanks. Carys often used to tell her she looked gorgeous, but it felt different coming from a man. Especially a handsome, hot-blooded Frenchman who, in her experience, only ever spoke his mind.

She shook off the thought. Ethan's opinion was the one that mattered to her. 'You're sure you don't want to come, too?' she asked.

'Sure.' As he whisked up a vinaigrette dressing with a fork she noticed he had oil stains on his fingers. He'd said he was going to deliver parts to Guy's garage today, but she guessed he'd stayed to help out again.

'Luc dropped off a black suit for you. It's hanging in my sewing room.'

'I told him not to.'

'I don't understand why—'

'It's not my thing. I won't know anyone.'

'You will. You'll know Luc and Natasha, Guy and Bob—'

'I'll look after Charlie.'

Her mouth snapped shut. A short silence followed. 'Fine.'

To be honest, she was relieved. It would be more straightforward this way: just her and Ethan. On a date.

The dog trotted into the kitchen with a hopeful expression. He must have heard his name.

'I'll walk him. Ten o'clock at the latest,' Alex vowed, tapping his watch, and she knew he was teasing her.

'I'm not *that* strict about routine.'

'Oh, you are. But don't worry. If I forget he'll come and tell me. He's a clever dog, aren't you?' He scratched the dog behind the ears.

'I can't believe how well you two get on now. What happened to keeping him away from you because you're allergic?'

'I bought some anti-allergy tablets and perhaps I've developed some immunity, too.'

A car engine made them both turn. 'That's Ethan,' she said.

She opened the door and invited him in. He looked incredibly smart in black tie and she loved that he was still taller than her even though she was wearing high heels. She introduced him to Alex and they shook hands.

'I've heard a lot about you,' said Alex. His tone was cool.

'You too,' said Ethan, sounding much friendlier. He

glanced at the Frenchman's sweater and black jeans. 'You're not coming to the ball?'

'No.' He offered no further explanation and his eyes glinted.

Liberty glared at him. It was clear he disliked Ethan, though she couldn't see why. Hadn't he encouraged her to date him? 'Alex kindly offered to stay and walk Charlie for me.'

Ethan smiled and nodded. She shifted from one foot to the other, feeling hot under the collar and desperately wanting to put some distance between the two men. It wasn't rational, but she was scared Ethan might sense something had happened between her and Alex.

'Right.' She picked up her purse. 'Shall we go? I'm so excited for tonight.'

Outside, she asked, 'What's your mum doing this evening?'

'Watching a film and sewing. She's been working really hard to get her quilt finished in time for the show.'

Ethan rushed to open the car door for her, just as he'd done on their first date. She thanked him, but found it mildly irritating this time. It felt a bit over the top and old-fashioned.

They arrived at the Old Hall where the entrance hall was already filled with people dancing. Waiters circulated around the edge of the dance floor with trays of champagne.

'Want to dance?' Liberty asked.

As she did so, she kept thinking of Alex at home by himself and wondered why he'd so obstinately refused to come. Then she told herself it was his choice, and he'd be fine.

After a while, they were both hot and thirsty. 'Shall we get a drink?' she suggested.

They wove their way to the edge of the room and Liberty accepted a glass of champagne. Ethan took an orange juice and they watched Evie pull Jake onto the dance floor. Usually Jake was strait-laced and reserved, but tonight he was making Evie laugh with some energetic dance moves. Liberty smiled. It seemed Evie brought out his fun side. On the other side of the room, Luc was dancing with Lottie, twirling the little girl around, making her giggle and squeal with delight. Natasha stood at the side filming them.

Liberty spotted Dorothy sitting by herself, so she went over to say hello. Ethan followed.

Dorothy greeted her with a smile. 'Liberty, where's your nice Frenchman? I've seen him in his leathers. He's quite a catch.'

Liberty flushed. 'He's not *my* Frenchman, he's my lodger.' Red-cheeked, she glanced at Ethan, who looked shocked too. She couldn't blame him.

Dorothy continued, 'You must come and have tea with me when you have a spare moment, Liberty. There's something I need to talk to you about.'

'Oh, yes? What is—'

A gust of icy wind made them turn towards the main door.

The music stopped abruptly and the guy muttered something about the machine playing up, but no one was listening. All eyes were on the doorway, their attention drawn to the unexpected appearance. There stood Alex, a dark figure in the entrance, hair all ruffled, wearing black jeans with a white shirt, collar open and a black tie hanging loose, as if he'd made the minimum effort to follow the dress code – or abided by it, but on his own terms and in his inimitable, unruly style. Her stomach tightened.

'The spitting image of James Dean,' said Dorothy, approvingly, and loud enough for everyone to hear.

Quiet laughter rippled across the room. Luc went over and slapped him on the back, greeting him in French, and closing the door behind him.

'Lib? Did you hear me?' She realised Ethan had been speaking to her and turned away from the door.

'Sorry. What?'

He pointed behind them to where Jake had climbed a little way up the staircase so everyone could see him as he began to speak. Evie joined him, stunning in a flowing dress the colour of cherry jam, which she'd made herself.

'Thank you all for coming here tonight,' Jake began. 'It means a lot to us to have you here and continue the age-old tradition of Willowbrook's Christmas ball. But tonight is very special because I have some news to announce.'

There were murmurs of *ooh*, and the crowd hushed to hear the rest. Liberty smiled. Even though she knew what he was going to say, it was still exciting.

'A year ago today I fell under the spell of a very special woman,' he said. He looked at Evie, and the expression in his eyes made Liberty's heart fold up. Evie beamed back at him.

Someone in the crowd whooped.

He went on, 'It was snowing, and I was grumbling about it, but she was smiling. And she made me see that you can choose to focus on the dark clouds in life. Or you can stand in the snow with your arms wide open and savour the beauty and the magic of snowflakes falling. It's fair to say that meeting Evie quite literally changed my life.' Jake blinked hard, and the crowd cheered. He soon recovered his composure and went on, 'Which is why we've decided to get married.'

There were gasps, then everyone began to clap and whistle.

'So please raise your glasses, everyone.' Jake turned to Evie and finished, 'Pollyanna, I want to thank you for the joy you've brought into my life. I love you, darling, and I'm looking forward to spending the rest of my life with you.'

'To Jake and Evie!' someone shouted.

The whole village cheered. 'To Jake and Evie!'

Chapter Fifteen

A lex wasn't sure why he'd made the last-minute decision to come. After Liberty had left, he'd stomped
around the kitchen, flinging salad into a bowl, dousing it
with oil and vinegar, banging a pan onto the hob and
firing up the gas ring. The flames had shot up fiercely,
engulfing the pan. He turned the gas down and glared at
the spot where Liberty had stood just moments ago,
dazzling in that long dress, glowing when he'd told her
so.

Then her date had knocked at the door.

Until then Ethan had simply been a name. But she was
right: it turned out he had all the looks. His blond hair
was impeccably tidy, his eyes were a striking blue, and
he was tall. Taller than Alex. He was everything Alex
wasn't, and he didn't like how that made him feel. He
wanted to push the guy out of the picture. And he wasn't
ready to examine exactly why he felt like that.

Alex had watched the guy hold open the door of his
dull, sensible car for her, seen her tense smile as she'd
thanked him, and then they'd driven away into the night.

Alone, Alex had sliced off a piece of butter and dropped
it into the frying pan. It sizzled and spat, then sank and

melted into a frothy puddle. Why did he care what Mr Blond looked like, or how radiant Liberty had seemed with him? She was absolutely right to continue dating. It had been her plan before, and nothing had changed. He swirled the melted butter around the pan and dropped in the steak. Charlie trotted into the kitchen.

'It's just you and me tonight, buddy,' Alex told him glumly.

He stopped. Was that what this was? After just three evenings together he was missing her? Seriously, Ricard, what the hell was going on? It wasn't like he was in the market for a relationship – or a kiss. Not even an accidental kiss.

Strange how the memory of that had stayed with him.

He shook his head and lifted the steak onto a plate. But when he sat down to eat, the salad was too vinegary, the steak overdone. He forced himself to chew, but got no pleasure from it, and when Charlie came over sniffing curiously, Alex pushed his plate towards him. 'Go on, have it.' He sighed, and watched the delighted dog wolf it down.

In the lounge he'd switched on the television and Charlie curled up beside him. Alex stroked him behind the ears. He flicked through the channels until he found an old cowboy film. But as Clint Eastwood climbed onto his horse, Alex's gaze strayed to the window. He pictured the Old Hall and wondered if Liberty was enjoying herself.

Cursing, he'd got up. 'Come on, Charlie, let's go for that walk.'

But even a brisk stroll in the cool night air hadn't

calmed him. When he got back to the cottage he'd paced up and down the hall, restless. Uneasy.

He'd picked up the keys for the quadbike and weighed them in his hand. He needed to return it anyway. Why not do it tonight?

So here he was, at the Old Hall, and while everyone was applauding Jake's speech, Alex searched the room for Liberty. She wasn't difficult to spot – her hair and height made it easy to pick her out in the crowd.

She looked stunning. Her long satin dress emphasised her tall slim figure, her skin was creamy pale with a dusting of freckles, her lips were glistening rubies. Ethan bent to whisper something in her ear and she smiled. Alex bristled. He needed to speak to her – alone.

Then Guy came over and offered to get him a drink, and he lost sight of her.

A short while later, he spotted Jake and handed him the keys for the quadbike. 'Thanks for lending it to me.'

Jake pocketed them and smiled. 'I wanted to thank you too. Guy tells me you've sourced parts for my Triumph. They're not easy to find.'

'Not a problem. I have a classic myself so I knew who to contact.'

'What brand do you have?'

'Yamaha. I take her out once a year and race her in the Moto Legends Cup.'

Jake nodded appreciatively. 'Cars are more my thing normally, but when I saw the Triumph I couldn't resist. I haven't told Evie yet.'

Alex sipped his drink. He scanned the room but

couldn't see the red hair he was looking for. 'You think she won't like it?'

'Actually, I'm worried she might like it too much – for herself.' Jake's mouth curved. 'Evie's the clumsiest person I've ever met. Put her on a motorbike and it would be an accident waiting to happen.'

Alex laughed. 'How many classic cars do you own?'

'Two. The Bentley I use every day, and I have a TVR in the garage.'

'I'd love to see them some time.'

'Want to take a look now?'

'Don't you have to . . .?' Alex waved a hand, indicating the guests around them.

'No one will miss us for ten minutes.' Jake winked.

Alex followed him outside to the spacious garage. He paused to admire the Bentley, but he was drawn to the sportier car, the TVR, and ran his hand over the curved bonnet.

'She's a work in progress,' said Jake. 'I like to buy and restore them to their former glory. Well, Guy does the restoring for me. I just pay him.'

Alex bent down to peer more closely at the interior, but his shoulder protested and he winced at the sudden shaft of pain.

'You okay?' asked Jake.

He nodded as the pain receded. 'Just an injury. So what repairs does this one need?'

'Oh, it's mainly superficial. The bodywork's badly rusted, as you can see, and there's a couple of other parts that need replacing. Guy's coming to pick her up next week.'

'How long will it take to restore her?'

'Who knows? Finding the original parts is the challenge, as you know.' He pointed to the Bentley. 'It took three years to get her in shape, but she was worth the wait.'

Alex liked how Jake referred to the car as 'she'. He did the same with all his bikes. Each one was individual, with its own personality and quirks, and getting to know it was part of the skill in being a good racer. Jake locked the garage and they walked back to the house.

'So you're a racer, Luc tells me.'

'I am.' Alex tensed. *Was.*

'But you like to tinker with the machines, too?'

'Only because I've got time on my hands. I came here to look for someone, but I've not had much success. And this week my bike was stolen. It's very frustrating.'

'You're recovering from an injury, too. Not an easy time for you.'

He didn't answer. His feet crunched over the gravel path and he kept his gaze fixed straight ahead. The windows of the hall glowed gold in the night, and silhouettes slipped past them. He wondered where Liberty was and what she was doing. Was she still glued to the blond guy's side? Was she dancing? Laughing?

'Congratulations on your engagement,' he said.

'Thanks.'

'I heard your speech, but I confess I didn't understand about the snow. And Pollyanna – who is this?'

Jake smiled. 'Did Luc tell you I lost my first wife?'

'No.' Alex stared at him. 'You were married before?'

Jake nodded. 'Maria died young. Very young. And I

took it badly. Partly because I blamed myself, but mostly because I got stuck feeling angry. Angry with the world, with myself, angry because she'd died when others lived . . . When I first met Evie I was in a bad place, totally focused on all I'd lost.'

Alex stared at him, trying to imagine the turmoil he was describing, but finding it difficult to picture anything except the calm, intelligent man who stood before him.

'But then I met Evie. And she taught me to count my blessings. She's an optimist so it comes naturally to her, whereas I had to learn to see the positives in life. But I'm glad I did.'

As Jake's words settled in the quiet night air, something about them hit home. Alex frowned. Was he focused on all he'd lost?

He was. Self-pity was never an attractive trait, but what had he been doing the last few weeks if not wallowing in it?

He sighed, disgusted with himself. He'd survived two serious accidents, but his injuries could have been worse. A lot worse. And he had no financial worries. He simply needed – no, wanted – to find a new purpose in life.

Back inside the Old Hall, Alex sipped his orange juice while he watched Liberty chat with Ethan. Even from this distance, he could see the stiffness of her smile. She was polite, not relaxed, and the guy was trying too hard, smothering her. As soon as he headed for the bar, leaving her alone, Alex seized the chance and crossed the room to speak to her.

'Alex!' She smiled. 'You changed your mind about coming, then? I'm glad. It's—'

'Why are you wasting your time with him?' Her smile vanished instantly. 'Anyone can see you don't have strong feelings for him.'

'Excuse me?' Her eyes blazed. 'Did I miss the part where I asked for your opinion?'

He shrugged. 'I'm simply pointing out what's obvious.'

She barked a laugh. 'And just what gives you the right to interfere in my life? Who I'm attracted to is none of your business.'

He raised his hands in mock surrender, but a silent voice told him he'd overstepped the mark. He should back off. 'Look,' he said, more gently, 'all I'm trying to say is just because you challenged yourself to date more doesn't mean you should date the wrong men.'

'Oh, and who would the right men be, then? Are you going to advise me on that too?'

He shook his head. 'All I know is you're wasting your time with Mr Bland over there. There's no chemistry between you, no passion. Anyone can see it. You know it too, but you don't want to admit it.' He hated how his accent had become more pronounced but he was fired up. He felt strongly about this, and although she was glaring at him, like a snarling cat, it felt good to finally let it out.

She frowned and followed his gaze to the bar, where the blond guy was patiently waiting to be served. 'Ethan's a really nice guy,' she began.

'And his mother likes quilting,' he said, rolling his eyes. 'I know.'

'That's not why I like him!' she said indignantly. 'He's caring and kind and settled—'

'And you want a family, so he'll do!'

She looked shocked. To be honest, so was he.

He said gently, 'You'll find someone else to start a family with. In the meantime, why not stop wasting your time by going down the wrong path?'

'Ethan's a good man,' she retorted. 'He works hard, he lives locally, he's . . . reliable.'

'That's the best you can come up with – nice? Reliable? And where he lives? You could be talking about an old-age pensioner.'

'I don't know what business it is of yours who I date or how I feel about them!'

'It's not. You're right. I'm just . . . concerned, that's all. Concerned that you're going for Mr Bland when you could do so much better. You wanted to find a partner and you've seized upon him because he's vaguely right. All those weirdos from the dating app have destroyed your confidence – so you've gone for the safe option. But it's obvious that he doesn't set your heart on fire.'

'Stop telling me how I feel!' she snapped.

'I'm just pointing out what you're too blind to see.'

'Are you? Or are you determined to spoil everyone else's fun because you're still feeling sorry for yourself about your career being over?'

Shocked, he stepped back.

'Butt out, Alex. I didn't ask for your opinion on my relationship and I don't want to hear it.'

She spun on her heel and stalked away, a whirlwind of blazing hair and dark satin.

She vanished into the crowd. Seconds later Ethan appeared with two full glasses. He frowned and asked, 'Have you seen Liberty?'

Alex gave a sharp nod. 'She went that way.'

Liberty fled down the hall and into the first empty room she found. It turned out to be the library, and she stomped back and forth, glaring at the tall bookcases, fighting the urge to kick one.

It was Alex she should kick, not Jake's furniture. How dare he? How *dare* he?

It took her a while to work off the worst of her anger, but when she had she stopped in front of the fireplace. Above it hung a huge gilded mirror. She gripped the marble ledge and glared at her reflection. Was there some truth in what Alex had said? Was she really so desperate to find someone that she'd latched on to Ethan? Was there no chemistry between them, no passion?

Her brain flew back to when she'd kissed Alex. *That* had been passion.

Or had it? She frowned angrily.

It had just been desire, a moment of madness. And even if it had been passion, so what? Passion didn't mean that two people were suited. Passion didn't give you safety or security. Passion flared and died unpredictably. It wasn't dependable.

She sighed and looked at the door to the corridor where

the lights were bright and the music was thumping. Ethan would be wondering where she was. She'd run here to get away, but only cowards ran away. And she wasn't a coward any more, was she? She didn't like what Alex had told her, but she refused to let it spoil her evening.

Drawing her shoulders back, she smoothed her hair and made her way back to the party. She was going to find Ethan and have a great time – and prove to Alex that he had no idea what or how she felt. None at all.

Ethan was looking for her, and his face lit up when he spotted her.

'Thanks.' She smiled as he handed her a glass. He kissed her cheek, and she was disappointed because she felt nothing. Not even a flutter in her stomach. But when she spotted Alex across the room, a shower of fireworks spilled through her.

She told herself that was because she was still angry, and took a long swallow of her drink. She tried to focus on what Ethan was saying – something about the karaoke machine skipping – but it didn't hold her interest. Her mind wandered, her gaze too. She found herself tracking the Frenchman as he moved around the room, and perhaps he was doing the same because whenever he looked up from his conversation he glanced her way and his expression was intense. Full of remorse too.

Something in her unravelled a little.

Frustrated, she told herself to ignore it. She preferred to stay angry with him: she didn't want to see an apology in his eyes or feel bad for the things she'd said to him. She was here with Ethan and he deserved her full attention.

Suddenly, on impulse, she turned to Ethan and cupped his chin. He broke off from whatever it was he'd been saying. 'Lib? What are you—?'

She kissed him hard and with all the passion she could muster, telling herself he was the man for her: he was intelligent, reliable, he shared the same goals . . .

It was no good.

Her thoughts were stuck on Alex.

Despairing, she broke away.

'Wow.' Ethan grinned. His lips were red and full. 'Dare I ask what brought that about?'

She threw him a fleeting smile. He looked puzzled, but pleased with himself, and she quickly drained her champagne.

'Liberty!' They both turned as Dorothy approached, a glass of sherry sloshing wildly in one hand and her walking stick in the other. She seemed extremely unsteady. 'There you are. Are you going to introduce me to your young man? I didn't catch his name earlier.'

Liberty rushed to her side and took her arm. 'Why don't we find you a seat first?'

'I'm not completely decrepit yet, you know. But there is a nice place to sit in the living room. Come with me, young man,' her blue eyes twinkled as she ran an appraising gaze over Ethan, 'and tell me all about yourself. Lib, would you mind getting me another sherry?'

Liberty wondered if perhaps she'd had enough sherry, but she watched them move away, then headed for the bar. As she crossed the hall, Gary the pub landlord was on stage singing 'My Way' on the karaoke. She paused to enjoy the spectacle, then continued weaving her way through the crowd. The room was a little less busy since a lot of people had left at eleven. The music suddenly stopped and jumped to a new song. When Gary looked queryingly at the karaoke guy, he shrugged and said, 'Machine's playing up. Sorry, mate.'

The new song began, and Gary turned back to his audience. 'I'm going to need a partner for this one. Ladies?'

Liberty smiled to herself, but her smile faded when he spotted her. 'Liberty!' He beckoned her over. 'Come and sing with me.'

For the millionth time, she cursed her red hair: it was guaranteed to draw attention. She shook her head and reached the bar where there was a small queue. She waited in line next to George, the retired fireman. If Carys were here she would have jumped onto that stage with Gary, no hesitation. Liberty could picture it: she'd have taken a bow, got the audience clapping along, she'd have sung and danced like a showman, entertaining everyone so they were still laughing about it well into the new year. Liberty, on the other hand, preferred to hide in the corner and remain invisible.

'Liberty is doing a challenge . . .' Gary announced to the room.

A spidery sensation touched her spine. She turned around. He wasn't – he wouldn't . . .

He grinned at her from behind the microphone. 'For the month of December she must say yes to everything. So I'll ask you again. Liberty, will you sing with me?'

People cheered, heads turned, and her cheeks filled

with hot colour as everyone waited for her reply. Memories flashed up of a school concert when she was small and a room full of parents all watching her on the stage. Her mum had been among them, glowing with pride. But when Liberty had opened her mouth to sing, the notes had stuck in her throat. Fear had paralysed her. Never again, she'd vowed.

'Don't look so scared, Lib,' George said kindly. 'It's only a bit of fun.'

The barman slid a couple of glasses of champagne towards him.

'Say yes, Lib!' someone shouted.

She cringed. She'd never sung in public – she avoided anything likely to draw attention to her. But if she refused, she'd have failed in her challenge.

Damn. First Alex's confrontation, now Gary's challenge: this evening was not going well. She glared at Gary, but he beamed back innocently. She looked around the room. It was half empty now. There wouldn't be too many witnesses . . .

What the hell? She grabbed a glass of champagne and downed it for courage. A little nudge from George propelled her towards the stage and Gary helped her up. He handed her a microphone and she looked at the screen where the lyrics for 'You're The One That I Want' began to roll. There wasn't time to feel nervous, and perhaps the champagne helped, too. Added to that, Gary's voice was a little off key but it didn't prevent him from singing with gusto, which made her giggle. Everyone was cheering and smiling anyway. But when it was her turn to start singing, the room hushed.

She faltered. Were they appalled? Anxious, she glanced at the crowd and saw wide eyes and open mouths. Alex came into the room and leaned against a wall. Her nerves tautened.

'Wow, the girl can sing!' said Gary. She heard the awe in his voice.

'She really can,' said someone in the crowd, sounding amazed.

Relief washed through her. Everyone began to clap, and a burst of satisfaction took her by surprise. Her nerves melted away, and she and Gary finished the duet.

As they took a bow, Gary winked at her, and Dorothy raised her empty sherry glass.

The karaoke machine had stuck again, so a short silence followed. 'Give me a minute,' said the karaoke guy.

Then Liberty heard a collective gasp. She reached up on tiptoe to see and noticed a commotion in the far corner of the hall. People moved back suddenly, and she saw that Natasha was staring at the floor in confusion.

'Your waters have broken,' Luc announced, shocked. 'The baby's coming.'

'No!' Natasha cried. Liberty's friend, who was normally organised and efficient, seemed to lose it and flew into a panic. 'What do I do? It's not supposed to come for another three weeks.'

'We need to go to hospital,' Luc said.

But Natasha's expression was one of terror. 'Something's wrong. It's too soon. What if it's another miscarriage?'

Liberty blinked. Natasha had miscarried before?

It explained why she looked so scared. The blood had drained from her face and when Luc put his arm around her she gripped his shirt as if it were a lifebuoy.

'The baby's just coming a bit early,' said Luc, although there was a slight tremor in his voice. 'Everything will be fine, don't worry.'

'No. Lottie was two weeks overdue. There's something wrong, I know there is.'

'Every baby is different, *chérie*. Don't panic.'

'It can't happen now. I'm not ready! Who will look after Lottie?'

Liberty scanned the room and spotted the little girl playing with a couple of other children. Fortunately, she didn't seem to have noticed anything and was absorbed in a game of chase.

'Evie said she'll do it,' said Luc.

'Yes. Where's Evie?'

Liberty looked left and right for her, but Evie was nowhere to be seen. Anyway, was it fair to ask her to babysit Lottie when she was hostess tonight and celebrating her engagement?

'Oh, no!' Natasha's eyes welled up. 'It's all going wrong. This isn't how it should be.'

Sensing her friend was on the verge of hysteria, Liberty hurried down from the stage. The crowd had dispersed, making it easier to cross the room.

'It's okay.' Luc was trying to calm his wife.

Liberty reached them. 'Why don't I take Lottie home and put her to bed?' she offered breathlessly. 'I know her routine. I can look after her.'

Natasha's shoulders dropped with relief. 'Oh, Liberty, thank you. Thank you so much.'

Luc smiled gratefully at her too, then turned to his wife. 'We should go to the hospital now, *chérie*.'

Lottie appeared, her friends in tow. She stared at the floor. 'Why is there a puddle, Mummy? Did you spill your drink?'

Natasha gave a nervous laugh, then crouched to speak to her daughter. 'Lottie, I have to go to hospital now, so Auntie Liberty's going to take you home.' She dug in her handbag and her hand shook as she gave Liberty her keys. 'Here. For the cottage.'

The music started up again, and they all glanced round to see that the karaoke was up and running again.

Scowling, Lottie folded her arms. 'I don't want to go home. I want to stay at the party.'

'Don't worry about a thing,' Liberty told Natasha, and picked up the little girl. 'You can stay at the party a little longer, honey. That's fine. We'll have fun together, won't we?'

Lottie nodded. Clearly, she didn't understand what was happening.

'How about we go and dance now?'

The little girl squealed with delight, and Liberty winked at Natasha. *Good luck*, she mouthed. Someone arrived with a mop, and Liberty let Lottie tug her back towards the dance floor. As she twirled the little girl and made her laugh, she glanced around for Ethan. Was he still with Dorothy? She hadn't seen him since she'd gone up on the stage to sing, or Alex, but she didn't want to think about him.

She felt a tap on her shoulder. As if she'd conjured him with her thoughts, there he was. 'Ethan!' She beamed.

He looked at his watch. 'Are you nearly ready to go? I have an early start in the morning. I'd better make tracks.'

Liberty blinked. 'An early start?' He hadn't mentioned this before.

'I'm going hiking.'

Nothing important, then. She frowned. 'Didn't you hear? Nat's gone into labour. I said I'd look after Lottie tonight.'

He glanced at Lottie. 'Ah. Children aren't really my thing, I'm afraid. Right, well, call me some time, okay?'

He seemed keen to get away. They kissed goodnight, but it was a chaste kiss. No sparks.

But there hadn't been any before, had there?

Sunday, 14 December, early hours

'Thanks for the lift, George,' said Liberty, when they got to Poppy Cottage.

George nodded. 'Any time, Lib. Looks like you're going to have an easy night. The little one's already out for the count.'

His car disappeared into the night, and Liberty shifted the sleepy child on her shoulder as she retrieved the key for the cottage. She carried Lottie upstairs to her room and laid her gently on her bed. While she was undressing her, the little girl woke and sat up. Noticing that this wasn't her usual routine, Lottie screwed up her nose and began to protest. 'Don't want to go to bed. I want to go with Mummy to hosp-al!'

'Hospital isn't as nice as your house. Your mummy will want to come home just as soon as she can. That's why you need to be here waiting for her. Now, let's get you ready for bed.'

'Is hosp-al a bad place?'

'No. But Poppy Cottage is definitely better.'

'*When* will Mummy be home?'

'Very soon, honey. Now, which are your favourite pyjamas?'

'Starry ones.'

'Want to show me where they are?'

Lottie scampered over to the chest of drawers and began to search through, scrummaging through all the neatly folded clothes and leaving them in a messy heap.

They read a story and Lottie sucked her thumb, then asked for the landing light to be left on and settled down for the night.

'Will you stay here all night, Libtea?'

'I will, honey. I promise.' The little girl nodded and her eyelids drooped. 'Goodnight, Lottie. Sleep well, honey,' she whispered.

A memory sprang up in her mind of her mum leaning over her when she'd been little, and Liberty felt a longing so strong it was like a vice around her chest. A longing to be a mother herself, to whisper those words to her own child. She tiptoed downstairs. Crikey, her body clock had really kicked in when she'd turned thirty, hadn't it? Was it normal to want so desperately to have children? She must remember to ask Evie if she felt the same.

In the kitchen she put the kettle on, shivering a little. The cottage was chilly, presumably because the heating had switched off for the night. She was exhausted, but she wanted to be sure Lottie had settled before she went to sleep herself. She looked around. Where would she sleep anyway? The cottage had three bedrooms: Natasha and Luc's, Lottie's, and the nursery which was all kitted out in yellow and cream with a cot ready for the baby.

She carried a cup of herbal tea into the lounge and wrapped a throw around herself, wishing she was wearing something warmer and more comfortable than a thin satin dress. She wondered how Natasha was getting on and checked her phone for messages, but there was nothing. Then she thought she heard a quiet knock.

It was past midnight. Had she imagined it?

A moment later she heard it again. It sounded like the front door. Who on earth was knocking at this time? She went to the window and nudged the curtain open a fraction. Even in the shadowy light of the moonless night she recognised the messy hair immediately.

Alex. Their angry conversation came back to her. She didn't know why he was here and he was the last person she wanted to see, but she was worried he might wake Lottie so she hurried to the front door.

'What are you doing here?' she hissed, as she opened the door a crack.

He threw her a pointed look that told her he didn't rate that as a greeting, but what did he expect? 'I brought you this.' His voice was low and deep. He held out the big tote bag she used to carry quilts to the post office and opened it for her to see. 'Thought you might need a few things for the night.'

Inside were her toothbrush, pyjamas, and dressing-gown. Plus a change of clothes for tomorrow: her favourite leggings and velvet tunic.

'Oh,' she said, unable to hide her astonishment. 'That's . . . thoughtful of you.'

Perhaps it was an apology or his way of making up for what he'd said earlier. She pictured him collecting all her belongings. He must have gone into her bedroom. It was an intimate thing to do: the kind of thing Carys would have done for her. And talking in hushed voices on the doorstep only added to that feeling of intimacy.

'I thought you might miss your sewing, too,' he said, and held up a handful of coloured scraps she'd begun piecing together for Evie and Jake's engagement present.

'Oh, wow! That's great.' Relief flowed through her that she had her sewing with her, and she blinked at him, astonished that he knew her so well. The clouds shifted and the moon appeared, a faint halo above his head.

'Can I come in?'

Liberty looked over her shoulder. She didn't really have a choice, did she? Not after he'd gone to all this trouble for her. She stepped back and let him past her.

'How did you get here?' she whispered.

'I borrowed a car from Jake.'

'They're his pride and joy. I can't believe he let you borrow one.'

'He's a good guy. And he feels he owes me because I've been helping with the work on an old bike of his.'

'At Guy's garage?'

He nodded. 'How's Lottie?'

'Asleep, I think. I was going to give it twenty minutes, then check on her.'

From upstairs a small voice called, 'Libtea?'

Liberty touched a hand to her mouth. 'Oh, no.'

There was a creak and she pictured the little girl sitting up in bed. 'Libtea! Who are you talking to?'

She laughed quietly. 'I guess she wasn't asleep, then.'

'I hope I didn't wake her,' Alex said apologetically.

'Libtea!' Lottie shouted. 'Is it Papa? Is Papa home?'

'I'd better go and see her,' said Liberty.

Alex nodded, and as she hurried upstairs she heard the click of the front door shutting. Her shoulders dropped and she was cross with herself for feeling disappointed that he'd left.

She tried her best to settle Lottie with another couple of storybooks, then sat with her, stroking her hair in the hope that she'd be reassured by her presence – but nothing worked. Every time Liberty tried to tiptoe out of the room, the little girl whimpered and woke, crying. She simply wouldn't go back to sleep. 'Why don't we go downstairs for a cup of hot milk?' Liberty suggested in the end.

Lottie nodded. She wrapped her in a blanket and carried her down to the kitchen, where she was startled to find Alex. 'I thought you'd gone,' she told him.

'No. I'm still here. Hello, Lottie. Remember me? I'm Alex.'

Lottie peered at him. 'You sound like my papa.'

'Yes, your papa is my friend. We knew each other when we were small, like you.'

Liberty balanced Lottie on her hip as she opened the fridge. 'Lottie couldn't sleep so we're going to make hot milk and read another story, then go back to bed.'

'Here, let me help,' said Alex, and took the milk bottle from her. 'Lottie, which cup should we use?'

Under the child's instructions, he poured the milk into her favourite cup and heated it. They carried it through to the lounge and Liberty and Alex exchanged a secret smile while she drank. Liberty read her a short story, then took her back to bed.

But Lottie began to cry. 'I want Papa, I want Mummy!'

'They'll be home soon, honey. Go to sleep and when you wake up they might be home.'

'I want them home now!'

The little girl became more and more agitated, so Liberty picked her up and rocked her. She paced up and down the landing, trying to soothe her. Lottie had never been upset like this before, and Liberty hated to see her in such a state. She didn't want to let Natasha and Luc down, either. Natasha had enough on her plate without coming home to an exhausted child.

'Let me help.'

She turned. Alex was standing in the doorway. He held his arms out to take the little girl, and spoke to her in French. *'Qu'est-ce que c'est qu'ça? Je croyais que t'étais une grande fille.'*

Lottie nodded and sniffed. 'I *am* a big girl.'

'Alors, si on s'arrêtait de pleurer, hein?' He began to sing

quietly in French, and her eyes became so round with astonishment that Liberty couldn't help but smile. Lottie stared at him for a long while, then stuck her thumb into her mouth and leaned her head against his shoulder.

He winked at Liberty, and as he carried Lottie back to her bed, where he sat and cradled her, Liberty tiptoed away. From downstairs she heard him talking quietly to her for a long while, then the baby monitor became silent and the stairs creaked as he came back down.

'Wow, I'm impressed,' she said, when he came into the lounge. She put her sewing down.

'We'll see if it lasts.'

'She sounded so surprised when you spoke French to her.'

'Yes. Most girls like that.' His eyes gleamed in the low lighting.

Her heart skipped a beat and she looked away quickly. He sat down on the sofa beside her. Natasha's lounge was smaller than her own at Damselfly Cottage, and it felt intimate. Or maybe that was her imagination. She picked up her sewing again and tried to turn her attention away from him. But it wasn't easy. She was aware of how his white shirt was stretched across his solid shoulders, aware of his masculine scent. He jabbed a hand through his hair and leaned back, one foot casually rested on his knee.

'Any news about the baby?' he asked.

'Nothing. I hope Nat's okay.'

'I'm sure she is.'

She shivered despite the throw she'd draped around her shoulders.

'Shall I light the fire?' he asked.

'It's okay.' She finished a row of stitching and snipped the thread. But she couldn't muster the energy to pick up another strip, so she laid the sewing aside and hugged the throw tighter. 'You can go if you like. You've done your good deed for the day. Lottie and I will be fine now.'

'She might wake again.'

'I can handle it. Not as well as you, obviously – I can't sing lullabies in French – but I'll manage.'

'I'll stay.' He got up and began to stack wood in the hearth.

Silence filled the room, and she wondered why he'd come to the ball when he'd been so adamant he wouldn't. What had made him change his mind? Her eyelids felt so heavy. The late hour was catching up with her and she was desperate to close her eyes and go to sleep.

Once the fire was lit, he sat down again.

'So how did you get so good at dealing with a screaming child?' she asked.

'I didn't know I was.' He threw her a crooked smile. 'I think speaking French just made her think of Luc. She was probably exhausted to start with so anything would have soothed her.'

Liberty picked a loose thread off her lap and rolled it into a tiny ball. The sound of logs crackling made her feel warmer already, but she couldn't relax. Not with Alex around, their angry words from earlier still going round in her head.

'I remember now,' said Alex. 'My mother used to rock me to sleep. She'd sing the lullaby I just sang for Lottie.'

He smiled at the memory. 'And when my brothers came along she had her hands full so I used to help with them. I guess that's why I still know the words.'

'Are you close?'

'What?'

'You, your mum and your brothers.'

He tilted his head to consider this. 'Yes. I suppose we are.'

The baby monitor stayed silent, but Liberty kept her voice low for fear of disturbing Lottie. 'When I was little I used to be jealous of families like yours.'

He turned to look at her. 'Why?'

'Because I was an only child. It was just me and Mum. I would have loved to have lots of siblings like you.'

'We all want what we don't have. I wanted a boring father with a dull office job. Someone who wasn't famous or rich and was always home.'

His rueful smile made his eyes crease, and it was disarming. Heat pooled in her middle.

She laughed softly and pulled the throw tighter, as if it could protect her against what she was feeling. But she knew it couldn't. The slow wind of desire was only growing stronger.

Chapter Sixteen

Alex wanted to kiss her.

His gaze slid to her long legs, slender ankles. She'd slipped her heels off and was barefoot, her toenails painted a deep plum. He watched as she hugged the throw tighter. She was still cold, and he wanted to draw her to him, hold her close, share body heat.

But he mustn't. Knowing all he did about her, it wouldn't be fair, and his conscience wouldn't let him. Still, desire held him in its grip.

'How old are your brothers?' she asked.

'Thirty-two and thirty.'

'Do they like motorcycle racing too?'

'They hate it – both of them. One is a teacher and the other works with computers.'

'Do you see them often?'

'When I can.' He'd be able to see them more now, he thought, remembering what Jake had told him about focusing on what he had, rather than what he'd lost, and his spirits lifted at the prospect of spending more time with his baby nephew.

The cottage was quiet, the only sound the crackling of the fire. They both watched the flames dance and arch against each other. The warm lighting made Liberty's hair glow, and her skin looked even softer than normal. Silence stretched. Their conversation at the ball had unravelled so badly. He wished he'd stayed at home tonight, like he'd said he would.

Liberty yawned. It was getting late and the fact that she didn't even have the energy to scw told him she was tired. But their angry words hung over him, so he decided to say what was really on his mind. 'How was your evening with Mr Bland?'

'Don't call him that!' Her brows knitted together in an angry scowl. 'His name's Ethan. And he's fine.'

'Did he enjoy the ball?'

'Yes. I think so.' Her tone was defiant. Fiery.

'He left early.'

She was clearly surprised he'd noticed. 'He has something on in the morning. A hike.' She rubbed one foot with the other.

He asked gently, 'You're disappointed?'

'What?'

'That he didn't stay. Were you hoping he'd go home with you?' He was careful not to sound combative, but as her cheeks bloomed the colour of cranberries he half expected her to tell him to mind his own business again. He shifted uncomfortably, irritated that she was hung up on Mr Bland. He wished she'd see that she could do better.

He also wished he'd stop interfering in her life.

Why didn't he?

Because living together made it difficult not to observe

at close hand the mistake she was making. At least, that was what he told himself.

But to his surprise, she admitted quietly, 'No.'

He stared at her. A log hissed and cracked. A flame leaped, then shrank back.

'You were right,' she went on. 'Earlier.'

'What?'

'I don't feel anything for Ethan.'

A wave of euphoria rushed through him. But he checked it immediately. It was simply relief, he told himself, because she was being honest with herself at last.

'But I wanted to,' she went on. 'I really wanted to.' A weak smile pulled at her lips, and her eyes were dark with sadness.

He felt a tug. 'Be patient. The right man will come along eventually.'

'No, he won't. Not in Willowbrook, anyway. No one new ever comes here – well, apart from you, obviously.'

The baby monitor lit up as Lottie stirred. She murmured something unintelligible and made a snuffling noise, then it went quiet again.

'And I'm tired of waiting anyway,' Liberty went on. 'I'm so envious of Natasha and Luc. I can't wait to have a family of my own.'

He admired her honesty. How could she say she wasn't brave when she was so open about her feelings? He hated discussing – or even thinking about – emotions. Analysing race times, bends and overtakes was much more his thing.

And yet this evening had been all about emotion.

When she'd come into the kitchen, her red hair

cascading around her shoulders, his breath had caught. When he'd arrived at the ball and spotted her with the blond guy, heads bent in intimate conversation. When he'd confronted her and she'd flashed fire at him. When he'd heard her sing, and the room applauded her and she was visibly astonished and delighted. And then here at Poppy Cottage, the closeness of being alone together now. The emotion had been building all night and now he sensed he'd reached a journey's end, a destination he'd been searching for.

But he didn't do intimacy with anyone – especially not Liberty McKenzie.

'I wish I could be more patient,' she went on. 'I wish I could just wait, like you say, for the right man to come along, but it's as if someone set a timer when I turned thirty and now I can hear it ticking, counting down every day.' She sighed. 'You probably think I'm mad, don't you?'

The throw had slipped while she'd been talking and his gaze dipped to the creamy skin of her throat, pale and flawless. He found it difficult to concentrate. 'I don't think that. My brother couldn't wait to have children either. I'm the one who's unusual.'

'You don't want a family at all? Ever?'

He shook his head.

'Why not? You won't be travelling so much now you're not racing.'

Solange's stricken expression flashed up in his mind. 'I'm not the settling type.'

'What about when you get older? Won't you be lonely?'

A tiny shiver touched the back of his neck. Alone was how he'd chosen to live. It was better this way.

Yet it had been a lot easier when he'd had a career. Alone on a bike or on a podium or celebrating with his team was very different from being alone with no career, no future, no purpose. But he'd have to get used to it, because he refused to let anyone get close to him. Memories of his father's infidelities splashed across the tabloids flashed up in his mind, like a red flag. His mother's pain and humiliation.

'I might,' he said. 'But I'm willing to take that risk.'

Her eyes widened. 'Why? You might find someone who enjoys travelling as much as you do.'

In the fireplace a piece of charred wood broke off, and ash crumbled down into the grate. Alex stared at the flames. 'It's not just about the travelling.'

She waited for him to go on. When he didn't, she asked, 'What is it about, then?'

He sighed, wishing he'd kept quiet. She didn't need to know any of this. He didn't want to tell her. He was a private person, not given to reflecting on these matters, never mind discussing them with others. Yet, for some reason, he felt he owed her an explanation.

'I've told you about my father, haven't I?'

'A little.'

'How he was unfaithful, never around for us. He made my mother suffer.'

She frowned. 'What does that have to do with you dating?'

'I am a lot like him.'

In the golden glow of the fire her lips looked full and dark. She paused before asking, 'What do you mean?'

'My appearance, my love of racing, of speed. There are many similarities.'

He felt her study him for a long moment. Then, 'I don't understand. So you both loved racing – what does that have to do with not wanting to settle down?'

He breathed in and realised he'd never spoken the words aloud. 'I'm scared I'm like him in other ways too. That if I was in a relationship I'd behave like him – get bored, leave. I have no desire to hurt someone the way he hurt my mother.'

Like Alex had hurt Solange.

'But that's ridiculous. Just because you like racing doesn't mean you're—'

'I did it already.'

She stared at him, puzzled. 'You did what?'

'I hurt someone. She didn't deserve it.'

Silence stretched for what seemed like minutes. The house held its breath.

'You were unfaithful?'

Guilt clung to him. What he'd done was just as bad. 'No. I . . . let her down.'

Memories filled his mind of all the excited plans Solange had made and the mounting pressure that had piled on him. The fear. Dread. Until one day he couldn't carry on and he'd ended it. The pain in her face would always stay with him.

Liberty waited expectantly for him to continue, but he clamped his lips together. He didn't want to go there.

'So because you had one bad experience, you're never going to have another relationship? Maybe she simply wasn't the right woman for you.'

He threw her a dark look. 'I'm not cut out for commitment, so I don't make promises I can't keep.'

'But how can you know if you don't try?'

'You asked why I don't do relationships and I told you,' he said impatiently.

'But it sounds like—'

'Can we change the subject?' There was a pounding in his temple.

Hurt flickered in her eyes.

'Lib, I'm sorry.' He sighed, annoyed with himself for snapping. He didn't like talking about his emotional life. Let's face it, he wasn't used to it because he hadn't had an emotional life for so long.

'You don't like to talk about your own life, yet you interfere in mine. Why?' Her beautiful eyes held his gaze.

Good question. He frowned. 'Because I . . . I care.' There was a pause. 'About you.'

Since they'd been snowed in together things had changed. Now he saw her vulnerabilities as clearly as her flaws and her strengths. And he felt protective. He wanted to look out for her. He didn't know why, he couldn't understand it, but that was how he felt.

She shook her head. 'I don't need you to care for me, Alex. I've looked after myself perfectly well for the last thirty years.'

He thought of her best friend in hospital, her cottage alone in the woods, and her rigid, solitary routine of dog-walking and sewing, and he opened his mouth to speak – but she got up.

'I'm going to try to get some sleep now,' she said briskly. 'Natasha told me Lottie's always up with the lark so I'll need to be ready.'

She delved into the bag he'd brought, pulling out her pyjamas and dressing-gown. He glanced at his watch. It was three a.m.

'Where are you sleeping?' he asked.

'Here. On the sofa.'

He nodded and slipped quietly upstairs, returning with a couple of blankets.

'Thanks,' she said, as he handed her one.

'I checked on Lottie and she's sound asleep,' he assured her, and laid the other blanket on the floor with a cushion for a pillow.

Liberty frowned. 'What are you doing? Aren't you going home?'

'I thought I'd stay here, if that's okay? It's late, and you might need a hand in the morning. How are you going to shower, for example, with Lottie around? I can help you.'

She bit her lip as if that hadn't occurred to her. She glanced up at the ceiling and he read her mind: she was wondering if she could sleep on Natasha's bed without actually getting into it.

'If Luc comes home in the night he'll need to sleep. I expect he'll be exhausted. Best if we stay down here.'

'What about Charlie?'

'I took him out before I came to the ball. I can nip back to Dragonfly Cottage in the morning, if necessary.'

'*Damselfly*,' she corrected. There was a long silence. Then she nodded. 'Okay.'

She left the room and came back a few minutes later wearing pyjamas and pulling the belt of her dressing-gown tight. When she saw he'd stripped down to his jeans her cheeks flushed but she didn't comment. He pulled the blanket over himself and told her, '*Bonne nuit*.'

She switched off the light in the lounge and they settled down to sleep.

In the darkness he listened to her quiet breathing and smiled to himself as he thought about her confession that she didn't feel anything for Mr Bland. It made him sing inside.

Yet he knew he was not the man for her. Her body clock was ticking so loudly it was deafening. He turned onto his side with his back to her. Be honest, Ricard. You want her. You want to hold her, run your hands over her milk-white skin, bury your face in her hair and lose yourself in—

He sighed, despairing at himself. Every conversation with her only emphasised how wrong for each other they were.

Yet his body wouldn't listen to reason, and the more time he spent with her, the closer he wanted to be to her. The closer he felt.

Liberty woke with a sharp intake of breath and it took her a few seconds to work out why she was curled up on a sofa with the smell of woodsmoke and the sound of a man's steady breathing.

Then it came back. Poppy Cottage. Lottie. Alex.

Her heart rate gradually returned to normal, and she closed her eyes to replay the vivid dream that had catapulted her from sleep. She'd been flying through the air on a rollercoaster, screaming, when it had flown off the rails and careered down a snowy hill towards a crossroads where a car was waiting for the traffic lights to change.

As Liberty drew closer, the driver at the wheel of the car came into focus and she realised it was Carys – Carys, whose mouth was wide with terror because Liberty was heading straight for her. Liberty panicked. She tried to stop, her feet stamped on the brake, but there was no pedal, nothing, and she couldn't do anything to stop—

Her eyes snapped open. It had just been a dream. Probably brought on by the alcohol she'd drunk, combined with the cocktail of complicated emotions Alex had stirred up when he'd come here. Breathe, Lib, breathe.

She peered into the darkness. Embers still glowed in the fireplace, and the baby monitor calmly glowed green. Alex's breathing was regular and quiet, but she wasn't sure if he was sleeping. He couldn't be very comfortable down there on the floor. She hoped his shoulder wasn't too sore.

Her whispered confession ran through her mind on loop: *I don't feel anything for Ethan.* The realisation had felt like a lead weight. She'd known in her heart that Ethan wasn't The One, so why had it taken Alex to point it out before she'd acknowledged it?

Because she'd wanted it to work. It would have been so safe and easy with Ethan, everything falling into place.

But maybe wanting it so much was precisely what had made her overlook that one vital element was missing: the physical, the spark, the magic. She glanced at the grey shadow on the floor.

She didn't light up around Ethan the way she did with Alex. He didn't even have to be near her: just the sight of him across a room was enough to make her feel heady, as if the sun had come out from behind the clouds.

Disappointment weighed her down. Wasn't it just typical that she felt lukewarm about the man who was perfect, and responded with fire and ice to the one who was totally wrong for her?

Don't get attached. I never stick around.

She thought of what he'd told her about his dad, about his past relationship. What had happened? Clearly he'd hurt someone. Did that surprise her? A man who lived for adrenalin rushes and high-speed racing was hardly likely to be the loyal dependable kind, was he? Still, it was sad that he didn't trust himself to commit to anyone again. Sad that he'd chosen to be alone.

She pushed this aside. It was nothing to do with her. He was just a lodger in her house, and he'd be gone by Christmas.

Alex sighed. 'You can't sleep either?'

In the darkness her head whipped round. His accent and the way he exaggerated his vowels had become so familiar so quickly, and she found it endearing. 'No,' she whispered.

She pictured him as she'd seen him earlier, wearing nothing but jeans, his chest bare, bronzed, muscular. Heat unfurled at the memory. Silence stretched. Her heart beat in a quick tempo beneath the blanket. A triangle of navy sky peeped through the top of the curtains where they didn't quite meet.

'Why did you come to the ball tonight?' she asked quietly. 'You said you weren't going to.'

There was a long pause before he answered. 'I changed my mind.'

'Why?' she insisted.

Another silence filled the darkness, although her eyes must have adjusted because now she could see the outlines of the coffee-table, the armchair and Lottie's toy box.

'I wanted to see you.'

'Me?'

'You.' She heard the smile in his voice.

'But you knew I'd be with Ethan.'

She waited, holding her breath, for the reply, but it didn't come. She sighed. 'I don't understand.'

'Neither do I,' he confessed finally.

The monitor lit up, a string of lights, as Lottie turned over. Then the lights flickered out.

'You looked stunning tonight,' he said. Was that his explanation, or was he changing the subject? 'That dress, your hair . . .'

Her thighs squeezed. Desire licked at her. She smiled weakly into the darkness. 'You should have used that as your opening line instead of passing judgement on my relationship with Ethan.'

'You're right.' She heard the regret in his voice. 'But I had to say it. I can't hide how I feel. It's not in my nature.'

'So . . .' she began, then swallowed.

Don't say it, don't go there, Lib.

But she couldn't stop herself. She needed to know. '. . . what are you feeling now?'

The pause before he answered lasted an eternity. Heat filled her cheek and she cringed. Oh, God, she'd blown it now. What had she been think—

'I'm feeling . . .', his deep voice reached her through the darkness, '. . . that I want you very much.'

She lit up with joy – and disbelief, too.

There was a rustle, and when his silhouette appeared in front of her she sat up. He perched on the sofa next to her. Their arms found each other and he kissed her. Tentatively. Queryingly.

Then it became feverish and urgent. Just like when they'd been snowed in, only this time it wasn't a surprise, and she wanted this. She longed for this. Desire had been simmering beneath the surface ever since that kiss among the feathers.

She slid her fingers through his hair, savouring its satin smoothness and breathing in his familiar scent. Her hands ran over his shoulders, back, biceps, relishing the heat of his skin, the rough curl of hair. She leaned back, drawing him to her, and her body sparked as he touched her. She arched against him, loving how he made her feel all woman. He excited her more than any man had before – why? Because she knew this couldn't lead to anything? Rational thoughts melted away as he began to drop kisses along her chin and her neck, and she pushed the blanket away, tugging at her pyjama top, wanting his lips to go lower. His knee slipped between hers and she gripped it, rubbed against it, breathing his name on a rush of air—

The sharp scrape of a key in a lock made them still. Liberty heard the front door open and click quietly shut.

'It's Luc,' Alex breathed. Reluctantly, he untangled himself from her and got up. She fastened her top and watched as he reached down for his blanket to wrap around himself. 'Can I put the light on?' he whispered.

'Um – yeah.'

She blinked against the bright light and heard him open the lounge door. 'Luc, hi. How's Natasha?'

'*Tout va bien.*' Liberty sat up and saw Luc's beaming smile in the doorway. He reverted to English for her benefit. 'We have a baby boy. Arthur,' he said proudly. 'It all happened quickly this time, but there were no problems and he's gorgeous. He looks just like Nat. Has her blue eyes.'

Liberty smiled. He was grey with exhaustion but his eyes were radiant.

'That's wonderful! Congratulations,' said Liberty.

Alex slapped his friend on the back. '*Bravo,*' he said, and muttered something else in French as he hugged him.

Luc looked a little dazed. The sound of Lottie stirring upstairs made them all glance up.

'Why don't you get some sleep and I'll look after Lottie this morning?' Liberty suggested, getting up. She could take the little girl out to the park, maybe stop for cake at the bakery.

'It's okay,' said Luc. 'I'm too excited to sleep. And I want Lottie to meet her little brother as soon as possible.

I'll take her to the hospital in a few hours. Give Nat the chance to rest first.' He looked from Alex to her and back again, then grinned. 'So you both stayed, huh?'

'Alex brought me an overnight bag,' she said quickly. 'And he helped me with Lottie. He was very good with her.'

'You two go home,' said Luc. 'Sleep in your own beds. It can't have been very comfortable on the sofa.' He winked, and Liberty blushed furiously.

Alex, on the other hand, seemed unfazed. 'If you're sure.'

They got dressed, collected their belongings, and left as quietly as possible so as not to disturb Lottie. The car Alex had borrowed was parked in front of the cottage. In the darkness she couldn't see what colour it was, but its shape was distinctive: a low sports car with an enormous bonnet that looked as if it had been stretched. It suited Alex perfectly.

'What is this car?' Liberty asked, not wanting to talk about what had just happened back there. Her cheeks were still hot at the memory of Luc's interruption. Imagine if he'd come into the lounge and caught them.

'A TVR.' Alex shrugged. 'I don't know this brand. Jake said it's British.'

The engine didn't catch on the first attempt and she watched him as he coaxed it to life.

'Probably very valuable.'

'Yes. I'm sure.'

Eventually, he got it going and pulled away. She noticed he drove carefully, easing the classic car round the bends, slowly through the sleeping village.

The streets of cottages huddled together in the dark, punctuated by orange spots of lamplight here and there. They drove over the bridge and pulled onto the main road, which was deserted. She cast Alex a covert glance. His jaw was set, and his hands were clenched around the steering wheel.

What would happen when they got home? Did she want to carry on where they'd left off?

Finally, they reached Damselfly Cottage. Alex killed the engine and turned to her. He looked as if he wanted to say something but couldn't find the words.

Her throat tightened. She needed time to work out how she felt, she wasn't sure what—

'It won't happen again,' he said quietly. 'I promise.'

She blinked. She hadn't seen that coming. It was a slap in the face.

Before she could say anything, he opened the car and got out. Stunned, Liberty watched as he strode towards the cottage.

Chapter Seventeen

Alex marched towards the front door. He hadn't drunk any alcohol last night, yet this morning he felt as if he had the worst hangover in the world.

Regret. That was what this grey ache in his head, in his stomach was. Regret and remorse – and anger with himself.

'Hold on a minute!' Liberty called after him. He stopped. She caught up, breathless. 'What do you mean it won't happen again?'

The sky was turning violet in anticipation of the sun. A crow called from somewhere high above.

What the hell was the matter with him? Ever since he'd arrived here he just kept screwing things up, saying the wrong thing. 'It shouldn't have happened. I shouldn't have let it—'

'*You* shouldn't?' She jabbed a finger at her chest. 'What about me? I was there too, remember? Does what I want count for nothing?'

Her hair was messy and its colour dulled by the bluish dawn light, but her eyes blazed and her brow was creased in a furious knot. She was vibrant. Fiery. Beautiful.

He said quietly, 'I'm thinking only of you, Liberty. I

don't want to hurt you.' He pushed a strand of hair back from her face and touched her cheek. It was as soft as the fleece lining of the mittens she'd made for him. 'We want different things, you know that. Which is why I can't believe I allowed that to happen . . .' He gestured in the vague direction of Luc's. She deserved so much better.

He rubbed a hand over his face and sighed. 'I promise I won't let it happen again.'

Wednesday, 17 December

It was only a couple of miles to Guy's garage, so Alex had walked there. He had all the time in the world, so why not? Through the woods, across the main road, then following the stream and the winding path it traced to Willowbrook village. Although it was winter and most of the trees had lost their leaves, nature was still lively: he'd spotted squirrels, rabbits, even a fox. He'd become aware of the orchestra of bird calls: the high trills of small birds, and the lower guttural rasp of crows and magpies. Details he hadn't appreciated when he'd first arrived in this tranquil place. And each day the stream played a different piece of music for him. After the snow had melted, it had gushed, loud and full; on clear days, it was calm and melodic.

By the time he reached Guy's garage, his head always felt clearer, his mood was brighter, and he was really looking forward to working on the Triumph. Guy had even given him his own overalls.

He was in the workshop taking apart the headlamp when a well-dressed lady came in. 'Mr Ricard?' she said.

Alex looked up. 'That's me.' A few weeks ago he would have been wary, but he'd found that no one here seemed over-impressed by his name or reputation.

She shuffled her feet. Wearing a smart tweed jacket and cashmere jumper, she looked out of place among the oil-stained metal and machinery. 'My name's Anna. I brought my car in yesterday and Bob mentioned you were helping here.'

'Ah. I'm sorry, Bob's not in today. Guy might know where you can find him.'

'Actually, it's you I came to see. About your letters. I heard you're looking for someone who . . . knew your dad.'

He put the lamp down. She had his full attention now. 'That's right. A woman whose name begins with M.'

What had she said her name was? Anna. She looked as if she might be in her late fifties. The right age.

Anna smiled. 'She was called Mary.'

His heart jumped. 'You know her?'

'No,' she said quickly. 'Not any more. She didn't live here long, just a couple of years. But I remember she met your dad when she was working at the hotel in town – the hotel where he stayed.'

His breath caught. A flurry of questions crowded his head, and it was difficult to know where to start. 'Do you know her surname?'

'Sorry. She rented a room in the house where my friend lived. I didn't know her well. But I remember she told everyone who'd listen about your dad and how they were dating.' Her lips made a thin red line. 'She was – how to put it? – a party girl. We weren't entirely surprised when she became pregnant. Sadly.'

The judgement and disapproval were evident. Alex tried to put them aside and focus on the facts. 'Do you have any other information about her or her baby?'

She shook her head. 'She left when her pregnancy became impossible to hide and she was sacked from the hotel. I'm afraid employers were less tolerant in those days. She moved away and we never saw her again.'

Disappointment filtered through him. The story was only getting more tragic. She'd been alone, pregnant, then lost her job too.

He scribbled his number on a scrap of paper and handed it to the lady. 'If you remember anything else – anything at all – please call me.'

She nodded.

'What else can you tell me about this Mary? What was she like?' he added, a little desperately.

'She was very taken by your father's fame and wealth. Mr Ricard, I know you're doing a good thing in trying to find her, and she must have had a hard time raising a little one by herself, but . . .', she appeared to choose her words with care, '. . . she wasn't an innocent, not by any means. And I think she saw your father as a meal ticket.'

'A meal ticket?'

Anna shifted uncomfortably. 'She was a gold-digger. And made no secret of it.'

As he watched her leave, Alex mulled this over. Did it make any difference? By the sound of it, she'd been young, but the outcome of her liaison with his father would have changed her life irreversibly. Whatever her intention had been, she was left jobless and with a child to raise alone.

No, he decided, it made no difference to him. In fact, what he'd learned today only made him more determined to help. He just hoped it wasn't too late.

Liberty was in the back room of the Button Hole, taking advantage of a quiet moment to press the seams of a new quilt top. It was made of long thin strips of fabric, which she'd machine-stitched together then laid diagonally; once it was finished and quilted Evie planned to display it in the shop to promote the packs of fabric strips known in the trade as jelly rolls. They made quilting a little easier for beginners because the fabrics were pre-cut and all the colours in a pack coordinated.

The iron hissed as she lifted it to slide the fabric along. As she worked, her mind was going over the difficult conversation she'd had with Ethan. They'd spoken on the phone two days ago and he'd been a little resentful at first, but then he'd admitted, 'I knew you didn't feel the same way about me.'

'You did?' She felt bad.

There was a moment's hesitation before he added, 'And I can't compete with a French racing driver.'

'Alex? But he – we're not—'

He gave a wry laugh. 'You talk about him all the time.'

'Do I?' She felt pale all of a sudden.

'And it's understandable, I suppose. The bike, the

money, the trophies – it makes the rest of us look dull in comparison.'

She was astounded. And he was so wrong. Bikes and money didn't excite her at all. Quite the opposite.

'Ethan, that isn't what this is about. I like you a lot. I just don't feel that – spark.'

His voice had softened. 'Thanks for being honest with me.'

Liberty put the iron down and finger-pressed the next section before gently lowering the iron again.

Everything had changed between her and Alex now. Oh, he was still friendly and the last couple of days they'd had dinner together, walked the dog, and spent evenings in front of the fire. They'd even made plans to visit Luc and Natasha tonight and meet baby Arthur for the first time. But there was an elephant in the room, and she wasn't sure how to deal with it.

She had tried to forget about the night of the ball, but it was difficult. He'd been so antagonistic towards Ethan, as if he was jealous. Then he'd been so considerate in turning up at Poppy Cottage and staying to help, and in the night when he'd kissed her and held her . . .

She couldn't shake off the memory. She'd replayed it so many times, but the intensity of it never faded. And he'd said he didn't want to hurt her, which was noble of him, yet as he'd spoken the words he'd touched her face with such tenderness, it had stolen her breath. It had been . . . unforgettable.

But she *had* to forget it. He was right: they had no future. He'd made that quite clear.

She put the iron down and yanked the plug out of the socket with more force than was necessary. She had to forget it, and she would.

With time, she was certain she'd put it out of her mind and move on.

'Luc's just changing his nappy. He won't be long,' said Natasha. She placed a tray on the coffee-table with steaming mugs of mulled wine and a plate of mince pies dusted with icing sugar and told Alex and Liberty to help themselves.

'Can I have a miss pie too, Mummy?' asked Lottie.

'Of course you can. Why don't you sit here with me to eat it?' Natasha sat down in the armchair and patted her lap.

'Are you going to France this Christmas?' asked Alex.

Natasha shook her head. 'We're going to have a quiet break here, just the four of us, although we might go over for the new year. What about you?'

'I've just booked my flight,' he said.

Liberty's head turned. She felt a stab of hurt that he hadn't mentioned it to her before now.

'I'm leaving on the twenty-third.'

Tuesday. She picked a crumb of pastry off her plate. She didn't know why she felt disappointed: she'd always known he'd leave before Christmas.

It was because of what had happened here, in this room. That heated moment had changed things for her. It had made her want things she couldn't have.

Footsteps sounded on the stairs and Natasha smiled. 'Here he comes.'

Luc opened the door and smiled warmly at his guests. 'Drumroll, please,' he said, as he approached the sofa where Liberty and Alex were sitting. He crouched so they could see the baby in his arms. 'Liberty, Alex, meet Arthur,' Luc said proudly.

'Oh, he's gorgeous,' whispered Liberty, peering at the baby's little face. 'He's utterly . . . perfect.'

'Do you want to hold him, Lib?' Natasha asked.

She grinned. 'Silly question.'

Luc placed his son carefully in her arms. Arthur weighed almost nothing, and was dressed in a soft cream Babygro with a thin cotton blanket draped around him. He gazed up at Liberty with serious eyes.

'He's happy there,' said Natasha. Little Lottie was curled up in her lap, her favourite, rather battered, doll in one arm.

'Give him a minute and he'll probably start to cry,' quipped Liberty.

He was so warm in her arms. She couldn't take her eyes off him. He smelt of baby lotion, and everything about him was delicate and tiny: his nose, ears, fingers that curled around hers and held on tight. Emotions rose in her, unexpected and overwhelming, making her throat squeeze.

'Lib, are you okay?' asked Natasha.

She blinked hard, fighting tears. 'Yes. Must be hormones or something.' She blushed.

'Liberty is feeling maternal,' said Alex, matter-of-factly. 'She'd like a family of her own.'

She gasped. 'Thanks for telling everyone!'

'It's obvious,' he shrugged. 'You look like you want to kidnap him.'

Everyone laughed and her cheeks became toasty.

Lottie jumped down from her mother's lap and came over. 'Libtea, you can't kidnap Arthur,' she said solemnly. 'He's Mummy's baby and mine.'

Liberty reached to stroke her blonde hair. 'I know, honey. Don't worry, I wouldn't dream of doing such a thing. Alex is being silly.'

A thought occurred and the little girl skipped over to her dad. 'Papa, Alex knows the same song you do and he sang it to me!'

'Did he? Which one?'

She rocked her doll as she sang the opening line.

Luc's eyes gleamed. 'Maybe he's practising for when he has a family of his own.'

Alex rolled his eyes.

'He can't,' scoffed Lottie. 'Only girls can have babies.'

'Maybe he'll find a girl he wants to marry.' Luc smiled at Liberty.

Embarrassed, she dropped her gaze and stroked Arthur's head. His skin was so incredibly soft beneath her fingers. She hadn't spoken to Natasha about the night of the ball – there simply hadn't been the opportunity – but Luc had clearly drawn his own conclusions.

Lottie turned to Alex. 'Which girl will you have a baby with, Alex?'

'Lottie,' Natasha said smiling, 'that's a very personal question.'

Lottie ignored her and dropped her doll in his lap. 'Will it be Libtea?'

Liberty didn't know where to look. Her cheeks burned so hotly that they must have been the same colour as the mulled wine Natasha had served them.

'I'm not going to have a baby, *ma petite*,' Alex said. He propped the doll into a sitting position and straightened her arms, as if she were gripping a steering wheel. He tilted her left, then right, so she mimicked driving a car.

Liberty tensed. She thought of what had happened on this sofa, and it hurt to hear him speak those words because she hadn't been able to forget about it at all. If anything, now she'd had a taste, she only wanted more.

'No baby at all?' Lottie was incredulous.

He shook his head.

'Why?'

'Lottie . . .' warned Natasha. She glanced at Liberty with concern.

Arthur began to grizzle. Liberty lifted him carefully onto her shoulder and rubbed his back.

Beside her, Alex was perfectly calm. And when she looked at him, his gaze met hers steadily. 'Because I like adventures,' he said. 'And adventurers don't make good fathers.'

Back at Damselfly Cottage Liberty sorted through her fabric stash, picking out half a dozen or so that went well together and would coordinate with Arthur's nursery. (She'd decided to put Evie and Jake's engagement quilt to one side while she made the baby quilt: cot-sized, it shouldn't take her long.) Her fabric selection included sage green, russet brown, cream, orange and slate. One or two had a cute woodland theme and were patterned with little foxes, squirrels and pine trees. The rest were geometric or plain, and it was this simplicity that gave Liberty's quilts their modern look. They were never fussy. For the backing she'd use one of the new fabrics that had just arrived in the Button Hole and featured the white silhouette of deer against a pastel grey background.

She laid out the material on her cutting mat, and decided that four-inch squares would be perfect for a small cot quilt.

As she measured and cut, she kept hearing Alex's words in her head: *I'm not going to have a baby.*

She couldn't wait to be a mother one day. Even more so now after she'd held little Arthur in her arms and seen his trusting gaze, heard him make those gorgeous contented gurgling noises and felt him nuzzle against her neck. She'd always loved going to Carys's house as a child: she'd liked the chaos, the noise, the energy of a big loving family. And when Natasha talked about Luc's big family in France, Liberty was envious. Family meant everything to her.

Which only drove home what she already knew: Alex was all wrong for her. She had to stop thinking about him and concentrate on finding her Dream Guy. The corner of the orange notebook was poking out of her handbag and caught her eye. She picked it up and thought about her challenge.

Tomorrow was another day, the chance for another yes. She'd meet someone who was perfect for her eventually. She would.

Thursday, 18 December

Brenda opened the door with a wide smile. 'I've almost finished it!'

Liberty stepped inside the house. Ethan's car wasn't on the drive, and there was no sign of him as she followed Brenda into the lounge either. She was relieved, but had the feeling he was avoiding her and she felt bad about that. 'The quilt for the show?'

Brenda nodded. 'I'm just stitching the binding, then it'll be ready to go.'

'Can I see?'

They spread the ninety-inch square quilt over the sofa and pored over it, Liberty admiring the complexity of her friend's needlework. Brenda brought in tea and a plate of delicious cranberry and white-chocolate cookies. Then they set to work, sewing.

'What's that you're working on, dear?' she asked Liberty.

'It's a cot quilt for my friend Natasha's baby, Arthur. He's four days old,' she said indulgently.

Brenda peered over her glasses at her. 'They're cute when they're that small.'

'Cute doesn't cut it! He's gorgeous.' Just the memory of holding Arthur made her heart sing.

'You like babies, then?' Brenda chuckled.

'Love them.' She couldn't hide the longing in her voice.

There was a pause before Brenda said, 'Ethan told me things didn't work out between you two. Don't worry, he didn't go into any details – he'd never do that – but I want you to know it doesn't change anything. For me, at least.'

'Or me, Brenda,' she said gently. 'And I'm still hoping you'll be well enough to come to the shop one day and pick your own fabrics.'

'Yes, well, on that subject – I've been seeing a very good counsellor and,' her eyes twinkled, 'I managed to go out into the garden the other day.'

Liberty gasped and put her sewing down to hug her. 'Oh, that's wonderful! How did it feel?'

'Awful. But I did it.'

'I'm so glad.'

'It's down to you, young lady. Well, the counselling has helped too, but mostly you.'

Liberty stared at her. 'Me? How?'

Brenda's lips twitched. 'You inspired me with your "saying yes" thing.'

'Really?' Her heart lifted with delight.

Brenda nodded. 'I thought if you can ride a motorbike and do all these terrifying things, then I should start to push myself too. You reminded me that no one else can do it for me. If I don't keep trying, nothing will change.' She stabbed a finger against her chest. 'I want to overcome this, and I want to do it for Ethan's sake. So he won't be tied down by having to care for me any more.'

'Brenda, I'm so proud of you.' Liberty blinked hard.

It was difficult to believe she'd inspired someone to do something so brave. And knowing what she did about Brenda's illness, she recognised that stepping outside had been a much greater feat than anything in her orange notebook.

'Don't cry, dear.'

Liberty grinned. 'Just got something in my eye.'

Brenda passed her a tissue. 'Ethan was over the moon.'

'I bet he was.' She put the tissue down and met Brenda's gaze square on. 'He – he's a good man. I'm really sorry things didn't work out between us. I really wanted them to.'

'Ah.' A penny seemed to drop, and it became clear Brenda had wondered about the reason for their break-up.

Liberty's respect for Ethan doubled, because he really hadn't shared any details of their relationship with his mum.

'But that's not always within our control, is it?' said Brenda. 'Who we have feelings for and who we don't.'

'Yeah.' Liberty gave a dry laugh. Didn't she know it! Her brain knew Alex was wrong for her, yet her body responded to him on another level. One that had nothing to do with her brain.

Brenda snipped a thread. 'There,' she said triumphantly. 'My quilt's finished and ready to go.'

Liberty smiled. 'Well done, Brenda. They're going to love it at the festival, I'm sure.'

'I hope so, dear. It's really given me a lift to think it will be hanging up in some beautiful French château for everyone to see. You can take it with you when you leave tonight.'

'Evie's going to post them tomorrow. Do you want to photograph it before it goes?'

'Oh, yes.' Brenda bit her lip. 'Ethan usually does that for me, but he won't be back until late.'

Liberty looked around at the small room. 'Why don't I photograph it in the shop tomorrow? There's more room and it will be at its best in daylight. Evie will help me.'

Brenda beamed at her. 'Good idea. Don't forget to send me the pictures so I can post them online.'

'You're online now?'

'I am. Another thing you converted me to. I've already made some new friends that way, and I love seeing pictures of everyone else's quilts all over the world. Very inspiring.'

Liberty smiled. 'I'm glad.' She was really happy for Brenda. It could only be a good thing to live in a world where borders didn't matter and a love of quilting brought people together.

Friday, 19 December

'It really is amazing,' said Evie, pausing in photographing Brenda's quilt to examine it more closely.

They'd hung it in the back room of the Button Hole where one wall was deliberately kept free for that purpose. Once upon a time Evie had used the track to hang the curtains she'd made before the shop had become a thriving business.

'Look at these tiny triangles here,' Evie continued.

'They're smaller than my thumbnail. And these T-blocks, see how intricate they are? That lady is seriously talented.'

Liberty nodded. 'And she has a really good eye for picking colours and patterns. Imagine what she could do if she could come here to choose the fabric herself.'

'I know. But the silver lining is that she's had the time to make this beautiful quilt.'

Evie finished snapping pictures, then draped the quilt over the work table for a few close-up shots. Once that was done, they folded it carefully and packaged it ready to send with two of Evie's quilts and one of Liberty's. The shop bell tinkled a couple of times, signalling that the lunchtime lull was over and they had customers.

Evie checked her watch. 'I'd better take these to the post office now.'

'When does the festival start?'

'The twenty-seventh of December.' She reached for her red coat.

'It's a strange time of year to run a quilt festival, don't you think?'

'Apparently it's very popular. I suppose people have more leisure time around Christmas.'

Liberty helped Evie tuck parcels under each arm before she picked up the two big bags. The parcels were heavy and bulky. She glanced at the queue of customers gathering at the till. 'If you wait a little while, I could give you a hand carrying them over.'

Evie shook her head. 'I'd rather get it done and tick it off my list. Today's the last post before Christmas, and the festival organisers are very strict about receiving submissions on time. A friend told me his quilt arrived late last year and the festival refused to enter it in the competition.' She hurried towards the door. 'Won't be long.'

Liberty served the string of customers buying last-minute sewing supplies and Christmas gifts. The patchwork cushion kits had been especially popular.

'I'm really looking forward to making these myself,' said a customer, buying two kits. 'I'll make one cushion for me and the other for a gift. It's quite special to receive something handmade, don't you think?'

'Absolutely.' Liberty smiled. An ambulance screeched past, making everyone glance outside. 'Would you like the cushion pads, too?'

'Yes, please. Save me making another trip. I've travelled twenty miles to come here, you know. It's such a treasure trove, this shop.'

The Button Hole had become a popular destination, drawing in customers from far and wide. Liberty served the line of customers as fast as she could, but cutting fabric was a slow process and she checked her watch, wishing Evie would hurry back. There must be an enormous queue at the post office: at this time of year everyone would be posting gifts and cards.

The shop bell rattled violently as someone threw open the door and hurtled in. Everyone in the shop turned to look.

'Liberty!' panted George. He put a pile of brown parcels down by the door.

Liberty frowned. What was he doing with Evie's quilts? And why did the packages look dirty and crumpled?

'Evie's had an accident!'

The rotary cutter fell from her hand, and memories of Carys's car crash fired through her head. 'What's happened?'

'She slipped on a patch of ice in the high street and hurt herself. An ambulance came.'

'What did she hurt? Is it serious?'

'I don't know any more than that, I'm afraid.'

'Does Jake know? I need to call him.' She picked up the phone.

George held one hand up. 'That's been done already. He's gone straight to the hospital.'

Panic gripped her. Evie was more than just her boss. If anything happened to her—

'Liberty? Liberty!'

George was standing in front of her. He held her by the shoulders. 'Don't worry. It was only a fall and she's in the best possible hands.'

'Right.' She tried to swallow but her mouth was dry, her throat tight.

'These parcels were on the ground where she fell. Where do you want me to put them?'

The quilts. 'They need posting. Today's the last post!' She glanced up at the clock on the wall and her heart sank.

'I'm afraid you've missed it,' said George. 'The post office closed half an hour ago.'

Chapter Eighteen

Saturday, 20 December

'You'd have thought all those quilts I was carrying would have cushioned my fall.' Evie looked ruefully at her sling.

Liberty smiled. She was so relieved Evie was all right and had only a broken arm. Her boss had been released from hospital earlier and was now sitting up in bed, her long hair spilling loose around her shoulders. Liberty had called round as soon as the Button Hole had closed.

'And the added bonus is I won't have to cook Christmas dinner now.' Evie's dimples flashed as she smiled.

'Too right,' said Jake. He came into the bedroom carrying a tray of hot drinks for them. 'You won't be doing anything but rest, given what could have—' His mouth snapped shut as if he'd said something he shouldn't, and he darted an anxious glance at Liberty.

Red spots darkened Evie's cheeks.

'What could have happened?' Liberty asked, puzzled.

'Nothing—'

'He meant—'

They had spoken in unison. They stopped and Evie blushed even harder.

Liberty glanced from one to the other before understanding dawned. 'Are you – pregnant?'

Evie nodded slowly.

Liberty gasped. 'Oh, Evie, that's wonderful!'

'It's early days,' said Evie. 'That's why I didn't want to say anything yet. The baby's due in the summer.'

Jake kissed the top of Evie's head. 'Now I've so successfully put my foot in it,' he said drily, 'I'll leave you two to it.'

Liberty hugged her friend. 'I won't breathe a word, I promise, and I'm so happy for you. You and Jake will make wonderful parents. Is that why you're getting married?'

Evie smiled. 'Actually, no. We'd already talked about it before I realised I was pregnant. But it does mean I'd like to get married soon.'

Liberty was thrilled for her friends. Yet the news derailed her, too. Natasha, and now Evie: she felt a piercing shot of envy. She tried to force that aside as another thought occurred. 'Did they check the baby was all right?'

'Yes. That's why I was in hospital so long. I had a scan and it's looking fine, thank goodness.'

'What a relief.'

'Do you know what happened to the quilts?' Evie asked hopefully.

Liberty hated to break the bad news. 'I'm afraid the post office was closed by the time I heard what had happened. George brought them to the shop.'

'Oh, no. That means we've missed the entry date.' Evie looked disappointed, but she quickly shrugged it off with her usual positivity. 'Oh, well. There'll be other quilt shows.'

'Not as big as this one, and not for a while.' Liberty thought of Brenda and how hard she'd worked to get hers finished in time. In fact, she'd been thinking about this all night.

'I'm sorry, Lib. Are you very disappointed?'

'Not for me. But for Brenda this show means a lot. I don't want to let her down.'

Evie's eyes were warm with sympathy. 'It's a shame, but there's nothing we can do now.'

'Actually, there is.'

'What?'

'I've had an idea,' Liberty went on. 'There's still time to deliver the quilts personally.'

'To the South of France?'

She nodded. 'I had a look online and I could fly there tomorrow, then back in time for Christmas.'

'That's a fab idea! Much safer than posting them.' Evie pulled a long strand of hair forward and absently wound the end around her fingers. 'But I thought you didn't fly.'

'I don't. Normally.' Liberty swallowed. 'But there were only a few seats left on the plane so I had to make a snap decision. I was feeling brave,' she added, with a not-so-brave smile. Her pulse quickened with fear.

Evie's eyes widened. 'You booked already?'

'I had to. Couldn't risk losing the last opportunity to get there in time.' She thought of Brenda and the hope in her eyes as she'd entrusted her quilt to her.

'Oh, Lib, are you sure you want to do this? I'm sure Brenda will understand if you explain what happened . . .'

'This is my month of being brave, remember?'

Liberty wanted to overcome this fear. Not being able to fly was preventing her from doing so many things she dreamed of. If Carys woke up she'd be so proud to learn she'd surmounted this huge obstacle. Perhaps they'd go to New York or Hollywood and visit all the places they'd seen in their favourite movies. 'I've booked to see someone today – a counsellor. He helped Brenda and he's going to do what he can to help me before I leave tomorrow.' As she spoke she checked her watch. She needed to get going.

'Wow, Lib. I'm in awe. This is huge. Let me pay for your flight, then. The postage costs would have been huge anyway. Are you sure you don't mind making the trip so close to Christmas?'

She thought of Alex. His flight home was booked for Tuesday, the day she returned. By the time she got home, he'd have left. This was just what she needed: a clean break would rupture the ties and help her move on to make a fresh start.

'I don't mind at all. But it will mean I can't work next week.' They'd planned to close the Button Hole on 23 December, so she'd miss the last two days.

'Don't worry about that.' Evie looked at her sling. 'Actually, I was thinking I might close a couple of days early because I can't do much one-handed. You've just helped me make that decision.'

Liberty smiled. 'There can't be many customers left

who haven't already been in. We've been so busy the last few weeks.'

'I know.' Evie giggled. 'It's been a really good month. Here, this is for you.' She handed her a cream envelope decorated with miniature gold acorns and oak leaves.

Inside was a Christmas card, which read:

To the best and bravest seamstress I know.
   Thank you for all your hard work throughout the year.
   Love, Evie xxx

'You shouldn't have,' Liberty said, holding the generous cash bonus Evie had also included. 'Thank you.'

'It's all true. You *are* the best, and you've been so brave with your challenge. I'm really proud of you – and Carys would be too.'

'I'm going to France to deliver the quilts, and I'm leaving tomorrow.'

Alex paused from wiping Charlie's paws and stared at Liberty. She was going away?

He'd just got back from Luc's, where he and Charlie had spent the afternoon being decorated in glittery pink capes and tiaras by Lottie. When he'd left, he'd said goodbye to Luc and Natasha because he was leaving soon. He'd believed he had a few days left before he said goodbye to Liberty. He'd never expected that *she*'d be the one to leave.

He put the towel down. 'Where will you stay?'

'I've booked a place in the village where the show is held.'

'Which village?'

'Tourmarin. I'm staying in a flat above a bookshop. It has views of the castle where the quilts will be displayed. And the drive from the airport shouldn't take too long.'

He felt his eyes widen. 'You're flying?'

'Yes.' He saw the effort it cost her to put on a brave face, and the fear she couldn't quite conceal. 'I'm not looking forward to the flight but I'm going to get through it. It's only short.'

Why was she doing this? He didn't need to ask. To help a friend. His chest tightened. How would she manage alone? What if she had a panic attack?

'Here, this is for you.' She handed him a large gift, wrapped in tissue paper and ribbon. 'Happy Christmas.'

He frowned. He hadn't bought her anything. He'd wanted to, had seen the perfect gift for her, but had resisted, telling himself she might get the wrong idea.

The parcel was soft and he had to unfold it before he recognised the orange and black quilt.

'You said they were your racing colours,' she explained, 'so I thought you might like to have it – to remind you.'

'Of my racing days?'

She nodded.

The only thing this would remind him of was her. The hours she'd spent hand-quilting it so the chevrons were softened by a pattern of waves and swirls.

'Thanks.' His voice sounded a little hoarse. He must

be coming down with a sore throat, he told himself. Couldn't be anything else.

'Charlie's going to stay with Evie, Jake and Smoke. Will you lock up the cottage before you leave?'

'No, I'll leave the door wide open and the three bears will be waiting for you when you return.'

She punched him playfully on the arm. 'It was nice meeting you, Alex. I'm sorry you didn't find your half-sister.'

He didn't reply. There was a look in her eyes he couldn't quite decipher. Guarded. Haunted. Was it fear, or something else?

She went upstairs to finish packing and he found himself alone in the kitchen. He stared unseeingly at Charlie, who was gobbling down his dinner. Why was he so shocked at her news? Because the home bird he'd met a month ago would never have had the courage to make this trip alone?

Yet he'd watched Liberty grow and change over the last few weeks. He knew she was a different person now. And he knew what lengths she'd go to for her friends. This was typical of her: always looking after everyone else. Anyway, what did it matter to him? He'd be leaving soon, too, going to France to spend Christmas with his family.

He heard her moving about upstairs. Who would know if she got there safely? And if she got home? Who would be looking out for her? He went up and knocked on her bedroom door.

'Yeah?'

He went in. A battered brown suitcase that looked a hundred years old was open on the bed. In it was a quilt, some clothes, and she was squeezing in her sewing bag. Another case filled with quilts lay open on the floor. 'Lib, are you sure this is a good idea?' he asked.

She stopped what she was doing. 'You don't have faith in me to do it?'

'I do have faith. I just . . .'

How did he explain this feeling? It wasn't rational, this knot in his chest, this worry because she was alone and he . . . cared.

'I know it's a big thing for you. It'll be your biggest challenge yet, won't it?'

She nodded.

'And this woman—'

'Brenda.'

'She's not exactly a lifelong friend, is she? How long have you known her – two weeks?'

Her eyes narrowed. 'It doesn't matter how long I've known her. This is really important to her,' she said defensively. Then she sighed. 'Anyway, that's not the only reason I'm doing this. Fear of flying is something I've wanted to conquer for a long time. It's held me back from seeing so many places and doing so many things. I don't want to be restricted any more.'

'But you don't have to do it. I mean, I admire all you've achieved this month, you know I do, but you don't have to say yes to everything. Sometimes it's okay to walk away.'

She picked up a pair of pyjamas and folded them

carefully, before putting them into the case and smoothing them flat. 'I know.'

The only sound was the quiet creaking and gurgling of the radiator.

'Will you text me when you arrive?' he asked. 'Let me know you got there safely.'

There was that look in her eyes again. What was it?

The corner of her lip curved. 'Why?'

'I'd just like to know you're okay, that's all,' he said. He went to leave.

His hand was on the door when she said his name and he stopped. He turned back and her gaze connected with his. 'I want to do this,' she said. 'It's important to me. And not just for the challenge. It's a demon I have to face.'

Admiration filled him. She didn't need him. She was courageous and determined, and he knew how proud she'd feel if she managed to do this by herself.

And he understood now what he'd seen in her eyes. She was telling him goodbye.

Sunday, 21 December

'You won't believe where I'm going today, Car.'

Liberty squeezed her friend's hand. She was excited about the trip. Nervous, but excited too, and she clung to that excitement, embracing it, welcoming it. She wondered if she would have felt the same a month ago, or if her fear of the unknown would have overshadowed everything else.

'I'm going to Provence. To a beautiful hilltop village in the Lubéron. I've seen pictures on the internet and it's gorgeous.'

She paused, studying Carys's still features, trying to imagine what her friend would want to know. What she was going to wear would be top of the list. 'I've checked the weather over there and it's cold but sunny so I'm wearing a jumper, jeans and knee-high boots to travel in, and I've packed a long dress – the green one with roses – in case I need to look smart. French women are always smart and chic, aren't they? Plus I have to deliver the quilts to a château and no one should turn up at a French château looking scruffy, eh, Car?'

One of the machines Carys was hooked up to blinked steadily. She wished her friend would wake up. She'd wished it so many times over the last six months but she'd never wished as hard as she did now.

Taking a deep breath, she forged on with her cheery chatter: 'I'm hiring a car at the airport and it's about an hour's drive from there. Can you imagine that? I've never driven abroad before.' She bit her lip, then admitted quietly, 'I'm really scared, Car.'

How would she find the place? She didn't even speak French. How would she buy food or navigate French road signs?

Deep breath, Liberty, she told herself, and remembered her phone call to Brenda, when she'd updated her on what had happened. This show meant everything to Brenda.

'But the hardest thing,' she confessed quietly, 'is knowing I'll never see Alex again.'

Her heart was begging her not to go, but her head knew this was the sensible thing to do. When she got back he'd have left.

'It's for the best,' she said, for her own benefit more than anything, and blew out a slow breath, trying to dispel the nerves, and reminding herself of all she'd achieved this month. 'And it's the perfect way to finish the challenge. A trip abroad to a beautiful place. With any luck it will be sunny, and I might even get a sneak peek at the other quilts as they're arriving for the show.' She rubbed her friend's hand. 'And don't worry, Car, I'll be back in a couple of days to tell you all about it.'

Liberty gripped the armrests as the plane began to trundle away from the airport and towards the runway. Her palms were sticky, her chest felt tight. She tried to do the breathing exercises she'd learned, but it was difficult when her eyes were fixed on the door, which was locked. This was what she'd dreaded: the walls closing in on her, making escape impossible, the air thinning so it was difficult to breathe. She didn't want to make a scene. She didn't want a repeat of what had happened last time. But last time the blinding fear had swamped her, the certainty that something terrible was going to happen—

Breathe, she told herself. You've got this far. You can do this.

The plane turned sharply, lined itself up on the runway, and stopped. Around her the other passengers seemed relaxed as they flicked through magazines and munched sweets. No one else appeared to share her fear. Boarding the plane, her legs had been so shaky she wasn't sure how she'd managed to climb the steps – but she had. And as she'd reached the door, she'd glanced over her shoulder, giving herself a silent pat on the back for getting that far.

It was all going to plan, even if it felt as if disaster was only a moment away. That's just the anxiety speaking, she reminded herself. You *will* arrive safely, the doors will open and you will get off. She closed her eyes and visualised this happening, then imagined the glowing sense of achievement she'd feel.

The plane began to move. In no time at all it gathered speed, the acceleration pushed her back in her seat, and she knew there were only seconds left until it left the ground. Her pulse raced. Her clothes were sticking to her. Then it lifted into the air.

Her heart was in her mouth as she watched the grass and the buildings fall away. Seconds passed – or minutes, who knew? – and she had to force herself to breathe, her fingers were still curled tight around the armrest. But the feeling of impending doom gradually weakened, and when the flight attendant's sing-song voice came over the loudspeaker she relaxed.

We're in the air and nothing bad has happened, she told herself, astounded. Amazed. She wanted to clap her hands because she'd got over the biggest hurdle.

'Everything okay?' asked a flight attendant. She'd explained to the crew about her fear of flying and they'd been checking on her at regular intervals.

'Yes,' she said, hearing the surprise in her own voice.

He winked and moved on. Liberty plugged in her earphones and listened to the audiobook she'd brought to distract herself. It wouldn't be long before she was landing in France and punching the air in celebration. It had been really important that she made this trip alone, and she had no regrets about that. She was proud she'd done it.

Still, there was one person she secretly wished was there to witness her achievement. Alex would be so proud.

Chapter Nineteen

A few hours later, Liberty picked up the key to the rental flat from the bookshop owner, then went upstairs. She unlocked the door and took it all in. It was gorgeous. The big windows looked on to the village square on one side, and she could see people sitting outside the café in the sunshine, wearing warm coats, scarves and sunglasses. She'd go for a drink there later, she promised herself. And from the bedroom window at the back of the flat she would see Tourmarin Château where, tomorrow, she'd deliver the quilts. Perched on a mound, the castle was simple yet majestic. Only a couple of fields away, it looked close, but she'd have to drive because the quilts were too heavy to carry that far.

Liberty quickly unpacked, changed into her dress, and texted Alex: *Arrived safely. Only made one mistake and went the wrong way round a roundabout. (Don't worry, nobody saw.) Going to café now.*

Her flight had arrived on time and, thankfully, all her luggage too, including the quilts. Propping her leather case on top of the shiny red one she'd borrowed from Evie, she'd wheeled them both across to the car-hire desk and joined a long queue snaking out of the door.

She shuffled forward, but the queue was getting longer, stretching out behind her, and people were becoming agitated.

'It's very busy,' she'd said to the lady next in line.

The woman replied in a language Liberty didn't understand – Russian perhaps? The woman tried again in broken English this time. 'Car' and 'strike', Liberty thought she'd said, but her accent was so strong the rest was incomprehensible.

Liberty had smiled politely and turned away, telling herself the car-hire desk was probably busy because it was nearly Christmas and everyone was simply trying to get home for the holidays.

Anyway, she'd reassured herself, she'd booked her car so there shouldn't be a problem. And there hadn't been. Once she finally reached the front of the line it had all been straightforward, and now she'd arrived she could finally relax.

The bookshop was closing as she made her way downstairs and the owner wished her a *bonne soirée*. Zipping up her jacket, Liberty picked a table outside and sat down. All around, people were enjoying their apéritifs. She ordered a drink and sat back, smiling to herself, still high on the satisfaction of having made the journey alone. Wasn't it pure sophistication, to be sipping red wine, watching the world go by, with jazz music playing in the background? Lots of her well-travelled friends would have thought nothing of making this trip, but for her it was a milestone and she was so proud of herself. She was definitely out of her comfort zone now – and loving every moment of it. She looked around, soaking up the magical scene.

The village square sparkled with tasteful white fairy lights and a large Christmas tree. Liberty spotted a man wearing a beret – a real beret! – and tiny black-rimmed spectacles that looked both intellectual and chic. She loved the sound of people speaking French. It was such a musical language, so expressive and romantic. If only Alex could see her now.

She tried to picture herself living in a place like this where everything was exciting, foreign and new to her. Imagine the possibilities. All the people she might meet, the new experiences she'd have. Although she couldn't speak French, she was confident she'd pick up the language soon enough. After all, Carys's family spoke Welsh at home and she'd picked up a few phrases without any problem. To think, if she'd let her fear stop her, she would never have seen this gorgeous place, with its narrow streets and pretty boutiques.

The challenge had changed her. She liked the person she'd become. Open-minded. Curious to try new things. Confident. Living life to the full.

Sewing was still her favourite thing, but she would have missed out on so many adventures if she hadn't pushed herself this month. She pictured the bouquet that had triggered all of this, and wondered if the sender had seen the change in her. Their gift had gone further than they could ever have imagined it would.

Her phone buzzed with a message from Alex: *Glad you got there. I left you a gift under the Christmas tree.*

She smiled, touched, and wondered where he was right now? At Damselfly Cottage, packing? Or was he out, having fun? She typed: *Let me know when you arrive in France.*

The waiter brought her glass of red wine and a bowl of peanuts. She thanked him and he answered in English, 'You're welcome.'

Damn, her accent must have given her away.

'You're visiting from America?' he asked, tucking his tray under his arm. He was handsome with dark hair, and seemed happy to stop and linger.

'From England. I'm delivering quilts for the show.' He looked blank. 'At the château?'

'Ah, yes! The festival. Yes, we have a lot of visitors for this after Christmas.'

She smiled. 'It's very famous. I'm so excited to be here.' It was just a shame she wouldn't see the show. Maybe next year she could come back. Perhaps with Evie.

'So you're . . .' the waiter glanced around '. . . here with a friend?'

'No,' she said, feeling ridiculously proud. 'I'm on my own.'

He grinned. 'Ah, well, my name is Louis, and if you need someone to show you around the village, you know where to find me.'

Wow, he was forward. No English reserve here, then. But she was flattered. 'Thank you. That's very kind.'

He was called away to serve another customer and she sat back, savouring her wine. As the sun set, the vibrant colours reminded her of Van Gogh's painting *Café Terrace at Night*. The indigo night sky, the warm glow of the café and the burgundy-coloured chairs and tables, the twin-kling Christmas lights strung around the square. An image formed in her mind of a new quilt design: using deep shades of blue for the background, she could appliqué a cluster of wonky squares in wine-coloured shades, with pale centres cut from glittery gold and white fabric that would take on a starry brightness.

Her phone pinged again. Alex had replied: *Why?*

She blushed. Good question. Why indeed?

Because she missed him and this was an excuse to prolong contact with him before they lost touch for good. She didn't write that. Instead, she typed: *Because I'd like to know you arrived safely. Like you did with me.*

He replied: *But my family will raise the alarm if I don't show up.*

Whereas she was alone, she interpreted. Her smile faded.

And it hit her then like a block of ice: all his concern about her arriving safely hadn't been because he cared but because he pitied her. Just as he'd pitied his half-sister and the woman whose letters his father had ignored.

She switched off her phone and slipped it back into her handbag. She sipped her wine and tried to refocus on the scene around her. But the magic had gone.

Monday, 22 December

The château was beautiful. The sandy gold stone rose up in turrets and towers, and glinted in the winter sun.

Majestic conifers stood proud around it, like green spear-heads, and as Liberty crossed the courtyard dozens of flags fluttered in the wind, representing the nationalities of all those who'd entered the quilt festival. Unlike the British castles she'd visited, which always had a distinctly damp and chilly edge, this one was well heated. It was the perfect backdrop for exhibiting quilts.

She deposited all of the quilts with their paperwork, and texted Evie and Brenda to say they'd been safely delivered. Then she took a quick peek at those that had already been hung for display.

'Beautiful, aren't they?' said a woman, holding a phone and a clipboard.

Liberty guessed she was one of the organisers super-vising the show. 'Amazing. I especially love these,' she said, pointing to a couple of Japanese Sashiko panels with their characteristically bold stitches and shimmering fabrics.

The woman eyed her appraisingly. 'Would you be inter-ested in helping as a steward at the show? One or two helpers have caught the flu so we're short of volunteers.'

Her heart jumped at the prospect – but her hopes instantly died. 'I'm afraid I won't be here for the show,' she said, 'but I'm free today, if you need any help setting up.'

The woman's eyes lit. 'That would be *formidable.*'

Liberty had already done a quick tour of the village this morning when she'd gone out to buy bread and pastries for breakfast, and had been planning to browse the gift shops and boutiques this afternoon. The prospect of helping here was far more appealing. She'd get a sneak preview of some of the quilts.

The lady led her to one of the château's large reception rooms and introduced her to the other volunteers. The day passed quickly as Liberty carefully unpacked quilts, hung and labelled them. She was surprised to see how far some entries had travelled, and it was fun chatting to other quilt lovers in broken English about the different techniques and fabrics that had been used. During a short break in the afternoon Liberty checked her phone. She had a message from the airline marked URGENT.

As she read it, her face fell.

Her return flight was cancelled due to a strike. Liberty's hand shook a little as she put her phone down.

That meant she could be stuck here for Christmas.

She asked the other volunteers if they knew about the strike. They did. Apparently there had been rumblings that it might happen. Perhaps that explained the long queue at the car-hire desk when she'd arrived. 'Will there be any trains running?' Liberty asked.

They shook their heads. 'All the transport workers are on strike. There'll be no trains or buses. Nothing.'

'What about my rental car? Could I use it to drive home?'

She dug out the number and one of her fellow volunteers called the rental company for her but shook her head. 'They need the car back tomorrow. They said you can leave it here and they'll collect it, but they can't extend your booking and they won't allow you to drive it out of the country.'

The woman next to her sent her a look of sympathy.

Liberty's shoulders sagged. 'Looks like I'm stuck here for Christmas, then.'

She'd better email her landlord and ask if she could stay a few days extra. And she'd have to go to the supermarket and stock up on food to see her through, perhaps buy some more clothes, too.

Breathe, Liberty. It's just Christmas. Think of it as part of your challenge.

It wasn't as risky as taking in a lodger, or as humiliating as her nightmare date with Sean and his vengeful ex, and it was nothing like as scary as flying. Her chin lifted with resolve.

She could do this.

Her phone was ringing insistently. In the car park at the supermarket Liberty put down her shopping and rooted in her bag until she found it. 'Alex?' she answered.

'Have you heard about the strike?' The urgency in his voice told her he was worried.

'Yeah. My flight's cancelled.'

'So is mine.'

She pictured him alone in Damselfly Cottage. 'What will you do? How will you get home for Christmas?'

'Not sure yet. Hitchhike, maybe.'

She couldn't tell if he was joking. 'Feel free to stay at the cottage. I don't mind.'

'I'll find a way. What about you?' he asked.

'The owner of the flat said I can stay here an extra

four days. Hopefully the strike will have ended by then.'

There was a pause before he asked, 'Are you all right, Liberty?'

'Of course I am.'

'It's just – I thought you might be worried. About spending Christmas alone.'

She smiled, touched by the concern in his voice. 'I was at first. But now I'm actually looking forward to it. For one thing, it means I can put off getting on a plane for a few more days, and for another . . .' She hadn't been looking forward to Christmas this year. Although it was really kind of Carys's family to have invited her, spending the day with them would have been a stark reminder of her best friend's absence. She would have put on a brave face, knowing their grief was far more acute than hers, but being alone might actually be easier. More relaxed. 'Well, it means I can do what I like.'

It was an opportunity to indulge herself. She'd bought lots of delicious food: duck breast, rainbow-coloured Swiss chard, cheeses, bread and patisseries, and wine. She'd used Evie's Christmas bonus to treat herself to a couple of new outfits, and she'd bought a stash of new fabric at the château so she had plenty of sewing to keep her busy on Christmas Day when everyone else was with their families. She was planning to go for a walk and soak up the beautiful views, and in the evening she'd call Carys's mum, Evie and Natasha. She'd wish Lottie a merry Christmas – she knew the little girl would be giddy with excitement about reindeer landing on the roof and the new doll's house Santa was bringing her.

It would be fine. She was getting good at challenges. Christmas by herself would be a doddle.

Tuesday, 23 December

Alex slid into the hire car and set off, joining the motorway and heading south. He reminded himself again that Liberty had somewhere to stay, she had food, and she'd assured him she was all right. But his thoughts kept returning to her.

As he joined the queue for the ferry.

As he gazed out at the turbulent, dark water.

As the car ate up hundreds of kilometres of motorway, heading south.

He knew he was lucky. He'd managed to get a car, and he'd booked himself onto one of the last ferry crossings before everything stopped. As long as he kept driving, he'd arrive at his mum's house in plenty of time for the festivities. Others around the country would not be so fortunate: the French news reports were already filled with accounts of people stranded far from home.

Like Liberty.

He hated to think of her alone. She'd said she was fine, but he knew she was being brave. And no one should have to be brave at Christmas. No one should be alone. She must be missing Charlie, missing home. He thought of her cottage and the tree they'd decorated, which now had one solitary gift placed beneath it, waiting for her.

He pressed the accelerator pedal and urged the car to go a little faster.

'Alex! You made it home in time,' said his mother, when he finally arrived.

He kissed her, he shook Bernard's hand, he answered their questions about the long journey he'd made.

They ushered him into the kitchen, a spacious room with a cosy, inviting feel. A bottle of red wine was open, and the smell of meat and garlic filled the air as his mother opened the oven.

'Take your coat off and sit down,' she said. 'You're just in time for dinner.'

She placed the casserole dish on the table and his stomach rumbled at the sight of the delicious-looking stew. It was tempting. After driving all night and most of the day he was stiff and his shoulder ached. A glass of wine and a good meal would have been perfect right now.

'Sit, sit!' his mum repeated.

'Actually,' he said heavily, 'I can't stay.'

She stopped. 'What?'

'I have to go.'

'But you've only just arrived. And it's Christmas Eve tomorrow.' His mum stared at him.

Usually he was the one who brought everyone together, who made sure everything was organised and ready. He helped with wrapping last-minute gifts, preparing the food. Tomorrow morning his brothers would arrive with their partners and families and the festivities would begin.

343

There'd be a family meal in the evening, followed by midnight mass.

'I know. Which is why I have to go. This is important.' He held her gaze. He'd turned this over and over in his mind all the way here; now he was certain of what he had to do.

She looked shocked. 'More important than Christmas with your family?'

'It's a friend. She needs me.'

His mum and Bernard exchanged a glance. 'Will you be back tomorrow?'

'I can't promise. I'm sorry.'

Liberty had the television on in the background while she cooked. If her brain heard the language, she'd thought, words and phrases might subliminally filter in and she'd learn French by osmosis.

It wasn't working.

The newsreader was jabbering on about the strike, *la grève*, Liberty had understood that much, but she still didn't know what had caused it or why the transport workers were protesting. She hadn't understood the weather forecast either, but she'd seen the big yellow suns dotted across the map of south-eastern France so she knew it would continue to be cold and sunny, which was wonderful. The bold cobalt sky and bright sunlight were so uplifting, and her flat was well heated and cosy.

She flipped the potatoes over and checked the duck in the oven. Now she'd got over her initial shock, she was quite looking forward to spending Christmas in Provence. She'd begun work on what she'd nicknamed her Van Gogh quilt, hand-stitching crooked squares of wine red and sunset orange onto a deep blue background (and she could picture the glittery gold fabric in Evie's shop that would finish it off perfectly).

The sharp ring of a doorbell interrupted her thoughts and made her jump.

She turned. It couldn't be her door, surely. She knew no one here. Then again, perhaps it was the flat's owner come to check on her. She switched off the hob and went to the living room window. Looking down, she saw the top of a dark head of hair – messy hair – and her heart jumped. She opened the window.

'Alex?' He looked up. Oh, that smile. Her spirits soared, and something unravelled in her. 'What are you doing here?'

'Let me in and I'll tell you.'

'Just a minute.'

She ran downstairs and flung open the door. She couldn't believe he was there, standing right in front of her. His chin was dark with stubble and there were shadows beneath his eyes. She wanted to fling her arms around him. Instead, she tempered her excitement and offered her cheek to him.

He laughed. 'You've already adopted the French ways.'

'Absolutely.' She showed him into the apartment, then asked again, 'Why are you here?'

His deep brown gaze met hers and held. 'I didn't like to think of you here alone for Christmas.'

Her heart sank. There it was again: pity.

Her pride didn't like this. Didn't like it one bit.

'But what about your family? Aren't they expecting you to be there tomorrow?' Natasha had told her that Christmas Eve was when the celebrations began in France.

'Let's talk about that in a moment. Can I have a coffee? I've driven a long way.'

'Of course. I was just cooking dinner. If you give me a minute I'll put more potatoes on. There'll be enough to share.'

'Thanks. I'm starving.'

She showed him where the coffee was, then tipped frozen potato cubes into the frying pan and prepared a large bowl of salad. His unexpected arrival had sparked a flurry of emotions in her. She couldn't believe he'd driven here, that he'd thought of her. She was so excited to see him. Like Charlie at the prospect of a walk, she was practically running round in circles. Calm down, Liberty, keep your cool.

'How did you find me?' she asked. 'I didn't give you the address.'

'You said your flat was above a bookshop. In a village this size, it wasn't difficult to find.'

She busied herself, getting plates and glasses, asking about his journey and the strike, all the time deliberately avoiding stopping and having to face him. How was she supposed to get over him now he was here, beside her? The night of the ball had made her realise how strong her attraction to him was, and although she was flattered that he'd come, she felt vulnerable too.

He didn't feel the same way. He hadn't come because

he missed her, but because he felt sorry for her, alone in France at Christmas.

'Liberty?'

She shook the frying pan of potatoes. She didn't want his pity, but she was so thrilled to see him her heart was spinning. She wanted him to leave – but she also wanted him to stay. The contradictions made her feel dizzy. She snatched a handful of cutlery and set it on the table with quick, frenetic movements.

'Lib, stop. Please.'

'Hm?' She straightened a knife.

'Liberty, look at me.' He was so close she caught a hint of coffee.

She stopped. 'What?'

'What's wrong?' he asked gently.

'Nothing. I'm just surprised, that's all. You didn't say you were coming. You could have texted or called, you could have warned me.'

'You're unhappy that I'm here?'

She wanted to laugh this off, to deny it. But that would be the easy way out, the coward's way. She refused to be a coward.

So she forced herself to meet his gaze. 'I'm thrilled that you're here, but it wasn't necessary. I don't want your pity, Alex.'

'Pity?'

'You keep saying you're concerned for me, that I have no one to check I arrived safely and no one to spend Christmas with, but I do. I have friends. It's just that this year I'm here and they're in England.' She took a deep breath. 'I don't need you to turn up and do the knight-in-shining-armour routine to rescue me. I'm fine on my own. Perfectly fine. No pity required.'

He looked stunned. 'That isn't why I'm here. I know you're fine. I . . .'

She waited, eventually biting back a sigh when he didn't speak. He didn't know what to say because she was right and he didn't want to admit it.

He pushed a hand through his hair, and she snapped. 'You always do that! Why?'

'Do what?'

'Mess your hair up. It's so annoying!'

'You know what I find annoying? You always have pieces of thread on your clothes!' He picked one off her sleeve to prove his point, then grinned affectionately.

She smiled too, the tension defused a little.

'I don't pity you, Liberty,' he said finally. And the look in his eyes was so earnest, she almost believed him. 'Far from it.'

'Then why are you here?' she asked quietly. Although she tried to stop them, her hopes lifted.

Seconds passed, feeling like minutes. Finally he said, 'Because I couldn't stop thinking about you.'

Her hopes sank. 'Feeling sorry for me.'

'No!'

'Then what?'

He appeared to fight a silent battle before he admitted, 'I wanted to be with you. I want to spend Christmas with you.'

She couldn't hide her surprise. 'Really?'

He nodded. What did this mean? He'd said he wasn't interested in a relationship or commitment.

'As a friend,' he added quickly. 'I think you'll enjoy it – to experience a French Christmas first hand. Different traditions and customs. And I want you to meet my family. You'll like them.'

There was a stunned pause. 'You're inviting me to your family's home for Christmas?'

'Wouldn't you have done the same for me if I'd been in England over Christmas? Included me in your plans?'

Of course she would. They both knew it. It was in her nature to look after everyone around her.

The timer rang, making them both turn. 'Dinner's ready,' she said, though her mind wasn't on the duck or potatoes any more.

'Why don't you think about it while we eat?' he said quietly.

They sat down and he took his jumper off, revealing a pink shirt. 'It's warm in here.'

'Toasty.' She smiled. 'I can't work out how to turn the heat down.'

The same could be said of her relationship with him.

They shared the duck, the potatoes and salad. After, she offered him bread and cheese, but he shook his head.

'So what do you say?' he asked. 'Do you want to stay here over Christmas, or come with me and spend it with my family?'

'They won't mind? They don't even know me.'

'They won't mind at all.'

She hesitated. It would be strange spending Christmas

with strangers, but it was also tempting. She was curious to experience the festivities in another culture.

'Go on, Lib.' His eyes twinkled. 'Come with me. It'll be fun.'

'I was going to count it as a tick in my book – spending Christmas alone.'

'Can't it be a tick to spend it with a French family? Wouldn't that be a new experience?'

He was right. It was better than spending it alone, sewing. In fact, now she saw that her plans hadn't been brave at all: she'd simply been reverting to her default settings.

She grinned. 'Let's do it.'

'Sure?'

'Yes. What was it you said? *Carpe diem*. It'll be fun to experience a French Christmas.' And she'd get to spend more time with him, a devilish voice whispered. She happily ignored it.

'A *Provençal* Christmas,' he corrected.

'Is that different from the rest of France?'

'A little,' he said, as they cleared their dishes. 'We have our own traditions around here, which are unique to the area. The thirteen desserts, for example.'

'Thirteen desserts? I'm sold already.' She put her plate by the sink and turned to him. 'And, Alex?'

'Yes?'

Their eyes met and held. 'Thank you,' she said.

'What for?'

'Coming here, inviting me to your family's home. I'm sorry if I was ungracious before, but I hate the idea of being the object of anyone's pity.'

'I don't pity you, Liberty. You're the bravest person I know.' A whirlpool of joy began to spin inside her. 'Most people don't acknowledge their own fears. They don't talk about them openly and they certainly don't take steps to face them and overcome them.'

'How do you mean?'

'I'm thinking of my father, who was afraid of responsibility, my mother, who's afraid of being in the limelight. I know people who are afraid of social situations, or being alone, or of confrontation. No one talks about these things but we're all afraid of something. We keep our fears to ourselves, like shameful secrets, but you are open about yours. You've faced them all and defeated them, like a dragon-hunter.'

'Dragon-*slayer*,' she corrected, with a giggle. Pride swelled in her and she didn't know what to say. There was a long pause. Then she asked curiously, 'So what's your fear?'

His brow creased as he thought about this. 'I don't know . . .'

She laughed. 'Of course, you're used to racing at three hundred miles per hour. You're fearless.'

While Liberty was in the kitchen, Alex called his mum to let her know he was coming home – and bringing a friend. He was excited she was coming with him, excited for his family to meet her. His mum was delighted, as he'd known she would be, and not just because he'd be home. He heard the hope in her voice as she asked about Liberty.

'Mum, it's not like that. She's just a friend. We'll sleep in separate rooms.' That night at Poppy Cottage burned his mind, but he hurriedly quashed the memory. He'd made a promise and he intended to keep his word.

When he'd finished the call he went over to the window, which looked on to the village square. The tall Christmas tree glittered in the night and the cafés were still busy even though it was late.

He could hardly believe Liberty had thought he pitied her. It couldn't be further from the truth. He admired her so much. He knew she'd been excited to arrive in France and discover this picturesque village and the castle – he'd heard it in her voice when he'd called her. But he'd also heard her vulnerability and bravado when she'd realised she was stuck here over the holiday, and it had stirred something in him.

Not pity, though.

What, then? Protectiveness? A sense of responsibility? A nagging sensation that he wasn't where he should be, that he needed to be where she was? Whatever, in the end it had won out and he hadn't been able to stay away.

He was simply doing the right thing, he told himself. He thought of the desperate, yellowed letters from M to his father. Alex refused to be the kind of man who abandoned people when they needed him.

And now he was here, he knew he was where he should be.

Liberty was his friend and they were going to spend Christmas together, that was all. He'd be with his family, and she wouldn't be alone. It was simply the convenient solution to a problem.

Liberty finished tidying, then went back into the lounge. She smoothed down her dress, a little tense, a little nervous. For the third time in three days her plans had been upended by unforeseen events and she'd had to adapt accordingly.

'When do you want to leave?' she asked. 'Tonight?'

Alex was standing by the window. It was late. The square below was noisy with laughter and chatter, footsteps fading. As she joined him, she looked outside and guessed the bars were closing.

'I drove all night and all day,' he said. 'It would be safer to wait until the morning – if that's all right with you?'

'You want to sleep here?'

A beat passed. 'Yes.'

Her heart flipped.

Immediately, she tried to quell the excitement. He'd rejected her only the other day, and she agreed that keeping her distance from him was the rational thing to do. The sensible thing.

But she wasn't feeling rational or sensible right now.

She felt daring. Audacious. Reckless.

And she wanted him.

She hadn't felt this temptation, this longing with Ethan. What she felt for Alex was so intense, so visceral, so different from anything she'd ever felt before – in any of her past relationships. It frightened her, but it was also exciting. Enticing.

'How many beds are there here?' he asked.

'One.'

'Ah.'

Her lips curved. Mischief tugged. Desire spiralled through her.

He looked around the room. 'I could sleep on the sofa.'

'You could . . .'

There must have been something in her tone because he turned back, one eyebrow raised. Their eyes connected and in that glance an unspoken message was communicated. She read his surprise, immediately replaced with caution. It made her smile. He was so honourable, always keen to do the right thing.

But tonight she wasn't interested in doing the right thing.

She stepped forward. 'But you don't have to,' she finished softly.

The air crackled with tension.

His eyes darkened as she reached to touch his lips. She traced them with the pad of her finger and hunger stormed her, deliciously sweet and tempting. When she lifted her lids to look at him, he seemed a little stunned. His eyes were dark as a forest night, and his breathing was ragged. She felt a surge of satisfaction.

'Liberty,' he whispered, 'I promised you it wouldn't happen again.' His brow was furrowed, and she could see he was fighting a battle with himself.

'But you want it, don't you?' Her voice was low. Seductive. She knew what *she* wanted. She was certain in her mind. She rested her hands on his shoulders. Their mouths were so close she could almost feel his warm lips on hers. 'There's a spark. You feel it too, don't you?'

'You know I do. But we mustn't . . .' His hands came around her waist, and their touch sent a dart of electricity shooting through her. 'I won't stick around. You know that.'

She held his gaze. 'That's okay.'

'It is?'

She smiled. 'I don't expect any more from you than you're willing to give.' She brushed the hair back from his face, giving her words time to settle.

'But – but you said you wanted a man who—'

She didn't let him finish. Need was making her impatient. 'I did. I still do. But that doesn't mean I can't have fun while I'm waiting for my Dream Guy to show up.'

She kissed him. It was as exhilarating – more so, even – than she remembered.

'I don't want to hurt you, Liberty. I don't want you to be disappointed because this won't lead to what you want.'

The regret in his voice made her heart fold up. He made it sound like she was fragile – but her challenge had changed her. Made her curious, more adventurous, eager to try things she'd previously written off as too dangerous. Now she was willing to take a chance. She was braver. And propositioning a man who wouldn't commit was a pretty brave thing to do, wasn't it?

They would be good together, she was certain of it. This might give her a taste of something she would never otherwise have experienced. For once she wanted to live in the moment and simply enjoy it.

'Don't look so worried. I'm sure this is what I want, and I'm brave now, remember?' She smiled mischievously. 'Anyway, this will count as a tick in my book.'

He gave an incredulous laugh. 'I'm not sure how I feel about that.'

'Well, how do you feel about this?' She dropped a trail of light, teasing kisses along his jaw and his throat. She unbuttoned his shirt and kissed his chest. He sucked in air and held her waist, as if to steady himself. She placed her palms flat against his torso and his muscles tightened beneath her touch.

'Lib, you're sure?' His voice was low and throaty, as if he was clinging to the last threads of his self-control.

'Very sure.'

His gaze locked with hers.

Finally, he seemed to be satisfied with what he saw there, because he closed his eyes in surrender, dipped his head and kissed her. Fiercely. Passionately. She lit up inside like a glittering chandelier.

He kissed her as if he'd waited an age for this, as if it meant the world to him too. She held on and poured all her longing into that kiss. He touched her cheek and she closed her eyes, savoured the heat of his fingers on her skin, heard his breathing quicken, felt her heart drum against her ribs. Everything else shrank away. She wanted this so much.

Of course he wasn't just a tick in her book, he was so much more.

But this would have to be enough.

356

Chapter Twenty

God, it felt good. To kiss her. To finally kiss her and let his body have the closeness it had been craving for so long. Alex wrapped an arm around her waist and drew her against him, burying his hand in her hair, filling his senses with the scent of her, her heat, her softness.

He'd been so sure he shouldn't do this, that he was wrong for her. It hadn't occurred to him that she might want a light fling. But Liberty McKenzie knew her mind. And, anyway, who was he kidding? A man would have to be made of steel to resist her. He wanted this, he wanted her.

He pushed her hair aside and kissed her neck. She gave a soft moan and tipped her head for him. The skin beneath her ear was pale and smooth, and he felt her pulse quicken beneath his lips, heard her breathing become shallow and rapid. His muscles coiled tight. She pressed herself against him, her hips locking with his, a perfect fit.

She'd already tugged his shirt open. Now he reached behind her to unbutton her dress. His hands were unsteady and he fumbled with the buttons, relieved when they sprang free. He kissed her again and as he did he drew the velvet fabric down, releasing her arms, and letting it fall in a puddle at her feet.

His breath hitched. He ran his gaze over her and whispered her name. Her eyes burned into him, dark with desire. His hands shaped the indent of her waist and the swell of her hips. She wasn't just beautiful, she was perfection.

And tonight he wanted to find a way to show her – without words.

Wednesday, 24 December

Alex opened one eye. He was lying on his front and his body was still so heavy from sleep, he couldn't even find the strength to turn over. The faint hum of cars and people's voices carried in the air, and it took him a moment to work out where he was.

When he did, he felt a jolt of panic. What had he done?

He remembered Liberty's words – *That doesn't mean I can't have fun while I'm waiting for my Dream Guy* – and relaxed again. The physical pull between them had been so strong that it was a relief not to have to fight it any more. He was only planning to stay in Provence for a week or so, and a week was too short for anything more to develop. Intimacy, closeness: they had no place in his life. Especially now, when he wasn't sure which direction his career was going to take him. By the end of this week the passion would have burned itself out, Liberty would return to Willowbrook and he – well, he'd go wherever life took him.

He stirred. Liberty was staring out of the window,

apparently in a daydream. She smiled when she saw he was awake and murmured, 'Morning, sleepyhead.'

Her face was soft from sleep, her hair tousled and spilled across her bare shoulders. 'You must have been exhausted from the long drive,' she said, moving closer so her face was next to his.

His gaze dipped to her full lips. 'Not just the drive.' He smiled because it had been late – very late – before they'd succumbed to sleep last night.

She propped herself up on one elbow and traced the scar lines across his shoulder. He let his eyes fall shut as her light touch lulled him.

'These injuries must have been so painful,' she said quietly.

He opened his eyes again, and pictured the cross-hatch pattern of lines and ridges on his shoulder and the ugly thick line that marked his spine. 'They look more dramatic than they were.'

'Don't believe you.' She bent to kiss his spine and he savoured the sensations. Her lips were warm on his skin and her hair brushed over him.

Then she lay down next to him and said, 'Tell me about the crash.'

He rolled over and gazed up at the chalk-white ceiling. 'Which one?'

She tucked herself against him. 'Both.'

'The first was in Malaysia.'

He heard a metal shutter being lifted and pictured the bookshop beneath them opening. Today would be busy with people doing their last-minute Christmas shopping.

'What happened?'

'It was a bad high side. I got thrown from the bike. Broke my back and a few ribs.' He stroked her distractedly and the memories trickled in. Strangely, they weren't bad ones. There'd been a little frustration, he supposed, because he was forced to take a break from racing, but he'd never doubted that he'd return. The doctors had operated, he'd recuperated and returned to training. Simple.

'Was anyone else hurt?'

'No.'

'What about the second crash?'

'A bad bend. I leaned in too much, lost traction.' He waved a hand in the air. He'd made a mistake. What more was there to say?

'What did it feel like? What were you thinking? Or was there no time to think because it happened so fast?'

'There's more time than you imagine. Everything kind of slows.' He'd known the moment it happened that the bike had tipped too far. He could still feel himself spinning across the track, relaxing as he'd been trained to do, bouncing across the gravel, gradually slowing, thinking he was lucky this time and he'd got away lightly – then the hard smack. 'That time my bike hit me.'

'Is that what hurt your shoulder?'

He nodded.

She released a slow breath. 'I can't imagine having a job where each day you could get injured. Or worse.'

'It was what I loved.' He realised he'd used the past tense. And where was the anger, the frustration? Something had shifted in him. Perhaps he was finally beginning to put it behind him.

He drew Liberty to him, not wanting to think. Just to feel. And when he kissed her, boy, did he feel. A rainbow of sensations filled his head, blotting out the past and the future, leaving only the present.

She lifted his scarred wrist to her lips. He watched as she dropped feather-light kisses down the length of the scar. It was unbearably sexy. Her lips moved slowly to his palm, his fingers. His muscles tightened. He was certain he'd never wanted or needed anyone as much as this. His fingers brushed her face, and their mouths were just centimetres apart. Every nerve ending was alert and sharp. He hadn't felt so alive in months – not since before the crash, in fact – and his heart soared like it used to when he crossed the finish line in pole position. Shivers of pleasure rolled through him until finally, with a ragged sigh, he drew her to him.

He kissed her fiercely. Passionately. No holds barred. As he'd been wanting to do for so long now.

'It's wonderful to have you here,' said Alex's mum, Babette.

'I'm so grateful to you for having me,' Liberty replied.

It was seven thirty on Christmas Eve and they were all seated at the wooden table in Babette's spacious kitchen, Alex's two brothers and their partners, his baby nephew, and of course Babette and her partner Bernard. Liberty was very grateful that they'd agreed to speak

English for her benefit. The little snatches of French she'd heard were unintelligible to her.

Babette waved away her words and smiled. 'This strike is a real nuisance.'

'Many people have been stranded because of it,' agreed Bernard. He was filling everyone's glass with red wine.

Liberty hadn't known him long, but she could already tell he was a modest man, as big and broad as a bear, but gentle and quietly spoken. Driving there, Liberty hadn't been sure what to expect: Alex hadn't really talked about his family much, and she remembered the stony look in his eyes when he'd spoken about his father. If he was always travelling, perhaps he didn't see them often, perhaps they weren't close.

But the moment she'd arrived at Babette and Bernard's house, she'd realised that wasn't the case at all. Alex's mum had enveloped him in a hug, then she'd done the same for Liberty. And Bernard had shaken their hands warmly.

'It's so sad,' Babette went on. 'Christmas is when families need to be together.'

Alex brought the food to the table. 'Here we are, everybody: *gratin de courgettes*.'

He'd explained to Liberty that whereas most of France feasted on Christmas Eve, Provençal tradition was to eat seven courses of vegetables or fish, but no meat before Christmas Day. The *gratin* he and Babette had prepared smelt delicious, and he began to serve.

'So tell me why you came to France,' Babette said. 'Alex said it was something to do with your work.'

'I was delivering quilts for the festival in Tourmarin.'

Babette's eyes brightened. 'So you quilt yourself? You must show me your work.'

'Gladly. I have lots of pictures.'

'I love quilts. I have them in every bedroom, but they're all shop bought, I'm afraid.'

Liberty smiled. 'Yes, I noticed them. The one in my room is beautiful.'

It was made from traditional French fabrics with a floral pattern in shades of faded red and grey. She'd seen many cheap imitations of old-style French quilts, but looking at the tiny hand-stitching, Liberty wouldn't have been surprised to discover that this one was a genuine antique. It suited her room perfectly. And she'd spotted more quilts when Alex had given her a quick tour of the rest of the house that afternoon.

'Is your room all right?' Babette asked warmly. 'Do you have everything you need?'

'It's perfect.' She and Alex had the two attic rooms. Painted white, hers was airy and the roof sloped steeply to a small window with stunning views over the vine-filled valley. She had a huge bed, and next door was a bathroom, which she shared with Alex, whose room was opposite hers. She hoped he wouldn't spend much time in it.

She thought of last night, and wanted to smile: it had been so different from any other relationship she'd had before, so . . . perfect.

'This is such a beautiful place you have,' she told Babette, and glanced at the French windows. It was dark now, but earlier she'd seen the big garden and forested hillside behind the house.

The whole place was light and bright, tastefully decorated with lots of whitewashed wooden furniture and gold-edged antiques. The style spoke of good taste, and Liberty guessed it hadn't been cheap.

'Thank you. We had a lot of work done before we moved in so it's exactly as we want it.' Babette shared a smile with Bernard, and the love in their eyes made Liberty's heart tug.

Alex finished serving and sat down next to her. The basket of bread was passed round and everyone looked poised to tuck in when Babette cleared her throat.

'While you're all quiet,' she said, addressing her family, 'this is a good time to tell you our news.' She smiled. 'Bernard and I have set a date for our wedding.'

'Your wedding?' Alex's eyes were wide with disbelief.

Sensing the tension, Liberty glanced nervously at Babette, but she simply smiled and said, 'Yes. In May next year.'

Was he upset his mother was remarrying? His brothers appeared relaxed.

Alex cleared his throat. 'It's very soon. Are you sure this is what you want, Maman?'

Bernard raised an eyebrow. Babette placed a reassuring hand over his.

'Yes,' she told her son. 'I'm very sure.' She smiled at Bernard. 'See? I told you he'd be overprotective.'

Alex raised his hands in the air. 'You know I like you, Bernard. I just don't want you to rush into this and regret it.'

'Like you did with Solange,' said his younger brother, Jules, and rolled his eyes.

His brother Victor shot him a hard look. There was a beat of silence. Liberty saw Babette glance at her, then quickly away.

'I've thought about it long and hard,' Babette assured Alex. 'We both have, and we're sure it's what we want. You don't need to worry.'

Alex nodded, and seemed to relax. 'Then I'm happy for you,' he said, with a wide smile. He reached to shake Bernard's hand. 'Both of you.'

'It's great news, Maman,' said Victor. 'Where will the wedding be?'

'Here. It will be a small affair, just family and a handful of close friends in the village church, with a meal at the house after.'

'Give us the date,' said Jules, 'and we'll dust off our suits.'

Alex was looking very thoughtful. Then he asked his mum quietly, 'Would you like me to walk you down the aisle?'

Liberty saw the sudden shine in Babette's eyes. 'Oh! I hadn't thought of that. Yes, I would like it very much. Thank you, Alex.'

Everyone smiled, and Liberty felt love settle around the room, like a warm blanket. It was particularly poignant knowing how unhappy Babette's first marriage had been. She sipped her wine.

'This house is the perfect setting,' said Victor's wife, Laure, as she bounced baby Maxence on her knee. He was around a year old, a happy little thing, eager to try the food on his mum's plate, which made Liberty chuckle.

'Yes, we love it here,' said Babette. 'The views and the forest behind, the village nearby, and everyone has been so welcoming. It's as if I'd never left.'

'You shouldn't have left, Maman,' said Alex.

'I didn't have much choice. Your father hated it. He used to say it was *un petit trou perdu.*'

'In the middle of nowhere,' Alex translated for Liberty. She wondered if he remembered that he'd used the same words to describe her cottage when he first arrived in Willlowbrook.

He turned to his mum. 'You should have stood up to him.'

She tilted her head, indicating she agreed. 'But at the time I thought it would make him happy to move to Paris.'

'I like it here,' said Laure. 'It's nice to get away from the city.' She'd explained to Liberty that she and Victor lived on the outskirts of Paris. They'd moved from the city centre to the suburbs a year ago when Maxence was born.

'And we're not too far from Nice if we need the shops,' said Bernard.

'Will you use the Citroën for the wedding?' asked Alex.

Babette explained to Liberty, 'Bernard has an old Citroën DS in the garage. He adores it, but it's not usable.'

'It will be,' Bernard corrected. His eyes danced with good humour. 'It just needs a few repairs.'

Babette tutted. 'The brakes are not working! That's a major repair.'

Bernard turned to Alex. 'Your mother won't let me use it until they're fixed.'

'Want me to take a look?'

'Yes, please.'

'Your old Yamaha is in there, too,' Babette told Alex. 'Are you going to be racing at Le Castellet?'

'Of course. It's my favourite race.'

Liberty tensed. When was he planning to tell his family he'd been forced to retire? It felt wrong that she knew something they didn't.

He turned to her and explained, 'On the sixth of January there's an event called the Moto Legends Cup. It's for classic bikes. I have an old Yamaha I like to race – for fun.'

'Not like your other races?' she asked.

'Nothing like that. It's for charity and to showcase the old bikes.'

Even so, she felt a small shiver of worry at the thought of him racing. What if the weakness in his wrist caused him to get hurt?

'I hope that old bike is safe to ride,' said Babette. 'You only use her once a year and you don't have a team of engineers to look after her.'

'I'll check her over and take her for a test run. Anyway, that race isn't about speed.'

Babette laughed and said to Liberty, 'He says that, but he's not happy if he doesn't win.'

'Well, this year maybe it won't matter as much if I don't win,' Alex said. He and Babette exchanged a look Liberty couldn't fathom, until he explained to her in a quiet voice, 'I used to enjoy beating my father in this race.'

Babette tutted again. 'And this was not a good reason for competing.'

'Maybe, but it felt good,' he said.

At the other end of the table, the conversation broke off as Victor lifted his glass. 'Let's make a toast to Maman and Bernard,' he said. 'To your happy marriage.'

'Babette and Bernard!' Everyone chinked glasses.

'So, Liberty and Alex, how did you two meet?' asked Victor.

'I stayed with Liberty while I was in England. She rented me a room in her house.'

'Ah, yes, and how was your trip?'

Bernard stopped eating and frowned.

'Uneventful,' Alex said.

'You didn't find her, then?'

'No. Sadly.'

'What are you going to do next?' Victor asked.

Liberty saw Bernard glance at Babette. She lowered her gaze and concentrated hard on spearing a slice of courgette.

Alex didn't seem to notice. 'I don't know. I could hire a private investigator, but I'm not hopeful I'll ever find her.'

Bernard cleared his throat and changed the subject. '*Alors*, who is coming to midnight mass with us tonight?'

While the others answered, Liberty watched Babette discreetly leave the table to refill a jug of water. She didn't need to understand French to have noticed the tension in the room, and she wondered what had caused it.

★

After dinner, Victor and Laure got baby Maxence ready for bed while the rest of the family planned to walk to the village church for midnight mass.

'Let's go now,' Alex suggested to Liberty. 'There's something I think you'll want to see.'

'What is it?'

But he wouldn't say.

The village was at the top of the hill, and as they climbed, she looked up. 'Wow,' she said, pointing. 'There are so many stars. Even more than we can see in Willowbrook.'

Alex stopped beside her. Together, they examined the expanse of purple studded with a million stars, which shone like tiny beads. 'This area is known for its lack of light pollution,' he told her. 'There's an observatory not far from here.'

'It's beautiful.' But beautiful didn't really do it justice.

They followed the road as it wound up the hill. It was quiet and still. Occasionally, they caught the delicious smells of cooking or baking.

'How are you finding it so far?' Alex asked. 'It's not too bad being away from home? My family can be very blunt at times.'

She smiled. 'They're lovely, and don't worry about me, I'm fine.'

But there was one thing playing on her mind, and although she tried to restrain her curiosity, she couldn't quite manage it. 'Alex?'

'Mm?'

'Who is Solange?'

'Ah.' His smile vanished and a moment passed before he answered. Their footsteps echoed in the empty street. 'She was my fiancée.'

Chapter Twenty-one

A lex kept his gaze down and concentrated on putting one foot in front of the other as thcy climbed the hill. Their breath left small clouds in the air. It was going to be a cold night.

'The ex you mentioned before?' Liberty persisted. 'What happened?'

'I got cold feet. Called it off.' He hoped his clipped reply would be enough, but he should have known better. Liberty didn't shirk from examining emotions, whether they were uncomfortable or not.

'Go on,' she said.

'It was just before the wedding.' He shook his head. 'I should have realised sooner that I couldn't go through with it.'

He'd never forget Solange's stricken expression. *Now?* she'd asked. *Two days before the wedding?*

'Why couldn't you?' Liberty asked.

He lifted his shoulders. Wasn't it obvious? 'I wasn't sure I loved her enough.'

'How can anyone ever know that?'

'Exactly. I preferred not to risk her happiness and mine for something that felt like a gamble.'

'Is that how you view love and relationships? As a gamble?'

He shrugged, but didn't answer. He supposed he did. His parents' marriage had hardly been inspiring.

'How did you feel afterwards?' Liberty went on. 'Did you have any regrets?'

'I regretted all of it. It was terrible for Solange, and I should never have asked her to marry me in the first place. But I was young, and I rushed into it.'

The faint croon of an owl carried in the air.

Liberty watched him curiously. 'Don't you think you're being too hard on yourself? I mean, these things can happen to anyone. We all make mistakes.'

He shook his head fiercely. 'I hurt her. Badly.'

'But imagine how much more hurt she would have been if you'd married her knowing you didn't love her.'

He glanced at her, sidelong, and felt something shift. 'Perhaps.'

'I think you did the right thing. You were honest with her.'

They turned the corner and the church and village square came into view.

'So since Solange you haven't had a serious relationship?'

'No. My career has been pretty full-on. Travelling all the time didn't make it easy for relationships to develop.'

It was simpler to live without the complications of emotions. It was easier to keep everyone away and focus on being the fastest, the best. With racing, he'd been in control. He could live without the unpredictability of emotions.

★

Liberty gazed around her as they reached the village centre. It wasn't as fairy-tale pretty as Tourmarin, but it was charming nonetheless, and seemed more authentic, populated by locals rather than tourists. The church and the village square were decorated with lights for Christmas, but she wasn't really paying attention: her mind was still on all Alex had told her.

She was glad he'd confided in her about this crucial event in his past. It all fell into place now, his warning to her: *Don't get attached. I never stick around.* After growing up with his father's infidelities and the pain they had caused, Alex must have hated being the one who'd hurt and humiliated his fiancée.

But everyone made mistakes. Surely it was time to stop being so hard on himself. Liberty had seen for herself how protective he was of his mum and how he looked out for his younger brothers. And that didn't fit with the image he'd built of a free spirit who cared only about winning. She puzzled over this. He'd made it sound like he was unreliable, but what she'd seen today contradicted this completely. His family was important to him. He was the best brother and son.

'The surprise is in the church?' she asked, seeing where they were heading.

He nodded. They joined the villagers streaming into the church, and inside he took her hand. 'Come and see this,' he said, leading her towards the front.

The smell of incense filled the air and to the right a small choir were singing carols. But the attention wasn't on them. Everyone seemed to be gathering in front of the altar where a handful of people were dressed in costumes and stood or knelt around a wooden crib. Sawdust and straw had been strewn across the stone floor of the church and candles burned on tall stands, lending the scene a golden glow.

'What are they doing?' whispered Liberty.

'It's *une crèche vivante*,' said Alex. 'A living crib.'

Liberty ran her gaze over their simple costumes and calm expressions. 'Are they actors?'

'No. Just villagers who volunteered. Even the baby's real. Chantal had him three weeks ago.'

'You know her?'

'Maman told me about the baby, but I used to know her. We were at school together.'

The woman's husband stepped closer to her and put his arm around her. She smiled at him and they watched the sleeping baby lovingly.

Liberty's heart folded. She thought of Natasha's son, Arthur, and how precious he'd felt as he'd nuzzled against her, warm and baby soft. The scene was peaceful and still, and warm air whispered through the church. Alex stepped away, but Liberty was mesmerised. She had the sensation of witnessing something ordinary yet magical. Mundane yet miraculous. This church at the top of the hill, the simplicity of the scene, the low hum of singing and the quiet snuffles of the sleeping baby.

It made her heart twist, and she knew she'd never forget this starry night.

A Winter's Dream

Thursday, 25 December

The next morning they woke late.

'Happy Christmas,' Alex said softly. He kissed her. 'What do you want to do this morning?'

'Shouldn't we help prepare lunch?'

'Jules and Caroline offered to do it, and it'll be ready around one. So until then we are free to do whatever we want.' He smiled seductively. He'd happily stay in bed a little longer.

'In that case, you could show me around the area.' He pouted in exaggerated disappointment and she smiled but continued, 'I'd love to see where you grew up, where you and Luc went to school, all the places that have meaning for you.'

'Okay,' he said slowly, his brain beginning to work out a route. He liked the idea of showing her round, sharing his memories with her, his past. He was glad to be back and hoped she'd love the place as much as he did. 'Do you prefer to go by car or bike?'

'Bike.'

'You're not frightened any more?'

'No. I trust you. You're a safe driver. And although the bike is noisy, I feel more in touch with my surroundings on it – the smells, the weather,' she smiled, 'even the bumps in the road.'

'Hopefully there won't be too many bumps.'

'And you won't go too fast, will you?'

He kissed her. 'Not unless you tell me to.'

'Do you have any helmets like Guy's where we can speak to each other?'

'I do.'

She grinned. 'What are you waiting for, then?'

Babette and Bernard's house wasn't in the town where Alex had lived as a boy, but it wasn't far and he'd had friends who lived in this village and those nearby. He hadn't been back much during the last twenty-five years, but the country roads, vineyards and fields had hardly changed. In fact, when he caught the smells of woodsmoke and rosemary they transported him back to his childhood, and the emotions that accompanied those memories surprised him.

He took Liberty to Château Duval first of all, Luc's family's estate, and he drove slowly past their vineyards. Then they followed the road down into town, passing fields, which, in summer, were filled with sunflowers or lavender. He pointed out the primary school he and Luc had attended, the café and the market square, which was, of course, deserted today, but he remembered it noisy with traders and locals, the air filled with the smell of hot food and fresh produce. Finally, he stopped near the main fountain and they dismounted.

They sat on a bench, and he swept his gaze over the square and the small playground nearby. The gravel area was empty now, but he was certain that later there'd be a handful of men playing *boules*, perhaps children on the slide too. Water flowed quietly from the fountain, and he remembered how on cold winter days it used to freeze.

'What's wrong?' Liberty asked him. 'You look troubled.' He'd lent her a jacket and her hair seemed even more vibrant against the black leather.

'Nothing.'

She arched her brows as if she knew better than to accept that.

'It's just . . . strange to be back. I haven't been here for – well, years.' He added, 'Apart from Luc's wedding, but that was a flying visit.'

'Why not? It's a beautiful place.'

Good question. Why had he stayed away so long? He leaned forward and touched his fingertips together as he considered it. 'I suppose I thought it would wake bad memories of my parents' unhappy relationship.'

'And does it?'

'Not as much as I'd expected.' Hardly at all, in fact. Mostly, he remembered the freedom he'd enjoyed as a boy, exploring with his brothers and Luc, cycling, climbing trees, building dens. He leaned back and gazed up. He'd forgotten how bold the blue sky was, and he pictured the place in summer with the tall plane trees in full leaf, the scent of sun-baked earth, and the tarmacked road shimmering in the heat. His lips remembered the sweet taste of freshly picked peaches.

Perhaps he hadn't been so aware of his parents' problems as a child, because warm memories flooded back of big family meals eaten outside in the shade with his grandparents, aunts, uncles and cousins. The sense of belonging hit him unexpectedly. Provence had felt like home.

And although his parents' marriage had always been troubled, his mum had been happy here. She appeared even happier now she was embarking on a new phase in her life, and that was a weight off his mind.

'It was a nice place to grow up,' he said finally.

Liberty smiled. 'I can imagine you tearing through the countryside with Luc. How old were you when you first learned to ride a motorbike?'

'Not as young as you might think. At six I was doing wheelies on a pushbike. But it wasn't until I was ten that I stole one of Dad's bikes to have a go.'

'You stole one? Why?'

'Because I desperately wanted to ride it, but I wasn't allowed.'

'No wonder if you were ten! You could have killed yourself. So when you stole it did you know how to ride?'

He grinned. 'I had no clue, but I'd had a dream the night before so I was convinced I knew it all.'

Her laughter echoed around the empty square. 'Oh, the arrogance! I hope you fell off and learned your lesson.'

He shook his head. 'Worse. I crashed it in a nearby field and damaged a wooden gate. The farmer dragged me home by the ear.'

'What did your dad say? He must have been so angry. You could have been hurt.'

He stopped laughing. 'He wasn't there. Just my mother.' The memory was still vivid. 'And she wasn't angry, she was sad.'

'Sad? Why?'

'Because she knew I'd inherited his passion, but she

didn't want me to follow his example and race for a living. She was scared I'd crash.'

'I'm guessing accidents happen often in racing,' she said quietly. 'She knew the risks.'

'Yes. There are dynasties of motorcycle racers where two or more men in the same family have died.'

'Their poor mothers and partners.' She shuddered. Then turned to him. 'When are you going to tell your family that you're not racing any more?'

His mouth flattened and he tensed at the prospect. 'Soon.'

Her phone pinged. She pulled it out of her pocket and read the message. Her eyebrows knotted.

'What is it?' he asked.

'A message from Evie. She's wishing me a happy Christmas and asking if I'm still doing the challenge.'

He grinned. 'I presume you haven't told her that I count as one of your ticks.'

Her cheeks flooded with colour. 'I – I was only kidding about that.'

He wasn't sure why that came as a relief. He became more serious. 'Do you want to continue with the challenge?'

'Definitely. I've got less than a week left, and nothing could be harder than getting on that plane. It seems silly to give up now.'

'But you decide the rules of the challenge, don't you? Doesn't being in a foreign place count?'

She tilted her head and considered this. 'Yes, it's a break from my routine, and spending Christmas with your family counts for today, but I'd like to find more challenges for the next few days. Exciting things to do or places to visit.'

'I can help you with that.' He winked.

She side-eyed him. 'I'm not sure that's a good idea. Your challenges will all involve high-speed or daredevil activities.'

'They don't have to. If you like I could show you the area. Provence stretches from the mountains right down to the coast.'

She held up her phone. 'Evie asked to see photographs of what I've done.'

'Not a problem. Leave it to me. I'll plan at least one new experience for each day you're here.' To be honest, he was excited at the prospect too.

'Okay. But I want to see the list first.'

He grinned and shook his head. 'It'll be more fun if each day is a surprise.'

'I think you should run your ideas by me. How will you know if I'll find them challenging or not?'

'I know you well enough, Liberty McKenzie.'

'But what if they're too scary? Too extreme? Or dangerous? I want to complete the challenge, but I have boundaries, you know.'

'The surprise will add to the experience. Trust me. I promise that by the end of this week you'll have finished your challenge and fallen in love with Provence too.'

Liberty watched as Jules carried the roast to the table. The noisy chatter paused as everyone oohed and aahed over the crispy golden goose. They'd already enjoyed a delicious smoked salmon starter and the wine was flowing freely. She'd had a fabulous day. Being stranded at Christmas was turning out to have been a stroke of luck, although she knew she'd landed on her feet because Alex's family were so kind and congenial.

'Who wants to carve?' asked Babette.

Everyone turned to Bernard. 'I'm no good at carving,' he said.

'Alex?' Babette asked.

He pushed his chair back and his mother handed him a knife. He set to work confidently, as if he'd done this many times before.

Meanwhile, Victor topped up their glasses. He held out the empty bottle. 'Is there any more?'

'It's in the cellar,' Bernard said. 'I'll go in a minute.'

They began to eat and the conversation resumed. Liberty had been telling Alex's mum about her challenge.

'What made you start this saying yes?' Babette asked.

Liberty thought back to her birthday. 'Because I felt my life was too quiet and predictable. I wanted to try being braver.'

'Liberty has a phobia of flying,' said Alex, who was sitting next to her, 'but she flew to France to enter her friend's quilt in the show.'

Babette's eyes widened. 'You are very *courageuse*.'

'Oh, not really.' Liberty smiled. 'Not compared to daredevils like Alex who race at terrifying speeds and get back on even after they've survived terrible accidents.' She thought of the scars that marked his body. They told the story of all he'd been through far better than words ever could. They filled her with admiration and wonder. He was brave. Fearless.

His mum pursed her lips. 'Ah, well, I'm not sure if that is courage or stupidity.' Her tone was disapproving but her eyes were warm with affection. She added, 'I worry about him so much.'

Alex held his mother's gaze and said quietly, 'Actually, you don't need to worry any more, Maman. I'm retiring from racing.'

Babette stilled. '*C'est vrai? Quand?*' In her shock she seemed to forget to speak English.

The room hushed.

'Now.' He lifted his wrist and pointed to the scar. 'This hasn't healed as I hoped it would. I tried everything, but the doctors are unanimous. It's game over.'

His words were met with a shocked silence.

Eventually Jules asked, 'What are you going to do? I know you're not stuck for money, but how will you fill your days?'

'I don't know. That's partly why I went to England – to get away while I thought about this.'

Babette smiled with relief. 'Well, at least now I can stop worrying that you might crash or get killed.'

A muscle ticked in Alex's jaw. 'Racing is my passion. It will be difficult to live without it.'

'I know. But perhaps it's a blessing too.'

His eyes narrowed angrily. 'What do you mean?'

'Do you think you're the first person on earth to have had his hopes dashed? Some people have their dreams crushed before they've even had chance to get started. At least you had a good go at yours. You won trophies and you've been world champion.'

There was a pause. Then Alex said, 'You're right. As always, Maman.' He glanced around the table. 'I'm going public with the news in a few days. I wanted you all to know first.' He stood up. 'I'll fetch more wine from the cellar.'

He left the room and the family sat in silence as the news sank in.

'Now I understand,' said Babette.

Victor agreed. 'I thought it was strange when he suddenly disappeared off to England. He never has long periods of time off normally.'

Babette looked at Liberty. 'He's not very good at dealing with this kind of thing. He likes to always win, always be the fastest, the best.'

Jules said quietly, 'I bet he sees it as some kind of failure.'

'He's taken it hard,' Liberty agreed. 'Once he finds an alternative career I'm sure he'll feel happier, but at the moment it's not clear what that will be.'

'He's just like his father,' said Babette. 'Gérard raced long after most men would have stopped. He had a fiercely competitive streak. Alex gets it from him.'

Liberty knew Alex would bristle at being compared to his father, but there was no escaping the traits that bonded a family.

Friday, 26 December

The next morning, Liberty was woken early by Alex whispering her name. She smiled, eyes still closed, and reached into the space beside her to touch him.

The mattress was still warm – but empty. Frowning, she opened her eyes. He was standing beside the bed fully dressed.

She sat up, her head muddled. 'What—'

He held a finger to his lips.

She glanced at the alarm clock. It was early, still dark outside, and he was wearing jeans and a sweatshirt. His hair was even more ruffled than usual, as if he'd only just got up himself. 'What's going on?'

He smiled. 'Time for today's challenge. Come on. You need to get dressed.'

She really didn't want to. The bed was so soft and warm. 'What is it?'

'It'll spoil the surprise if I tell you. Trust me.'

She groaned and slumped back against her pillow. 'Wouldn't you rather stay in bed?' she asked, arching an eyebrow seductively.

His eyes gleamed. 'I got dressed first so you couldn't tempt me. It will be worth getting up for, I promise.'

She bit her lip. He seemed excited about whatever this surprise was. 'Okay,' she said, with an exaggerated sigh.

He beamed. 'Get dressed and wear sensible shoes. You've got five minutes.'

★

They tiptoed downstairs to the back door and into the garden.

'I can't see anything,' she whispered, as they crossed the lawn and headed towards the forest.

Alex held a lantern torch, which cast a wide beam of light onto the ground ahead, but the night around them was dense. 'Hold my hand,' he said, 'and follow in my footsteps.'

The only sounds were of their feet crunching on dry twigs and her ragged breathing as they climbed the steep hill. It reminded her of her daily walks with Charlie, only here the woods smelt less damp and peaty, and the scent of pine was stronger. She held Alex's hand and followed him blindly through the trees. His touch made her tingle with awareness.

'Nearly there now,' said Alex, as the trees thinned and his torchlight illuminated a rocky ledge. 'Keep tight hold of me. If you slip it's a long way down.'

Liberty gripped his hand and edged forward. When he sat down on a large stone, she followed suit, glad to stop and rest.

'You all right?' he asked, propping the torch up between them so it lit their faces.

She nodded, still a little breathless from the climb. He must be super-fit because he didn't seem even slightly tired. The torchlight drew patterns of light and dark shadow across his face, emphasising his cheekbones and the straight line of his nose. Above him was a cluster of stars, but the moon must have been hidden behind the trees.

'We're just in time,' he said.

'For what?'

'Look over there,' said Alex, and pointed in front of them.

He switched off the torch and Liberty realised the light had begun to change. Wispy grey perforated the darkness so the silhouettes of the trees came into focus.

Across the valley, behind the low hills in the distance, the sky became bluer, then tinged with coral pink. A warm glow laced the edge of a solitary cloud. Alex pulled out his phone to film it.

'Is this why you brought me here?' Liberty whispered, without taking her eyes off the horizon. Little by little, the colours were changing, unfurling like a flower. Gold and orange swam into pale aqua, and the valley below had turned ink-blue.

'*Oui.*' She heard the smile in his voice.

The sun crept up from behind the hills and added a velvety rich red to Nature's display.

'It's so beautiful,' she murmured. The colours would make a gorgeous quilt: peach, gold and ruby spliced with dusky blue and grey.

When the sun had risen and the jewel colours were replaced with blue, Alex pointed the phone at her and said, 'Smile – to prove you were here.'

She grinned. 'That was amazing! And you were right – it was definitely worth getting up early for. How did you know it would be so spectacular?'

He put the phone away. 'It often is. As boys, we used to come here to see the sun set, then race down the hill in the dark. Ask Luc – he'll remember.'

High above them, a distant plane left a pink thread in its wake that slowly dissolved into the blue sky.

She reached out and took his hand. 'Thank you for sharing it with me.'

'I knew you'd like it.'

Alex bounced baby Maxence on his knee, hiding his face behind a muslin cloth, then whipping it away. Each time the baby roared with laughter and waved his chubby hands with delight.

'He's never going to tire of that game,' Victor said, as he heated the baby's bottle.

'Who?' Jules joined Alex at the kitchen table. 'Alex or Max?'

Alex rolled his eyes at his younger brother. 'Very funny.'

He covered his face again, and this time he let the baby pull the cloth away. Although he hadn't thought it was possible, this delighted Max even more. The little guy's helpless chortles would make anyone smile.

'Right. Time for a bottle,' said Victor. 'Why don't you feed him, big bro? He's happy and you did it so well earlier.'

Alex shrugged. He didn't mind. Leaning back, he settled the baby in the crook of his arm and took the bottle Victor gave him. The baby sucked hungrily and the kitchen fell quiet. He heard the murmur of voices and the odd tinkle of laughter from upstairs. The four women were going through Babette's old dresses. Laure, Caroline and Liberty had all been excited when Babette had mentioned the names of the French and Italian designer labels she was clearing out. Bernard had walked into the village on the pretext of buying groceries, but he'd stop at the café while he was there for a drink with his friends. It pleased Alex to see how quickly he and Babette had settled into village life.

'All that slurping is making me thirsty,' said Victor looking at his son. 'Is it too early for an apéritif?'

'You read my mind,' said Jules.

Victor brought over three beers and sat down. They chinked bottles.

'So tell us more about your retirement,' said Victor.

Alex frowned. It had been a relief to get the news off his chest, but he didn't want to talk about it. 'I already told you. There's not much else to say.'

'You're okay?' Victor worked as a maths teacher in a secondary school, and Alex could picture him sitting down with a troubled pupil and adopting the same concerned expression.

He found it unnerving. Normally, he was the one checking that his younger brothers were all right. 'Course I am.'

He almost missed the look Jules and Victor exchanged. 'What?' he protested. 'I am.'

Max's noisy guzzling quietened a little as the milk drained, and his eyelids grew heavy.

'Seems like you met Liberty at the perfect time,' Jules observed.

'What do you mean?'

'Well, now you're retired you'll be able to settle down.'

Alex laughed. 'You've misunderstood. Lib's just a friend.'

'Yeah, right.'

His brothers' sniggers made his hackles rise. 'She is.'

'But you're—'

'Just a friend, Jules,' he cut in firmly. 'She got stuck here because of the strike and I didn't want her to spend Christmas alone.'

He tipped the bottle up, as Victor had shown him, so the baby could get the last of the milk without taking in air.

Victor shook his head. 'Maman said you drove all the way here from England, then the minute you arrived you left again to go to Tourmarin.'

Irritation began to simmer inside him. What was it about little brothers that they pressed all his buttons? 'Because I was concerned. She was alone.'

The last of the milk disappeared and he set the empty bottle down.

'He says "concerned",' Jules said to Victor. 'He means "in love".'

'I do not!' Max opened his eyes, startled, and whimpered. Alex rocked him back to sleep, then finished more quietly, 'I'm not ready for a relationship. I haven't even figured out what I'm going to be doing next month, never mind next year.'

'Perhaps that's less important than who you'll be doing it with,' Victor suggested.

Jules grinned.

'That didn't come out well,' said Victor, 'but you know what I mean.'

Alex rolled his eyes. 'Will you two ever grow up?'

'I'm serious,' said Victor. 'Perhaps it's time you did things differently, Alex.'

'What do you mean?' He took a swig of his beer.

Victor grew serious. 'You've always been there for us. You were more than a big brother, but . . .' He hesitated.

'What?' Alex sighed.

'. . . perhaps now it's time you did something for yourself.'

He frowned. 'You don't think I have already? My whole career has been about me. Winning races, coming first, getting all the glory – you can't get more selfish than that.'

'Or lonely,' said Victor. The word echoed around the kitchen. 'Perhaps it's time you found a more . . . meaningful way of life.'

Their eyes rested on Max asleep in his arms.

Alex huffed. 'You're not going to tell me I should become a father, are you? Just because you—'

'Actually, I was going to say you might enjoy a more rewarding career, like teaching. But having a family would suit you too. You'd be good at it. After all, you were like a father to us, making sure we didn't go off the rails, keeping the family together.'

'Yeah, you were bossy,' Jules chipped in. He was picking the label off his beer bottle.

Victor went on, 'And Lib's a great girl.'

'She's just a friend!' Alex protested again.

But guilt clawed at him because how could he say they were just friends when they were sleeping together? Maybe he shouldn't have brought her here. Maybe it had been a mistake to let their relationship stray into this grey area. But he didn't want to regret something that felt so good. Liberty wasn't making any demands, she'd been open with him, and their relationship was straightforward.

His brother ignored him. 'She stands up to you. I like her. We all do. A lot.'

'It's not like that,' he bit out.

'Why not?'

He sighed. Why wouldn't they let this go? 'Because she wants a family and I don't do . . .', he gestured to the child in his arms, '. . . all this. You know I don't.'

'Why not?' Victor drained the last of his beer. 'And please don't tell me it's because of Solange.'

Alex threw him a dark look. It was easy for his family to say he should let go of the past, but they didn't know how devastated Solange had been. They hadn't been there to see her stricken expression. He couldn't erase it from his mind. He'd hurt her in exactly the same way his father had hurt his mum – countless times. He hated himself for that.

But, worse, he'd been relieved to break it off.

Which proved just how much he was his father's son. He couldn't do commitment even if he tried. Which was why he'd vowed never to make another promise he couldn't keep.

Victor shook his head. 'I knew it. How long are you going to beat yourself up about that?'

'You know she's married, don't you?' Jules said casually.

Alex stilled. 'Is she?'

His youngest brother nodded. He was still peeling the

label off his beer and there was now a small pile of paper shreds on the table in front of him. 'I bumped into her a couple of years ago. She has three kids and seemed happy.'

'I didn't know that.'

Victor turned to him. 'Well, there you are. Her story ended well. Why shouldn't yours?' He got up. 'Another beer?'

Alex shook his head, and took in this news. Solange was married? He was glad. She'd moved on. Good.

Did this change anything for him? Not really. Liberty had been quite clear that he wasn't – what had she called it? – her Dream Guy. This was temporary. It would be over in a week. She'd return home and he'd go . . . Well, he didn't know where yet.

Saturday, 27 December

'You're not waking me up for another challenge, are you?' Liberty asked sleepily.

He kissed her slowly. Seductively. 'Not for a challenge, no.'

'Mm. That's a relief.' He felt a thrill as she arched against him, and his hand slipped under her, shaping the hollow at the base of her spine and the back of her thigh that wrapped around him. She sighed with pleasure. 'What is today's challenge, then?'

He smiled against her lips. 'Can't tell you.'

'When will it happen, then?'

He pretended to give this serious consideration.

She idly ran her fingers over his jaw, and slipped one into his mouth. He kissed it and closed his eyes in pleasure, wondering how she did this. Every time he thought he was in control, she flipped it. A touch or a look were all it took to bring him to his knees.

'This morning?' she asked.

He shook his head and took her hand, feeding one fingertip after another into his lips.

Her eyes became dark. 'This afternoon?'

'No.' He smiled. His plans meant they could stay in bed as long as they liked.

'This evening, then?'

He nodded, and moved over her, caught in a contradiction. Emotionally, he didn't want to get any closer than the friendship they already shared, yet physically he couldn't get close enough. He wanted to hold her all night, wake up with that glorious red hair pressed against his cheek. He wanted to make her smile and laugh or frown in concentration as she mastered yet another challenge for her book.

'Tell me what it is,' she said. Her eyes were closed, her head tipped back.

He kissed the hollow of her neck.

'Tell me.'

'Can't.'

'You can.'

'It'll spoil the surprise.' He wanted to make her stay here as exciting as possible. He wanted her to love Provence as much as he did, though he couldn't explain why. He told himself he wanted to support her in her challenge and for her to take away good memories of her Christmas here, yet he wasn't sure that was the whole truth. He brushed it aside as yet another contradictory emotion he didn't want to understand and focused instead on the physical. That was simple and straightforward. Perfect.

'It won't.'

'Not knowing will create anticipation.' He kissed her. 'Tension.' He kissed her again. 'Promise.' With each kiss he felt his body wind tighter. The need was almost over-whelming, but he held out.

'I'd still like to know.' She smiled.

He settled himself between her legs. He nudged a little, and she breathed a sigh of pleasure. 'Okay. I'll tell you, but no more questions and I won't give you any more clues or explanations.' His body rubbed gently against hers. Every nerve was fraught, every sense on high alert.

She opened her eyes. They gleamed like polished wood. 'Agreed.'

He kissed her one more time before telling her, 'I'm taking you to visit a Christmas village.'

'What's that?'

He held a finger to her lips. 'No questions, remember?'

She smiled and nodded. Then her lashes fluttered shut as they finally succumbed to the pull of desire.

Even driving there, Alex still wouldn't tell her what a Christmas village was or give her any clues. Liberty wasn't sure what to expect, but when they parked at the bottom of a steep hill, she could see coloured lights stretching all the way up to the top.

'Is this going to involve another climb?' she asked, as he slipped his hand into hers and they set off. He'd advised her to dress warmly so she'd borrowed a stylish hat from Babette, and wore her warm winter coat.

'It is, but it'll be so gradual you won't notice.'

It turned out that the residents of this tiny Provençal village opened their homes to the public once a year, with each house giving over a room to an artist or artisan who welcomed visitors and brought a touch of Christmas magic to the place. Some sold local crafts or foods, others provided entertainment, while restaurants and the little bakery opened their doors too. Everyone was invited to visit them as they followed the trail to the top of the hill where children would find Father Christmas in his grotto.

Alex was right: Liberty hardly noticed the climb as they went from one stall to the next, listening to a flautist, watching someone throw clay on a pottery wheel and shape a tall vase, pausing to inspect the miniature figurines called *santons*, which had originated in Provence.

'Want to have your palm read?' Alex asked Liberty. He pointed to a woman in a turquoise headscarf sitting behind a curtain.

'Nah. They just tell you what you want to hear.'

'You're right. I can do that for free.' He pulled her to one side and cupped her face in his hands, pretending to channel telepathic waves or whatever it was that supposedly made them psychic. 'Let me see now . . . In ten years' time you will be married with a baby or two.'

'Just two?' She grinned. 'Four, actually. I'd like a big family.'

He frowned. 'But Damselfly Cottage is too small. You'd have to move.'

'You said it right!' she gasped.

'What?'

'Damselfly.'

He smiled. 'Why is it called that by the way?'

'Because there are damselflies, of course. In summer. They like the pond nearby. And to answer your question, I'd convert my sewing room into a bedroom with bunk-beds and move my sewing things into my bedroom. They'd just about fit.' Although, now she thought about it, it wasn't impossible to picture herself in a different house, one with French shutters, still rural but perhaps near a forest of pine trees and a night sky thick with stars . . .

She hurriedly brushed aside the thought.

He laughed and released her face. 'You have it all planned out.'

They walked on, leaving the fortune-teller behind and heading for a restaurant. But his light-hearted talk had made her curious. 'Where do you hope to be in ten years' time?'

'I don't know . . .' He thought about it. 'I hope I'll have found a new passion to replace racing. A new challenge.'

She looked at him. 'You don't think there'll be more to your life than just your job?'

'I need adventure of one kind or another. You know that.'

She nodded quickly and turned away so he wouldn't see her disappointment. They stopped outside a restaurant.

'Fancy this place for dinner?' he asked, and pointed to the chalkboard. 'I'm afraid the menu is fixed – soup, stew and a crème caramel for dessert – but it will all be home-made.'

She forced a bright smile. 'Sounds delicious.'

As they were served bowls of creamy leek soup and a basket of bread, Liberty silently mulled over his words. He'd always said he didn't do commitment, he didn't stay still, yet something didn't add up.

She broke off a piece of bread and puzzled over it. She'd seen him with his family and he was close to his mum, protective and supportive of his brothers. So what drove him to avoid commitment? It couldn't just be his bad experience with Solange, surely? He'd said he was scared of hurting others, but she wasn't so sure. She was curious to know more.

When they'd finished their soup, she asked him softly, 'Tell me about your dad.'

His expression hardened, as she'd anticipated it would. 'What do you want to know?'

Chapter Twenty-two

'What was it like growing up with him?' Liberty asked. Alex tensed. He didn't discuss his father. He deflected questions, changed the subject or closed it down, irrespective of how brusque that made him seem.

But tonight he felt the crack of a tiny fissure opening, and Liberty squeezed past his defences with her inquisitive brown eyes and her warm, interested tone. Many people were hungry for information about the famous racer, but she was the first to ask how it had felt to be his son. 'I don't know,' he said. 'I grew up without him – most of the time, anyway. He lived his own life. He wasn't home much, and when he was it was . . . difficult.'

'Difficult? How?'

'He was a selfish man. He had no sense of duty or responsibility. Actually, no, that's not fair. He made sure we were provided for very well financially – but emotionally, he wasn't how a father should be.'

'He wasn't hands-on?'

He gave a dry laugh. 'That makes it sound like he didn't change nappies or play with his children.' It had been so much more than that.

A complete lack of interest in his family. Even in Alex,

who'd followed in his footsteps professionally and been even more successful. World champion. But that hadn't been enough. 'He didn't care about us. When he came home, which was rare, he wanted no part in our lives. It was clear that he felt nothing for us. He couldn't wait to get away.'

'Yet he kept coming back? Why?'

Alex had no answer. Except perhaps that his parents' relationship had been more complicated than he, as a child, could understand.

Her eyes were dark, deep pools filled with pity. Alex bristled. He didn't want pity. He hated his father, and his death hadn't changed that. He'd always hate him.

'How awful for you,' she murmured.

'Not for me – for Maman.' She was the one who'd been hurt. The one who'd suffered repeatedly at his indiscretions. 'He was incapable of being faithful, and living in the public eye meant all his adventures were splashed across the papers. The shame, the humiliation – it never got any easier for her.'

Alex felt as angry for her as for himself. It was a double dose of hatred.

'Did they divorce?' Liberty asked.

'You would think so, wouldn't you?' he said bitterly. 'If they had, it might have been easier for her. She could have separated herself from it and moved on. But no, he refused.'

Liberty's eyes widened and he saw the rainbow of fairy lights reflected in them. 'Why?'

'For selfish reasons, I guess. Maybe he liked the idea

of a home and family to come back to when he felt like it. Or maybe he used it as an excuse to get rid of people when he grew tired of them. Who knows? But a divorce would have freed her.'

'He was a racer, too, wasn't he? So he travelled a lot with his job?'

He nodded.

She threw him a cautious look, as if she was picking her words carefully. 'Do you think he was lonely, spending all that time away from home? Could that be why he had affairs?'

'It's no excuse,' he snapped. 'And, no, I don't think so. He was away more than he needed to be.' Much more. Alex saw in his mind the grainy paparazzi shots of his father in bars with women on his lap, or on yachts, near naked. Even through the prism of years gone by, he still felt the same disgust. How must it have felt for his mum to see those pictures?

Once Alex was old enough he used to hide them to protect her. But it wasn't always possible. And once his father had retired from racing, the infidelity became so blatant that even the press lost interest. The bastard had kept several partners shacked up in various places across the world and treated life as one big holiday in the sun. He had no respect for those he hurt in the pursuit of his own pleasure.

'Why do you think he was like that?' asked Liberty.

'I don't know. He was so competitive he had to win at all costs. He was ruthless, he had . . . no heart.' Alex paused. It had been a long time since he'd tried to understand his father. 'He was raised in an orphanage and never knew his own parents. Perhaps that made him emotionally detached.'

'Maybe he never knew how to love,' Liberty suggested softly.

He waved away this suggestion. 'We all know how to love.'

Liberty met his gaze steadily. 'I'm not so sure. They say that cycles of behaviour repeat themselves through the generations. If he wasn't loved growing up . . .'

He shook his head, refusing to accept this. Refusing to allow anything to excuse his father's behaviour. He remembered how many times his mum had forgiven the man, how each time he came home she'd hoped that this would be the time he finally stayed and settled down.

He never did. And Alex would never forgive him for that.

Sunday, 28 December

'I brought you breakfast in bed.' Alex put down a tray. On it was a big cup of tea and a plate of waffles with syrup. He added, 'I thought you might be missing your routine.'

Liberty's heart did a little somersault. 'Oh, Alex, that's so thoughtful.'

'Are you missing it?'

'Erm . . .' She realised she'd hardly thought about home since arriving here. She'd been so caught up in getting to know his family and visiting new places. Getting to know him better too, and . . . well, enjoying herself.

Before, she'd clung to her routine, but this trip had taught her that the unknown could be exciting, magical, wondrous. She was so happy. Her confidence had grown and now she couldn't imagine going back to her old timid ways. 'Actually, no. I'm not missing it at all. I love it here.'

'I miss it,' he said.

She blinked. 'You do?'

He nodded. 'I miss our walks in the woods, and helping in the garage.'

She wasn't sure what to make of that, but told herself it had probably been a throwaway remark. 'I do miss Charlie,' she said. 'In fact, I'll call Evie now and check he's okay.'

Evie picked up straight away and assured her Charlie was fine. 'He and Smoke are getting on really well – except when Charlie eats Smoke's food.'

Liberty giggled. 'Ah, yes. Labradors are greedy.'

'Oh, and we had an incident with a cocktail.'

'An alcoholic cocktail?'

'Yes. Jake's sisters came to visit and he made drinks for them. His sister Louisa left hers on a coffee-table and Charlie came in, drank it, then walked into a door.'

'Oh, no! Is he all right?'

Evie laughed. 'He's fine. And we've been really careful to keep everything out of his reach since. Did the quilt-show people call you?'

She'd lost track of the days and only remembered now that the festival started today. 'No. Why?'

'They rang me just now. Brenda's quilt won in the Traditional Quilt category,' Evie said excitedly.

Liberty gasped. 'Oh, that's amazing! She'll be so thrilled.'

'And yours came third in the Modern category.'

Her eyes widened. 'That's brilliant.' But Brenda's news was what mattered most. It made it all worth it: this trip, the flight. Everything.

'So how's it going over there?' Evie asked.

Liberty smoothed the quilt and glowed as she thought of how she'd slept curled up in Alex's arms last night. It was such a tiny thing, yet it had felt so . . . right. 'It's wonderful.'

'Good.' She heard the smile in Evie's voice. 'Do you know when you'll be back?'

'I'm not sure yet. In the new year.'

'Well, don't rush on our account. The shop's staying closed for now and Charlie's happy.'

'Thanks, Evie.'

The garage was quiet, apart from the sound of sand-papering as Alex rubbed away a patch of rust above the wheel arch. Bernard had the bonnet open and was leaning over the engine of the old car. As they worked in companionable silence, Alex found it ironic that he had more in common with his stepfather-to-be than he'd ever had with his real father. Actually, that wasn't true. He and his dad *could* have shared a huge amount – racing, bikes – but his dad had chosen not to spend time with him discussing or sharing these experiences.

Bernard rubbed his lower back as he straightened up.

'When are you planning to announce your retirement publicly?' he asked.

Alex paused from his task. 'There's a press release going out in the next couple of days.'

'Maybe this could be a new career for you.' Bernard waved a hand to indicate the car and the repairs they were carrying out.

'It's just a hobby,' Alex said. 'I'm not a trained mechanic.'

'You could be.'

He considered this. 'I suppose.'

'You clearly enjoy it.' Bernard wiped his screwdriver on a rag. 'You know, it's unlikely you'll find another career that can give you the same things racing did. What you need to do is look for an occupation that you enjoy, that you can see yourself doing for the next few years.'

Alex gave this some thought. There was some wisdom in Bernard's words. Perhaps he'd been searching for the impossible. Nothing could ever match racing. He'd always tinkered with his own bikes, finding ways to adapt them to suit him better or improve their performance. 'While I was in England I helped out in the local garage, did some work on an old Triumph. She was even older than that one.' He nodded at his old Yamaha in the corner. 'And it turned out to be a good way of meeting people and chatting – you know, because I was trying to get information about my half-sister.'

There was a long pause. 'You said you didn't have much luck with that.'

'No. I can't decide whether to stop searching or hire a private investigator.'

Bernard looked at him. 'Perhaps you should stop.'

Alex glanced up. Bernard's mouth was flat. Why? 'Someone came into the garage and told me she remembered a woman called Mary who went out with him. Trouble is, she didn't know her surname.'

Another long silence followed before Bernard asked, 'Have you really thought about what will happen if you find her?'

'Yes, of course.' He frowned, puzzled by the question.

'What about your mother? It could be difficult for her if you do find this girl – and her mother. Babette would do all she could to welcome the girl into the family but . . .' He tipped his head, as if the rest should be obvious.

Alex stared at Bernard with a growing sense of dismay. 'It would be a painful reminder,' he said, as understanding dawned.

His father's betrayals had been many.

'Yes,' said Bernard. His gaze met and held Alex's.

Alex swallowed, appalled with himself. How had he not thought of this before? He'd been so wrapped up in his own problems, he'd raced off to England convinced he was doing an honourable thing – not pausing to think about how she would feel. Of course his mum would find it difficult. He was ashamed he'd behaved so thoughtlessly.

'Maybe you could be happy with the family you already have,' Bernard suggested. 'Your brothers and Babette, they all love and need you.' He picked up the spanner and leaned into the engine again.

Monday, 29 December

The road was narrow and winding. It was edged by a low wall, a foot or so high to Liberty's right, then there was nothing. Just a steep drop, hundreds of feet down to the bottom of the hill. Terrified, she sat rigid and gripped her seat, trying not to look at the vertical slope, which seemed only inches away from her.

Alex wanted her to visit a hilltop village, which he said dated back to medieval times and had fabulous views. She'd been keen to visit too, but now they were halfway up she'd changed her mind.

'You're very quiet,' said Alex as he steered the car round another bend at triple the speed she would have felt comfortable with.

'I'm scared.' She had to force the words out because she could hardly breathe.

He glanced at her, smiling. 'What are you scared of?'

'Don't look at me! Keep your eyes on the road!' she blurted. 'I'm scared of plunging to my death because this road is too narrow and you're going too fast.' She could picture their car tumbling and rolling down the hill.

He laughed. 'Trust me, Liberty. I'm in complete control of this car.'

'How can you say that?'

'I'm used to driving at speed, remember? Anyway, I'm really not going fast.'

'What if the brakes fail? What if a car comes the other way? You won't have time to –', she gasped as he rounded another blind bend, '– react.'

'I will.' He was so confident, so certain.

As if on cue, a beaten-up van appeared in the opposite direction. It came hurtling towards them, taking up more than its fair share of the road and leaving no room to pass.

'He's on our side of the road!' she gasped, and covered her eyes. 'There isn't going to be room. He's going to—'

'It's fine,' said Alex, and slowed.

She peeped from between her fingers. The passenger in the van waved as they passed, and Alex held a hand up in greeting too. She couldn't believe it. Was everyone oblivious to the possible dangers except her?

'See?' said Alex, when the van had gone.

'You might be in control but they weren't. This road is so dangerous!' Liberty's pulse drilled furiously in her temples. She wasn't sure her blood pressure could cope with this.

Alex accelerated away again.

She sneaked a glance at him and noticed he was smiling. 'You're enjoying this, aren't you?' she said, appalled.

He shrugged, still smiling. 'It's a challenging drive, yes. But I'm not enjoying seeing you so scared, if that's what you mean. You're a very nervous passenger.'

'We're so different, you and me,' she muttered, under her breath, and tried to keep quiet. But she couldn't uncurl her fist, which was clenched around the door handle.

'Would you rather drive?' he asked.

'Yes!' Anything would be better than being frightened and powerless like this in the passenger seat. 'But there isn't room to stop.'

'There's a viewing point coming up soon.'

'How do you know?'

'We used to come here when we were kids.' He turned a couple more corners. 'There it is.'

He pulled over and stopped the car. She breathed a sigh of relief and jumped out, glad to feel solid ground beneath her feet.

But when she got into the driver's seat, she had second thoughts. She could handle the gear stick being on the wrong side, but how would she know if she was too far to the edge of the road? 'Actually, I'm a bit scared.'

'Just take it slow and you'll be fine.' He winked. 'I'll let you know if you get too close to the edge. Will it count for today's challenge?'

'Definitely!'

Five minutes later, she glanced in her mirror at the string of cars behind her and bit her lip. This was harder than it looked. One of the drivers hooted, making her jump. 'I can't go any faster!' she said, feeling sick at the thought of the steep drop.

'Ignore them,' said Alex. 'You're doing fine. Locals are always impatient.'

He turned round and pointed the phone behind him. 'What are you doing?' she asked.

'Just filming the view for Luc.' She heard the smile in his voice and knew he'd caught on film the line of cars. Luc would be rolling on the floor with laughter when he saw this.

★

'I can't believe I did that!' Now she was safely out of the car and off that terrible ravine-sided road, Liberty was high on a rush of relief and pride.

'I know. A whole journey in second gear is a record,' he teased.

She stuck her tongue out at him, then grinned again. 'It was terrifying but I did it! I got us here in one piece.'

'Why do you sound so surprised?' asked Alex as he tore off a piece of bread and ate it.

They were seated on the terrace of a restaurant with stunning views of the countryside. From this height the vines were seams in the fields that stretched away into the distance. The sun was shining and the sky was denim blue with not even a smudge of cloud. And behind them loomed the ruins of an ancient château, accessible via tiny cobbled lanes that could have sprung from the pages of a story book. It was a beautiful magical place and she felt on top of the world. Quite literally.

She took a sip of her drink. 'Because a month ago I wouldn't even have dared try. Now I feel – I could be anything I want to be.'

'Of course you could.'

'I'm so happy.' Her heart felt like it might burst.

He smiled. She loved how he understood her fears and, although he didn't share them – far from it – was patient with her. She loved how calm he was behind the wheel and how talented (even if driving at speed wasn't a skill she particularly admired or encouraged). She loved his confidence, his energy, his willingness to take risks and embrace danger full on. She loved the person she was with him. She loved him.

Her hand stilled, the glass of water midway to her lips. *She loved him?*

How had that happened? He wasn't her Dream Guy. He was so far from it, why had her brain locked on to him?

It hadn't. Her heart had.

And she realised she'd loved spending the last few days with him. She didn't want their time together to end. The thought made her head spin.

He leaned back in his chair. 'When this trip is over and we say goodbye, I hope you'll remember this: that you *can* be anything you want.'

And just like that her spirits fell.

She'd been thinking how much she loved him; he was thinking of when they'd part ways. She looked away, swallowing hard.

'Lib? You've gone pale. What—'

'I'm just going to the loo,' she said quickly, and pushed her chair back.

In the marble-tiled Ladies, she stared at her reflection. 'You stupid, stupid girl. How could you? How could you fall in love with him when you knew – you knew he would never love you back?'

Her hand shook as she pushed a strand of hair off her face, and her mouth was drier than it had been on the winding road to get there. When she'd arrived in France she'd been on a high. She'd overcome her fear of flying; she'd made the journey alone to a beautiful French village and delivered her friends' quilts in time; she'd been all set to spend Christmas alone in a foreign place. She'd felt she was capable of anything, brave enough to face a bear if necessary; more than brave enough to sleep with Alex, despite all she knew about him.

But now the high had worn off, she'd come back down to reality – and she was scared. How arrogant she'd been to think she was in control. She should have known better. She should have stayed away from Alex Ricard.

Shaking her head, she closed her eyes and took a deep breath. Fear and anger gave way to something gentler.

Perhaps love wasn't something anyone had the power to prevent. After all, it had crept up on her slowly, hadn't it? Like tiny neat quilting stitches, appearing three at a time, almost imperceptible yet doing their work of slowly but surely binding her heart to his.

She loved him. She couldn't change that.

She could only hope he might, in time, come to love her too.

Chapter Twenty-three

'You didn't mind spending Christmas here in Provence?' his mum asked, as Alex helped her strip the beds. She folded the quilt and laid it on a chair.

His brothers had left, returning home for the new-year celebrations. Alex and Liberty would also be leaving tomorrow, heading to the coast for a surprise he hadn't yet told her about, but he planned to return in the new year. They hadn't really discussed it and Liberty hadn't yet booked her flight home, but he hoped she'd stay for the classic bikes race at Le Castellet.

'Why would I mind?' He tugged a pillow out of its case.

'Because we've spent every Christmas for the last twenty-five years in Paris.'

He remembered how fraught Christmas had been, everyone on tenterhooks wondering whether his dad would show up. He wasn't nostalgic for those days. 'It doesn't matter where we are. It's being together that's important. You, me, Victor, Jules. Bernard too.'

She pulled off the mattress cover and threw it on to the floor with the rest of the sheets, then started on the cot. 'I'm glad you like Bernard. It means a lot to me to have your blessing.'

'I never thought you'd love again. Not after what Papa did. Weren't you afraid of getting hurt again?' He helped her remove the tiny sheets and cotton blanket.

'A little. But I knew when I met Bernard he was nothing like your father. He's considerate, loyal.' She picked up a rattle, which had fallen between the mattress and the side of the cot, straightened and side-eyed him mischievously. 'I'd like to see you settled, too. I like Liberty. She's a nice girl.'

'I know.' He sighed. No matter how many times he said it, his family simply wouldn't accept that Liberty was just a friend. 'That's the problem.'

'Why is it a problem?'

'I don't want to hurt her.'

She studied him. 'You still blame yourself for what happened with Solange,' she observed sadly.

He didn't reply. Of course that wasn't the only reason. But the more time went on, the less clear his reasons were.

'You have to let that go, Alex. We all make mistakes, we're all only human. Even your father had good qualities, you know.'

He was shocked to hear her say that. 'Oh, yeah? Like what? And please don't tell me he was good in bed.'

'He was gregarious, and charming. He was laid-back—'

'You can say that again.'

'When I first met him I thought this was an attractive trait. A man with no cares.'

He scoffed. 'No responsibility, more like.'

'Can't you see? Every character trait has a good and

a bad side. Someone relaxed can be irresponsible, someone anxious can be conscientious.' Her eyes filled with regret. 'I'm afraid that you grew up too early and it's my fault.'

'Your fault? How? You were the perfect mother. You were mum *and* dad for us.'

She shook her head. 'You took on the role of father as soon as you realised he wasn't doing it. You carried the world on your shoulders, and I should never have allowed you to do that. I wish I could turn back time.'

'Don't regret it, Maman. It was hard for you. You did what you could while he swanned about.' He couldn't keep the bitterness from his voice.

'He muddled through like the rest of us,' Babette said gently. 'It doesn't help to be so angry with him.'

He stared at her, incredulous. 'When he hurt so many people?'

'Perhaps he didn't mean to. Perhaps he was searching for something he never found. You know something? Now he's gone I feel sorry for him. I can even . . .' She searched around, as if unsure, then nodded. 'I forgive him.'

'Really?' He was genuinely astounded.

'Yes. Perhaps it's time you stopped being angry with him and looked forward instead – to your own future.'

'You mean a new career?'

'Not just that.' The rattle jingled as she pressed it into his hands, then winked.

Their conversation had come full circle – back to Liberty. He groaned and shook his head, sorry to disappoint her.

'I'm not planning to settle down, Mum. Not with Liberty or anyone else.'

What would it take for her – and his brothers – to understand that he didn't need a relationship, and it simply didn't feature in his plans for the future?

She raised a brow. 'I've seen the way you look at her.'

He bit back a sigh of exasperation, and said gently, 'Perhaps you're seeing what you want to see.'

Putting the rattle down, he scooped up the sheets to be laundered and headed downstairs. His mum didn't reply, but as he left the room he glanced at her – then did a double-take. He frowned and hurried away, but her expression unsettled him.

Why had she smiled like that?

As if he was the one who didn't understand.

Liberty lay awake, staring at the stars through the skylights. Alex had been fast asleep for hours, his long lashes resting on his cheeks, lips slightly parted. Her fingers curled around the edge of the quilt, anxiously gripping the faded cotton.

She loved this room high up in the attic, away from all the noise, where she and Alex enjoyed the privacy and space to talk, laugh, make love. It was snug and warm, yet at the same time she felt close to nature up here where the rain tap-danced on the roof, the wind whispered against the windows, and the stars glittered and blinked, like a secret spectacle for her. Tonight the moon joined them, a swollen lantern steadfastly beaming its silver light into the room.

By the end of this week you'll have fallen in love with Provence, Alex had told her. She closed her eyes briefly. She'd done far more than that. She'd fallen in love with him too, and now she was torn: should she tell him? Or keep her precious secret close to her heart and leave at the end of the week with it untouched and unspoiled? That would be the easier option.

But what if he had feelings for her?

He didn't.

He might. He could. Look at all the thoughtful things he'd done for her: driving to find her in Tourmarin, making her waffles on Sunday, showing his support whenever she faced a challenge, and his pride in her when she achieved them. She remembered his anger at the ball when he'd confronted her over Ethan, and his adoring expression when he'd held her after they'd made love an hour ago.

He shifted in his sleep and rolled away from her. His leathery scars looked dark and angry in the pearly light.

Despite everything she knew about him, she still clung to the hope that maybe he returned her feelings. It was a fragile hope, but her heart clung to it because the alternative was too dreadful to face.

And that was why, while there was a chance – even a minuscule, million-to-one chance – that he might love her too, she had to say something. Be brave, think of your challenge. Resolve filled her.

It was risky, it went against all they'd agreed – but she had to tell him how she felt. The only question was, when?

A Winter's Dream

'I can't believe there are just two days left in December,' Liberty said, as Babette's house came into view. They'd been for an early-morning walk, enjoying the winter sun but well wrapped up against the icy wind. On the way back they'd stopped at the *boulangerie* to buy croissants and bread still warm from the oven.

'Two days left of your challenge,' Alex told her, 'and I've saved the best till last.' Excitement made his dark eyes sparkle.

'Really?' she said absently. She couldn't stop thinking about whether now was the right moment to tell him about her feelings.

He nodded. 'We're driving to the coast tomorrow and you need to pack a dressy outfit. Black tie.'

Her curiosity was sparked and he had her full attention now. 'Black tie? Why?'

Alex hesitated, clearly torn between keeping it a surprise and wanting to share his excitement with her. In the end, excitement won and he watched her reaction as he said, 'We're going to a New Year's Eve party . . .' he paused '. . . on a yacht. In Monaco.'

'Wow,' she gasped, and felt the quiver of butterflies. This was going to be way out of her comfort zone. On the other hand, it would also be a fabulous once-in-a-lifetime opportunity. 'Whose party is it?'

'One of the MotoGP teams is hosting it. All my ex-colleagues will be there.'

Wednesday, 31 December

Liberty stepped out of the car onto a red carpet and blinked, dazzled by the glittering lights. The tang of sea air carried in the breeze. This was surreal. She was in Monaco for a celebrity-studded party on a yacht! Wait until she told Carys.

Security men in sleek suits made sure the handful of paparazzi stayed behind the barrier, but as the cameras spotted Alex, they came alive with clicks and blinding flashes.

Suddenly nerves hit her.

What was she doing here? Would the paparazzi laugh when they saw this ordinary girl made up like a film star? Breathing fast, she ducked her head and smoothed down her dress. It was one of the vintage designer frocks Babette had been clearing out, floor-length black velvet with a jewelled neckline, and had needed only slight adjustments, which Liberty had made. But now she felt exposed in front of the enormous cameras. She felt sick.

Alex appeared at her side. Her fear must have shown because he asked, 'What's wrong?'

'Bit nervous,' she confessed.

He took her hand and her heart started pounding. 'Why? You look beautiful.'

She tried to relax but knew her fear must be written all over her face. This was his world. Glamorous. Exciting. She didn't belong here.

'Hey, you're brave, remember?' Alex leaned forward and whispered in her ear. 'You've got this.'

He was right. She *was* brave. *Fake it till you make it.*

She took a deep breath and smiled at him, then at the cameras.

'Is this your new girlfriend, Mr Ricard?' one of the photographers shouted.

'Are your injuries healing well?' asked another.

'How are you feeling about your enforced retirement?'

She felt Alex stiffen, but he didn't respond and led her away quickly instead.

Nothing could have prepared Liberty for how spectacular the evening would be. She'd foolishly imagined the yacht to be a large boat with a generous deck and maybe a tiny cabin below. In fact, the yacht was bigger than most houses, and as she and Alex made their way through one noisy room to another, then upstairs to another level, she wondered if she'd be in danger of getting lost when she looked for the bathroom.

But the people Alex introduced her to were not at all intimidating, and greeted her warmly. She smiled as they slapped their former teammate on the back like a long-lost friend. Staff circulated with trays of artistically presented canapés and drinks. As Liberty sipped champagne, she sneaked surreptitious glances at the stunning dresses and jewels, trying to commit every detail to memory because she was certain she'd never experience anything like this again. No wonder Alex had been appalled to find himself at her poky cottage. No wonder he'd found Willowbrook too quiet initially. It was a world away from all this, and she wondered whether he missed his old life. She glanced at him and felt a pang.

One day, when she was Old Dorothy's age, she'd tell her grandchildren about this night. But she wondered if the handsome Frenchman would be long gone – only ever part of a memory.

Alex nodded at former acquaintances as he wove his way through the crowded room, anxious to return to Liberty's side. She tipped her head back, laughing at something his ex-manager, Eric, had just said. She looked relaxed, as happy and comfortable here as in Willowbrook's village pub.

He was relieved she was enjoying herself, albeit still confused by the blast of emotion that had hit him earlier. When they'd arrived at the party and stepped out of the car to meet the paparazzi, her face had become as pale as the moon.

And he'd felt something so powerful it had momentarily stunned him.

Seeing the fear in her eyes he'd wanted to shield her, enfold her in his arms and whisk her away. He couldn't put his finger on what this sensation was, but it made his heart rev like an engine on full throttle.

A waiter offered him champagne and he realised it was almost midnight, time to toast in the new year. He took two glasses and continued through the satin gowns and dazzling jewellery towards the beacon of glossy red hair. Her conversation with Eric ended and she turned, scanning the room until she spotted Alex. Their gazes locked, and when he finally reached her, he leaned in to kiss her.

He smiled as lust coiled itself around them, deliciously sweet and impossible to resist. At the beginning of the week he'd told himself this passion needed oxygen and space, and in a few days' time it would have burned itself out.

Yet it hadn't. Instead it was becoming overwhelming. His muscles wound tight, reminding him of when he used to lean the bike through the tightest corners, his knee skimming the ground, the bike balanced at a precarious angle. A fraction too far and it was all over, the tarmac coming to greet you.

He drew back and offered her a glass. 'Champagne?'

She took it with a smile, but he gripped his own. Was he growing attached? Was that what this was, this pull he felt to be near her? This need to be in her slipstream, close by, looking out for her. The thrill for her, the swell of pride when she smiled at him, delight when she'd surprised herself with what she was capable of. Her happiness felt more important than his own.

He frowned and distractedly stroked a loose strand of hair away from her face. No, he wasn't becoming attached. Definitely not. He'd been clear-headed about this from the start – as had she. She'd assured him she didn't expect commitment. They were having a good time, that was all, and they'd agreed it wouldn't last.

'How does it feel,' she asked, 'to see all the people you used to work with?'

He glanced around the room. 'It's a little strange.' He hadn't been sure how he would feel about meeting his former colleagues and rival racers again. But it had turned out that everyone was genuinely pleased to see him and curious, too, about the injury that had sealed his fate. And on his part, far from feeling a rush of anger or loss, he felt only acceptance that that part of his life was over. And it surprised him. 'But I'm ready to move on.'

When had the change happened? When he'd returned to Provence with its gentler pace of life? Or before that, in Willowbrook? When his bike was stolen and he'd gone cold turkey, perhaps. He thought of the woods, the breeze on the leaves, birdsong, the stream rippling close by. He couldn't pinpoint when his attitude had shifted, but while racing had once been his all-consuming passion, now he felt ready to embark on a new phase. He saw possibilities and opportunities. He felt hope.

'Shall we go outside?' he suggested. 'Not long until midnight, and the fireworks are bound to be spectacular.'

Up on deck the night air was fresh. He took off his jacket and draped it around her shoulders. All around the port people were gathering in anticipation.

'Is this how your life was before?' Liberty asked, gesturing with her champagne flute to the guests around them. 'All glam parties and razzle-dazzle?'

'Razzle-dazzle?' He chuckled. 'Not really. I had lots of invitations, but didn't accept many.'

'Why not?'

'It's not my scene.'

He'd hated this aspect of his old life: the parties, networking, posing for the cameras. His father had adored it, but Alex found it superficial, even soul-destroying. He'd much rather escape somewhere quiet with Liberty.

She giggled. 'That's a relief. Maybe we have more in common than we thought.'

'You're not enjoying it?'

'I am . . .', she slanted him a coquettish look, '. . . but I'll be equally happy to go home where we can be alone.'

He felt a rush of desire and was suddenly impatient for the fireworks to be over. 'It's a deal,' he said, his voice low.

They decided to walk back to the apartment, taking the longer route along the seafront, and when they reached a quiet beach they slipped off their shoes and walked along the water's edge. Alex was relieved to have left the noise and lights behind. The distant laughter of party-goers carried through the darkness but it was peaceful here. The water whispered against the sand, and the stars were silver pinheads in the navy sky. Liberty's hand felt warm in his.

'This trip has been magical,' she said, eyes sparkling.

'I'm glad you've enjoyed it.'

'Provence is a really special place.'

'It is.'

She squeezed his hand. 'I'm so glad you brought me here. Thank you.'

His chest tightened at the note of finality in her words, and he frowned, realising he didn't want her to leave.

What did he want? His feet sank into the wet sand.

More of this. Uncomplicated friendship and passion.

But Liberty would want to go home and resume the

search for her Dream Guy. A man who would give her the family she hoped for and the security she craved.

That wasn't him.

Who, then? Mr Bland? Another blind date? The thought set his teeth on edge.

Perhaps she wouldn't leave yet. She'd said she was happy here, she got on well with his family, she loved Provence and the unspoilt beauty of the quieter, inland areas. Perhaps they could continue with this a little longer.

Spontaneously, he stopped. 'Actually,' he said, 'we're not finished.'

Her head whipped round. 'What do you mean?'

He checked all around. The small horseshoe of beach was overlooked by a few shops, all in darkness, and there was no one else about. He grinned. 'How about outdoor swimming to finish your challenge?'

She hugged his jacket to her. 'But – it'll be freezing!'

He tipped his head to one side. 'You're not going to say yes?'

She looked down at her velvet dress. 'I haven't got my swimming costume.'

He winked and began to strip. 'Underwear is fine. Once you're wet it's all the same.'

Biting her lip, she looked around at the deserted stretch of sand.

He tossed his trousers on to the ground beside his shirt and tie. 'What do you say, Liberty McKenzie? Is it a yes?'

She laughed and reached to unzip her dress. As she ran down the beach into the water, she shouted, 'Ye-es!'

A Winter's Dream

Liberty leafed back through the pages of her orange notebook. They'd wrapped up warm to have breakfast on the terrace, enjoying the view of the Mediterranean and the tranquillity while most people still slept. Now they lingered over coffee.

Clouds had pushed in, but that didn't bother Liberty as she read back over the last few days' entries: the Christmas village, the hairy drive up that winding road to the beautiful hilltop village with incredible views, and last night's glamorous party on the yacht with a stunning firework display. Her week in Provence had ended, quite literally, with a bang.

'You've done a lot in one month, *hein*?' said Alex, leaning in to read it too.

Pride swelled in her and she nodded. 'And it's changed me. I'm not the same person any more.'

'What have you learned from doing this challenge?'

She brushed a crease out of the skirt of her green dress and thought hard. 'I've learned that the idea of doing something is often worse than the reality. The voice in my head used to stop me doing so many things by telling me I wouldn't cope, I might get hurt, or focusing on everything that could go wrong. Now I don't let it.'

She'd set herself this challenge because she'd believed her life was lacking excitement, risk, love. And because she'd felt lonely. But during the last month she'd learned something, and not just that she was more courageous

425

than she'd believed. She'd learned to value her life, quiet as it was, and to accept who she was.

Yes, she missed Carys, and she might still be alone, but now she appreciated how lucky she was to live in a place where friends were like family. She could count on Natasha and Evie to be there when she needed them. She adored her cottage, her walks with Charlie, her job, and she couldn't wait to get back. Willowbrook was her home, and she knew now that she could get along just fine by herself.

Although she hoped she wouldn't be by herself.

Alex got up and leaned against the balcony rail, his features relaxed as he looked out over the slate-coloured water and the darkening sky.

She swallowed, because there was still one difficult, frightening thing she hadn't done. She'd put it off, tried to push it away – but she knew the time had come to bite the bullet.

Alex watched the waves jump and curl. The sea was agitated, the sky masked by a dirty grey filter.

'Alex, there's something else.' Liberty's voice made him turn. It sounded thin. Uncertain.

She was standing beside him and he touched her cheek. 'What is it?'

'There's – something I need to tell you.'

A sober feeling washed through him. Why did she look so unhappy, so afraid? His skin prickled uncomfortably.

'It's quite simple, really,' she said quietly. Her smile was watery. She fiddled with the belt of her dress, twisting the end around her finger, then unwinding it and starting again. 'I love you.'

He blinked. The words settled like dust after an explosion. Horror snaked through him and he fought the urge to jump up and run. Or throw his head back and sigh with exasperation, because he'd been so clear about his position on this.

'I know it's a shock,' she went on, 'and, to be honest, I'm as surprised as you are. I mean, I didn't think you were my type and – well, it doesn't make any sense. But there you are.' She gave a small shrug. 'This is how I feel.'

Silence stretched. His heart thudded angrily.

He should never have let things get to this stage. He shouldn't have gone after her in Tourmarin – he shouldn't have done any of this. He noticed she'd twisted the belt so tight her finger was white. Deep grooves dug into her brow.

He swallowed. 'Lib, what do you expect me to say?'

She tilted her head and considered this. 'You could tell me how you feel. So I know where I stand.'

He felt a hammering in his temples. He was pretty sure she didn't want to hear that. Choosing his words carefully, he said slowly, 'You know how I feel. We've talked about this before. Our worlds are too different.' His voice carried a warning note.

'They're not so different, though, really. I have Charlie and Carys, and you care about your mum and your brothers.'

'I'm talking about how we live our lives, not who's

important to us. You like your routine, village life. I don't live like that.'

She watched him as if he held her heart in his hands. He bit back a curse. It was Solange all over again. 'But you could. You don't need to move around any more,' she said, in a small voice.

He didn't have an answer for that. The hope in her eyes made him twist with guilt. He didn't want to hurt her, but he couldn't give her what she was hoping for. 'I don't – I can't . . .' His throat felt thick. 'I'm sorry.'

Silence stretched. Then she placed her hand on his and said, 'It's okay.'

The small gesture of compassion was so unexpected, his head lifted. He stared at her, steeling himself for tears or the slamming of doors. But she met his gaze square on and told him, 'Really. It's fine. I promised I wouldn't ask more than you were willing to give and I understand you don't return my feelings. But I still love you.' She moved to go back inside. 'I'll find a hotel and stay there until I leave.'

He blinked. Her honesty – her fearless honesty – took his breath away. 'You're leaving?'

She nodded. 'I'll book a flight for tomorrow.'

'So soon? You'll miss the race . . .'

'Are you still going to take part in that?'

'Yes.' It wasn't overly competitive but it might be one of the few opportunities he had to race. He'd hoped she'd be there, but now . . . Now he didn't know what he hoped any more.

'I'm worried you might get hurt.'

He shrugged off her concern. 'It's nothing like MotoGP. It's old bikes and sometimes old men too. My father took part in it every year until two years ago. I enjoyed beating him,' he added wryly.

'You don't have anything to prove now, Alex.'

'I know.'

She nodded and said quietly, 'I'll go and pack.'

He raked a hand through his hair, frustrated and confused. She loved him but she was leaving. He didn't do love, yet he didn't want her to leave. But he didn't want to hurt her, either. This was all spinning out of his control. 'I thought you liked it here.'

'I do. But my life is in Willowbrook. My cottage, my job, my friends, and Charlie. This has been fun, but I need to get back.'

Putting some distance between them was exactly what they should do now. Cut the ties and walk away – for her sake. So why did it feel as if his world was splintering?

She added quietly, 'You could come with me. You don't have any ties, after all.'

His features hardened. No. Not now she'd told him she loved him. 'I told you, I don't do commitment.'

She smiled and asked gently, 'You say you don't, but if your mum and your brothers need you, you're always there for them, aren't you?'

'That's different.'

'Is it?' She blinked hard and he saw the hurt in her eyes. His chest tightened, yet he couldn't step forward and take her in his arms. He couldn't.

She continued, 'I think you're afraid.'

'Afraid? Don't be ridiculous. I'm—' Anger reared up in him, hot and vivid. 'Okay, believe that if you want to, but the only thing I'm afraid of is that I might hurt you like I hurt Solange!'

'For goodness' sake, stop using her as an excuse!' Her cheeks flooded with colour. 'That happened years ago. You were young and she wasn't me.' Her pulse flickered angrily at the base of her throat. She took a deep breath, obviously trying to compose herself, and said more quietly, 'You know what I think? You're not just afraid of hurting me. You're afraid of being hurt yourself.'

He stiffened. 'No.'

'Like your dad hurt you.'

An icy chill trickled down his spine. He stared at her.

She forged on: 'But love doesn't always have to hurt, Alex. You know that, somewhere deep inside you. You're just afraid to take a chance and risk your heart by letting anyone into your life.'

'I'm not afr—' he began.

Her sigh cut him off. 'Goodbye, Alex.'

As she turned and made her way indoors, her words ricocheted through his head. Was he afraid? Had the belief that love hurt embedded itself in him?

He knew love was possible: he'd seen how happy his mum was now, and his brother was happily married, Luc too.

He shook his head. Liberty was wrong. He wasn't afraid. He was just doing the right thing, the responsible thing.

So why, as she walked away from him, did it feel so wrong?

Chapter Twenty-four

Friday, 2 January

Liberty cried all the way home. She sobbed like a child. Or, rather, like a grown woman whose heart had been ripped in half. Who had she thought she was, saying she was brave enough to love him even if he didn't love her back? Her stupid challenge had made her over-confident. It had pushed her too far and given her false hopes – unrealistic hopes – that he would return her love.

Well, now she was getting her comeuppance. This was what happened when you got too big for your boots, Liberty McKenzie. You were hit by pain stronger than a rocket's g-force.

She went straight to the Old Hall to collect Charlie, who leaped into her arms and made her cry because he was so uninhibitedly pleased to see her.

'Lib?' said Evie, seeing her tears. 'Are you—?'

'I'm fine,' she said quickly, and swiped at her wet cheek. 'Just tired from the journey – you know, I don't like flying and all that.'

It was a white lie. It turned out that having a broken

heart had been the best distraction from her fear of flying. She'd barely noticed the plane leaving the runway. She'd been so inconsolably wrapped up in her heartache.

'Better go,' she choked, bundling Charlie into her car. 'See you at the Button Hole tomorrow.'

When she got home, she lit the fire and poured herself a large glass of red wine. It didn't normally feature in her routine for Friday nights, but stuff it. A small gift beneath the tree caught her eye. Its red packaging glinted. She picked it up, remembering Alex had said he'd left it for her. Her fingers lifted out a silver chain and pendant on which a damselfly was engraved, and the words:

She believed she could, so she did.

Her heart drilled and her fist closed around it as the tears began to flow once more.

Saturday, 3 January

'So you're back on vanilla slices, then?' Evie asked.

'Yup. I completed the challenge, I collected my winnings, so January is going to be all about routine. Nice, safe, boring, predictable routine. It's great!' she said bitterly, and took a huge mouthful of vanilla custard filling. She licked her lips. 'Delicious.' At least, it would be when she was back to feeling normal.

Evie's eyebrows knotted in sympathy. 'Are you okay? You look a little . . . tired.'

Liberty laughed. 'I look terrible, you mean.'

'I didn't say—'

'You didn't need to. I know I look a mess. I've got puffy red eyes and blotchy skin and – and—' Here they came again, the sobs, racking her body, making her nose run. She hadn't thought it was possible to cry as much as she had in the last two days.

Evie scurried to the door, flipped the shop's 'open' sign to 'closed', then steered her through into the back room. 'Sit down,' she said softly, and placed a box of tissues beside her.

Liberty did as she was told.

'What happened? Tell me everything.'

So she did. From Alex's unexpected appearance in Tourmarin to the New Year's Eve party in Monaco and . . . well, everything.

'So we spent a week together and it was exciting and eye-opening and wonderful and I fell in love with the place – and with him. But he doesn't love me.' His look of horror when she'd told him she loved him would stay with her always.

'Oh, Liberty, you poor brave girl.'

'If I hadn't fallen in love with him I would still be the person I was before. I wouldn't be hurting so much I can't last an hour without sobbing!' She sniffed.

'You can't help your feelings. And just think of all the things you'd have missed if you hadn't gone to France and spent that time with him.'

She thought of the nights, making love, sleeping curled up against him, having whispered conversations. Of celebratory meals with his wonderful family and seeing all those beautiful places: châteaux, hilltop villages, forests, the Mediterranean Sea. The quiet moments, the living crib, and watching him sleep. And the nights.

She made a choking sound, half laugh, half sob. 'You're right.'

'It might not feel like it right now but this has made you stronger.' Evie hugged her. 'I'm sorry it didn't work out. He's a fool. But you are a beautiful, sweet, caring girl and one day you will meet someone who will appreciate that and love you as you deserve to be loved.'

Liberty rested her cheek on Evie's shoulder and hoped her friend was right.

Tuesday, 6 January

Alex leaned against the wall, arms folded.

'Ready in fifteen minutes, Mr Ricard?' asked a marshal.

He nodded. The marshal moved on.

After yesterday's qualifiers he was starting in pole position. He didn't even need to worry about the competition or his race plan, he thought, sighing because the distraction would have been welcome. Instead, he had time to kill and only his thoughts for company. He kicked his heel and glared at the sullen sky.

He used to believe that being alone was the best way for him to be. He'd been happy alone before. But now Liberty had gone it felt as if the life had been sucked out of his world. Everything was slow, soundless, hollow. He kept opening his mouth to tell her something or ask her opinion, but she wasn't there.

He pictured her at Damselfly Cottage and wondered if she had gone back to her old routine or if her challenge had changed that. He thought of Willowbrook village with its tiny cottages and friendly residents. He missed working in the garage and Guy and Bob's friendly banter, being able to pop into Luc's for a chat over coffee. He missed the calm of walking in the woods and the centring effect those walks had had on him. He even missed the damn cottage with its lethally low doorways and cosy rooms. It was calm and homely, and he missed Charlie too.

But most of all he missed Liberty.

He'd love to be there with her, walking Charlie in the forest, sitting with her by the fire. Little things but, he realised now, meaningful things.

Well, he'd simply have to get used to it. This was how it had to be. It was best for everyone, and he had to stop dwelling on it.

'Mr Ricard?' a woman asked.

He looked up. What now?

A young woman stopped beside him. Her headset and hi-vis jacket marked her out as another race official. 'We're ready for you to go through. Good luck with your race.' She eyed the track. 'Conditions are good. I'm sure you'll smash it.'

Liberty guided the last of the quilt through the sewing-machine and snipped the threads. At least that was one job done, she thought irritably. She hadn't derived any pleasure from working on this king-sized quilt, a bespoke order for an online customer. Black and white in a Rail Fence design, the zigzag pattern had sent her cross-eyed as she'd quilted it.

She stood and stretched her back, then spread out the quilt to check it. The shop bell tinkled, signalling they had a customer – only the third today. January was usually quiet, but today had been deathly. It was as if everyone could sense her black mood and was keeping away. Probably wise. Good job Evie was out there to give them a cheery welcome. She folded the quilt and was about to check Evie's notes for which fabric to use to bind it when a crease caught her eye. She stopped and peered closer at the quilt's backing, and her hand automatically reached to smooth the deep crease in it. It remained fixed there – quilted into place by her.

She swore. 'Please tell me this isn't happening,' she ground out, and unfolded it.

'Lib?' Evie appeared in the doorway.

'I've just finished quilting this and look.' Liberty held it up for her to see. The crease ran right down the middle.

'Oh,' was all Evie could find to say. There was no silver lining this time.

There was nothing for it but to unpick her work. Every last damn stitch. Liberty resisted the urge to stamp her feet – or punch something.

'Dorothy's here to see you,' Evie said.

'To see me?' Liberty frowned. Dorothy sometimes came in to buy knitting patterns or wool, but she wasn't usually picky about who served her.

Glad to leave the accursed quilt, she went through to the shop.

Dorothy's white hair trembled as she waggled a finger at Liberty. 'You forgot to come and see me.'

She frowned, then remembered – at the ball, Dorothy had said something about having tea. 'Oh, Dorothy, I'm sorry! There's been so much going on.'

'I heard about your adventures.' Her eyes twinkled. 'Why don't you pop in after work tonight?'

Liberty was tired and grumpy, and all she wanted was to change into her pyjamas and relax. 'Well, actually, I'm—'

Dorothy shook her head. 'No excuses, young lady. I'll be expecting you.'

'Oh. Okay. Um – what's it about again?' She probably just wanted a chat. Dorothy could talk for England and she got lonely.

'I'll explain this evening.'

Dorothy lived on Love Lane, a cobbled road too narrow for cars and only a short walk away from the Button Hole. A wreath of pine cones and mistletoe hung on the door of her terraced cottage, and the porch light glowed like a firefly in the dark winter's evening as Liberty approached.

Dorothy must have been waiting near the door because it opened as soon she knocked.

'I'll take your coat. You sit down, dear.' Dorothy pointed to the living room where a vigorous fire was burning and a plate of mince pies lay on the coffee-table.

Liberty obediently took a seat on the sofa and sank into the soft cushions. She didn't feel like discussing knitting patterns or 'that nice Frenchman' tonight, but it was clear Dorothy had gone to some effort, so she reined back her impatience. She couldn't stay too long anyway because Charlie would need to go out.

'Sherry?' Dorothy had already poured them each a tiny glass.

'Actually, I'm—'

'Take it.' Dorothy added, under her breath, 'You might need it.'

Liberty took it and frowned. 'Why will I—'

'It's about the flowers you get every year on your birthday.'

She froze. 'You know who's sending them?'

Dorothy nodded. But she had a strange expression, one Liberty couldn't read, and she gulped down her own sherry (although, on reflection, that wasn't so unusual).

'Well? Who is it?'

She hesitated, and Liberty could see she was fighting a battle with herself. The person must have sworn her to secrecy, just as they had done the florist.

Finally, piercing blue eyes met with hers. 'Someone who loved you very much.'

'Loved?' Past tense. Liberty held her breath and waited for her to go on.

But Dorothy didn't. Instead, she asked, 'Can't you guess? I think you know deep inside.'

Frustration bubbled up inside her. She'd spent the last twelve years trying to guess and hadn't worked it out.

Loved.

But she'd only considered those who were still here.

Her voice was a whisper. 'Was it – Mum?'

Dorothy nodded.

Liberty shook her head. 'No, it can't be . . .'

Her mum had been there the first time she'd received a bouquet and had sworn it wasn't her.

'You must have made a mistake, Dorothy. Maybe you misheard something or—'

'No mistake, dear.' Liberty blinked. 'It was your mum. She set it up, arranged it all.'

Stunned, Liberty ran this through her mind. Had she denied it? Or had she simply been evasive – *What me? Organise something like that?* – and led her daughter to dismiss the idea? How many people knew gerberas were her favourite flowers? Not many. But her mum had died not long after Liberty's eighteenth birthday. 'How? I mean, I can't . . .'

'Drink your sherry, dear. Just a sip.'

The fiery liquid tasted foul, but the rush of heat was welcome. Her mum? How had she arranged for them to come every year after she'd gone?

'Better?' asked Dorothy. 'I told you you'd need it.'

'But you knew Mum. She couldn't even organise her sock drawer! Planning wasn't a word in her vocabulary.'

'She did it for you.'

Those words settled like spring blossom fluttering to the ground. Her mum had planned for her to receive this gift each year on her birthday. Liberty felt the warm wash of her mother's love and it made her heart swell.

'She loved you more than anything.'

The sudden spring of tears made her blink hard. 'I – I know.' She'd never doubted it. 'Why did she do it? What are the flowers supposed to mean?'

With an unsteady hand, Dorothy refilled their sherry glasses. 'She was worried that as a teenager you'd become quieter and a little shy, and she always wondered if growing up without a father figure in your life had affected your confidence.'

'What a ridiculous idea!'

Dorothy put the sherry bottle down. 'She sometimes worried that she wasn't enough.'

Liberty's eyes filled. 'How could she think that? She was the best mum.'

'Anyway. The flowers were supposed to get you thinking about all the people in your life who cared about you. Make you realise that you had a lot to feel proud of, confident about.'

She remembered her mum asking, 'Is there anyone you've helped in some way or been kind to?' And Liberty had thought about all the good deeds she'd done. 'Is there anyone who admires you, maybe from a distance, or a friend who's too shy to say how much your friendship means to them?'

The realisation dawned that her mum had been encouraging her to examine her life and see that she was surrounded by a community that cared and was rooting for her. She felt a smile spread across her face. 'How ironic,' she said. 'Mum sent those flowers to boost my confidence, and they were the very thing that triggered me to feel I was too timid and stuck in a rut!'

But in doing the challenge she'd faced her fears and discovered she was braver than she'd realised.

'Your mum would be proud of your challenge. She'd be cheering you on all the way.'

Liberty nodded, her throat too tight to speak. Even in death her mum was still sending her love, encouragement and support, and that was just typical of her. How had Liberty not guessed?

Dorothy patted her hand. 'She loved you and isn't it wonderful that she found a way to tell you so even after she was gone?'

'She always was creative.'

Dorothy laughed. 'She certainly was. I hope I did the right thing in telling you. It was supposed to be a secret, after all. A mystery. But . . .' Her thin lips pressed flat.

'But what?' Liberty asked, with a rush of concern.

She hesitated, then admitted, 'The doctor's been doing a few tests and – well, I'm worried. I won't always be around, love.'

'Oh, Dorothy! What tests? What's wrong?'

Dorothy waved away her concern. 'Nothing to worry about. I'm just not as young as I used to be, that's all. But I don't want you to be sad if one day when I'm gone the flowers stop coming.' She grinned. 'I'm not sure your mum thought *that* far ahead.'

A little later Liberty walked back to her car, her head

filled with this news, her heart lighter. She couldn't wait to tell—

She stopped herself.

Damn. Why was Alex still the one she wanted to run to with her news?

He was gone. She had to remember that.

The race should have been a walk in the park. The opportunity to showcase the bikes of a bygone era with all their classic beauty and historic value. And now Alex's father was no longer around there was no real competition. The other racers were simply not in the same league to challenge Alex's place in pole position, even with his weak wrist. Engine revving on the starting grid, he expected it to be a breeze.

But Fate had other ideas.

On the third corner the guy next to him leaned in a little too close and Alex tried to adjust. Perhaps his mind was still on Liberty, or perhaps he was out of practice after a month away. Perhaps he over-adjusted or his tyre lost traction – he'd never know. But for the third time in two years he felt the bike separate from him and he sailed away from the track, skimming the ground towards the barriers.

It was déjà vu – yet it was different.

He'd had two serious crashes before and each time he'd done what he'd been trained to do: relaxed his body, let himself roll and slide, resigned to whatever the outcome was to be.

Not today.

This time blinding white fear gripped him. He didn't want to die.

Liberty's face flashed up in front of him. He saw her smile, her hair, her beautiful eyes. He couldn't leave her. He had to live.

But his body continued to roll and bounce, and the barrier loomed larger and closer – until he smashed against it.

And the lights went out.

Chapter Twenty-five

Charlie was curled up asleep next to her sewing table and Liberty was getting ready to go to Brenda's for the evening. She dropped into her bag the gold squares she'd cut ready to stitch on tonight. She'd almost finished the Van Gogh quilt and if she held it to her nose and inhaled, she could smell the gorgeous perfumes of Provence: pine trees, sunshine, a salty hint of the sea. It reminded her of the day she'd arrived in France and the high she'd felt.

Reminded her of Alex.

She put the scissors down and waited for the sharp, jagged pain to pass. Sometimes it was so raw it stole her breath. She knew it would ease eventually, but that day was far in the future. Her best form of defence was not to let herself think of him at all, to keep busy, fill her mind with quilts and colours and plans for the future.

But tonight she was tired, and for once she didn't have the strength to prevent her thoughts from wandering to him. She wondered where he was, what he was doing. Did he think of her? Did he miss her at all?

A thought suddenly occurred, and she checked the date. His race had been two days ago. Had he won?

She glanced over at her laptop. Leave it, Lib. You must move on.

But, unable to resist the temptation, she sat down and typed in a search for the results. He hadn't come first.

She frowned and scanned the list. Finally, she found his name near the bottom:

Alexandre Ricard – DNF.

'DNF? What does that mean?' she said.

Charlie opened one eye, then went back to sleep. She typed in another search, and her pulse quickened. *Did not finish.* Why not? She tapped furiously, searching for a write-up of the race. A journalist's report came up, and as Liberty read it her skin began to prickle. No!

The report said he'd crashed – early on. A handling error, it said. Unusual for him – as if his mind hadn't been on the race, the journalist speculated. Alex had been thrown from the bike, hit the crash barrier and blacked out. He was airlifted to hospital and his family were with him, but there'd been no updates since.

Liberty gripped the table, feeling sick, winded. He'd told her the race wasn't high level, that it involved nothing like the speeds he was used to. She snatched up her phone and texted him: *Just heard about your accident. Are you okay?*

She waited five minutes. When he didn't reply, she dialled his number. Stuff her pride. She needed to know. But his phone didn't connect and went straight to voicemail.

What should she do?

It took her less than ten seconds to decide. She went

back to the laptop and looked up the next available flight to the South of France.

Alex felt a kick as he spotted the first sign for Willowbrook. But the traffic lights switched to red so he grudgingly slowed to a stop, cursing under his breath. As he'd lain in hospital, then as he'd travelled here, he'd had time to think – to really think – about what Liberty had said a week ago.

Was she right? Was he afraid? He, who'd had a passion for speed since the moment he could ride on two wheels, did he fear opening his heart and getting hurt?

He revved his engine and waited impatiently for the lights to turn green. He'd watched his mother suffer time and time again. He'd witnessed her pain, her torment. He'd tried to help but most of the time he'd been helpless. As he'd grown older she'd leaned on him because he could at least help in practical ways, but the anger he'd felt at his father had been about *her* hurt.

Or had it?

A memory struck unexpectedly. He pictured himself as a young boy the night before Christmas: tense, anxious, unable to sleep. But not because he was fantasising about reindeer and sleighs.

Christmas had been either a time of tension or of absence. Always of hurt.

How many times had he lain awake, wondering why his father couldn't be content with them – his family? Why was he never interested in his son, who'd done all he could to impress him, even surpassing his own professional achievements? Pain corkscrewed through him. He'd desperately wanted his father to acknowledge him – not just as a motor-racing champion, but as his son.

He hadn't. And that had hurt.

Liberty was right, he realised now.

He pictured the hurt in her brown eyes, the tears she'd furiously blinked away, and the corkscrew dug in deeper. He'd encouraged her to be brave with her challenge, when all along he'd been avoiding relationships himself and living by the belief that love hurt.

He'd been afraid of his feelings for her.

He thought of how she'd said yes to so many things she'd found terrifying – the bike ride, the flight to France, spending Christmas alone in a country where she didn't speak the language – and knew he couldn't let his fear hold him back any longer. He couldn't live his life constantly on the run, heading for the fire escape each time someone began to get close to him. He had to give their relationship a chance, even if it meant risking his heart – and hers.

He gripped the handlebars anxiously. If only he could see into the future and be sure it would work, he'd be back at her side in the blink of an eye. But no one knew what the future held, did they?

He stopped. Why was he assuming the future was out of his hands?

If he'd learned anything from his poor excuse for a father, it was that relationships were about being there and sticking around, even when things were less than perfect.

And Alex was good at that. He'd always been there

for his mum and brothers: why couldn't he be there for Liberty?

The lights finally changed and he charged forward with the same purpose and determination he used to have on the starting line of a race.

He slowed right down as he turned off for her cottage, and inhaled the fresh woodland scents of bark, wet leaves and fertile soil. He couldn't bring himself to get off and walk the rest of the way, he was too impatient to see Liberty.

His heart slugged hard. Liberty had been the only thing on his mind as that barrier had come rushing at him. She was the only thing that mattered. As he drew up outside the cottage, a curtain jerked open and he saw a flash of red hair before she darted away. The front door opened and she flew out, Charlie hot on her heels. Alex killed the engine, dismounted and unclipped his helmet. Joy pounded through him at the sight of her.

'I've been trying to call you,' she said urgently. 'They said you crashed.' Her eyes were round with fear and concern, and he wanted to draw her to him.

'I did. But I'm fine.'

By some miracle, he hadn't been seriously hurt. Once he'd come round, though, he'd already been lifted into the helicopter. He'd insisted he didn't need any checks, but they'd flown him to hospital anyway. He was discharged the same day.

He knew he'd been lucky. He knew how close he'd

come to losing everything. *You're like a cat with nine lives,* his mum had told him.

He was still here, he'd been given another chance, and this time he wasn't going to waste it. From now on, he wasn't going to take anything for granted: things were going to be different.

'Thank goodness,' Liberty said, flattening a palm to her chest. 'I was so worried.'

Her visible relief made his heart swell. 'Sorry about that. My phone battery died halfway here. That's why you couldn't get through.'

She nodded, and his instinct was telling him to kiss her, but she hung back. Charlie, on the other hand, jumped up and Alex rubbed his ears. 'Hello, Charlie.'

The dog did a couple of excited circles, then cocked his leg against the back tyre of his bike.

'*Merci,*' Alex muttered drily. He turned back to Liberty and searched for the words, which, all the way here, had been so clear in his head, but now they fluttered out of reach. 'Lib, when I lost control of the bike there was a long moment when I wasn't sure what was going to happen.'

'You thought you were going to get hurt again?'

'Or worse.' He took a deep breath. 'And in those moments all I could think of was you . . .'

Her eyes widened. Fear and hope quivered in him, like butterfly wings, but he told himself there was nothing for it but to take a deep breath and say the words. Take the leap of faith he'd been too cowardly to take before.

'I love you, Liberty. I want to be with you.' He went on, 'I love that you visit Carys every Sunday without fail and you refuse to give up on her. I love that when you sing it's so beautiful I get goose-bumps. I love that you're so talented and passionate about sewing. I love that when I'm with you I don't want to be anywhere else. I love that you're brave even when you're scared, and I love that you weren't afraid to say you loved me even when I pushed you away. You're the bravest person I've ever met, Liberty, and I love you.' He grinned, and found that saying the words brought unexpected pleasure. A sense of peace, too, of everything suddenly coming into focus.

Her eyebrows knotted. 'But I can't ask you to make sacrifices for me. You love travelling, I'm a home bird.'

'I love that you're a home bird. You love the simple things in life. And I don't miss travelling. I miss you. I miss this place.' He gestured to the blanket of trees above them and pictured the hum of wildlife that filled it by day. 'I want to live here. I'm going to talk to Guy about restoring classic bikes, and I want to be by your side for the rest of my life . . . So what do you say?'

He held his breath, waiting for her answer.

'You know my answer, Alex Ricard,' she said quietly. She took his face in her hands and her smile made his chest constrict. 'I love you.'

Their lips met, and he pulled her to him, impatient for this, impatient to begin this new chapter in his life. In *their* lives.

'I'm going to love you like you deserve to be loved,' he promised, 'full throttle, no holds barred.'

Epilogue

Sunday, 25 January

It was a Sunday like any other. They'd walked Charlie through the woods, up the hill towards the Old Hall and back again, enjoying the little signs that spring would soon be on its way: the call and response of a pair of pigeons, the clenched buds of a camellia bush, the first clusters of snowdrops. They'd made waffles with chocolate sauce. And now they'd come to visit Carys at the hospital.

Later, Natasha, Luc and the children were coming to Damselfly Cottage for a Sunday roast, and Liberty planned to present the cot quilt she'd made for baby Arthur.

But for now her attention was focused on her friend. Carys slept on, her breath steady, her expression soft and calm.

'So, once Alex has found some premises, he's going to set up a workshop specialising in restoring classic bikes. He'll pay a team of mechanics to do the dirty work and he'll manage the place, tracking down the parts and quoting for work and so on. At least, that's what he says.' She glanced up at Alex, who was sitting on the other side of the bed, and they shared a smile. 'Knowing him like I do, I'm sure he'll end up in the workshop tinkering too, but it should keep him busy.'

'Keep me out of trouble, you mean.' He smiled.

'Exactly.'

Liberty sat back. She tried to think if there was any more news she could share with her friend, but the last few weeks had been exciting in a low-key way. Alex had moved into Damselfly Cottage (she'd decluttered to make room for his stuff, but it turned out he didn't have many possessions – only a handful of motorbikes) and their time had been filled with walking Charlie together, spending cosy nights in. Nothing to write home about, yet she couldn't imagine anything more perfect.

Alex looked at his watch. 'Do you think we should make tracks? I need to start thinking about getting the food into the oven.'

Liberty nodded. She squeezed Carys's hand and leaned forward to kiss her cheek—

Then blinked and looked down.

Had she felt her own fingers being squeezed?

She looked at Carys's hand in hers. Was it a muscle spasm? Was that even possible for someone in a coma? Carys's fingers uncurled, and her thumb rubbed Liberty's ever so slightly.

She gasped.

'Did you say something?' Alex stopped at the door and glanced back at her.

'Wait,' she said breathlessly, and beckoned him over. 'I think – I thought I felt something. Carys? Car?'

Her friend's eyelashes fluttered a little, then lifted and closed again.

Liberty gasped again. She was vaguely aware of Alex standing behind her. 'Did you see that?' she asked, without taking her eyes off Carys.

'I did,' he whispered.

'Carys?' she said, a little louder. She was gripping her friend's hand in excitement now.

'Should I get a nur—' Alex began.

Carys's eyelids opened again. This time they stayed open, and her gaze slowly turned towards Liberty.

Liberty couldn't breathe, she couldn't move or even speak. Excitement brimmed in her. Their eyes connected, and her heart somersaulted. She was certain – no doubt at all – that Carys could see her. Properly. She was fully conscious.

'You're back,' she whispered. A sob of happy laughter choked her, and tears made her friend's face swim.

Alex squeezed her shoulders. 'Looks like you need to introduce us.'

Acknowledgements

Apologies to all the friends and family I complained to when I was writing this book because I thought I'd never finish it on time. You were right – I did.

Thank you to all my wonderful Facebook friends who gave me stories of naughty things their dogs had done, and especially Lizi Pepper and Mike Collins whose dog Frankie inspired Charlie's cheeky antics.

Thanks to Marian Keall and Maureen Scapens for checking the sewing bits. Also, love and thanks to Bowdon Quilters.

As always, thanks to Jacqui Cooper for her encouragement and support.

And I'm so grateful to Adrian Leach who chatted to me about motorbikes and patiently answered my long list of questions (any mistakes are mine).

Thanks to my mum, Brigitte, for checking the French spellings.

Finally, thanks to my agent Megan Carroll and editor Kimberley Atkins for being so wonderful to work with and for believing in me and my books.

Discover more from
Sophie Claire . . .